Praise for *Da*

'She's a thriller queen . . . . . . extraordinary
piece of writing'
Sunday Times Culture

'Bauer takes astonishing risks but – like a brilliant
ski-jumper – arcs down to the perfect landing'
Independent

'She can do tragic brilliantly and she can do grim,
but every now and then humour breaks into the
tale – and she does that almost best of all'
Guardian

'I would press this one on anyone who loves
Kate Atkinson, Bauer really is that good'
Alice O'Keeffe, *The Bookseller*

'Outstandingly good'
Literary Review

'A barnstorming follow-up [to *Blacklands*] . . .
Bold, mordant, compassionate'
Sunday Times

'Impressively original and convincing. Read it
and you'll see what I mean!'
Sophie Hannah, *www.express.co.uk*

'Tense and imaginative'
Guardian

www.penguin.co.uk

More praise for Belinda Bauer

By Belinda Bauer

Blacklands
Darkside
Finders Keepers
Rubbernecker
The Facts of Life and Death
The Shut Eye
The Beautiful Dead
Snap

And writing as Jack Bowman

High Rollers

DARK SIDE

BELINDA BAUER

CORGI BOOKS

TRANSWORLD PUBLISHERS
61–63 Uxbridge Road, London W5 5SA
A Random House Group Company
www.transworldbooks.co.uk

DARKSIDE
A CORGI BOOK: 9780552158886

First published in Great Britain
in 2011 by Bantam Press
an imprint of Transworld Publishers
Corgi edition published 2011

Addresses for Random House Group Ltd companies outside the UK
can be found at: www.randomhouse.co.uk
The Random House Group Ltd Reg. No. 954009

The Random House Group Limited supports The Forest Stewardship
Council® (FSC®), the leading international forest certification organisation.
All our titles that are printed on Greenpeace approved FSC® certified paper
carry the FSC® logo. Our paper procurement policy can be found at
www.randomhouse.co.uk/environment

Typeset in 11.5/15pt Caslon 540 by Falcon Oast Graphic Art Ltd.
Printed in the UK by Clays Ltd, Elcograf S.p.A.

11

To Dad, too late

Forty-six Days

The sounds of the hospital came back to Lucy muffled and from far away. She became aware of a big hand holding hers – tough, dry and warm.

Jonas, she thought with a twist of guilt.

Stiffly she moved her head and opened her eyes, expecting to read worry, relief – even anger – in his eyes.

Instead, for one crazy moment, she found she had been sucked through a tear in time, and that she was married to a small boy wearing a look of such terror on his face that she flinched and clutched at his hand as if *he* were the one who was falling.

'Jonas!'

Her throat burned and the word came out as a harsh caw, but it aged him like a slap in the face and immediately his eyes filled with all those emotions she'd expected to see when she first looked up at him – even the anger.

Lucy didn't care. She brimmed with tears. Jonas held her in his arms – a man again – and she overflowed into the crook of his elbow while he bent over her and said quiet, tender things into her hair.

'I didn't mean it,' she sobbed, but she couldn't even understand her own muffled words.

And anyway, she wasn't certain they were true.

Twenty-three Days

Margaret Priddy awoke to the brilliant beam of light she had been anticipating with fear and longing for years.

Finally, she thought, I'm dying. And tears of loss mingled with those of joy on her lined cheeks.

Ever since her fall she had lain here – or somewhere very like it – slack and immobile and dependent on other people for her most basic needs. Food, water, warmth. Toilet – which the nurses carried out as if her dignity were numbed, not her body. Company . . .

The nurses tried their best.

'Morning, Margaret! Beautiful morning!'

'Morning, Margaret! Sleep well?'

'Morning, Margaret! Raining again!'

And then they would either run out of paltry inspiration or jabber on about their night out getting drunk, or their children's seemingly endless achievements at school. A relentless rota of cheerful bustle with big busts and bingo wings. The break in silence was welcome at first but, in the face of inanity, Margaret quickly longed for solitude.

She was grateful. Of course she was. Grateful and polite – the way an English lady should be in the circumstances. They had no way of knowing about her gratitude, of course, but she tried to convey it in her eyes and she thought some of them understood. Peter did, but then Peter had always been a sensitive boy.

Now – as the light made her eyes burn – Margaret Priddy thought of her son and the tears of loss took precedence. Peter was forty-four years old but she still always thought of him first as a five-year-old in blue shorts and a Batman T-shirt, running down the shingle in Minehead on the first beach holiday they'd ever taken.

She was leaving her little boy alone.

She knew it was silly, but that's how she felt about it.

She was dying and he'd be all alone.

But still she *was* dying. At last. And it was just as she'd imagined – white and wonderful and pain-free.

It was only when she sensed the press of weight on the bed that was her home that she realized this was not the start of her journey to the Hereafter, but someone in her room with a torch.

Someone uninvited, invading her home, her room, her bed, the very air in front of her face . . .

Every fibre of Margaret Priddy's being screamed to respond to the danger.

Unfortunately, every fibre of her being below the neck had been permanently disconnected from her brain three years before when old Buster – the most reliable of horses – had stumbled to his knees on a patch of ice, throwing her head-first into a wooden telegraph pole.

So instead of screaming, punching and fighting for what was left of her life, she could only blink in terror as the killer placed a pillow over her face.

He didn't want to hurt her. Only wanted her dead.

As he suffocated Margaret Priddy with her own well-plumped pillow, the killer felt a rush of released tension, like an old watch exploding, scattering a thousand intricate parts and sending tightly wound springs bouncing off into nowhere as the bounds of the casing broke open around him.

He sobbed in sudden relief.

The feel of the old lady's head through the pillow was comfortingly distant and indistinct. The unnatural stillness of her body seemed like permission to continue and so he did. He pressed his weight on to the pillow for far longer than he knew was necessary.

When he finally removed it and shone his torch into her face, the only discernible change in Margaret Priddy was that the light in her eyes had gone out.

'There,' thought the killer. 'That was easy.'

*

First Lucy – and now *this*.

PC Jonas Holly leaned against the wall and took off his helmet so that his suddenly clammy head could breathe.

The body on the bed had played the organ at his wedding. He'd known her since he was a boy.

He could remember being small enough not to care that it wasn't cool to be impressed by anything, waving at Mrs Priddy as she went past on an impossibly big grey horse – and her waving back. Over the next twenty-five years that scene had been repeated dozens of times, with all the characters in it evolving. Margaret growing older, but always vibrant; he stretching and growing, coming and going – university, Portishead, home to visit his parents while they were still alive. Even the horse changed, from a grey through any number of similar animals until Buster came along. Mrs Priddy always liked horses that were too big for her; 'The bigger they are, the kinder they are,' she'd told him once as he'd squinted up into the sky at her, trying to avoid looking at Buster's hot, quivery shoulder.

Now Margaret Priddy was dead. It was a blessing really – the poor woman. But right now Jonas Holly only felt disorientated and sick that somehow, during the night, some strange magic had happened to turn life into death, warmth into cold and this world into the next.

Whatever the next world was. Jonas had only ever had a vague irreligious notion that it was probably nice enough.

This was not his first body; as a village bobby, he'd seen his fair share. But seeing Margaret Priddy lying there had hit him unexpectedly hard. He heard the nurse coming up the stairs and put his helmet back on, hurriedly wiping his face on his sleeve, hoping he didn't look as nauseous as he felt. He was six-four and people seemed to have an odd idea that the taller you were, the more metaphorical backbone you should have.

The nurse smiled at him and held the door open behind her for Dr Dennis, who wore khaki chinos and a polo shirt at all times – as if he was in an Aussie soap and about to be whisked off in a Cessna to treat distant patients for snakebite in the sweltering outback, instead of certifying the death of a pensioner in her cottage on a damp January Exmoor.

'Hello, Jonas,' he said.

'Right, Mark.'

'How's Lucy?'

'OK, thanks.'

'Good.'

Jonas had once seen Mark Dennis vomit into a yard of ale after a rugby match, but right now the doctor was all business, his regular, tanned face composed into a professional mask of thoughtful compassion. He went over to the bed and checked Margaret Priddy.

'Nice lady,' he said, for something to say.

'The best,' said Jonas Holly, with feeling. 'Probably a blessing that she's gone. For her, I mean.'

The nurse smiled and nodded professionally at him but Mark Dennis said nothing, seeming to be very interested in Margaret Priddy's face.

Jonas looked around the room. Someone had hung a cheap silver-foil angel over the bed, and it twirled slowly like a child's mobile. On the dresser, half a dozen Christmas cards had been pushed haphazardly aside to make way for more practical things. One of the cards had fallen over and Jonas's fingers itched to right it.

Instead he made himself look at the old lady's body. Not that old, he reminded himself, only sixty-something. But being bedridden had made her seem older and far more frail.

He thought of Lucy one day being that frail and tried to focus on Margaret lying on the bed, not his beautiful wife.

Her lips flecked with bile and soggy painkillers . . .

Jonas pushed the image away hard and took a deep breath. He focused and tried to imagine what Margaret Priddy's last words might have been before the accident that crushed her spine and her larynx in one crunching blow. Final words spoken in ignorance three years before the demise of the rest of her body. Jonas thought probably: 'Get on, Buster!'

'Glad you're here, Jonas,' said Mark Dennis – and

when he turned to look at him, Jonas Holly could see concern in the doctor's face. His instincts stirred uneasily.

'Her nose is broken.'

They both looked at the nurse, whose smile disappeared in an instant. She hurried over and stood beside the doctor as he guided her fingers to the bridge of Margaret Priddy's nose.

'See?'

She nodded, a frown making her ugly.

'There's no break in the skin or apparent bruising,' said Mark Dennis in the annoying, musing way he had. 'I'm no CSI, but I'd say a sharp blow was not the cause.'

Jonas hated people who watched American television.

'You want to feel, Jonas?'

Not really. Still, he was a policeman and he should . . .

He swallowed audibly and touched the nose. It was cold and gristly and made Jonas – an ardent vegetarian – think of raw pork chops. Mark Dennis guided him and Jonas felt the break in Margaret Priddy's nose move grittily under his fingers. Gooseflesh sprouted up to his shoulders and he let go and stepped back. Unconsciously he wiped his hand on the dark-blue serge of his uniform trousers, before realizing that the silence – coupled with two pairs of eyes looking at him questioningly – meant he was supposed to take charge;

was supposed to do something professional and police-man-like.

'Yuk,' he said.

*

The detectives from Taunton must watch a lot of American television, too, thought Jonas as he observed them striding through Margaret Priddy's tiny home, bumping into antiques, clustering in the hallway, and thumping up and down the narrow stairs like US Marines invading a potting shed.

Despite their expertise in the field of suspicious death, Jonas secretly wished he'd never called them in. Of course, *not* calling them was not an option, but even so . . .

Jonas was equipped to handle nothing beyond the mundane. He was the sole representative of the Avon & Somerset police force in seven villages and across a good acreage of Exmoor, which rolled in waves like a green and purple sea towards the northern shore of the county, where it met the Bristol Channel coming the other way. The people here lived in the troughs, leaving the heather-covered peaks to the mercy of the sun, wind, rain, snow and the thick, brine-scented mists that crept off the ocean, careless that this was land and not water, and blurring the boundary between the two. People walked on the exposed peaks but their lives were properly conducted in the folds and creases of Exmoor, out of the view of prying eyes, and where sounds carried only as far as the next looming common before being smothered by a damp wall of heather and prickly gorse.

These shaded vales where people grew held hidden histories and forgotten secrets, like the big dark pebbles in the countless shallow streams that crossed the moor.

But the homicide team now filling the two-hundred-year-old, two-up-two-down cottage with noise and action never stopped to listen to the undercurrents.

Jonas didn't like Detective Chief Inspector Marvel, not only because the spreading, florid DCI's name sounded like some kind of infallible superhero cop, but because DCI Marvel had listened to his account of the finding of Margaret Priddy with a look on his lined face that told of a bad smell.

It was unfair. Jonas felt he had recovered well after launching the investigation with the ignominious 'Yuk'.

He had ascertained that the nurse – a robust fifty-year-old called Annette Rogers – had checked on Mrs Priddy at 2am without noticing anything amiss, before finding her dead at 6.15am.

Despite the obvious answer, he had dutifully quizzed Mark Dennis on the possibility of a woman being able to somehow break her own nose during the act of sleeping while also paralysed from the neck down.

He had escorted Mark Dennis and Annette Rogers to the front door with minimal deviation to maintain the corridor of entry and exit to the scene.

He had checked the bedroom window and quickly found scrape-marks surrounding the latch. It was only a four-foot drop from the sill to the flat roof of the lean-to.

He had secured the scene. Which here in Shipcott meant shutting the front door and putting a note on it torn from his police-issue notebook. He'd considered the content of that note with care, running from the self-important 'Crime Scene' – which seemed merely laughable on a scrap of lined paper – through 'Police! Do Not Pass' (too bossy) and 'No Entry' (too vague), finally ending up with 'Please Do Not Disturb', which appealed to everybody's better nature and which he felt confident would work. And it did.

He had alerted Tiverton to the fact that foul play may possibly be involved in the death of Mrs Margaret Priddy of Big Pot Cottage, Shipcott, and Tiverton had called on the services of Taunton CID.

Taunton Homicide was a team of frustrated detectives generally under-extended by drunken brawls gone wrong, and Jonas thought Marvel should have been grateful for the call, not openly disdainful of him. He understood that in police hierarchy the village bobby – or 'community beat officer' as he was officially called – was the lowest of the low. He also knew that his youth worked against him. Any policeman of his age worth his salt should be at the top of his game – swathed in Kevlar, armed with something shiny, clearing tall buildings in his pursuit of criminal masterminds and mad bombers – not walking the beat, ticking off children and corralling stray sheep in some sleepy backwater. That was a job for an old man and Jonas had only just turned thirty-one, so it smacked of laziness or stupidity. Therefore Jonas tried hard to appear neither lazy nor stupid as he ran through his notes with Marvel.

It made no difference.

Marvel listened to the young PC's report with a glazed look in his eyes, then asked: 'Did you touch her?'

Jonas blinked then nodded – reddening at the same time.

Marvel pursed his lips. 'Where?'

'Her nose. Dr Dennis said it was broken and I felt it.'

'Why?'

Jonas felt his face burn as everyone in the room seemed to have stopped what they were doing to watch him being grilled.

'I don't know, sir. Just to see.'

'Just for fun?'

'No, sir, the doctor said it was broken and I checked.'

'Because you needed to confirm his diagnosis? Are you more highly qualified than him? Medically speaking?' Marvel dripped sarcasm from every pore, and from the corner of his eye Jonas saw the Taunton cops grin and roll their eyes at each other.

'No, sir.'

'Anyone else touch her?'

'The nurse, sir.'

'Was *she* more highly qualified than Dr Dennis?'

'No, sir.'

Marvel sighed and flapped his arms once helplessly like a man who has given up chasing down a mugger. The flap said, 'There's only so much you can do.'

'So the doctor touched her. Then you touched her. Then the nurse touched her.'

Jonas didn't correct Marvel on the sequence of events.

'Yes, sir.'

'Anyone else?'

'No, sir.'

'You sure? Not the milkman? The village idiot? You didn't get one man and his dog up here to give her a little poke?'

There were snorts of amusement all round.

'I'm sure, sir.'

Marvel sighed, then asked: 'What's your name?'

'PC Holly, sir.'

'Have you ever heard of a crime scene, Holly?'

'Yes, sir.' Jonas hated Marvel now. The man was grandstanding in front of his team and Jonas shouldn't have touched Margaret Priddy's nose, but still . . .

'Have you ever heard of *contaminating* a crime scene, Holly?'

'Yes, sir.' The heat of embarrassment was leaving Jonas and being replaced by a cool and distant anger, which he found easy to hide but which he knew he would nurture for ever in that very small and stony corner where he kept all that was not kind, responsible and selfless in his heart.

'And you understand that it's a *bad* thing, don't you?'

'Yes, sir.'

'A stupid thing.'

Jonas wanted to punch him.

'Yes, sir.'

Marvel smiled slowly.

'Then why would you do that?'

Jonas was eight years old and Pete Bryant had put a cricket ball through Mr Randall's greenhouse roof. Pete had run, but Jonas had dithered – and Mr Randall had gripped him in a single meaty claw and shaken his arm while shouting that same question into his face. Eight-year-old Jonas could have told Mr Randall that it was Pete who had thrown the ball, but he didn't. Not because he was scared; not because he wasn't a rat; just because it was too late; the damage was already done. The glass was already shattered, Mr Randall already angry, his bicep already bruised, his tears already flowing and his self-worth already pricked. All that was left was for him to get home as quickly as possible so he could shut his bedroom door and cry at the unfairness of it all without alerting his mother.

Now the thirty-one-year-old Jonas swallowed that same bitter pill and unfocused his eyes so he could look straight over Marvel's greying hair.

'I'm very sorry, sir.'

Marvel regarded the tall young policeman with a little disappointment. He'd really have preferred the fool to have got defensive and angry. He loved a good fight. Instead PC Holly had rolled over like a puppy and shown the world his belly.

Ah well.

Marvel turned away before speaking.

'You can go,' he said.

In small defiance, Jonas bit back his 'Yes, sir' and left without another word. Halfway down the stairs he heard Marvel say something he didn't catch, and the laughter of the big-town cops.

*

Some investigation, thought DCI John Marvel, as he stared out at the leaden Somerset sky. A dead old woman with a broken nose. Big deal. But a suspicious death was a suspicious death and helped to justify the funding that kept his Task Force (as he used to like to call it over late suppers with Debbie) in existence. So if they could whip suspicious death up into murder, then all well and good.

Marvel had spent twenty-five years as a homicide detective. Half his life. To Marvel there was no other crime worth investigating – nothing that came close to the sheer finality of death by the hand of another. It kicked assault's arse, rode roughshod over robbery and even trumped rape in his book. Of course, there were degrees – and not every case was a thrill. Some were one long slog from beginning to end, some went off like firecrackers and turned into damp squibs, while others started off quietly and then spiralled wildly out of control. There was no telling at the start how it was going to finish, but the thing that kicked each one off was what sustained Marvel after all these years. The body. The corpse. That stabbed, strangled, beaten, shot, dismembered, poisoned used-to-be-person hung over his head every day like a cat toy – endlessly fascinating, tantalizing, taunting, always reminding him of why he was here and the job he had to do.

The burgled replaced their televisions, bruises healed on the beaten, and the raped kept living, kept going to work and buying groceries and sending post-cards and singing in the choir.

The murdered were dead and stayed dead.

For ever.

How could any true copper not love the murdered and the challenge they threw down from beyond the grave?

AVENGE ME!

Marvel could never hear that ghostly voice in his head without also imagining some kind of broad, dark cape billowing in righteous vengeance.

It was stirring stuff.

And Marvel was always stirred.

Eventually.

Even by a case like this in a place like this, he knew he *would* be stirred once death by violence was confirmed. He had to sort of *grow into* being stirred.

But until then, he was just a bit cheesed off.

Marvel sighed.

Margaret Priddy's body had been removed to civilization – or what passed for it in this neck of the yokel woods. He hated to be out of town. He'd been born and brought up in London. Battersea, to be precise, where the stunted lime trees grown through lifting, cracking pavement were all the green he felt anyone should suffer. Once he'd carved his name in the bark and been repelled by the damp, greenish flesh his penknife had exposed. Sometimes as a kid he'd hung around a bus stop close to the park, but had rarely ventured in. Only on the occasional Saturday for a kickabout, and even then he'd never warmed to the muddy, olive-green grass. Playing behind the garages or under the railway arches was cleaner and faster. Grass was overrated, in Marvel's opinion, and it was his constant gripe that most of the Avon and Somerset force area where he'd ended up working was covered in it.

Now here he was in this shit-hole village in the

middle of a moor that didn't even have the niceties of fences or barns on it, with the miserable prospect of having to conduct a murder investigation surrounded by the vagaries of gorse, yokels and pony shit instead of the sensible amenities of self-service petrol stations, meaningful road-signs and his beloved Kings Arms.

The Divisional Surgeon had already found cuts and bruising inside Margaret Priddy's mouth where her lips had been crushed against her teeth, and the pathologist might find even more. All it would take now was for the Scientific Investigations Department in Portishead to confirm that the saliva and mucus on the well-plumped pillow found lying next to Mrs Priddy belonged to the victim, and they would have their upgrade to murder and their murder weapon all in one neat forensic package.

Marvel looked at the empty bed over which three white-paper-clad CSIs crouched like folk off to a costume party dressed as sperm.

'I like the son for this,' Marvel told DS Reynolds. Marvel loved saying that he 'liked' someone for something. It made him feel as if he were in a Quentin Tarantino film. His south-London accent was a handicap but not a bar to such pronouncements.

'Yes, sir,' said DS Reynolds carefully.

'Sick of watching his inheritance pour down the home-nursing drain.'

'Yes, sir.'

'So what have we got?'

'So far? Hairs, fibres, fluids—'

'Semen?'

'Doesn't look like it, sir. Just what was on the pillow, and urine.'

'I thought she was catheterized?'

'I think the bag must've burst.'

'So the perp could be covered in piss.'

'Yes, sir.'

'Lovely. Anything missing?'

'Doesn't look like a burglary, sir. If something was taken then the killer knew exactly what he was looking for and where to find it.'

Marvel glanced around the room with its old dark furniture. A lifetime of use was evidenced by the wear around the dull brass handles on the chest of drawers. Nothing looked disturbed; even the lace doily on the dresser was flat and un-mussed.

'I want the names of all the nurses employed and hair samples from everyone at the scene.'

'Yes, sir.'

'Prints?'

'Not so far.'

It was a bitterly cold January and the killer could have worn gloves for that reason alone. But Marvel hoped he was not just some opportunist burglar who had overreacted to finding a woman watching him silently from the bed in what he'd thought was an empty room. Marvel hoped he'd planned ahead. Whether he'd planned burglary or murder ahead was open to question, but the fact that it looked unlikely that they would find prints made the whole case more interesting to Marvel. He hated to waste his talents on the low and the stupid, and – since coming to Somerset – he'd started to tire a little of the flailing drunks who'd turned from nuisances to killers because of the unfortunate coming together of heads and kerbs, and of the glazed teenagers whose generosity in sharing their gear had been repaid by their ingrate friends dying curled around pub toilets with shit in their pants and in their veins.

No, the gloves made the killer a more worthwhile quarry in Marvel's eyes.

Just *how* worthwhile remained to be seen.

*

Four hundred yards before the sign that read PLEASE DRIVE SLOWLY THROUGH SHIPCOTT was the house Jonas had grown up in, and from where his parents had been carried to their graves. Not house really, more cottage – although cottage sounded nicer than it really was, as if it were the picture on a box of souvenir fudge. This cottage was squat and tiled rather than thatched, and attached to its only neighbour like a con-joined twin. The pair of them sat and glared across the narrow road at the high hedge beyond it, which cut off both light and the view from the downstairs windows. Both twins had identical silvered-oak nameplates on their garden gates: Rose Cottage and Honeysuckle Cottage. The John and Mary of adjoining country homes. Rose for Jonas and Lucy, Honeysuckle for old Mrs Paddon next door.

Jonas parked the garish police Land Rover behind Lucy's Beetle in the track beside Rose Cottage and felt his heart quicken.

He had to keep hold of himself.

Had to step out on to the dry, freezing mud slowly and walk normally through the front door, and clean the bathroom and fill the washer-dryer, and make the tea – just the way Mark Dennis had told him he must.

'*Lucy needs you. You can't fall apart on her, Jonas. Now more than ever.*'

He wouldn't fall apart. He would keep hold of himself. Even though every day for the past three weeks he had walked up the cracked and un-weeded stone pathway with his heart squeezed into his throat with fear, and his keys jingling like wind chimes in his trembling hands. The dread was almost overwhelming – the dread that he would push open the front door and it would once more wedge softly against the body of his wife. Or that he would call her echoing name and finally find her in a bath of tepid, pink water. Or that he would walk into the house enclosed in winter darkness and feel her bare feet nudge his face as they dangled in the stairwell.

Jonas shook himself on the doorstep, forcing his breathing back to normal so he wouldn't cry with relief when he saw her, and pushed open the door.

'Yuk' had made it home before him.

Lucy greeted him with the word and a single questioning eyebrow as he walked into the living room. If he'd had to hazard a guess he'd say that Mark Dennis had told his receptionist, who'd passed it on to Mr Jacoby or someone in Mr Jacoby's shop. From there it could have been anyone who finally brought it to the Holly household. Steven the paper boy, old Will Bishop the milkman, or one of the several visitors Lucy received sometimes on her couch, between the horror movies which Jonas ordered by mail for her in a never-ending supply, and which she watched with indecent joy from behind her favourite tasselled cushion.

He gave a mock-sigh and shrugged expansively, making her laugh. It lit up her face. Lucy was always beautiful to Jonas, but when she smiled, that became a universal truth – even after the ravages of disease and the strain of recent weeks. Her boyish face with its upturned, freckled nose and widely spaced green eyes – together with her cap of cropped auburn hair – gave her an elfin look.

He kissed the top of her head and she took his hand and became serious.

'Poor Margaret.'

Poor Margaret indeed. But it was a relief. A relief to speak of death like common gossips for whom it was merely a passing notion, instead of a time bomb in their pockets.

'What have you heard?' It was a village in the middle of Exmoor; she could have heard anything.

'That somebody killed her.'

'Possibly. Taunton have it now.' He squeezed her hand, feeling with relief that it was warm and steady, then turned and sat down beside her on the edge of the couch. 'How are you feeling, Lu?'

It was a question he'd been asking daily in one form or another for nearly three years. Sometimes it came out sounding strange to his ears, other times it was a studiedly casual 'All right, Lu?' He could reduce it to a mere questioning look from across the room, which she would answer with a smile or a shrug.

Sometimes he didn't even have to ask.

Those were the days when he came home to find her curled and gasping in the rib-crunching spasms of the MS 'hug', or jabbing at a broken plate and spilled food with the dustpan and brush, her spastic hands that had caused the mess in the first place unable to make it right. Sometimes when he found her like that he pulled the rug over them both on the couch and tickled her arms languorously until she relaxed and finally slept; other times he held her while she shook and cried and slapped at her own failing body with her angry, twisted hands. Jonas had never cried with her – never given in to the self-pity that that would imply.

After she had been diagnosed, everything had changed – at home and at work. He had withdrawn an application for Anti-Terrorism and applied instead for this backwater posting where he was largely autonomous and could fit work around home rather than the other way round. They moved into Rose Cottage, which had been closed up after the death of his parents. Jonas had never wanted to come back but he knew the place; he knew the people; he knew it would be easier to do his job on Exmoor than learn the ropes somewhere new, and that that would make it easier to take care of Lucy.

But sometimes even the comfort of familiarity was not enough to ease his mind. Sometimes – as he gave walkers directions to Dunkery Beacon, or spoke to the parents of a teenager with a half-bottle of vodka and an attitude – Jonas would feel the almost overwhelming urge to jump in his car and race back to check on Lucy. The first time his heart had clenched that way he had given in to the impulse and driven home blindly through winding lanes at 60mph. He'd burst through the front door shouting her name and she'd come running down the stairs of their little cottage in a panic, almost tumbling the last few treads. He'd caught her at the bottom and babbled his usual question, 'Are you OK?' and she had thumped his arm for scaring her so.

That was when Lu could still go up and down stairs properly. Jonas wanted to get a loan for a stair lift, but she said she liked the couch and the TV through the days and liked the challenge of inching upstairs on her bottom to the bathroom.

'Keeps my triceps in shape,' she'd teased him at the time. 'Other women pay a fortune for that kind of workout.'

He'd laughed to please her, and left the elephant in the room unremarked upon – that three years previously Lucy Holly could have walked upstairs on her hands if she'd fancied it. She'd been the fittest woman Jonas had ever met. Even straight out of training in Portishead he'd had to work to keep ahead of her on the five-mile runs they'd regularly taken together. Lucy was no gym-bore. She ran, she swam, she rode horses and bikes and, for the first winter after Jonas had got the posting back home on Exmoor, she'd turned out occasionally for the local girls' football team, Blacklanders Ladies. Jonas smiled a little now at the memory of his petite wife going nose-to-nose with the ref, her eyes flashing and her pony-tail flicking until the cowed man reversed a poor penalty decision in her favour. Once a week for ninety minutes 'Ladies' was just a euphemism.

It seemed forever ago.

Just yesterday he'd found her white and drawn and although she'd insisted she was fine, he'd tasted the salt on her lips that told him she'd been crying.

Now – three weeks after the pills – the question he'd got so used to asking was fraught with new fear.

'Good,' replied Lucy, bringing him gently back to the present. 'I'm good.'

He searched her eyes for the truth and found it had already been told. He felt the tension that had been squeezing his guts relax a little.

'I planted bulbs. Daffs and tulips out front and anemones in the tubs.'

He studied her hand and saw the red-brown earth under her short, practical nails and knew the effort it must have taken for her to organize and complete that task. The bag of compost, the trowel twisting awkwardly in the weak hands and floppy wrists, the effort of breaking into the earth made hard by winter. He almost asked how long it had taken her, but knew it must have been most of the day. Instead he got up and went outside to look for himself. The fact that she didn't get up to point things out to him was proof of how much it had taken out of her. He came back in, smiling.

'And then you . . . ?' He left it hanging for her.

'. . . had a nap,' she finished dutifully and they both laughed ruefully.

'I got your stuff,' he said. They called it her 'stuff'. Her analgesics, her anti-depressants, her anti-convulsants, her anti-virals, her job-lot hypodermics . . . the list seemed endless and ever-changing, which did not instil confidence in their efficacy. Just saying the names had become depressing – Decadron, Neurotin, Prothiaden, Symmetrel . . . 'Stuff' covered them all and had the power of robbing them of their doom-laden titles.

'Oh, Jonas! On a day like this! It could have waited. It's only the Symmetrel I'm out of.'

'No trouble,' he shrugged, although they both knew it was a thirty-mile round trip through narrow lanes to the nearest dispensing chemist's in Dulverton. Jonas's beat included a clutch of tiny villages and had to be covered by Land Rover, but edging out as far as Dulverton when a woman had died in Shipcott was still more than an inconvenience.

Still, he did it, and she appreciated it. That was how they worked at life. They cared for each other.

The very first time Lucy had met Jonas she'd recognized something in him that reminded her of the children she taught in kindergarten. Something that she knew any amount of gung-ho police training would never quite erase from him. There was a softness, a childlike uncertainty, a silly humour in Jonas that meant he would spend the day in riot gear fending off Molotov cocktails and then demonstrate to her at night wearing a pudding bowl and armed with a spatula. When he turned out for Police XV against Army, Lucy watched in embarrassment as Jonas joined his team-mates in a testosterone-packed pre-match ritual of chanting, grunting and chest-beating. Chest-beating! Like gorillas in shorts! Halfway through the spectacle, he'd caught her eye in the stands and they'd both dissolved in such helpless laughter that his captain was still bitching at him at half-time.

Jonas's dark-brown eyes were too far apart, his nose too long and his mouth too full to be called handsome, but Lucy never could get enough of looking at him and craved more. When they'd first moved into his parents' old home, she'd looked for photos of him as a boy. When she'd failed to find any, he'd joked about being 'too ugly to show up on film'.

In her eyes, at least, it was far from true.

'Who told you about Margaret?' he asked, even though it didn't matter.

'Frank.'

Frank Tithecott. The postman. Of course. The postman and the milkman covered the same area as he did but without the same confidentiality. Jonas was suddenly glad Frank had brought his embarrassment home – at least it had made Lucy laugh for the first time in three weeks.

'Are you going to be busy with that?'

'I doubt it,' he shrugged. 'I don't get the impression they'd welcome my assistance.'

'Then they're idiots and I hate them all,' she said sharply, as if Jonas was a boy to be protected from playground bullies, and not a strapping six-foot-four officer of the law.

Jonas rolled his eyes at her sharp words but smiled to show he enjoyed her support, even if it was hopelessly biased. Lucy shifted her legs to make room for him on the couch and Jonas sat down, draped his legs over one end and lowered his long frame gently backwards into her arms. The chores could wait.

The TV was on, the sound down. For several minutes Jonas stroked Lucy's arms with the backs of his nails as they idly watched a blood-spattered teenager being chased through a house by a man in a mask. Without screams and music it was hypnotically dull and soon their breathing slowed and synchronized in the way they both loved.

Lucy slid a single finger between the buttons of his white uniform shirt and ran it tenderly along a rib. The moment caught her unawares and her eyes burned with sudden tears.

To stop them before they could overwhelm her, she kissed his ear and murmured, 'They don't know what they're missing.'

*

DCI Marvel knew *exactly* what he was missing.

Sky TV.

His team were billeted in quarters so basic that he was surprised no one had started whining.

But it was only a matter of time. Marvel liked to have little private wagers with himself. His money was on Grey, Pollard, Rice and Singh to start whining in that order. Rice and Singh were Elizabeth Rice and Armand Singh, and in his experience women and

ethnics either never made waves or made effing great
tsunamis. Rice and Singh were both pretty easy-going
that way, although he had once seen DC Rice knee a
grabby drunk in the balls when she thought no one
was watching. Pollard was solid and stolid, and worked
best when others did the thinking for him, but Grey
was more bolshy and thought he had rights. Marvel
wasn't counting Reynolds. His sergeant was not *with*
him but was too nervous to be *against* him. Like a
whipped dog.

Police budgetary constraints meant they had been
booked into a stable block outside Shipcott. Oh, sure,
the sign at the end of the long and rutted track read
'Farmhouse Accommodation', but the low, ugly row of
'cottages' were no more than converted stables with
window-boxes. And the owner, a bent and arthritic
crone improbably named Joy Springer, apparently
thought that tiny televisions and giant microwave
ovens were enough to justify the tagline 'All Mod
Cons'.

At home he had Sky on a 48-inch screen, complete
with a set of Acoustic Energy Aelite 3 home-cinema
speakers. There were six in the set and they easily
filled the spaces left by Debbie's furniture. The
precious 1970s Habitat suite she'd brought into their
relationship was now squeezed uncomfortably into her
mother's house, elbowing the over-stuffed mock-
leather into corners and competing for floor-space with
the Formica coffee table. So he'd have somewhere to

watch the TV from, Marvel had bought a cheap couch and taken pleasure in putting his feet all over it – often in his shoes.

Now he surfed through the channels for what felt like the hundredth time. It didn't take long. BBC1, BBC2 and ITV1, though BBC2 was grainy and flickering. Channel 4 and Five were seemingly beyond the reach of this part of the moor. He imagined the second test match from Australia dancing and crackling somewhere above his head, searching forlornly for a receiver high enough to be welcomed by, before finally weakening and sputtering out over the heather, lost to him for ever.

Fucking Timbuktu.

He looked at his watch. Ten thirty pm.

The night was young.

Unfortunately, so were his team. They were like babies, the way they were all in bed by ten. Not like his days in the Met, where they'd roll off duty when they ran out of arms to twist and spend the rest of the night in Spearmint Rhino. DS Reynolds was a reasonable cop but Marvel couldn't imagine his sergeant stuffing a twenty into a G-string any more than he could imagine him doing a shampoo ad. DS Reynolds's hair grew on his head in unfortunate tufts. Sometimes they almost joined up; other times he was nearly bald. Reynolds claimed it was stress-related. Fucking nancy boy.

Marvel ran a hand through his own hair and

wondered how long it would be before he was shedding like a Persian cat. His hair would go first, then his teeth. Then his joints, he imagined. Or maybe his eyesight. Already he needed to squint at the menu at McDonald's drive-thru. Once he'd tried to order a McFury, imagining it must be some hellishly well-peppered new burger. He and the pimpled girl in the window had almost come to blows before she worked it out and told him with some degree of triumph that a McF*lurry* was a kiddies' ice-cream. He'd ordered it just to spite her, and lobbed it vaguely towards a bin as he drove out.

Just imagining his teeth falling out made them twinge, so he stopped thinking about dying and concentrated on Margaret Priddy. He'd spoken to the nurse, Annette Rogers, and was reasonably satisfied she was in the clear. She seemed to be going through the motions of sympathy in a way he'd expect a professional nurse to – as if she was simultaneously wondering what she would have for tea. That was fine by Marvel; if she'd wept and wailed over Margaret Priddy's death, he would have had her in custody before her ugly white shoes could touch the ground.

There were two other nurses who had split shifts with Annette Rogers. He had asked Reynolds to track them down for interview.

He pulled the flimsy file towards him and checked. Lynne Twitchett and Gary Liss. A male nurse. Marvel would have snorted if there'd been anyone in the room to hear him pass comment on male nurses. In his head he knew Gary Liss was large, soft, blond – and camp as a row of tents. He'd lay good money on it.

He lost focus on the TV while he thought of how the investigation would proceed, all the elements that he needed to ensure worked together. When it came to leading a homicide investigation, Marvel liked to think of himself as a swan, sailing majestically along while under the surface his team paddled like crazy to keep the whole thing moving smoothly in the right direction.

Marvel mused on Margaret Priddy. It was a strange one. He had been working murders since he was twenty-four years old and his instincts were pretty sharp, but they didn't have to be honed to know that it's hard for a mute and bedridden old woman to make enemies.

But he also knew that friends could be just as dangerous.

In the morning he'd speak to Margaret Priddy's son.

*

After smothering Margaret Priddy, the killer had gone home, showered, and made himself a cheese and bacon sandwich. There was an old black-and-white film on TV – a wide-eyed Hayley Mills lying her earnest way out of trouble over the sound of his teeth on salty meat and sticky bread. He didn't like to turn the volume up. He watched the girl clambering over rocks, spying on a church picnic, jumping on the back of a white pony. The killer switched off the TV and threw away what was left of his sandwich. He curled into a foetal ball on the couch, slept like a baby, and when he awoke he felt like a new man.

Twenty-two Days

The first snow of this winter came in blustery little flurries, like handfuls of frost thrown across the moor by a petulant god. It gathered on the ground only in pockets and made the moor look merely wan rather than truly white. In the villages it made the pavements slippery without making them pretty first, and for that sin the hardy residents of Exmoor – ponies and people alike – hunched their shoulders and doggedly ignored the stinging flakes.

Despite getting off on the wrong foot, Jonas called Marvel before leaving the house, to offer his local knowledge to the investigating team. It was only professional.

There was a brief pause on the other end of the crackly line, then Marvel said, 'I think we'll manage without you—' before the line went dead. He might have been cut off – mobile signals were notoriously poor on Exmoor – but Jonas was pretty convinced he'd just been hung up on.

He put the phone back in its cradle and Lucy looked at him curiously.

'Business as usual then,' he shrugged, feeling like a fool.

By 9am the snow had stopped and by ten it had started to melt away.

Jonas had a routine. Park at the edge of each village he covered and walk up one side of the main street and back in a rough loop. He would pop into tiny shops or post offices, check on old folk, referee neighbour disputes, have a Coke in the pub. Only when he was sure all was well would he move on to the next village. It let the locals see what their taxes were buying in the way of policing. In winter each village took half the time it did in summer. Summer meant stopping to chat, giving directions to tourists, enjoying the sunshine, buying an ice cream. Winter was all brisk pace and hurried hellos so people could get back to their work or their hearths.

But the Exmoor grapevine had been active and today everybody wanted to talk about Margaret Priddy. Doors opened as he passed and warmth wafted from cottage doors as women stood on doorsteps and asked about what had happened, while passers-by hurried over to hear the latest.

There was no latest, of course. Not that *he* knew

about anyway – and by early afternoon Jonas was sick of saying 'I don't know,' and seeing the surprised, embarrassed looks on the faces of the locals.

In Exford he asked old Reg Yardley to walk his dog by the river and not on the green – for only about the hundredth time – and the man strode off muttering something about catching *real* criminals. Jonas let it go, but it didn't help his guilt or his rising sense of frustration that he was at the frontline of public relations but without any inside knowledge of the investigation to make him seem anything more than a barrier between the people and the information. Not that he could or would have told people much more than he was able to now, but being able to say 'we' instead of 'they' when talking about the murder hunt would have reassured people that their local bobby was taking an interest, and made him feel like less of a fraud. Jonas was not a self-important man – when Lucy had been diagnosed with Multiple Sclerosis he had left his future behind him and never looked back – but for the first time in his career he felt he needed the validation of being an insider. It made him abashed to admit it, even to himself.

Finally back in Shipcott, he walked past the flapping blue-and-white tape cordoning off Margaret Priddy's cottage at the end of the row. The Taunton cops had put it up to keep people out, but, of course, all it had done was draw attention to the scene. Since Sunday morning when it went up, he'd seen local boys daring each other under the tape to knock on the door, and now he noticed that Will Bishop had left milk on the doorstep. It had frozen in one of the bottles and pushed the silver-foil lid up into the air, where it perched like a jaunty cap on a misshapen column of crystalline calcium.

Jonas knew the milk would be sure to piss Marvel off. He'd have to do something about it.

As he walked through the village he'd grown up in, Jonas was reminded that in the years he had been away from Shipcott, not much had changed but plenty had happened.

Mr Jacoby's shop had become a Spar; Mr Randall's son Neil had left his right leg beside an army checkpoint in Iraq, and the bones of poor Mrs Peters' lost son had been found at last up on the moor. The consequences would have been imperceptible to anyone but a local. When he'd first come back after the death of his parents, Jonas had noticed that everything in Mr Jacoby's shop had a price label on it now, so Mr Jacoby's eidetic recall was surplus to requirements – which made Mr Jacoby sort of surplus to requirements too; that Neil Randall was getting drunker and more bloated by the day, so that his woven way home along narrow pavements on his poorly fitted prosthetic was becoming a hazard to traffic; and that Mrs Peters no longer stood at her window waiting for Billy to come back.

A stranger wouldn't have understood.

But Jonas did.

While never wondering why he was so blessed – or cursed – Jonas understood how almost everything important happens underneath, and away from public view – that signage and medals and headlines are just the tip of the village iceberg, and that real life is shaped long before and far below the surface in the blue-black depths of the community ocean.

Linda Cobb complained about the boys getting under the tape and banging on Margaret's door and windows. Jonas said he'd have a word.

A little way up, Mrs Peters opened her door. 'What's happening with Margaret?' He told her what he'd been telling people all day.

'And what are *you* doing?' she asked bluntly.

'Nothing,' he said, and when Mrs Peters cocked her grey head and peered up at him intently, he hurried on: 'I mean, they're the experts in this sort of crime.'

She eyed him for a disbelieving second, then snorted.

Jonas got a sudden uneasy flash of the day her son had disappeared. Jonas had been at school with Billy. In the not-quite-dark summer evening he and his friends had buzzed with the sick thrill of a boy gone missing. For a short while they had roamed the streets, made adult and brash by the self-proclaimed tag of 'search party'. Then later, when he was alone, there had been the more sobering – more *real* – sight of torches on the moor and lazy blue lights pulsing past the windows, until his mother came into his room, yanked his curtains together, and told him if she had to come in one more time, then his behind would be the first to know about it. He remembered lying in the dark afterwards, sure of what must have happened to Mrs Peters' little boy, and fearing it would happen to him too . . .

'They'll catch him, Mrs Peters,' he said now, and tried to put as much feeling into it as he could. More than anyone in Shipcott, she deserved to be reassured that she was safe – that her family was safe.

She didn't look reassured. 'Poor Margaret,' she said by way of goodbye. Then she turned into the house and closed the door.

He really should be doing something. Or at least come up with a better answer than 'nothing' the next time somebody asked him. He hadn't realized how bad it sounded until he said it out loud.

Up ahead he saw the milk float bump on to the pavement . . .

Will Bishop told Jonas that he'd been paid a month in advance.

'But there's nobody there, Will.'

'Yur, but her's paid me to provide a service, see. Can't just take the money and then stop doing the job just on account of Mrs Priddy being dead, can I?'

Jonas knew that the 'her' who had paid Will Bishop was Peter Priddy. Older locals still blurred their genders that way. He looked at the milkman. He was seventy if he was a day. Whip-thin, weathered, and as crumpled as a brown paper bag. Been delivering milk on this part of the moor seven days a week for over fifty years.

Jonas admired his devotion to duty but he also knew that the logical option – halting the deliveries and giving Peter Priddy his money back – had not even crossed Will Bishop's mind. If there was a tighter fist on Exmoor, Jonas would not have liked to have felt its grip. Had Margaret Priddy's house been picked up and swept away by a twister, Will Bishop would have continued to place a pint on the lonely doorstep every day until he'd discharged his duty. And the very day the bill was overdue, he'd have left a note instead: *Pay yor bill or I will see you in cort*, or *Pay yor milkman or pay the consuquenses*. Jonas and Lucy had had such a note themselves which read: *Milk bill dew. Pay up OR ELSE*.

Jonas hated to pull rank, but . . . 'You're not supposed to cross the police tapes, Will. It's a crime scene.'

Will looked up at him witheringly with his small, bright-blue eyes: 'I seen them roller-skate boys bang on the door plenty.'

'I know, but they don't leave a pint of milk there as proof that they've been.' Jonas sighed. '*I* don't mind. I know it's harmless. But Taunton is handling the investigation now and they *will* mind.'

Will waved a hand of dismissal and hopped back

into his float. 'Let 'em sue me then! I'll see 'em in court!'

His getaway was slow and electric, but Jonas still felt as if he'd been left eating the milkman's dust.

*

The CSIs had finished with Margaret Priddy's home and so, in the absence of a local police station – and with the stables too far from the village to make an effective base – Marvel had arranged to meet her son there. Once foul play was confirmed, he'd be able to call in a mobile incident room and work from that.

In any case, Marvel liked to question suspects or would-be suspects at the scene of the crime whenever possible. He had seen too many guilty men crack under the weight of memory to discount it as an investigative tool. So he got Reynolds to tell Priddy to meet them outside, and then Marvel led them into the kitchen.

Peter Priddy was a tall, broad man, but with the unfortunate face of a toddler. His cheeks were too rosy, his chin too pudgy, his eyes too blue and his hair too wispy-yellow to fake adulthood, even when perched atop such a frame. But Marvel noted that the man's hand engulfed his own when he shook it. He also noted the shiny black work-shoes that spoke of a uniform in another context.

'Prison officer,' said Priddy when he enquired. 'At Longmoor.'

'Interesting,' said Marvel, which was what he always said when he had no interest.

Priddy spoke slowly and carefully and in the country twang Marvel hated so much. He made tea – thick and milky – and then searched pointlessly through the cluttered kitchen cupboards for a packet of Jaffa Cakes he claimed to have brought on his last visit, while Marvel and Reynolds sat at the table.

'Not real ones,' Priddy added hastily, to allay any soaring expectations. 'Spar ones. Copies.'

'Generic,' supplied Reynolds helpfully and Marvel frowned; Reynolds couldn't bear to hide his education – even when it came to biscuits.

'Please don't trouble yourself,' said Marvel formally, but Priddy got on his haunches in case someone had hidden them behind the bleach under the kitchen sink.

'I know they're by here somewhere. I brought them myself and Mum weren't a big biscuit person.'

'Could she eat anything? With her injury?'

'Only all mushed up.'

Reynolds grimaced at the idea.

'Was that the last time you saw your mother?' asked Marvel.

'Yes.'

'How long ago was that?'

'Errrrr . . . About two weeks.' He straightened up and stared at the door of the refrigerator. 'This is daft.'

'I understand she was unable to speak?'

'That's true,' said Priddy with his head in another cupboard, 'but she could blink and smile and so forth. I'll bet them fucking nurses have had them.' He slammed the door.

Marvel and Reynolds exchanged brief looks. For the first time since they'd arrived, Peter Priddy looked at them properly. He sighed, leaned on the kitchen counter and threw his hands briefly in the air in anger. 'Have you seen the size of them? Them nurses? I'm amazed there's a bloody thing left in these cupboards.' Then his big baby-face screwed up and he let out a single bubbly sob.

'Sorry,' he added and blew his nose into a crumpled handkerchief.

Marvel hated shows of emotion and ignored them whenever possible. 'Is anything missing from the house?'

Priddy looked confused. 'Not that I've noticed. They wouldn't let me upstairs.'

Reynolds looked sympathetic. 'We can assign you a family liaison officer, Mr Priddy. They'd keep you informed of the progress of the investigation.'

Priddy shook his big baby-head and stared at the new contents of his handkerchief before stuffing it back into his pocket.

'Who paid for your mother's care, Mr Priddy?'

'She did. She had savings.'

'What's that cost nowadays?' said Marvel, turning to Reynolds as if he would know. 'Five hundred, six hundred quid a week? Savings don't last long at that rate.'

'More like seven hundred,' supplied Priddy with a grimace. 'She had my dad's pension too, but it weren't going to last for ever.'

'No. Precisely. And what would have happened then?'

Priddy sighed and shrugged. 'Would have had to sell up and go into a home, I suppose. On benefits.'

'Once she'd spent all her savings?'

'Yes.'

'All your inheritance.'

'That's the way it goes nowadays,' said Priddy with a long-suffering air. 'She would have wanted to stay here though. That's why I got the nurses. I'm glad in a way that she died here and never had to go into some shitty nursing home.'

'Oh yes. Much better she die in her own bed, hey?'

Marvel watched for his response but the barb was lost; Priddy was staring at curling photos stuck on the fridge. Horses mostly, several with Margaret on them. One of a chubby child in a Batman T-shirt.

'Did you ever get the feeling that your mother was in danger, Mr Priddy?'

'No,' said Priddy, returning his attention to Marvel. 'Who from?'

'One of the nurses perhaps?'

Priddy shook his head, surprised. 'I don't think so. Why?'

'Anyone else?'

'Like who?'

'*You* tell *me* like who,' Marvel said – and the words hung between them, their slightly harder tone changing the very air in the room.

Peter Priddy's gaze hardened. 'Not like me,' he said very slowly.

Marvel shrugged, his eyes never leaving Priddy's. 'All that money pouring out every week. *Your* money, really . . .'

'That's sick.'

'People *are* sick,' said Marvel sharply. 'Most people are murdered by someone they know. Someone they love. I'm just asking.'

'And I'm just telling you,' said Priddy stiffly.

'Well,' said Marvel, pushing himself off the chair with the help of a heavy hand on the kitchen table, 'thank you, Mr Priddy.'

Silence.

Reynolds flipped his notebook shut and looked uncomfortable.

'We'll be in touch,' added Marvel as he started towards the front door.

The big man watched them leave with contempt in his baby-blue eyes.

At the front door Reynolds turned back. 'Thanks for the tea, Mr Priddy,' he said.

Priddy snorted as he swung the door closed. 'I can't believe I was trying to find the Jaffa Cakes for you.'

They walked to the car.

'That went well,' said Reynolds.

'Shut up,' said Marvel.

*

At the shop Jonas bought a Mars Bar and peeled the price off a can of pineapple chunks so that Mr Jacoby could exercise his dormant talent and tell him they were 44p.

He came outside and saw a slip of paper under the windscreen wiper of his Land Rover. This was how a village worked – gossip over garden fences, Chinese whispers from the postman or the milkman, idle chats with Mr Jacoby or Graham Nash in the Red Lion – and these little flyers. They were run off on home PCs and displayed a wild variety of grammatical competence while offering a wide range of content: Young Farmers' Club discos, car-boot sales, the Winsford Woodbees doing *South Pacific*, cats lost and umbrellas found. He slid the flyer from under the wiper and got into the car, which was still warm because he'd left the engine running. He knew it was against the rules but this wasn't Bristol; this was Shipcott, where he knew all by sight and most by name; nobody was going to steal his car except possibly Ronnie Trewell, and if Ronnie stole it, Jonas would know where to find it, so that wasn't so much stealing as it was borrowing really, when you thought about it.

Jonas unfolded the flyer, expecting to crumple it immediately and throw it in the plastic Spar bag he kept for litter.

Instead he felt as if he'd been punched in the stomach.

Call yourself a policeman?

Jonas stared at the words in dumb shock. It was so unexpected. The note was only pen on paper but contempt came off it like something sharp and physical. Whoever wrote it hated him.

Hated.

Him.

Jonas couldn't think for a moment or two – just gripped the scrap of paper so tightly that his fingers went white at the tips, while his stomach clenched painfully.

Then he felt the heat of shame rise up his neck and into his ears.

Whoever had written this note was right. He was a policeman. The *only* policeman in Shipcott! And protecting people was his job – his whole reason for being. If he couldn't protect people, he had no right to the title. The logical part of his brain started to complain that he could not have known that Margaret Priddy was in danger, but it was quickly smothered by the guilt. It didn't matter. He *should* have known. Mrs

Priddy was a member of *his* community; she was *his* responsibility. And yet someone had climbed through Mrs Priddy's window and crammed a pillow on to her face and stolen her life from her, such as it was. He, Jonas Holly, was here to stop things like that happening. He'd failed, and she'd died – simple as that.

Jonas bit his lip. He looked around to see if anyone was watching him – maybe a clue as to who had written the note in this odd, spiky hand. His eyes scanned the empty street and darted from parked car to parked car, seeking a watchful silhouette or the sudden ducking motion that could denote culpability. Then his gaze flickered over the windows of the brightly painted cottages that crowded the narrow main street, waiting for a twitching net to give the guilty party away.

Nothing moved apart from Bill Beer's fat border collie, Bongo, snuffling his way up towards the shop where he spent every day door-hanging for treats and gently removing sweets from the unwary hands of passing toddlers.

Jonas felt like a stranger in his own home. Somebody knew he'd failed in his duty. Worse than that . . . that *somebody* wasn't on his side. Jonas had always felt that the local people held him in warm regard. Now a small dagger of ice had pierced that warmth and everything had changed in an instant.

Call yourself a policeman?

Jonas tore the note into small pieces and squeezed

those pieces together into a shapeless lump in his hand, before dropping them in the litter bag behind the passenger seat.

Then he looked around at the village once more and – with a hollow sense of foreboding – drove slowly away down its curiously silent street.

*

Lucy watched *The Exorcist* in slices between her inter-twined fingers. So silly! She'd watched it a dozen times; it was dated; the story was so copied it was a retroactive cliché; the effects were all pea soup and puppetry – and it scared the crap out of her every time.

Lucy had a degree in psychology. She knew that demonic possession was rubbish – that it was the way religions had for centuries explained conditions like schizophrenia and multiple-personality disorders. She knew that. She reminded herself of that. She believed it to be so. But the idea of a little girl possessed by the devil, of a mother's reluctance to accept the fact as her golden-haired child descends into apparent madness – and the final showdown in all its hellish hamminess. It ticked all the right boxes for Lucy.

She had always liked horror films. As a teenager they had just been a way to allow a boy to put his arm around her at the movies without feeling as though she was being a slut. Then she got addicted to the thrill – the jumps and the gore. How many ways *could* a head come off a human being? How far *could* blood squirt from a severed artery? And over what? Or whom? Lucy applauded every new method of murder, exalted any clever new way to make her jump out of her skin, bowed down in awe to any film that could leave her wishing that turning on the lights on a winter's afternoon was a quicker affair than hauling herself across the room on sticks and pressing the switch with her chin.

But she always came back to *The Exorcist*.

Often, when she thought about her life and death, Lucy wondered about her passion for horror. She had finally come to the conclusion that it was born out of a deep-seated sense of security. Until the MS was diagnosed, Lucy had led a charmed life. She had meandered through school and university in the manner of many very bright students – neglecting her studies with a vengeance and yet still managing to pick up her First and lifelong friends along the way. She had dabbled with cannabis and yet never had a trip worse than the one where she suspected her best friend, Sharma, had stolen her new Max Factor mascara. She had been on three protest marches – Animal Rights, Tibet, and Tibet again – without ever having her name taken by police. She'd got drunk only in the company of friends who made sure she got home safely, she'd never lost a close relative and she'd never had her heart broken. Probably, she reasoned, she enjoyed horror because nothing even vaguely similar had ever happened to her or ever would.

At least, that's what she told Jonas.

But it was not as strictly true as it had been before she was diagnosed. Since the MS had started to take over her life, she grudgingly recognized some need to *test* herself through horror, to push the boundaries of her own strength and resourcefulness to reassure herself that she was not yet helpless – even if the test was just in her mind.

She watched the films for fun; she studied them like manuals.

No longer could she simply see a pretty young girl walk through creepy woods or a dark house without some part of her wishing she was there – and handling it better.

Lucy Holly would *never* turn round and call out, 'Who's there?' in that tremulous voice. *She*'d duck suddenly into the trees, circle silently back through the undergrowth and get behind the lurching zombies. See how *they* liked it!

She'd *never* creep downstairs in the dark with a knife shaking pathetically in her hand to confront an intruder; *she*'d stay at the top of the stairs and tip the landing bookcase on to the bastard as he crept ignorantly up towards her.

If she could stalk a zombie; if she could squash an intruder . . . how hard could it be to repel the killer in her own body?

Sometimes, when she felt mentally strong enough,

Lucy would stand naked and watch herself in the mirror. That was what it felt like – *watching* herself, not *looking*.

She had been beautiful. She knew that – although it was behind her now.

The year of steroids was over and she had lost all the weight and more. She had hated being fat and puffed up almost more than she hated the disease – had not wanted Jonas to touch her, even when she wanted to touch *him*. But now even she could see that things had gone too far the other way. She was so thin and wobbly that when she stood before the mirror she almost fancied that, if she only looked hard enough, she could see the very beast that was consuming her from the inside out. Sometimes she even thought she caught a glimpse of it – a tic in the skin stretched over her hip, an odd bulge under her ribs that disappeared with the light. She would feel sick at the thought that one day she might be looking into this mirror and see a sharp claw split her belly, a scaled hand emerge, and the cold-eyed reptilian disease open her skin like curtains on the final act in the play of her life.

Lucy shivered, even though their heating bills were ridiculously high and she had the rug snuggled up to her chin. She thought of the real-life horror that had played out less than a quarter of a mile from where she lay now on the couch. Had Margaret woken before dying? She must have. Even if it was only when the pillow was already over her face. The terror. The helpless terror. Lucy felt compassion overwhelm her. Poor Margaret.

Shamefully hot on the heels of compassion came the usual question: what would *she* do?

She thought that she would bite an assailant to make him let go of her. Biting was weird, and taboo enough to be unexpected. So, bite him in the face like a pit bull. She imagined the taste of his unshaven cheek and the howl of pain and outrage as his grip loosened . . . Then she would jerk upwards and sideways to throw him off the bed and on to the floor – like *this*! – then she would twist, fling the bed covers over his head, stamp on the place where she'd last seen his face and run next door to Mrs Paddon to use the phone.

There!

She was mentally breathless, but drew real strength from her imagined actions, reassured that if anyone ever tried anything like that with her when Jonas wasn't around, she'd done as much as she could – and more than most people – to prepare herself.

There was a faint rumbling noise, then the sound of the garden gate squeaking and a tentative knock on the door. Lucy changed channels to the *Antiques Roadshow* and called, 'Come in, Steven!'

A gangly sixteen-year-old sloped into the room with white earphones in, making only shy eye-contact.

'I brought your paper, Mrs Holly.'

As if he'd be doing anything else. The DayGlo sack

resting on his hip with *Exmoor Bugle* emblazoned across it was the giveaway, just as the rumble of his skateboard wheels on the road outside the front gate was his weekly herald.

'Thanks, Steven. How are you?'

Steven Lamb had been delivering their paper since they moved in, and Lucy had watched him change from a boy into a teenager in weekly increments. First he'd been a scrawny thirteen-year-old, small for his age, and so shy that he had reddened and stammered at the mere idea that he might actually *come in* to deliver the paper instead of push it through the letter-box. Only the five-pound tip Jonas Holly pressed into his hand every month seemed to convince him that the policeman was serious – that he should indeed enter their home and give his wife the paper in person.

'It's what people *do* here,' Jonas had fibbed to Lucy at the time. 'Make sure she's all right and call me if she's not,' he'd told Steven privately – just as he'd requested of Will Bishop and Frank Tithecott and Mrs Paddon next door.

It had taken almost a year before Steven had even engaged in conversation beyond a flushed and mumbled 'Hello,' but he took his gratuity seriously and, on the occasions when Lucy failed to answer his knock, he would wait and knock again, or go round and check the garden. He never left without finding her, and once had called Jonas to tell him his wife was crying upstairs, and then waited for nearly an hour on the chilly doorstep for him to come home.

Now Steven would come in and say, 'I brought your paper, Mrs Holly,' then Lucy would ask him to sit down for five minutes and he would do that – always on the most uncomfortable chair in the room – and he would face the TV and watch with her whatever was on. Sometimes it was *Countdown*, sometimes it was one of those shows about buying houses or selling antiques, mostly it was a horror movie and they would flinch together in companionable silence. Lucy no longer minded that Steven saw her using her tasselled cushion for protection, and she never mentioned that she often saw him gently shut his eyes in moments of extreme tension.

Steven had eyes that often looked distant, as if something was troubling him. She imagined it must be his homework or girls, but she never asked. She was afraid that if she did, he would shy away from coming again.

And Lucy loved having him there.

She'd been a kindergarten teacher before the disease had taken hold of her, and missed children with a passion – their fresh openness, their honesty and lack of guile. The way they would look to her for comfort, or come in with a joke they'd been saving up for her, give her misshapen lumps of painted clay for her birthday, and the way they didn't mind being babied if they skinned their shins on the jungle gym.

Over the years Lucy had tried offering Steven a cup

of tea or a biscuit, in the hope that he would extend his stay, but he had never accepted. He would get a little frown line between his eyes as if he was really considering it, and then always say the same thing: 'Ummmm . . . no, thank you.' So she'd stopped asking that and instead now and then asked him about himself. He would answer briefly without turning away from the TV, and with a refreshing indifference to his own ego that made his life so far sound like the most tedious sixteen years in human history. He lived with his mother and grandmother and little brother Davey. They did nothing and went nowhere. School was all right, he supposed. He liked history and he wrote a good letter. Once he'd brought her a bag of carrots he and his Uncle Jude had grown. Another time it was beans. 'I don't like them, but they're fun to grow,' he'd said, watching police frogmen drag a bloated corpse from a river. 'Water destroys all the good evidence,' he'd added sombrely at the screen, making Lucy look away to smile.

Occasionally, as time wore on, Steven would volunteer something even if she hadn't asked.

His mother had a new job cleaning at the school and now was always there when he got home. He was planting onions, which his nan had promised to pickle. 'Makes my mouth go funny just thinking of them.' It was his friend Lewis's birthday and Steven had bought him a catapult. 'And ammo,' he added mysteriously.

Lucy was fascinated by it all.

Now she hit mute on the *Antiques Roadshow* in the hope that Steven would fill the space with random boy-speak.

After a few dead-end questions from her, she struck gold when Steven mentioned that his nan had bought slippers at Barnstaple market and then insisted on keeping them even though they were both left feet. 'She looks like she's always going round corners,' he said seriously, and seemed pleasantly surprised when Lucy laughed.

He turned back to the telly. 'I've seen this one,' he sighed at a woman with an ugly Majolica pot, and stood up. Ten minutes a week – maybe fifteen – was all Steven Lamb ever gave her, but Lucy cherished the time.

'Bye, Mrs Holly,' he mumbled.

'Bye, Steven,' she said and listened to the squeak and then the rumble that was him leaving for another week. She thought about his life unfolding – somewhere else away from her – and sighed. Now she understood why her mother called so often.

When she switched back from the *Antiques Roadshow* she'd missed *The Exorcist*'s head-spinning scene and rewound. Then she watched the demonic girl's neck twist and creak in sickening circles – while all the time she yearned for a child.

Twenty-one Days

The heating in the stable was on the blink and short flurries of overnight snow seemed to have come through the TV aerial because even the few available channels were now only visible through a white swirl of static. After cursing the tepid water and aborting a shave, Marvel decided he needed to yell at someone, so called Jos Reeves a good hour before he was due to arrive at the lab.

'Well,' said Reeves calmly at the other end of the line – and Marvel itched as he heard the man light up a cigarette before continuing – 'we've got seven hairs, dozens of fibres and we rushed through the saliva on the pillow.'

Marvel didn't acknowledge the rush. 'Is it hers?'

'Yes. Looks like you have your murder.'

'Good,' said Marvel, devoid of tact. 'Prints?'

'No fingers, no feet.'

'Fuck,' said Marvel. 'Semen?'

'Nope. No blood, no semen. Some urine though.'

'She had a bag. It burst.'

'Oh dear,' said Reeves.

Marvel was now irritated anew by the fact that he'd chosen to call and yell at one of the few people he couldn't intimidate. Jos Reeves was so laid back he was supine. Not for the first time, Marvel wondered about the contents of the cigarette he could hear Reeves sucking on now and then. He wished he'd called Reynolds instead and demanded something unreasonable. Watch his head get all patchy. He told Reeves to keep him updated when they had results on the hairs and fibres and hung up while he still had a reasonable reserve of vitriol.

Marvel walked across the wet concrete courtyard and knocked officiously on Joy Springer's door. Even though it was 7am and still dark, the old woman was up and dressed and had a hand-rolled cigarette clamped in her drawstring mouth. Another setback in his quest for the upper hand.

'There's no hot water,' he snapped.

'Well, it's not *cold*, is it?' she snapped back.

Marvel was wrong-footed. 'It's lukewarm,' he said feebly.

'Lukewarm in't cold. Did you let it run?'

'No,' he said grudgingly.

'You got to give it a chance to come through, bay. Specially when there's a freeze on.'

Marvel glanced past her and saw the bottle on the kitchen table. It looked like breakfast.

Joy Springer saw his gaze and moved forward to hustle him backwards. She clutched her big old woollen cardigan with leather buttons together at her wrinkled throat and gestured at the open door with one gnarled hand. 'And now you'm be letting my heat out.'

Marvel withdrew gracelessly and went back to his quarters, wishing he could start the morning again. He let the water run and it finally came through hot, but only if he almost closed the tap to a trickle. Finally he boiled the inadequate travel kettle and shaved with the proceeds.

He banged on Reynolds's door half an hour before they'd agreed, but his DS was ready to go.

'I'm arresting Priddy,' Marvel said by way of good morning.

Reynolds knew better than to openly disagree. 'OK,' he said neutrally as they walked to the car.

'If it was burglary gone wrong then the killer knew the nurses' routines and he knew what he was looking for, in which case it's got to be one of the nurses or a friend or family. If it was murder, then it's personal and ditto.'

Marvel glared at Reynolds, daring him to protest. When he didn't, his own theory lost some of its shine and he dumped the clutch irritably.

'I suppose we can always ask him for a DNA sample

once the results on hairs and fibres are in,' said Reynolds with a mild-mannered shrug. 'Confirm it then.'

Marvel gripped the steering wheel more tightly. Trust Reynolds to ruin everything with his slavish devotion to the niceties of evidence. Nobody played a hunch any more.

*

Marvel could go and screw himself.

That was the thought that kept rolling around Jonas Holly's brain. This was *his* patch, these were *his* neighbours, and Margaret Priddy has been *his* responsibility.

And if Marvel wasn't going to let him on the team, he would simply fly solo. He had his usual work to do and no one – neither Marvel nor anyone else – could keep him from asking a few questions, keeping his eyes peeled, and responding to whatever he heard or saw. That was the job he was paid to do, after all.

After a restless night, Jonas rose at 5.45am, kissed a sleeping Lucy goodbye at 6.30, checked that Mrs Paddon had taken her milk in and was therefore still alive, walked down the pitch-dark road into the village, and knocked on his first door at 6.45am to be sure of catching the four or five residents he knew would shortly be off to work themselves, leaving empty houses behind them for the day.

By the time the school bell rang at nine, Jonas had

covered about thirty houses, asking the same questions again and again and again up and down Barnstaple Road. What did you see? What did you hear? Anything suspicious? Anything that might help? Do you have my number?

All morning, as he made careful notes of random comments, Jonas had the uncomfortable feeling that he was being watched.

It was the note. The note bothered him. *More* than bothered him. There was no home that Jonas asked questions in where a little voice in his head did not ask another question: Was it *him*? Was it *her*? Did *they* write the note?

The very fact that he had not discussed it with Lucy was proof of how badly it had shaken him. Jonas was not in the habit of hiding things from his wife. So he knew that this guilty itch at the back of his neck and his urge to turn around suddenly was most likely due to keeping a secret from Lucy.

Since Monday morning when he'd found it, Jonas's jaw tightened every time he approached the Land Rover; his eyes swept the screen, fearing another accusation – another truth. And at night when he helped Lucy upstairs to bed, it was the note he thought of as often now as the way his wife was wasting away beneath his hands. She had been through the steroids that made her fat but now he could feel the ribs in her back, the knobs of her spine, the blade of her pelvis poking rudely at the place where her smooth and pretty hip used to be. His wife was disappearing and it was his job to keep her from falling backwards into the abyss.

Lucy needs you. Now more than ever.

She was going through the motions – getting up every day and getting dressed; planting daffodils and anemones too late in already-frozen ground, reading the *Bugle* and asking him about his day. But he knew it was all brittle brightness. The way she felt the need to smile at him when she caught him looking. The way she said 'I love you' with her lips while her eyes were always searching the perimeter wall for a way out.

The last thing *she* needed was to worry about *him*.

And if she knew how the note had made him feel, then she *would* worry. Because it had made him feel terrible.

Uneasy, guilty, paranoid.

Ashamed.

How could he tell her about the note? The weight of that cruel slip of paper might be enough to break her. Again.

No . . . Lucy had enough to carry. He would carry the note alone.

*

Marvel didn't arrest Peter Priddy, of course. He didn't even see Peter Priddy. He told Reynolds to continue the house-to-house in Shipcott and then spent the morning shouting at various imbeciles at HQ in a bid to get a mobile incident room assigned. Stuck out in the middle of all this air and weather, Marvel needed the grubby confines of a glorified caravan to feel a sense of purpose.

By the afternoon Marvel's Task Force were all gossiped out. Unlike movie imaginings of the secretive, sinister life of a small village, Shipcott residents couldn't wait to give their opinions of who-dunnit, and have their shaky recall tested by questions about what they saw on the night Margaret Priddy died. The team felt overloaded by pointless inform-ation. Snippets and digs, Miss Marple theories and bad blood.

As the light started to fade from the overcast winter sky, the Task Force met Marvel in the Red Lion to pool their information, and quickly discovered that their collective picture of a possible perpetrator amounted to a sole suspect in the shape of a local thief called Ronnie Trewell. To add insult to injury, between them at first they thought they had *three* promising leads. It took them nearly an hour to realize that Skew Ronnie, Ron Trewell and 'the boy what walks funny' were all the same person – and a mere car thief, to boot.

Despite that, Reynolds made a dutiful note of the name, wrote 'alias, Skew Ronnie (limp?)' next to it in his book and felt like one of the Famous Five doing it.

The team also reported that several residents had

been short with them because they'd already spoken to the local bobby.

'That idiot who waggled the vic's nose?' frowned Marvel.

'I suppose so,' said Reynolds. 'PC Holly.'

'Very festive,' said Elizabeth Rice, and Grey over-laughed as if he thought she just might sleep with him for doing so.

Marvel's already lined face got even more rumpled and he flicked a fingernail repeatedly against his glass of bitter lemon as if all would be well with the world if only he had a proper pint.

No one had had anything to report from Saturday night that was out of the ordinary because by now they all knew as well as any local that Neil Randall getting drunk and falling over was a regular occurrence, and – as they'd heard from at least four separate sources – that in the throes of passion, Angela Stirk in Bellbow Cottage *always* yipped like a dog.

'Got an Asbo for it, apparently,' said Grey with just a hint of admiration. 'And her husband's away on the rigs!'

Marvel stared into his drink as the reality dawned on him.

'Nothing,' he said. 'They've told us precisely nothing.'

'Maybe there was nothing to tell,' said Reynolds placatingly.

'Or maybe they told it all to their mate Holly already.'

'It's a possibility,' said Singh mildly.

'Fucking yokels,' said Marvel too loudly, and Reynolds glanced guiltily at the regulars at the bar and hogging the fire. None of them appeared to have heard. At least, no one was coming at Marvel with a pitchfork.

'Seems Mrs Priddy had no enemies,' Reynolds shrugged, steering them back to the victim. It always helped to be reminded of the victim in these cases – made everyone focus again when they were drifting or bickering.

'Yeah. I'm starting to think it was a random thing,' said Rice, downing her lemonade and wiping her mouth in a way that made Marvel wonder if she was a lesbian.

'Nothing is random,' he told her. 'There will be a reason – even if that reason makes no sense to anyone but the killer.'

*

The killer observed Jonas with a cold eye as he made his calls. Saw him bang his head against Will Bishop's odd logic, saw him step off the narrow pavement for Chantelle Cox with her ugly ginger baby in its cheap buggy, despised the way he scanned the street for the watcher he could feel but not see.

Jonas Holly was supposed to be the protector.

If he had done what he was supposed to, then the

killer would never have started – and might have been stopped.

The killer was here because Jonas was not doing his job.

And as long as he continued not doing his job, the killer would only get stronger.

Twenty Days

Jonas got an anonymous call from Linda Cobb to say that Yvonne Marsh was on the swings in her knickers. He knew Linda's voice and she knew that he knew it, but anonymity was hard to come by in a village as small as Shipcott, and he liked to respect it wherever possible. Nobody liked to be a tattle-tale.

Yvonne Marsh was indeed on the swings in her knickers. Despite the frozen ground, the dull brown sky and the stares of the boys on the nearby skate ramp, she sat slumped and flaccid in a greying bra and semi-matching briefs.

Not for the first time.

Jonas took a scratchy grey blanket from the Land Rover and walked towards the mother of his old school friend. As he got closer he could see her pale flesh raised in goose-bumps, mottled purple from the cold.

'She's been there half an hour!' one of the skaters called to him. He looked over at them but couldn't tell which of them had spoken, so just raised one hand in a vague gesture of acknowledgement. The boys – four of them – were lined up on the top of the ramp, watching, their fingers tucked into their armpits and pockets, their skateboards captured with easy dominance underfoot like dead colonial lions.

'Hello, Mrs Marsh,' he said cheerfully. 'Bit nippy for swings, isn't it?'

Her distant stare shifted to him without real focus. She didn't recognize him and he was grateful for it. He thought of the day he and Danny had jumped out of the bathroom window holding Mrs Marsh's brand-new Egyptian cotton sheets as parachutes. He could still feel the garden hitting his feet – the jar of it running up to his armpits – and Danny's high-pitched yowling in the flower bed.

He focused.

Her breasts were almost on her thighs, the way she sat. In between were three distinct rolls of cold, pale fat.

'Want a blanket?' Jonas stepped forward and, when she did not object, draped it over her shoulders and gathered it at her throat. 'Here, you hold on to that for me, Mrs Marsh,' he said as he unfurled her left hand from the chain and moved it to the blanket. She gripped the wool, still vacant, and he straightened up.

'Got the heater on in the car. And a flask of tea. You want to jump in there and warm up a bit?'

'All right then,' she said. 'But I lost my sandals in the lake.'

'No problem, Mrs Marsh, I'll send one of my lads out to find them.'

There was no lake. He had no lads.

She staggered as she rose from the swing and he caught her with one arm around what used to be her waist, and helped her to the car – slowly because of her bare feet on the frosty grass and then the rough tarmac.

He settled Mrs Marsh into the passenger seat and leaned across her to fasten the seatbelt. He caught a scent of unwashed body and remembered a different Mrs Marsh sunbathing in her tiny back garden, the sleek lines of her tanned skin, the smell of coconut lotion, the stolen peek at the swell of her full breasts and how they sloped away from her body to be captured by the meagre turquoise cups of her bikini . . .

'I remember you, Jonas Holly,' she said suddenly and with a sly lilt that made him blush as if they were back in that summer garden and it was *that* Mrs Marsh who had caught that long-gone boy peeking.

He said nothing, willing her to shut up.

'Sticking gum in Danny's hair!' she teased, and fluttered her lashes at him. 'And mud all over my best sheets that day he fell in the roses!'

Jonas hoped this wasn't the start of a sudden shower of remembering after a long dry spell.

But she just laughed again and sighed. 'You boys!'

He gave a rueful smile and shut the door on her. By the time he had walked round the back of the Land Rover and opened his own door, she had forgotten who he was.

Danny Marsh answered his knock and Jonas watched his expression flit from surprise to wariness and then to concern as he registered that Jonas had his near-naked mother in tow.

'My sandals are in the lake,' she said as he drew her indoors, gently handing her over to his tight-lipped father and watching them disappear into the kitchen, where it was always warm. Jonas could hear Alan Marsh murmuring quietly and his wife's confused responses growing more muffled as they went.

For a moment he and Danny stood awkwardly, both looking down the hallway at nothing at all. Then Danny cleared his throat and said, 'Thanks, mate.'

'No problem.'

It was the first time they had spoken in twenty years.

*

While the rest of his team went on knocking on hope-less doors, Marvel drove to Margaret Priddy's under a sky the colour of an old bruise. He wanted to be able to think, without Reynolds being clever beside him.

Three boys sitting hunched on a bench at the edge of the playing field shared a cigarette and watched him lock his car.

'Double yellows there, mate,' one of them pointed out.

'Shouldn't you be in school?' he said and they all looked at him as if he were speaking Dutch. Shut them up, though.

Marvel faced the playing field. One hundred yards to his left was a sign saying THANK YOU FOR DRIVING SLOWLY THROUGH SHIPCOTT. He knew that the back of it read PLEASE SLOW DOWN THROUGH SHIPCOTT. Or something like that; it had been blurred when he'd passed it. He'd also driven by several cottages dotted singly or in pairs at the roadside, part of the village but separate from it. But Margaret Priddy's home, with its dirty peach walls, was the first one inside the tenuous boundary marked by the sign. He wondered whether that was significant – whether the killer had come from the east and broken into the first house he reached. That would say something about his state of mind. It would speak of desperation and recklessness. But the killer had left no prints – not even shoe prints – which didn't fit with recklessness.

The playing field had goalposts without nets, and sloped alarmingly towards the furthest corner flag. In London the flags would have been stolen. Behind the posts nearest the village were three swings, an old metal slide of the type that most council Health & Safety committees had long since sold for scrap, and a low half-pipe skateboard ramp with a railing along each end – presumably to keep the village children from loop-the-looping into the narrow stream that ran along the back of the field, marking the foot of the moor. While Marvel watched, a lone fat collie meandered over and took a shit on the penalty spot.

Marvel could see dark footprints in the frosty grass leading to and from the swings and more to the ramp. Skating before school. Or maybe instead of school. Truants? Drop-outs? Or something more sinister? Apart from his good nose for a killer, Marvel's greatest gift was that he could see the bad in anyone. He had already seen enough in his career to justify a healthy dose of misanthropic suspicion and, in his mind, a half-pipe ramp and a crime scene in anything like close proximity was good enough reason to pull in any passing skater for a grilling. If the killer wasn't Peter Priddy, he'd put good money on it being some zit-covered hoodie with his fake Calvin Kleins poking out of his half-mast jeans.

'You skate?' he asked the boys, then – when they looked confused – he jerked his thumb at the ramp. They all turned round and stared at it as if it had suddenly materialized from outer space.

'Nah,' said one. 'We smoke.'

Slow sleet started to fall straight down from the sky

like broken plumb-lines, and the boys got up as one and hurried off. Marvel pulled the collar of his overcoat up around his ears and ventured out on to the grass. Past the side of Margaret Priddy's home and round to the bottom of the garden, which was enclosed by buckled sheep wire on concrete posts and – now – a strip of police tape which an over-enthusiastic somebody had used to wrap around the entire house and garden like a birthday bow. Pollard, most likely. He lacked the imagination to make a bad job of anything.

The sheep wire sagged and bowed in several places, loose between the posts, and he had no trouble stepping over it. As he did he noticed that his dull-brown brogues were going dark with water, and made a mental note to buy some boots. He walked up the overgrown back garden, ridiculously trying not to put his feet down in the wet grass. He passed broken terracotta flowerpots showing dead roots, a pile of old metal door strips, a couple of plastic carrier bags pressed against the boundary fence, while a ramshackle kennel spoke of a long-ago dog. As if on cue a small brown terrier started to bark at him from next door, running up and down the line of the fence as if it might break through and tear him limb from limb, even though it was barely taller than his shin.

'Piss *off*!' Marvel feinted towards the dog and it yelped and rushed behind a garden shed, from where it peered and growled.

'All mouth and no bloody trousers,' muttered

Marvel, then swore and lurched sideways to avoid stepping in what looked like vomit in the grass between the back door and the lean-to. He stood for a moment staring down at it while large wet drops of ice plopped into it like little meteorites. Vomit! There was vomit at the murder scene and no one had spotted it! Not surprising – the vomit was only really visible from directly above – splashed through the tufty, unkempt grass like modern art. Marvel stood hunched over it, protecting it from the sleet, then realized that he couldn't do that for as long as it would take for some-one to get down here from the lab. They were lucky it had been pretty dry since the body was discovered.

There was an old steel dustbin on its side and he looked around for the lid. When he found it he put it carefully over the splash.

He pulled out his mobile phone and glared at the lack of signal bars on it. He'd discovered that they came and went here, seemingly on a whim, sometimes lingering for hours, sometimes teasing with a fleeting appearance and then winking out as quickly as they'd come.

The bloody sticks.

He looked up at the bedroom window. From here he could see how easy it had been for the killer to get into the house. The green wheelie bin that must have been used as a ladder had been carefully wrapped and taken to the lab for examination. His eyes traced the obvious path from the lean-to roof to the window. A man would have to be fit to pull himself up to force the latch and then over the sill, but he wouldn't have to be Superman.

Marvel tried the back door and felt a little stab of irritation when it opened, even though it saved him having to go round to the front door and using the key he had. He'd find out who had been responsible for leaving the house secure and give them a bollocking.

Inside, the place already felt abandoned. The kitchen where he and Reynolds had drunk tea just the day before yesterday was now cold and dingy. Their mugs were still in the sink with the dregs in the bottom. He wondered whether Peter Priddy had found the Jaffa Cakes after they'd left.

He tried the lights and they came on, although even they seemed dull and sickly.

Upstairs he stood in the bedroom doorway and stared for several minutes at the bed where Margaret Priddy had died. The linen had been stripped from it and taken away to the lab. All that was left was a blue mattress with an old yellow-brown stain on it. On the bedside table was a lamp with a stand made of a chipped plaster cherub, and a shade the same colour as the stain.

There was also an alarm clock, a box of tissues, and a dog-eared copy of Frank Herbert's *Dune*. Distant planets, spice wars and giant worms. One of the nurses was a man, he remembered. Gary Something. Liss. Gary Liss. Marvel guessed that the book belonged to him.

Lightning flickered and the lights went out with a resigned click. There was a long second when Marvel missed the tiny sound of electricity, and then he adjusted. With the fading light and the storm clouds, the house was all but dark now and Marvel could feel his heart pumping more urgently. Marvel had never liked the dark. Stupid! It was a power cut – that was all. Nothing to be afraid of. He took a rechargeable penlight from his pocket and switched it on. Strangely, it made him feel worse, not better. As if everything outside the narrow beam was now even blacker and more dangerous than it had been before.

Half a dozen Christmas cards were curling with damp beside the bed. He glanced at each; they said safe, meaningless things and were signed with the names of old people.

Love from Jean and Arthur. Best wishes from Dolly, Geoff and Family.

He opened the drawers and the wardrobe and examined the detritus of a life. The wardrobe contained few items of clothing but what there was smelled of damp. A winter coat, two dresses, a skirt, two blouses, carefully folded underwear, two pairs of sensible shoes speckled with mould. Enough to be going on with had Margaret Priddy ever been the subject of a miracle rather than a murder. The drawers were mini scrapyards of single earrings, old lipsticks, foreign coins and what looked like a pair of spurs. Right at the back of the bottom drawer was a jewellery box, which he opened with a modicum of anticipation, but all it held were yellowing invitations to weddings and christenings and a few fragile letters. He unfolded one . . . *wasn't at the Ridge when we arrived so we had coffee in the conservatory and waited . . . the going was bottomless so we all got into a fine mess and I was glad to hand the nappy beast back at the yard and walk away without a backward glance . . . naturally Raymond opened the '63 – always the snob . . .*

Marvel refolded the letter, closed the drawer and flicked off the penlight. His fingers were covered in fingerprint powder, which he wiped on the chintz curtains. Debbie would have gone mad to see him do it.

The window sill and frame were similarly daubed with powder and he ran a practised eye around the square of the frame, seeking anything the CSIs had missed. He always thought he might and was usually disappointed. They knew their job and did it well. The vomit was a rarity, but it wouldn't stop him giving Jos Reeves an earful first chance he got.

Outside the sleet had turned to rain.

He looked out at the moor, which rose so steep and close behind the houses that it stole the remaining light from the room.

What a place to live.

What a place to die.

He shivered and turned away from the window. Before he came back he'd get Grey to check the fuses; the man fancied himself handy.

Halfway down the stairs he heard a sound. He froze and held his breath. It came again – a scrape, a clink. His eyes followed his ears to the front door and he started to move again – with surprising stealth for a man his age and size. Another scrape. Someone was at the door. Trying to be quiet. Trying to break in? He put his hand to his pocket, felt his phone, but knew there was no signal . . . knew he'd have to deal with this alone . . . felt his heartbeat pick up again and adrenaline spurt into his guts at the thought.

Despite his job, it had been a long time since Marvel was in any actual personal danger. Homicide detectives, by their very nature, arrived *after* the killer had done his deed, and retro-engineered the crime from there. Sure, sometimes the killer was still at the scene – in the shape of a glazed-drunk teenager or a husband who had snapped and was already confessing. But being in imminent threat of violence was so rare that – if pressed – Marvel would have had trouble remembering when it had last happened.

Now he was shocked by how nervous he felt. How his breathing got too short and too loud and how he was suddenly aware of how *noisy* he was! His shoes creaked, his palm squeaked on the banister; his thigh-length coat scraped the woodchip wall in papery warning. Everything gave him away. And in a way he wanted it to. In a way he wanted the person who was now trying to gain access to the scene of Margaret Priddy's murder to hear him and run off. Then Marvel could open the front door and stare belligerently up and down the narrow street and pretend he was sorry to have missed his chance.

He suddenly remembered how a lot of people in Quentin Tarantino movies ended up.

He reached the bottom stair, the gloomy tiled hallway, ran his eyes over the door catch – bog-standard Yale – and braced his feet apart for balance. He raised his hands and saw that they were trembling like a drunk's. Outside, the scrape came again. A little whisper of cloth on the other side of the wooden door. He held his breath. All he had to do was quietly twist the knob, grip the handle and *pull* . . .

The brass knob slipped from his sweaty grip, the door hit his foot and rebounded, making him shut his eyes; he grabbed at it and caught the tip of his finger between it and the frame, sending a needle of pain running up his shoulders and neck like voltage.

Fuck!

Marvel finally gripped the door and focused.

Jonas Holly stood on the doorstep with a guilty look on his face and three pints of milk clutched to his chest.

'What the *fuck* are you doing?'

Marvel slammed the door behind Jonas and strode through the dim house to the kitchen. As he did, his fear and pain segued seamlessly into an anger that was fuelled by the dread that the younger man might have seen the panic on his face in the seconds he took to fumble the door open like some crappy amateur magician bungling a trick.

Jonas followed, as the DCI's angry stride demanded of him, still holding the icy bottles.

In the kitchen Marvel turned on Jonas.

'Explain yourself.'

Haltingly, Jonas did. He explained about Will Bishop, the relentless milkman. He tried to lighten the mood with the joke about the twister but it went nowhere. He got back on track by suggesting that the cordon of tape was doing nothing but flapping a challenge to local boys who were daring each other underneath it and annoying the neighbours; he dangled a comradely escape route in front of Marvel in the shape of a comment about how everyone in the village was understandably on edge with the killer still at large. Marvel ignored the comradeship *and* the escape.

And so – because he didn't really know what else he could usefully say – Jonas Holly made a serious mistake.

He apologized.

'I'm sorry, sir,' he said, 'if I gave you a fright.'

The glamorous assistant with a sword through her leg, the dead rabbit in the hat.

'You didn't give me a *fright*, you fucking moron! I almost fucking *killed* you, that's all! You don't know how close you fucking *came*!' Marvel bumped round the Formica table and held his thumb and forefinger a hair's breadth apart an inch from Jonas's nose.

'*This* close! This fucking close!'

'Yes, sir,' said Jonas, unable to meet Marvel's eyes to lend honesty to his answer.

Marvel glared up at him and Jonas felt himself starting to detach. He'd done all he could here. He'd done the right thing. If it hadn't worked then he would just have to let Marvel decide how this would play out.

Marvel watched Jonas's face go blank and knew he was hiding his real feelings. Knew he was hating him inside. Somehow that made Marvel feel a little better – that Jonas had to hide his feelings, while he – as the senior officer – was allowed to give vent to *his*.

'What was your name again?

'Jonas Holly, sir.'

Jonas felt cool now. Felt no need to justify himself or his actions. Felt comfortably distant. He'd seen the panic in Marvel's eyes as he cocked up the simple task of opening the door. He'd offered the man a graceful exit from embarrassment and Marvel had not only declined to accept that offer but Jonas had the distinct suspicion that the DCI was going to make him suffer for it.

'What's your take on this, Holly?'

'On what, sir?'

Marvel rolled his eyes and waved a brief arm at Margaret Priddy's house. 'This! What do you think of this case?'

Jonas was careful. He shrugged. He looked around. 'Um, I'm not sure, sir.'

'None of us are *sure*, Holly. If we were sure, we'd have caught the killer.'

'Yes, sir.'

'You think it's a local?'

'No, sir.'

Marvel raised his eyebrows. 'Interesting,' he said.

Jonas didn't like Marvel questioning him. He felt like a calf being corralled into the corner of a barn. Nothing bad was happening right now, but a veal crate was always a possibility. 'I only mean that I know everyone in Shipcott. Pretty much. Not everyone in the other villages, but in Shipcott I do. And I can't think of anyone who might have done this.'

Marvel pursed his lips and nodded as if it was all sinking in. Which it was.

'What about this Ronnie Trewell?'

'Skew Ronnie? He's a car thief.'

'Maybe he's moving up in the world.'

Jonas couldn't help smiling. 'Have you spoken to him, sir?'

'Not yet.'

'He's not moving anywhere. He's harmless. He's not . . . quite . . . right.' Jonas waved at his temple with his forefinger. 'You know?'

'The Yorkshire Ripper wasn't *quite right*, Holly.'

'Yes, sir.'

'What about Peter Priddy?'

'As the *killer*?'

'No, for president.'

Jonas ignored the sarcasm. 'I think it's highly unlikely.'

'Because you know him?'

'No, because I know what he's *like*.'

'And what is he like, Holly?'

'He's all right. Nothing special. He's just a good bloke.'

'So Trewell is harmless and Priddy's a good bloke. Convincing,' said Marvel waspishly.

Jonas was sick of standing in the corner of the barn. 'Don't you have any forensic evidence, sir?'

'That you didn't put your grubby great mitts all over?'

Jonas flushed deeply and realized he'd backed into the crate all by himself. Marvel wasn't being nice. He wasn't sharing. He'd just been waiting for his chance to get Jonas back for the fright at the door – he could see that now, but it was too late.

'And now I hear you've been doing our fucking *job*, Holly – bumbling about asking questions before we can go in.'

'People keep asking what we're doing, sir. What *I'm* doing. As the local officer I thought I should be doing *something*. That's all.'

After their first encounter Marvel had marked Jonas Holly down as spineless and stupid. Now he expanded his opinion of him to encompass spineless, stupid, and with ideas above his station. There was something about Jonas that brought out the bully in Marvel – made him want to cut the lanky young man down to size.

'You think you should be *involved*, do you, Holly?'

'Sir, I only—'

'Be part of the investigation? Get a bit of glamour in your life? Local bobby catches killer?'

'That's not what I—'

'OK then!' Marvel clapped his hands together and rubbed them as if he was about to partake in a truck-pull. 'Far be it from me to keep a good man down, Holly. I've got just the job for you.'

Jonas said nothing. He felt he could only make things worse.

But even his silence fed Marvel. 'Killers,' he said, 'like to return to the scene of the crime. Right?'

'Some do,' said Jonas warily.

'Then I want you to wait for him.'

Jonas was confused.

Marvel headed back to the front door, gesturing for Jonas to follow him. He opened the door and pointed at the now-empty step.

'I want *you* to stand *there* until further notice.'

'You're joking!' The words burst out of Jonas before he could stop them. He almost added 'sir' in an attempt to mitigate them, but that bird had flown.

Marvel was unruffled.

'Maintain the integrity of the crime scene. Report suspicious activity. Consider yourself *involved*.'

Jonas said nothing. Marvel cocked his head and put a hand behind his ear. 'I didn't hear you, PC Holly.'

Jonas had one last stab at resistance: 'What about *my* job? I'm not under your command. Sir.'

'What job? Cats up trees and taking fags off school kids? Do me a fucking favour. This is a murder investigation and I'm the senior investigating officer so you're under my command if I say you are. Got it?'

Again he cocked his head. Again the hand behind the ear.

'Yes, sir,' said Jonas. 'I got it.'

*

Marvel's shoes were ruined and they were the only pair he had with him. He turned the heating up to Full and put his brogues on the radiator, stuffed with the sudoku and horoscope pages from the *Daily Mail*; each as pointless and confusing as the other. Debbie used to read his stars to him; at him, really. Taurus. The Bull. Bull*shit*, more likely. She'd always said they were a perfect match. Well, look at them now: him sat in a stable with wet shoes, her back with her mother like some impecunious student, having chosen the retro couch over him and his growing collection of empty Jameson bottles. A match made in heaven.

Fuck. He suddenly remembered the vomit. He

pulled his phone out of his pocket more in hope than expectation, but was surprised to see five full bars of signal inviting him to make the call while he still could.

'Reeves?' he said. 'It's me.'

Jos Reeves had obviously been asleep and Marvel glanced at his watch. It was only 11.10pm, the bloody stoner.

'Yeah,' said Reeves. 'What?'

'I found what looks like vomit outside the vic's back door.'

'Vomit?' said Reeves through a yawn.

'Yes. Your boys must've missed it.' Marvel didn't say he'd have missed it himself if he hadn't almost stepped in it.

'OK, I'll send Mikey down in the morning.'

'What's wrong with tonight?' said Marvel, uncomfortably aware that he'd forgotten all about it until this minute.

Jos Reeves laughed as if he'd meant to make a joke and Marvel hoped this case never came to hang on the freshness or otherwise of said vomit, or he'd have to do some serious verbal sword-dancing to avoid the whole bloody thing collapsing around his ears. He knew that Jos Reeves wasn't going to send a man down at this time of night, and knew it was unreasonable to ask him to do so.

'Well, it's not getting any fresher,' he said petulantly, 'and it's pissing down.'

'Yeah, it's raining here too,' said Reeves mildly in that conversational way that got under Marvel's skin so badly.

'It's a lot wetter here,' he said, and hung up before Reeves could further irritate him with some eyebrow-arching clever remark about the wetness of water.

Marvel wrinkled his nose and sniffed the air like a dog, before realizing that the reek came from his steaming shoes releasing pungent foot-smell into the room.

Tomorrow he would get some wellington boots and put them on his expenses.

*

Jonas had cleaned the bathroom and kitchen, put on a load of washing, ironed a shirt for the morning and made supper of fake steak, oven chips and broccoli. The only real meat Lucy insisted on nowadays was bacon and the occasional McDonald's, which she craved as if pregnant. The nearest outlet was a forty-minute drive away in Minehead, but sometimes they'd make a day of it, laughing at their own bumpkin quest for what Jonas always called 'the fabled Golden Arches'.

At least you could pick up a burger with your hands, thought Lucy ruefully as she struggled to cut her fake steak. Sometimes her hands could do these things and sometimes they just couldn't. Jonas leaned over and did it for her, without missing a beat and – somehow – without making her feel patronized or pathetic.

He told her he was now involved in the investigation. He didn't tell her how it had come about, or that the Senior Investigating Officer apparently thought he was a moron. He also didn't tell her that his involvement would consist of standing on a freezing doorstep with the wholly spurious aim of spotting the killer as he sauntered compulsively back and forth past the scene of the crime.

Basically he didn't tell her any of the details that he knew would get her so angry on his behalf.

And although she knew he was hiding something, Lucy didn't ask. She just squeezed his hand as well as she could, told him she felt safer because he was on the case, and thanked him for bringing home the extra milk.

Nineteen Days

Jonas was on Margaret Priddy's doorstep by 8am, which meant a trickle of schoolchildren had nearly an hour to stare and whisper and giggle at him on their way to school. The cordon of tape had been attraction enough; Jonas standing there like the policeman outside 10 Downing Street was a black hole of fascination that sucked kids in from all over the village.

Linda Cobb from next door brought him a cup of tea at eight thirty. He accepted politely and then had to stand pointless guard while sipping now and then from a mug which read *World's Best Mum*. It was just fuel on the irritating little fire that was the Schadenfreude of the mocking children. They were nice children; Jonas knew all of them. And he knew too that it was only the odd alignment of the murder, the cordon and his sudden silly vigil that had made them bratty – but right now he wished the lot of them would quietly disappear. His wish came true when the school bell dragged them to the other end of the village at a collective run.

At nine thirty it started to rain – icy droplets that drummed off his helmet. Jonas had worn his black waterproof windcheater but his legs from the thighs down were soon soaked. Linda Cobb collected the mug and brought him an umbrella. With flowers on it.

At 10.01am Jonas decided to walk the perimeter to keep warm. After all, he reasoned, if the killer returned to the scene he might just as easily return to the back of the house as the front.

He trudged through the muddy grass of the playing field at the side of Margaret Priddy's home, and round the back – much as Marvel had the day before. Just as Marvel had done, he made his way up the garden, past a small pile of metal strips at the end, noting the old kennel as – right on cue – the terrier next door rushed the fence, its whole body quivering every time it barked.

'Hello, Dixie,' said Jonas calmly and the dog wagged and stopped barking to hear its name.

The wheelie bin was gone – to the lab, most likely – but in his mind's eye he saw it there still beside the lean-to, the easy route on to the flat roof and from there through the bedroom window.

Call yourself a policeman?

Jonas swallowed hard. How easy it had been. Everything the killer needed was right there. Even the smaller steel dustbin that was left behind would probably have been enough to allow a fit man on to the lean-to roof. He took the lid off and turned it upside-down, then stepped on to it, keeping his feet close to the edges so he wouldn't punch a hole right through the base, teetering like an elephant on a beach ball.

The felt of the lean-to roof was gritty under his hands but it was no great feat to pull himself on to it. Then he took a few creaking paces across to the window, where dusky fingerprint powder still clung to the paintwork. It was a sash-style window and the latch was at the limit of Jonas's height. A shorter man – which he assumed the killer must be – would have had to work with his hands over his head, looking up. Awkward but possible. All it really required was a thin strip of metal forced between the paintwork and pushed against the latch to shove it aside. A knife – or a piece from the little collection of junk at the end of the garden might have done just as well. From here the grooves and nicks in the paint around the latch were more obvious than they had been from the inside, and Jonas noticed that flecks of lemon-coloured gloss had sifted to the dark roof below. Once the latch was conquered it would just be a matter of sliding the window up. Jonas put his hands against the frame to see what kind of resistance it afforded. Not much, but maybe this was an easy slider. His palms squeaked slightly against the glass. The window going up might have woken Margaret Priddy, but who cared? Even if she heard, she could not move, could not raise the alarm, could not call for help . . .

Horrific.

Jonas stepped back slowly, hardly seeing the window any more in his mind's eye. He looked up to the sky to let the rain fall on to his face. Big drops on his eyelids. He opened his mouth and let it fill up, then walked to the edge of the roof and spat on to the garden, feeling cleansed.

As he swung himself off the roof back on to the upturned dustbin, Jonas noticed a small curve of something plastic in the gutter. He cocked his head to get a better look and saw it was a button lying half covered in the muck; if it hadn't been at eye-level he wouldn't have seen it. It was maybe half an inch across, four holes, black – very like the button on his own uniform trousers. He quickly checked that he had not pulled a button off while climbing on to the roof, but he was all present and correct. Jonas resisted the urge to pick the button up and turn it in his fingers, but he could see from here it was nothing special – apart from the fact that it was here on the roof outside the window of a room where a woman had been murdered. Apart from *that*.

'Hello,' said a voice and Jonas looked down to see a middle-aged, bespectacled man.

'Mike Foster,' the man said, with a cheerful smile. 'I've come for the vomit.'

'Vomit?'

'Outside the back door, apparently,' said Foster.

Jonas felt a pang of irritation that Marvel had not told him there was something back there; he could have stepped in it, ruined it.

'Nobody told me,' he confessed as he dropped back to the concrete.

They both looked for it, treading carefully now, exchanging pleasantries, mostly about the lousy weather.

Foster was remarkably upbeat for a man who'd come sixty miles in the rain for the sole purpose of scooping sick into a bag. Jonas said as much.

'Oh, it's lovely stuff, vomit!' Foster exclaimed. 'If the vomiter is a secretor then you can get DNA. Or diet, at the very least.'

'Even after it's been rained on?'

'It's not the rain so much as the age. The acid in the vomit eats at the DNA, fragments it. Still, you never know your luck.'

They couldn't find it.

Foster called the office and then called Marvel, grimacing to try to hear the DCI over the terrible connection.

'There is no bin lid,' he said, looking questioningly at Jonas.

'Only on the bin,' said Jonas.

When Foster relayed this information to Marvel, Jonas could hear the man's blood pressure rising with his voice. It was funny really, even though it was serious.

Foster listened and covered the mouthpiece. 'He says he covered it with the bin lid.'

Jonas shrugged. 'The lid was in place when I came round here. I had to take it off to turn the bin upside-down.'

Foster relayed this to Marvel, then frowned at his phone before saying to Jonas, 'I think he got cut off.'

There was a short silence while Jonas felt bonded to Foster through the common experience of being hung up on by DCI Marvel, then Jonas told him about the button on the roof. Foster said he was the vomit guy really but then seemed quite excited about taking a look anyway.

He wasn't short but neither was he fit, so Jonas cupped his hands and boosted him on to the roof and pointed out the relevant section of guttering.

'Ooooh,' said Foster with a happy smile. 'Did you move it at all?'

'No.'

'Excellent.'

He asked Jonas to hand him his field bags and bemoaned his own stupidity at only bringing plastic instead of paper bags too.

'Only expected vomit, you see?' he reminded Jonas. 'But you should always be prepared.'

He continued to chat happily as he took several minutes measuring and photographing the button in situ, then he picked it up with tweezers and put it in an evidence bag before lowering himself gingerly off the roof and on to the upturned bin which Jonas held steady for him.

He held the plastic bag up to the questionable light and they both examined the button as if it were a goldfish they'd won at the fair.

'Nice spot,' smiled Foster and, for the first time in days, Jonas felt like a real policeman.

'It was *right here*!' Marvel stood in the freezing rain holding the dustbin lid like a riot shield and pointing at his feet. 'Right *here*!'

He glared at Jonas, who deflected the look to Mike Foster, who shrugged for them both.

'Maybe someone moved it,' said Foster in a helpful tone that showed Jonas he had no first-hand experience of DCI Marvel.

'You *think* so?' said Marvel furiously. 'The lid's on the grass covering the vomit. Then the lid's on the bin and the vomit is all washed away. You think someone moved the lid? You think so? You're wasted at this forensics shit! You should be a fucking *psychic*!' He hurled the bin lid across the garden. Dixie rushed from his hidey-hole all noise and thunder and little white teeth as the lid rolled into the fence and toppled to a standstill.

'Couldn't we have fingerprinted that to find out *who*?' said Reynolds tentatively.

'*Shit!*'

While Marvel stomped across the wet grass to retrieve the bin lid, Jonas and Mike Foster exchanged guilty looks, as if they were jointly responsible for whatever it was Marvel wanted to blame them for.

'I touched the lid,' Jonas said quietly.

Reynolds rolled his eyes. 'I'll tell him.'

Marvel returned, holding the lid by an edge.

'Jonas found a button on the roof,' said Foster with just the right note of submission.

Reynolds raised an interested eyebrow, but it was wasted on Marvel.

'I don't give a shit if Jonas found the fucking Rosetta Stone on the roof. I want to know what happened to the *vomit*.'

'I don't know, sir,' said Jonas when it became clear Marvel expected a response and that Foster was too cowed to give one.

'It was your job to keep the scene secure. Your fucking *job*!'

Jonas flared a little. 'With respect, sir, you said my *job* was to stand on the doorstep and wait for the killer to come back.' From the corner of his eye, Jonas saw Foster and Reynolds exchange puzzled looks. Good. Let them know Marvel was a prick.

Marvel glared at him, then turned away dismissively and muttered darkly, 'Can't protect a puddle of fucking *sick* . . .'

Nobody knew what had happened – and no amount of haranguing from Marvel could enlighten them. Finally he jerked his head at Reynolds and stalked away down the garden in his porous shoes. When

Reynolds caught him up and asked where they were going next, he told him they were going to put the squeeze on Peter Priddy.

Jonas helped Mike Foster put his bags into his car and almost felt like hugging him goodbye. He was the first sensible official Jonas had met on the case.

*

Squeezing Peter Priddy didn't go quite to plan.

For a start, Peter Priddy blubbing in his dead mother's kitchen while in search of Jaffa Cakes was a very different person from Prison Officer Priddy, angry, embarrassed and defensive about being pulled off shift on a wing full of nosey cons to speak to homicide detectives.

Marvel squeezed and Priddy pushed back and the worry lines on Reynolds's brow got deeper and more indicative of imminent hair loss the more evident it became that they were really just there taking a flyer.

'Of course my hairs are going to be on the bed!' said Priddy. 'She's my mother! I don't stand at the door and *shout* at her!'

'But you didn't visit her on Saturday night?'

'I told you.'

'Were you in Shipcott on Saturday at all?'

'No! I *told* you!'

Marvel nodded slowly as if he agreed 100 per cent with what Peter Priddy had told them. 'Because we have a witness who saw your car parked on Barnstaple Road at . . .' He stopped for Reynolds to fill him in on the details but never took his eyes off Peter Priddy's face, so was perfectly placed to see the big man's fair skin flush a deep red.

'Between 8.45pm and 6am,' supplied Reynolds.

'Bollocks!' Priddy pushed his chair back from the staff-room table with a loud rasp.

'We have a witness,' said Marvel with a careless shrug.

'Who? Where? They're lying.'

'No need to get agitated, Mr Priddy,' said Marvel in a tone guaranteed to agitate.

'Fuck off.'

'Are you saying you weren't there, Mr Priddy?'

'Yes I am.'

Marvel raised his eyebrows in open disbelief. 'Well, maybe they're mistaken.'

'Yes they bloody *are*. Or mischief-making.'

'Why would anyone want to make mischief with you, Mr Priddy?' said Marvel. 'You've just lost your mother in the saddest of circumstances. Why would anyone want to make life harder for you?'

Peter Priddy got up, not looking at Marvel or Reynolds. 'I don't know. Like you said, people are sick. I have to get back to work.'

'Mr Priddy,' said Reynolds soothingly, 'we're just going through a process of elimination. We're speaking to everybody like this.'

'Bollocks.'

'We *are*,' said Reynolds, hoping it would be true before too long. He looked at Marvel for confirmation and got a grudging nod. 'It's our job. You're in law enforcement, Mr Priddy; *you* understand. We're on the same team here.'

The flattery worked and Priddy softened a little. 'Yeah. OK.'

Some of the tension drained from the room.

Reynolds cleared his throat. 'Before you go, I wonder if I could ask you for a DNA sample?'

Priddy stared at the two men with undisguised disgust. Reynolds looked away and got out the kit. In silence he got the swabs from the sterile plastic. In silence, Peter Priddy opened his mouth and allowed Reynolds to scrape the inside of his cheek.

'I've got to get back to work. And you do too, because the more time you waste with me, the more time you're not trying to catch the man who killed my mother. And that really pisses me off.'

In the silence that followed him slamming the door behind him, Reynolds closed his notebook, turned his palms upwards and sighed. 'Can't blame him, I suppose.'

'I'll blame him for whatever the bloody hell I want,' snapped Marvel.

As if Reynolds didn't know that.

On their way out, the prison staff were noticeably less friendly than they had been on the way in.

Eighteen Days

Annette Rogers had been interviewed at the scene and had already moved on to care full-time for an elderly man in Minehead, but Gary Liss and Lynne Twitchett both worked part-time in Shipcott at Sunset Lodge, a large detached stone house in its own grounds set back from the road and conveniently adjoining the grave-yard behind the church. As they got out of the car, Marvel wondered at the horror of growing old and infirm within a geriatric stone's throw of your final rest-ing place.

The home's owner, Rupert Cooke, was a chubby, happy-faced man with the habit of bending slightly forward and turning his head attentively when he listened, even though Marvel wasn't seated in a wheel-chair. He offered Marvel and Reynolds his office for privacy and Reynolds thanked him politely.

'I'll give Lynne and Gary a shout,' he said.

'Don't,' said Marvel. 'We'll find them. Have a look around at the same time.'

'If you don't mind,' added Reynolds hurriedly.

'Of course,' said Cooke. 'Be my guests.'

'Not for a while, I hope,' said Marvel drily. Too drily, apparently, as nobody laughed.

He and Reynolds wandered through the large airy rooms where a few residents sat and did jigsaws or knitted. An old man with an oxygen mask on and ears so big he looked like a spaniel peered fixedly at an enormous television with the sound down so low that it was all but inaudible. Seemed that past a certain age, one functioning sense at a time was all any resident could really expect to enjoy.

Reynolds peered into a large aquarium. 'They've got a Japanese fighting fish in here. Beautiful.'

Marvel ignored him. Ridiculous hobby, fish-keeping. Making yourself a slave to guppies.

A middle-aged woman in a blue uniform bustled towards them and Marvel stopped and raised his eyebrows. 'Lynne Twitchett?'

'In the garden room, I think,' smiled the woman, pointing in the direction they were already heading.

The majority of the residents were in the garden room and Marvel understood why the moment they entered. It was hot. Saharan hot – even in the middle of winter. With its long windows and glass roof, the garden room was no more or less than a greenhouse for cultivating old folk. And it seemed to be working. At least two dozen old women with identical hair sat around the perimeter of the room, sunning themselves like lizards in wing chairs, sucking up the heat as if they'd outlived the capacity to make their own. Several of them wore hand-knitted cardigans and crocheted knee-rugs just to be on the safe side. A large tin of cheap biscuits was being passed around the room and examined at each station as if it were the Holy Grail. Ahead of the tin was all craning white heads and expectant muttering, behind it was silence and crumbs.

Lynne Twitchett sat at the upright piano against the far wall of the room, playing a faltering version of 'Jingle Bells' while perched on a piano stool. At least, Marvel assumed that was what she was sitting on. From behind it looked as if Lynne Twitchett's giant blue arse had simply sprouted four spindly wooden legs, so completely had her bulk consumed the rest of the furniture.

Reynolds leaned in to him and murmured, 'Who ate all the Jaffa Cakes?' – the first funny thing Marvel had ever heard come out of his mouth.

They talked to Lynne Twitchett for less than five minutes in the office. Her near-impenetrable Somerset accent made her sound like one of Marvel's yokels, but even Reynolds felt it was less a misleading anomaly than the cherry on the top of her dubious intellect.

Marvel loved dumb people. If guilty, they either

confessed or were so transparent in their lies that there was never any doubt about their culpability. Similarly, if they were innocent it shone through despite their nerves or their rambling or their accidental self-incriminatory statements. Dumb people were a breeze and Lynne Twitchett was right up there with the breeziest he'd encountered. Added to which, he had discounted her as a suspect the moment they saw her; the thought of Ms Twitchett tiptoeing unnoticed past Annette Rogers, or bounding gracefully on to the lean-to roof, was comical. Reynolds thanked her and released her back into the greenhouse, where she would no doubt grow even bigger on a mulch of the residents' biscuits.

They found Gary Liss changing beds upstairs, where it was cooler and apparently empty of old folk.

Gary Liss was nothing like Marvel had imagined. He was a small and lithe thirty-five-year-old. He had dark hair, an olive complexion and narrow blue eyes. He looked like a circus acrobat who had been reassigned to bedpans and taken to them like a duck to water. He didn't miss a beat while they talked, and his military bed-making was hypnotic to watch. Marvel and Reynolds followed him from room to room asking their questions, and Gary Liss stripped beds, bundled dirty sheets, shook out fresh ones and then wound mattresses in them as neat and as tight as if he was working in the gift-wrap department of the Great Pyramid at Giza. Marvel wondered how the hell the old folk managed to fight their way between the top and bottom sheets every night, and had a mental image of residents spending years shivering above the covers, too frail to gain entry to their own beds.

Despite the efficiency of recall that his phenomenal work-rate promised, Gary Liss was almost as useless as Lynne Twitchett when it came to the details leading up to Margaret Priddy's death. He had been on the early shift before she was killed – seven in the morning until three in the afternoon – and had gone to the pictures that night.

'Alone?' said Marvel.

'No,' said Liss, then volunteered, 'with my girlfriend.'

'What did you see?'

'Some old French crap at the art-house place.'

'Not a film buff?' asked Reynolds.

'Not all that foreign bollocks.'

'Can you remember the title?' persisted Marvel – it was a fact that could be checked.

'Mister Somebody's Vacation, I think.'

'*National Lampoon*?' suggested Marvel.

'Nah, something French.'

'*Monsieur Hulot's Holiday*?'

Trust Reynolds.

'Yeah,' said Liss. 'Total junk.'

'I agree,' said Marvel, although he hadn't seen it. It was just to piss Reynolds off. 'Give me Will Smith any day.'

'Exactly,' said Liss, turning a sheet over a blanket and tucking it in ruthlessly. '*I, Robot*.'

'How about *Dune*?'

'Yeah. You a fan?'

'No. You left a book at Margaret Priddy's.'

Liss looked blank for a second, then smiled. '*That*'s where it is!'

'How did you get into this line of work?' Marvel asked Liss as they moved to the next room. The man was starting to interest him.

Liss shrugged. 'I cared for my father while he died. Lost my job because of it, so when I started looking again, it was just something I knew I could do.'

'What did you do before that?'

'Nothing special. Factory work. Glad to lose it, the way things worked out.'

'What did your father die of?' asked Reynolds.

'Lung cancer,' said Liss without emotion. 'And I didn't help him along, if that's what you're thinking.' He winked at Reynolds, who at least had the decency to look embarrassed.

'So how did you get on with Mrs Priddy?' Marvel asked.

Liss looked a little confused by the sudden switch, but that was good – to catch them off balance . . .

'Wasn't much to get along *with*.' He shrugged. 'She couldn't say anything or even let you know how she was feeling.' He stopped bustling and stood still for the first time since they'd started talking to him. 'It was fucking awful, 'scuse my French. I mean, the people in here, they're old and lots are sick, but at least they can let you know what they want, but *her* . . .' He picked a bundle of used sheets off the floor. 'It was like she was already dead. If she hadn't died I'd have left soon. Depressing.'

They followed him to the next bedroom.

'You think maybe it was a mercy killing then?' said Marvel carefully, but Liss was not fazed by the question.

'Could be,' he said and flapped open a new sheet.

'You could understand something like that?' Marvel asked.

Liss didn't hesitate. 'If she was my mother I'd have done it myself.'

Reynolds and Marvel didn't speak for a long time as they drove back to the farm.

Reynolds broke the silence.

'You think that was a confession? A kind of double bluff?'

'I don't know,' said Marvel. It was not something he often admitted to, but on this occasion he felt it was OK to be a bit confused.

'He had a door key, he hated the job, he obviously has no compunction about euthanasia . . .'

'But to say it right out loud like that – to *us*!'

'I know,' said Reynolds. 'He'd have to be a psychopath.'

Marvel shrugged. 'Yes, he would.'

*

Less than an hour after Reynolds and Marvel got back to Springer Farm, Grey and Singh returned from interviewing Skew Ronnie Trewell and everyone crammed into Marvel's room to hear how they'd got on.

'It's not him,' said Grey.

'Yeah, boss, I don't think he's our man,' said Singh more tactfully.

Marvel was unwilling to let the only tentative lead they'd got from their sweep of the village go so easily.

'He got an alibi?'

The two detectives exchanged looks.

'Well, he says he was asleep,' said Grey.

'At home all night,' added Singh.

'Compelling,' said Marvel sarcastically.

'He just doesn't seem the type, sir,' said Grey. Then, when he saw Marvel's face tighten angrily, he added, 'I didn't get a vibe off him. Nor did Armand,' he said, turning to Singh, 'did you?'

'No,' said Singh. 'I didn't get any vibe at all. The guy's a car thief through and through. Obsessed. Couldn't stop talking about them even while we were asking him about a murder!'

'Yeah,' added Grey. 'His only interest in Mrs Priddy seemed to be that she used to own some sporty BMW.'

'A three-litre CSi,' remembered Singh.

'Good car,' said Grey approvingly and Pollard nodded in agreement.

Marvel glared at them all. He thought about Margaret Priddy dropping down through the cracks of society from horsewoman and BMW-owner to being bedridden while her savings ran out of her bank account like water from a punctured paddling pool. He thought about Peter Priddy and how he must have felt about that. He thought about Skew Ronnie Trewell and wondered if he should leave it at that or go and intimidate the little thief himself. It irked him that Jonas Holly had dismissed the man as a suspect; part of him *wanted* Ronnie Trewell to be the killer, for that reason alone. But Grey and Singh were good men. He trusted their judgement. Usually. While these thoughts whizzed through his mind, his eyes never left the two DCs, who became more and more uncomfortable.

Unaware of Marvel's train of thought, Singh decided to add another helpful observation. 'He just didn't seem . . . quite *right*, sir.'

'No,' said Grey, nodding in enthusiastic agreement. 'Not quite right.'

Hearing Jonas Holly's words echoed by Grey was what did it for Marvel. He made an all-purpose sound of disparagement, picked up the keys to the Ford Focus, and stomped out of the room to judge Ronnie Trewell for himself.

*

The boy was standing on the front step, squinting into the dim sun as it fell behind the moor. Ronnie Trewell was skinny and so gaunt he looked like an extra from a prison-camp movie. He had a shock of home-cut black hair, and a brow permanently creased by the confusion that was his life.

He saw Marvel pull up, threw down the roll-up he'd been smoking and backed towards the door.

'I want to talk with you!' Marvel yelled at him through the passenger window, and the boy stopped and waited.

Marvel liked a meek thief. He got out and went up the weed-strewn front path.

'DCI Marvel,' he said. 'You Ronnie Trewell?'

'Yeah,' he said. 'I haven't done a thing. I spoke to your lot already. I haven't done a thing. Is that a Zetec?'

Marvel was caught a little off-balance by the sudden change in direction. He glanced towards the Focus. 'I haven't come here to talk about cars, mate. Come about a murder.'

'Yeah I know,' shrugged Ronnie. 'But I told the others about that already. Can I have a drive?'

As he spoke, he stepped off the porch and headed for the car. Marvel found himself in undignified pursuit.

'No. Tell me where you were Saturday night.'

'Here. Asleep. I said already. Just a quick one. You can come too. I'm not gonna nick a police car, am I? Not with you *in* it, anyway.'

'Shut up about the fucking car, all right?' Marvel was already starting to feel that he was wasting his time here. 'You got any witnesses?'

'Nope. Not an ST though, is it?' said Ronnie with a little sneer in his voice as he peered through the window. Marvel didn't give a shit what the Focus was or wasn't, but that little sneer made him feel suddenly protective towards the pool car.

'Goes well though,' he said, feeling foolishly like he was seventeen again with his first learner motorbike – a 125cc Honda Benley with a hand-painted tank – trying to talk it up to the older, richer boys with their RD250s . . .

'Yeah?' said Ronnie. 'Believe it when I see it.'

It nearly worked. For a second Marvel was all ready to jump behind the wheel and do a donut in the mud at the end of the lane beside the dirty little bungalow. Floor the accelerator and spray the kid with gravel. Maybe even let him feel the kick for himself . . .

'Nice try, Ronnie,' he said, not without a little respect.

Marvel opened the door of the Ford and thought he'd better go out on an authoritarian note. 'Don't go anywhere, all right?'

'Where am I going to go?' said Ronnie Trewell, with

a shrug at the darkening moor around them. He seemed genuinely at a loss.

Marvel ignored the question and drove away.

Ronnie Trewell wasn't the killer. He wasn't . . . *quite right*.

Seventeen Days

The mobile incident room arrived and it was shit.

Just the way Marvel liked it.

There were soggy Polo mints in the desk, mud up the walls, two black bags filled with junk-food wrappers, and someone had used indelible green ink on the whiteboard and then what looked like some kind of wire brush to try to remove it.

Marvel felt himself relax into the squalor of the unit in a way he just couldn't into the rusticity of Springer Farm. The rutted driveway, the mossy roofs, the smell of manure repelled him. But this squalor was different. He *wanted* the stained coffee pot, he *liked* the muddy lino, and the sour reek of the grubby little fridge was napalm in the morning to him.

Didn't mean anyone else had to know that. 'Clean this place up,' he growled at Reynolds, who made a note in his book.

'What are you writing?' said Marvel irritably.

'Sir?'

'What are you writing in your little book? I said "Clean this place up." Doesn't need a fucking memo, does it?'

'No, sir.'

'Then clean this place up.'

'Yes, sir.'

'Don't let Rice do it.'

'No, sir.' Before Reynolds could ask why, when Rice was the only member of the team who might make a decent job of it, Marvel had trudged down the steps and slammed the door.

The unit was parked at the edge of the playing field alongside Margaret Priddy's home. Nonetheless, Marvel drove the four hundred yards to the shop.

He asked for wellington boots but was told he'd have to go to Dulverton or to somewhere the large, docile man behind the counter called 'the farm shop' – the directions to which were so complex that Marvel stopped listening after the third dogleg.

'You're the chap in charge?' asked the man, and Marvel nodded. 'Any progress?'

'Early days,' said Marvel. It was all he ever said in response to enquiries by civilians – right up to the point where he stood in his funeral suit and only decent tie to hear the verdict of the jury. Before that, nothing was sure.

'Poor Margaret,' said the shopkeeper. 'Although it was a blessing really.'

'Hmm,' nodded Marvel, but was not sure he agreed.

Outside, he saw the small brown dog from next door to the Priddy home, and introduced himself to the owner, Mrs Cobb. He asked whether the dog had barked on the night of the murder and she said 'No' as if it was the first time it had occurred to her.

Typical, thought Marvel. The dog barks at *me* but not at the bloody killer.

He went back to the unit, where Reynolds had made a poor enough job of cleaning the unit to satisfy the most ardent slob. He was now standing by for plaudits, but Marvel merely glanced around and grunted, then answered his phone. Jos Reeves told him they had the hair matches. Two from Peter Priddy, two from Dr Mark Dennis, and one each from Gary Liss and Annette Rogers.

'Nothing from Reynolds? He usually sheds like a fucking Retriever all over the scene.'

'Nothing from Reynolds.'

'You said there were seven.'

'One unidentified,' said Reeves.

Marvel accepted the news with grudging silence. 'What about fibres?'

Reeves sighed. 'Nothing of significance yet.'

'Let me be the judge of that,' snapped Marvel.

'OK,' said Reeves mildly and started to recite their results so far in a relentless monotone. 'Carpet, white cotton, black cotton, blue cotton, red wool, blue wool—'

'Email me,' said Marvel and hung up.

Sixteen Days

Mike Foster and his enthusiasm for vomit proved to be the highlight of Jonas's first few days on the doorstep. Linda Cobb brought him increasingly infrequent cups of tea and his novelty quickly wore off with the schoolchildren. None came out of their way to stare at him and whisper at each other now, and the few who passed gave him barely a glance. He had tried to maintain the illusion, even in his own head, that he might at some point spot the killer, but he really wasn't even rooting for himself. He felt it was a pointless exercise and had no wish for Marvel to be proven right through some weird fluke, even if it *did* mean catching the perpetrator of a horrible crime.

No, that wasn't true, thought Jonas, shamed. Catching the killer of Margaret Priddy would be worth any kind of humiliation. But he'd prefer it if they caught him another way – a way that wouldn't give Marvel the option of an 'I told you so.'

It was a long, cold day.

*

Jonas got home to find Lucy asleep on the couch with the phone in her hand and *Rosemary's Baby* playing silently on the TV.

'How are you, Lu?' he asked softly as she stirred.

She blinked in confusion for a few seconds and Jonas watched recognition float back into her eyes.

'My legs hurt,' she said grumpily. 'And Margaret Priddy's son called you. He didn't say why.'

She shifted up and he sat down and pulled her bare legs on to his lap, covering them up again with the brown tartan rug.

Jonas started to massage her calves.

'Are you going to call him back?' she said.

'In a minute.' He shrugged.

Onscreen Mia Farrow was over-acting at the sight of the devil-child she'd spawned.

'Let's have a baby,' said Lucy.

He didn't stop massaging her, but he also didn't answer her. Or even turn his eyes from the TV.

'Jonas?'

'Can we talk about it later?' He still caressed her, but she could tell now that it was perfunctory.

'I want to talk about it now.'

Jonas sighed and looked at her. 'We've talked about it, Lu. You're ill . . .'

'That's not it.' She drew her legs up and away from him, and curled them under herself. Now it was her turn to look at the TV.

He said nothing. They had last had this conversation almost two years ago. He'd hoped they wouldn't have it again.

But Lucy wanted it again. 'You wanted children before we got married.'

'I didn't.'

He said it automatically and saw her eyes widen.

'You *said* you did.'

There was no way out of it now. His mouth had betrayed him and he couldn't take it back. '*You* said I did.'

'You never said you didn't.'

'Well . . .' shrugged Jonas with a helpless lift of one hand. 'I don't.'

Lucy bit her lip, determined to be an adult about this. This was an adult conversation between two adults. The fact that she wanted to slap him and cry on the floor like a child was an aberration.

'Why?' she said and hated the tremble in her own voice.

'I just don't.'

'I think I deserve a better answer than that, Jonas.'

Jonas thought she did too. *Knew* she did. But stayed

as silent as a coward, which he knew was his only defence.

Usually Lucy let it go. They never fought and weren't quite sure how to, but tonight Lucy was finally hurt enough . . .

'Don't you want something to remember me by?'

Jonas stood up in an instant, and as soon as Lucy saw his face she wished she could take it back. For a second she was actually frightened.

He walked out of the room and she heard him pick up his car keys and phone from beside the flowers on the hall table.

She nearly called out to him, but then held her tongue.

She had a right to say what she was feeling! If things were the other way round, Lucy would have moved Heaven and Earth to have Jonas's child. She could barely believe that – for once – he did not want the same thing as she did. Disagreeing was one thing, but refusal to even discuss such a vital issue was quite another. She felt her throat constrict in self-pity. She wasn't dead yet! Her vote still counted!

Didn't it?

She heard the front door shut quietly behind him.

Jonas drove away.

He had no idea how to tell her the truth: *I can't protect a child.*

Because in his head he always heard her ask *Why?*

And then he'd have to tell the truth again.

Nobody can . . .

*

Marvel sat with an unopened bottle of Jameson whiskey in one hand, the TV bunny aerial in the other, and watched *Coronation Street* for the first time in about twenty years. He was shocked and confused to find that at some point Tracy Barlow had served time for murder, and while he was trying to work out how that could legally happen to a five-year-old girl, someone knocked on his door.

He hadn't heard a car but he thought it might be Reynolds, who had taken the DNA swabs to Portishead. Marvel could have gone too, but had finally decided that going back to the future at this point would make it that much harder to return to Exmoor.

He was therefore more than a little surprised to find PC Jonas Holly standing in the dark.

'I need to speak to you about Peter Priddy.'

Marvel held open the door by way of invitation, and immediately felt the cold night air invade his cottage, giving him an unexpected pang of empathy with Joy Springer and her jealous guardianship of warmth.

But Jonas didn't come in. Instead he stood hesitantly in the yard, then asked if they could go to the pub. Marvel needed no second bidding. He abandoned Tracy Barlow to her fate and grabbed his coat.

It was warm in the Land Rover. Holly swung it round expertly in a tight turn. As he did, Marvel noticed Joy Springer peering at them from behind her kitchen curtain.

They turned right at the bottom of the drive – away from Shipcott – and headed up the hill across the moor.

'Not going to the Red Lion?'

'I thought it would be better to go somewhere away from the village to discuss work.'

Marvel nodded. Holly was different tonight. There was nothing of the junior officer about him. His manner was surprisingly brusque and he looked as if he was brooding about something.

'I spoke to Peter Priddy. He's got a right cob on.'

Marvel didn't understand the reference but got the gist. 'Mr Priddy doesn't understand the process of elimination.'

'He feels victimized.'

'He had motive, opportunity and probably inclination.'

'It's his *mother*!'

'You think nobody kills their mother? Or father? Or their own kids? What do you think this is, bloody Toytown? Grow up, Holly, for fuck's sake!'

Jonas said nothing and put his foot down.

Marvel watched the empty ribbon of tarmac lined

by dirty brown moor race at them out of blackness and disappear as soon as the lights had passed over it. It was like travelling through space, or a lower intestine. The blackness could have been infinite or claustrophobically close, there was no way of telling – and the motion was timeless and hypnotic.

'Where's the pub?' he said.

'Withypool,' said Jonas just as curtly, as he stopped at a T-junction.

A porcupine of white wooden signposts bristled out of the opposite hedge.

'Withypool two and a *quarter*!' read Marvel in exasperation. 'This place is like Middle fucking *Earth*.'

Jonas turned right and floored the accelerator again, his jaw set. Marvel was starting to enjoy needling him.

'He was with a woman at the time. Not his wife.'

Marvel rubbed his hands together. '*Now* we're talking! In Shipcott?'

'Yes.'

'Yeah, we had someone who saw his car on Saturday night. He with her all night?'

'I guess so.'

'*Guessing* so does not *make* it so. You spoken to her?'

'No.'

'A miracle! Someone you *haven't* fucked about with before we could get there. Who is it?'

Jonas tightened his fists on the wheel. This wasn't going as planned. He should have thought it through before calling Marvel. He'd thought he was doing

Peter Priddy a favour – that Marvel would accept his word about an alibi, but now it was all getting away from him. His head had started to ache as soon as he'd walked out on Lucy and now it throbbed cruelly as the tunnel of road and moor rushed at him like a video game. He should never have gone to see Marvel when he felt this way but he'd needed something to take his mind off her words. He couldn't bear to think about them – to think of her being gone. Of her being *not there*. Of having to have something to *remember* her by . . .

He'd had to stop thinking of it. He'd called Peter Priddy; he'd picked up Marvel. Now he tried to focus on what they'd said and what he'd said to them, piling words up like ashes on embers, but *her* words still glowed and flickered underneath. Now those words had been lit, he couldn't imagine they'd ever go out, and he felt their burn at the base of his skull.

The pony came out of nowhere, filled his vision and struck the car all in the same frantic second. By the time Jonas hit the brakes, it was behind them.

The car slewed briefly and stalled with a lurch.

'*Shit!*' said Marvel.

The engine ticked quietly in the silence.

Marvel looked in his wing mirror and saw the dark shape of the animal in the road twenty yards behind them, lit faintly by their brake lights.

'I think it's still alive,' he said. 'We'd better go and see.'

He looked at Jonas but the younger man just stared at him blankly, as if he hadn't heard.

'We'd better go and look at it,' he repeated, and this time Holly registered what he'd said and looked in his rear-view mirror. Then he backed up the car until they were just a few feet from the horse.

Marvel got out. It was much colder up here on the moor, and drying out too – as if the sky was sucking the moisture from the air and preparing for something much more spectacular than mere rain. He walked round to the back of the Land Rover. By the dull red of the tail lights, even Marvel could see that the pony's front leg was broken at a sickening angle. The animal was trying to get up anyway, heaving itself on to its chest then flailing helplessly – its hoofs drubbing the tarmac and leaving pale scrapes in its surface – before collapsing back on to its side, snorting, ribs heaving under its shaggy winter coat, and its eye rolling wild and white around the edges.

'Its leg's broken,' he said, looking up for a lead from Jonas, and surprised to find him not there. He looked round. Jonas had got out of the car with him but was still at the door of the Land Rover, silhouetted against the stars.

He raised his voice. 'It's got a broken leg.'

Through the vague red darkness he saw the silhouette nod its head.

'What are we going to do?' asked Marvel.

'I don't know.'

'Well, *you*'re the bloody local! People must hit these buggers all the time.'

'I'll call the hunt,' said Jonas after a pause.

'What?'

'I'll call the hunt. They'll come out and shoot it and take it for meat.'

'Meat?' Marvel was utterly confused.

'For the hounds,' said Jonas.

'You're fucking *joking*!' said Marvel.

'No,' said Jonas, 'I'm not.'

Marvel tried to regain a sense of normality. Two minutes ago, he had been off to the pub. Now he was confronted with a dying horse, a remote companion, and the mental image of a pack of hounds tearing the dark-brown hide from a still-warm beast, while faceless men in scarlet stood by laughing.

And he wasn't even drunk.

Maybe he was in shock. Maybe Jonas Holly was too, with his monosyllabic responses.

He had to keep things in perspective. Be practical.

'We should put it out of its misery,' said Marvel, knowing that he wouldn't be able to, but hoping that a countryman like Jonas would take control.

He knew nothing of horses. He wasn't sure he'd ever touched one, but something made him hunch down now beside this pony's head and reach out to it. The animal let out a shrill whinny, driving his hand away from it briefly. But because Jonas had already seen him scared at Margaret Priddy's house, he reached out again.

This time he touched the horse's neck. The coat was thick but surprisingly soft, and slightly damp. He let his hand sink into it until he could feel the hot skin.

For a moment his touch seemed to calm the beast and he felt the faint throb of the pulse under his fingers. Then it squealed and started to thrash about, knocking Marvel on to his backside in the road. Disorientated, he opened his eyes to see its hoofs blurring close to his face. He put up a protective hand and it was immediately kicked aside. He shouted in pain, then felt a rough tug at the scruff of his neck and was dragged out of range of the flailing hoofs.

His hand was agony. In his head he ran through every expletive he'd ever heard, but in reality he just bit his lip, laid his cheek on the cold tarmac, squeezed his hand in his armpit and tried to stem the tears of pain that threatened to drown his eyes.

Jonas stared numbly at the pony in its death throes. It must have been injured internally because blood was now spurting from its nose as it made bubbly, squealing sounds, still trying to heave itself upright in a pointless but instinctive bid for survival. In the wild, the horse that could not get up was doomed. This one was doomed anyway, but still tried to get to its feet in a terrified panic at being left behind by its herd to be picked off by predators.

To watch it suffering was sickening. To smell it was worse. Under the fear and the blood Jonas could smell its olde-worlde horse smell of dusty pelt and grass and sweet manure. For some reason he couldn't explain, *those* smells disturbed him more than anything.

Finally it gave up.

Its head flopped heavily to the tarmac at Jonas's feet while blood continued to run out of its nose. Its flanks heaved more shallowly, and its eye started to lose focus.

Jonas felt nauseous without the capacity for vomiting. He felt tired without the capacity to sleep. And the embers of the headache had flared to white heat in his brain.

Distantly, he watched the blood from the dying pony's nose pool towards his shoe; in this light it looked black and oily. The animal grunted once, then sighed hugely as the last of its breath left it.

'Is it dead?' said Marvel.

The younger man said nothing; Marvel took that as a 'yes'.

'It kicked the shit out of my hand.' Marvel's voice was shaky and he leaned over to study his hand by the lights of the car. In the redness he couldn't see anything wrong with it but it hurt all along its outer edge. He straightened up and looked left and right to where he knew the narrow ribbon of road draped over the moor.

'Suppose we'd better get it out of the road.' Marvel bent down. 'You want to take a leg?'

Jonas didn't bend down. 'It's too heavy,' he said instead.

'You think so?' Marvel grabbed a hoof and leaned back. The leg stretched but the horse didn't budge. 'You going to help me?'

'No.'

Marvel squinted at him as if he hadn't heard Jonas correctly. 'What?'

'I said no. I don't like horses.'

'You don't have to *like* it, for fuck's sake! It's *dead*! Just grab a bloody leg!'

Jonas didn't move; Marvel dropped the leg and the hoof hit the road with a clunk. 'We can't just leave it here.'

Jonas shrugged.

Marvel nodded at the Land Rover. 'You got a winch on that thing?'

While Jonas prepared the winch, Marvel had a cigarette. He didn't smoke often – it was all so bloody awkward nowadays – but out here in the middle of the moor in the middle of the night, he puffed furiously, loving the way the end of the cigarette fired up in the darkness every time he sucked on it.

He thought about touching the pony's living skin through its thick fur, and remembered Margaret Priddy. How warm she once was, and how cold she was now.

And *there* was the little stir he always got sooner or

later. *There* was the moment when her death stopped being a job for him and became a personal crusade. It had taken a dying horse to remind him of how every murdered body he stared down at was once alive and terrified and facing lawless death. Marvel was relieved to find that rudder of personal affront, which he knew would keep him steady now throughout the investigation.

Jonas drove slowly and bumpily into the heather, then got out and walked around to free the pony, hardly noticing the deep, wet vegetation forcing water through his trousers, socks and work shoes. His only thought, drubbing in time to the jackhammer in his brain, was to get it over with before his head exploded. He wound out some slack and nudged the cable loose enough with his toe so he could lift it back over the muddy fetlock.

The pony lay stretched out as if bounding easily across the moor, looking strangely fleet of foot in death. Jonas knew that within hours foxes would have found it, and at first light the crows would take its eyes, which were already fading to dull grey pebbles in its skull.

He got back in the car and turned towards Shipcott.

'What about the pub?' Marvel said a little petulantly.

Jonas said nothing.

They drove in silence to the stables and the Land Rover swung round in the yard and gravelled to a halt.

Marvel snorted when he saw that Reynolds was back with the car. He could have waited an hour, avoided getting kicked by a dying horse, and still have had a couple of pints.

He got out of the Land Rover and peered back in at Jonas. He hoped he wasn't going to start up about Peter Priddy again, but the man looked distant and tightly wound. Probably thinking about the paperwork he'd have to do tomorrow on the police Land Rover.

'Thanks for the drink.' Marvel was half joking, but because Jonas said nothing in ironic response, the words hung there and then soured into something far more sarcastic – even bullying.

What the fuck. The night had been a disaster from start to finish. He should have stuck with Tracy Barlow.

Marvel swung the door shut and watched the young policeman drive away.

It felt like four in the morning but it was only 10.30pm. Through a chink in Reynolds's curtain he could see his DS was watching *Who Wants to Be a Millionaire*. Marvel almost laughed out loud. Typical! The bloody clever clogs! Showing off even when he was alone! Still, he felt like company – felt like sharing his adventure. He was about to knock when he saw Joy Springer's kitchen curtain twitch. On a whim he went over and knocked on her door instead. She opened it a hair's breadth and glared at him.

'We hit a horse up on the moor,' he said.

'So?' she said, while ash drooped dangerously off the end of her cigarette.

Marvel wasn't in the mood to beat about the bush.

'I'm a bit shaken up. You got anything to drink?'

She poked her head outside so she could make sure he wasn't about to bring in a whole legion of free-loaders, then opened the door.

The kitchen was stiflingly hot – just the way Marvel liked it. Joy Springer got two odd mugs off the dresser and poured from a bottle.

'Sit down if you want,' she said.

Underfoot were flagstones covered in a virtual rug of cat hair. There was a cat on the kitchen table and, with only a brief glance, Marvel noticed another four dotted about on various mismatched armchairs and a sofa. He chose one end of the sofa and almost fell through its sagging bottom. She handed him a drink and he took a sip and grimaced.

'What the hell is that?'

'Dubonnet,' she said spikily. 'If you don't want it, you can pour it back in the bottle.'

He shrugged and took another sip. 'I've got some Jameson's in my room.'

'We'll have that tomorrow then,' she declared.

*

The bathroom at Rose Cottage was quick to steam up and slow to clear, so that the moisture hung in the air for ages, like an extension of the moor itself. It was so thick that the windows were curtained with steam, and they never bothered with the blinds, even at night. Jonas stood utterly still and let the shower cleanse him of the night's activities, just as he let the sound of the water drown out his memory, leaving him pristine and empty. He stood like that until he felt the chill of death leave every part of him, then turned the water off, grabbed a towel and stepped over his clothes, which lay in a damp pile on the bathroom floor.

He wrapped the towel around his waist and did his teeth. Habit made him stare into the mirror while he brushed, but the glass was opaque and he didn't bother wiping it. Instead he watched the diffuse half-shape that was also him moving in time to his own ablutions. It was hypnotic and comforting, like a distant twin who was living another life behind the steam, similar but different to his, where all the edges were comfortingly fuzzy and nothing had to be faced in harsh focus. Jonas brushed for longer than normal, until his mouth burned with minty freshness. He stuffed his clothes into the laundry basket and – despite the hour – cleaned the bath and the basin. It was one thing to tick off his list of chores.

Lucy was asleep in bed. She liked to make the effort to get upstairs even if he wasn't there to help her. Sometimes she could crawl up quite fast; sometimes it took her half an hour. She'd taken to leaving a book halfway up the stairs so she could stop and rest without getting bored. The book there at the moment was a novel called *Fate Dictates*. Like his woolly thinking on the afterlife, Jonas was unsure about whether or not he believed in Fate. Who knew how life was going to work out? What weirdness was just around the corner? Could it be controlled? And if it could, would you *want* to control it?

He towelled his short, dark hair hard and fast and slid into bed beside Lucy before he could lose the wonderful warmth of the shower.

As he did, she stirred and rolled towards him.

'Where were you?' she murmured sleepily.

'Wet and cold and not with you,' he whispered, stroking her hair.

'I'm glad you're home.' He could hear the lazy little smile in her voice and felt her hand sneak on to his hip. He smiled in the darkness at the way it made the night's events disappear behind him as if they'd never been.

She lifted his hand and placed it over her small round breast.

'I'm glad you're home too,' he said, and kissed her with intent for the first time in months. At the same time, he whispered into her mouth: 'I'm sorry.'

Fifteen Days

Jonas walked down into the village at eight o'clock the next day feeling truly happy for the first time in many weeks.

The morning was so bright it hurt his eyes. The sky was already a pale Mediterranean blue, while the moor below it sparkled like quartz under a thick frost. Every breath he took was menthol in his nostrils. His work shoes were still soaked from the drama the night before, so he'd put his walking boots on, with three pairs of socks for warmth.

The fall-out from last night had been minimal. The Land Rover's bull bars had protected the lights and bodywork, and he'd reported the dead horse to Eric Scott, the local park ranger, first thing this morning. Then he'd called Bob Coffin, the huntsman with the Blacklands Hunt, to tell him where he could find the carcass. His headache had gone so completely that

Jonas could barely imagine what a headache felt like, and although Marvel had not exactly said he'd leave Peter Priddy alone, at least Jonas had raised the alibi with him as he'd promised he would.

Mostly, though, he felt better for having failed to take Marvel to the pub. It was a childish victory but a victory none the less. Of course, thanks to Marvel he now had all day to stand on the doorstep and savour it, while waiting for that wholly predictable killer to return like iron filings to the magnet of the crime scene.

Jonas smiled ruefully.

Oh well. At least it wasn't raining.

The boys were skating as he came down the hill. In the quiet air he heard them before he saw them – a sound like little trains on short journeys, each ending with a clatter, a laugh, a sound of approval or a sharp expletive that floated faintly upward from the playing field. The ramp came into view below him. Three boys. Steven Lamb, Dougie Trewell and one of the Tithecott boys. Chris? Mark? He couldn't tell from here.

Jonas stood and looked down on them for a moment, admiring their lazy grace – even all bundled up in their thick winter jackets, their motions were elegant. He'd seen plenty of bad skaters on that ramp since coming back to Shipcott – had taken Lalo Bryant and his broken ankle to hospital himself – but these three boys were good to watch, especially on a morning like this, where the white playing field around them was painted orange by the late-rising sun, and their tracks through the frost gave the scene a festive feel. The reminder of the Christmas just past made Jonas uneasy. The silence; the tight white face of Lucy's mother bustling up and down stairs; the false smiles and season's greetings, the unwrapped gifts under the unlit tree. Most of all, the sight of Lucy – wan and silent – in their bed, when she could just as easily have been dead. Before Christmas Day even dawned, Jonas had pushed the tree nose-first into the bin, lights, tinsel and all.

As he started to walk again, Jonas's eye was caught by something yellow at the edge of the playing field. He backed up a couple of paces to regain the view through a gap in the hedge.

There was something in the stream that bordered the field close to the ramp. Probably a plastic bag, but Jonas's gut stirred uneasily.

He hurried fifty yards down the hill to where the hedge was interrupted by a rusty five-bar gate, bent from the time Jack Biggins had roped a cow to it without using a baler-twine loop.

Now Jonas climbed those same bent bars until he'd gained another three feet to add to his existing six-four. From this height – and closer to the stream – he could see it was not a plastic bag.

Jonas leaped off the gate into the field and ran down the hill. The bright morning suddenly seemed surreal.

He shouldn't be running with this fluttering in his guts on such a morning, with frost crackling under his feet. At the bottom of the field he vaulted the stile on to the playing field and ran faster. Now he was on the flat he couldn't see the yellow thing any more, but he'd taken bearings in his mind, and ran straight and true past the swings and then the ramp, towards the crooked blackthorn that leaned drunkenly over the stream.

He reached the bank and there it was.

The body.

Yellow T-shirt bunched around the waist, pink knickers, blue-white skin.

He knew. He *knew*!

Jonas slithered down the bank, half falling, feeling the frozen mud on one cheek of his backside. The boots he'd worn that day for warmth cracked through the delicate plates of ice that had formed at the edges of the stream, and filled with water as he splashed the few feet to the body and turned it over.

'Mrs Marsh! *Yvonne!*'

Jonas dropped to his knees in the icy water and cleared her mouth, then started to breathe into the woman he knew was already dead.

Shit.

He dragged her to the water's edge. He couldn't get her up the bank – not alone – but he needed a firm surface. He balanced her awkwardly, knelt over her and pumped her chest, then breathed into her again.

'Mrs *Marsh!*'

He slapped her face hard, then breathed again, pumped her chest, then breathed again . . . felt everything in the world going awry.

The three boys from the ramp were above him, pale-faced and big-eyed.

'Call an ambulance!' he yelled.

The Tithecott boy fumbled his phone open and said, 'No signal.'

'Run to the houses!' Jonas yelled, before forcing more air into Yvonne Marsh's spongey lungs.

The boy took off, running. Without a word, Dougie Trewell slid down the mud into the stream and helped to keep Yvonne Marsh's upper body on the bank while Jonas worked on her. Steven Lamb sank to his knees in the white grass and just watched.

Jonas knew it was pointless. Yvonne Marsh was dead and had probably been dead for hours. Now he thought about it, there had been a little crackling sound as he'd tugged her body over on to its back – the sound of ice breaking around it. She had been there for a while, held still by the branches of the blackthorn and by the delicate ice that had embraced her. Maybe overnight. Who knew?

Danny Marsh might know. Or his father. And even if they didn't know *that*, thought Jonas wearily, they would know *this* for sure – that all their vigilance and their locks and their love and their care had not been enough to stop one vulnerable woman from wandering out into the freezing winter in bare feet, knickers and a baggy T-shirt, to drown in a freezing stream.

Everybody had to sleep some time, and that was the truth.

It was this thought that finally made Jonas give up. He looked across the stream at the rising moors, keeping all his air for himself now.

'Is she dead?' said Dougie Trewell tremulously.

'Yes,' said Jonas. All the energy he'd been filled with this morning had gone. 'You'd better get out of the water, Dougie.'

Dougie let go of the body and Jonas felt how much of its weight he'd taken in trying to help. 'Thanks,' he said, and the boy nodded mutely. He was Ronnie Trewell's younger brother and so always skirting the edges of delinquency – but he'd shown some character today. Something to hope for. Jonas turned to the other boy, who looked a million miles away. 'You want to help Dougie home, Steven? Make sure he gets warm?'

Steven focused slowly on him again.

'What?'

'Help Dougie, Steven. Take him home.'

'OK.'

Steven reached out and helped Dougie up the bank, and they walked away in a daze.

Jonas realized he hadn't given them instructions on getting help for *him*. The ambulance could take ages on icy roads. The boys might not have the presence of mind to think about him. He tried to manoeuvre his phone from inside his jacket, but the operation proved impossible while he was holding Yvonne Marsh. Finally he knew he'd have to let go of her body to do it, so he did, and felt the slow current start to pull it away from him. Her legs were still in the water. Jonas clutched at the yellow T-shirt with one hand while he flipped open his phone. There was one bar of signal. Miraculous. Maybe he should make all his mobile-phone calls from running water. He had been half kneeling on the bank, but now stood up in the water; his legs almost gave way under him, they were so cold. He stood in the way of the body and called Marvel while the current pressed the dead Yvonne Marsh insistently against his legs.

It wasn't until he spoke to Marvel that Jonas realized he might be standing up to his knees in a crime scene. He'd only called him because he was police and there were no police closer to Shipcott than Marvel was, and he needed help getting the hell out of this water before his legs fell clean off. But Marvel was immediately suspicious. Jonas figured that was how it was to be a homicide detective – every death was guilty until proven innocent.

'Don't touch the body!' Marvel snapped as soon as Jonas told him he'd found one.

Jonas said nothing, feeling guilty – and angry at himself for feeling that way.

'You fucking touched it, didn't you?'

'I tried CPR.'

If there was a Scorn Olympics, Marvel could have sighed for England.

'Well, don't touch it again, for Christ's sake! Stand by and wait for me!'

Jonas was wet, cold, traumatized and tired of being spoken to like a car-park attendant. 'Listen, *sir*. I'm up to my arse in ice, trying to stop the body floating downstream, so either get down here *fast* and help me out, or I'm going to let it go and your crime scene'll stretch all the way from here to bloody Tiverton!'

Jonas snapped his phone shut and hoped Marvel wouldn't be churlish enough to take his time.

He wasn't.

In less than five minutes, Marvel was watching Pollard and Reynolds help a shaky Jonas Holly out of the water.

He sent Grey and Singh down the icy bank to retrieve the body. There was little point in leaving it in situ now that Holly had already altered the scene by dragging it from the water.

The ambulance tipped off the village that something was happening down at the playing fields, and within ten minutes of its arrival the entire populace, made jumpy by one murder, was standing on the playing field, craning to see from behind the blue-and-white tape that Rice had rolled out from the lamp-post outside Margaret Priddy's across to the far goalpost, making a single cordon which now encompassed two crime scenes.

Maybe.

Marvel was unsure for about sixty seconds, and then he nodded as Dr Mark Dennis pointed to the livid finger-shaped bruises under Yvonne Marsh's wet hair.

'Not the throat, see?' Marvel told Reynolds. 'He held her like this . . .' He clawed his hands and hovered them over the back of the dead woman's neck. 'I think he held her face-down in the water and drowned her.'

'Could be,' said Mark Dennis.

'Pathologist will tell us for sure,' nodded Reynolds.

'*I'm* telling you for sure,' snapped Marvel. 'He'll just confirm it.'

Reynolds pursed his lips and tried hard, but finally couldn't help himself. 'Do we still like Peter Priddy, sir?'

'Fuck off, Reynolds.'

Reynolds withdrew a few paces from the scene and took out his notebook.

'That's F-U-C-K,' Marvel said and Reynolds put his notebook away again without writing in it.

'Pollard's in charge of the press,' Marvel told him.

'There *is* no press,' said Reynolds – and to all intents and purposes that was true. Marvel was all for the new breed of lazy, desk-bound journalists who Googled instead of bothering him for proper answers. Margaret Priddy's murder had elicited a few calls from the local rag, the *Bugle*, but the *Western Morning News* had been content to pick up a few paragraphs from that.

'There will be,' said Marvel in a doom-laden voice. He knew that one old woman being murdered was a shame, but two in the same tiny village in just over a week had the thrilling ring of serial violence about it, and it was only a matter of time before reporters started to arrive with their pushy ways and their cock-eyed views. He wanted Dave Pollard in charge of the press because he was the dullest and least forthcoming of the team. He had no fear that Pollard would suddenly get all star-struck and blab too much at a press conference just because the reporter who'd asked the question was wearing a push-up bra.

Two paramedics, finding their intended patient was past help, had instead turned their attentions to Jonas and stripped his trousers, socks and boots from him with professional disregard for his dignity. They had wrapped him in a foil blanket, followed by a scratchy grey one very like the blanket he himself had draped around the shoulders of Yvonne Marsh just a couple of days ago. At that thought, Jonas stopped trying to fight the chattering of his teeth and let them drown out all sound, like snare drums between his ears.

He'd known as soon as he saw the body in the water that it was Yvonne Marsh. He could have saved her. Could have followed her into the house that day and talked with Danny and his father about their options, the help available, safety locks. He could have given them the number of Social Services for respite care, or quietly asked Rupert Cooke up at Sunset

Lodge whether he had room for another resident.

Could have, would have, should have. Now that Yvonne Marsh was dead, Jonas could think of a million ways of keeping her alive.

Because once Marvel pointed out the bruises to Reynolds, Jonas knew that the man who had killed Margaret Priddy had also killed Yvonne Marsh. Knew it in his gut.

More easily, too, he imagined. Jonas would bet good money that the killer had not had to break into the Marsh home to find his second victim. No doubt Yvonne had just wandered out into the confused night of her mind to go to the shops, or to pick little Danny up from school, or to find her sandals in the lake.

Instead she had found her killer, or he had found her.

And Jonas had failed again.

''Vonne!' He heard a jolting, whimpering sound and looked up to see Alan Marsh running awkwardly across the playing field in the oily blue overalls and steel toe-caps he wore to work. The man's usually dour face was twisted open by emotion. Twenty yards behind him was his son, barefoot in jeans and a T-shirt, careless of the cold – and the Reverend Chard, too tubby to travel at more than a brisk walk.

Grey tried to stop Alan Marsh from just rushing the scene, but the older man ran past him as if he wasn't there, and fell to his knees beside his dead wife.

Jonas expected tears and wailing, but Alan Marsh

calmed right down when he saw his worst fears confirmed. He didn't even touch the body – just knelt and
looked at it and shook his head. Danny allowed himself to be slowed by Grey, and then stood with his
hand on his father's shoulder.

Jonas wished he had his trousers on, but this wasn't
about him. Holding the blanket around his hips like a
sarong, he went over to the tableau of sorrow and stood
in Danny's eye-line.

'I'm sorry, Danny. Mr Marsh.'

Danny looked at Jonas, dazed. 'What happened?'

'We're not sure yet. I found her in the stream.'

'She drowned?'

Jonas ignored Marvel's unnecessary warning look.
'We don't know yet. I tried CPR but I think she'd
been in the water a while. Hours, maybe.'

Danny nodded and bit his lip until he could speak
again. 'We didn't even know she were gone. Not until
we heard the ambulance.'

Jonas nodded.

'You can't watch her all the time,' said Danny dully.

'I know,' said Jonas. 'I know.'

He saw the tears gather in his former friend's eyes
and looked away.

'You can't watch her *all the fucking time*!' Danny
shouted suddenly. '*Every fucking DAY!*'

Jonas touched Danny's shoulder. His hand was
knocked away but he put it back and this time Danny
let it stay. He led Danny away from the crowd and

towards the stream. The two of them stood and stared across the singing water at the white-frosted moor. Jonas didn't look at Danny as he cried. There was very little sound from behind them, considering the whole village was just a hundred yards away. The morning was still beautiful – facing this way, at least – and Jonas was seized with a sudden notion to take Danny by the arm and lead him through the stream and up on to the moorland opposite and just keep walking, leaving everything behind them and never looking back to see the horror of reality.

He didn't, of course, but he could taste in his mouth what it would be like to do it.

Finally Danny spoke softly.

'She hated being that way.'

Jonas nodded.

'You remember what she was like?'

'Of course,' said Jonas and Danny sighed.

'Sometimes *she* remembered. How she'd been. That was the worst part, you know? Not her going nuts, but her *knowing* that she was going nuts.'

Jonas nodded. He understood.

'At least that's over now,' Danny said, and turned back towards the surreal scene of his mother lying dead near the corner flag while the whole village watched silently from the far touchline, as if they'd come to see a match and stayed to watch a murder. His father was in the back of the ambulance now, with the two paramedics fussing over him.

Jonas saw that someone had put a blanket over Mrs Marsh's body and he was stupidly grateful, because it was a cold day, despite the sunshine.

Danny sniffed, sighed, and shook a B&H out of a crumpled pack he found in his jeans.

'You all right, Jonas?'

Jonas glanced at him, perplexed. *He* was all right! *He* wasn't the one whose dead mother had just been hauled out of a frozen stream like an Arctic seal. Why the hell would Danny ask him *that*?

He said nothing and Danny didn't ask again.

Nearby a blackbird burst into song and Jonas allowed it to fill him up. With his back to the body there was nothing but beauty in the world.

Danny squinted as he blew the only cloud into the clear blue sky. 'We should have a drink,' he said.

'Some time,' said Jonas, and hoped Danny realized that that meant 'never'.

Danny smoked half the cigarette and flicked the rest into the stream. 'Yeah,' he said. 'I'll see you soon, Jonas.'

Marvel watched Danny Marsh walk away from Jonas Holly and back to his father. Without averting his gaze, he spoke quietly to Reynolds, who stood beside him with that damned notebook open.

'What's the link?'

'Pardon, sir?'

'The link. Between Margaret Priddy and . . .' He nodded at the corpse.

'Yvonne Marsh.'

'Yes. Assuming this is murder and it's the same killer. What's the link?'

Reynolds thought for a second. 'Both in their sixties. Both women . . .' He dried up.

Marvel looked at Reynolds directly now. 'Both a burden on their families, wouldn't you say?'

Reynolds nodded his thoughtful agreement.

'Could be two families finally snapping. But if it's not, then what's the link? More important, *who*'s the link?'

'I don't know, sir.'

'Well, nor do I,' said Marvel. 'Yet.'

He told Pollard to bag up PC Holly's clothes for Jos Reeves at the lab. The crime scene here was a joke – in the open air and on a field that half the village used, trampled by Holly and the skateboarders at the very least, and the body had been in water and then moved, just to add to the complications – but he might as well preserve everything he could, if only for the purpose of elimination. He walked back towards the car, his feet making a satisfying crunching sound on the frosty field, and called Jos Reeves to tell him to be sure to compare forensics in the Yvonne Marsh case with Margaret Priddy's. Reeves got in a huff with him. Got all offended that Marvel thought he didn't know his own job. Prima donna. Next time he'd have Reynolds call Reeves.

He sent Singh, Pollard and Grey to do *another*

house-to-house, asking all the same questions but about a different time, place and victim. It was a chore but it had to be done.

Later he took Elizabeth Rice to meet the Marshes. He told them she would be their family liaison officer, staying with them twenty-four hours a day for support, and keeping them informed of how the investigation was progressing.

'Anything you want, or anything you need to know, you just ask her,' he said with surprising kindness.

He told *her* they were both suspects until further notice.

*

After Jonas had given a preliminary statement to one of Marvel's DCs, the paramedics dropped him off at home so he could finally get some trousers on. They wanted their scratchy blanket back, and Lucy looked up in surprise as he walked into the cottage wrapped from the waist down in silver foil. She made a mermaid joke, then saw his face. He told her what had happened and watched her get quiet. *More* quiet; Lucy was always calm – even when told about what looked like the village's second murder in eight days.

'You need to get warm,' was her verdict. She insisted on coming upstairs with him, so he carried her on legs that throbbed painfully now, cramping as the blood got going again. Without her sticks she moved carefully and with a break in her stride that made it look as if she might fall at any minute. Still, need gave her strength, and she bossed him and ran him a bath while he stripped off and bundled his clothes into the laundry basket. He thought he might as *well* be a mermaid, he'd been so wet in the past twelve hours. His good shoes and another pair of work trousers were still on the radiators from last night. He could hear Lucy painstakingly laying out a fresh uniform on the bed – doing her wifely thing in jerky slow motion – while he stepped into the bath, sending needles of hot pain up his legs.

Their bath – which had a view of the moor on one side and the fields sloping up to Springer Farm on the other – was the biggest that would fit into the tiny bathroom, but it was no match for Jonas. It was why he preferred the shower; in the bath he had to sit up to keep both his legs submerged. As his legs warmed and he listened to Lucy moving around – making all that effort for his benefit – he slumped back against the cold enamel and a great weariness overtook him. The shock of last night, and the bigger shock of this morning. Two murders. *Two murders!* Perhaps if he'd watched more American television, he wouldn't feel so appalled. Perhaps being a policeman and having two murders in quick succession on his patch would not feel so surreal if only he'd tuned in to *NYPD Blue* a bit more dutifully in his formative years.

Somewhere out there was a killer. It seemed

unbelievable, but a killer had come to town and – like the shark in *Jaws* – had apparently decided to stick around.

Call yourself a policeman?

The words hit him again, but this time they seemed to be not just an accusation but a warning. Was it the killer who had left him a message? The idea jolted him. Was the killer taunting him? Letting him know how ineffective he was? Was Yvonne Marsh another display of his dubious skills? If so, how many more people might the killer be planning to murder? Where would his appetite end?

The shame he'd felt as he read the note came back to Jonas hard, along with this new fear and a fresh wave of helplessness. He was the *protector*. He should be out there on the high seas hunting down the killer shark, when all he was doing was standing on the jetty with a shrimping net, hoping it would swim past and wave a fin. And if the killer *was* here to stay, then all he really wanted to do was stock up on canned goods, barricade the doors and wrap Lucy in his arms until it all went away.

Except that what Lucy really needed protecting from was *never* going to go away . . .

A loud sob escaped him and he clapped a hand over his mouth, feeling the tears heat his eyes as efficiently as the bath had heated his legs.

'Jonas?'

He bent his knees and slid quickly down the

enamel and under the water, so that when she came in, there would be a good reason why his face was wet.

*

The killer was angry.

Margaret Priddy had been unavoidable in a way, but Yvonne Marsh should never have had to happen. If Jonas had understood the first message, then he'd have done his job – and if Jonas had done his job, then Yvonne Marsh would still be alive.

To the killer it all seemed very simple.

He didn't know why Jonas had to make it so complicated.

*

Marvel had rather grudgingly told him to take the rest of the day off, but Jonas knew he couldn't stay at home and out of sight for all of it – not after a second murder in the village he was charged with the care of. He also didn't want to leave Lucy alone. He knew he'd have to at some point, but today was too raw, too soon.

So that night he took her to the Red Lion, ostensibly for a drink, but they both knew it was so he could be seen; be seen to be part of things.

The mood in the pub was paradoxically sober and the moment they walked in Jonas knew it had been a bad idea to come. Everyone wanted to talk to him, everyone wanted to speculate and everyone wanted to know what the police were doing. This would have been bad enough if he'd been alone – telling them that all he was doing was standing on a doorstep, effectively doing nothing while villagers were being slaughtered – but with Lucy in tow, it was truly shaming. She squeezed his hand under the table at one point, which made it even worse. People weren't rude about it, but he could see the esteem in which he'd been held slipping as they realized that, while they'd been treating him like one for years, he wasn't a real policeman after all. All very well to drive about the place in a flashy Land Rover with bull bars and a winch, but when it came down to the nitty gritty, they might as well have a scarecrow for a village bobby, if all he was going to do was *stand* there.

Jonas felt a sweat starting and got up and went to the bathroom, just to get away from them all. He shut himself in a stall and tried to think clearly.

If he could only go back to his usual routine it wouldn't be so bad. At least then he'd look as if he was doing what he did best while leaving the murder investigation to the experts. But Marvel wasn't going to give him a break. He felt that instinctively. He may not keep him on the doorstep for ever, but there was no way he was going to release Jonas while he was still smarting over some imagined slight. He'd give him some other shit thing to do; keep punishing him. Jonas saw his days stretching out in front of him, pointless, boring, undermining his position in the community, and – most importantly – not helping to catch the killer. It was a grim picture.

He stepped out of the stall, still deep in thought, and went over to wash his hands. As he raised his eyes to his reflection in the scarred and pitted mirror over the basin, he noticed the writing on the door behind him. Graham Nash had painted all the toilet doors with blackboard paint inside and out, and provided chalk so customers could write on them. It was a nice idea and gave people something to read while taking a shit, but, of course, it always threw up a mixed bag of dirty limericks, four-letter words and local libel, which required that the whole lot was washed down and erased on a regular basis.

Jonas frowned and turned to look at the door to the stall he'd just come out of. There was a single message in an oddly familiar, spiky hand:

Do your job, Crybaby

A cold prickle ran over his skin.

Who knew? Who the *fuck* knew that he'd cried in the bath? His mind scrabbled for purchase on the idea that someone had seen him, or heard him, or just plain *knew* that he'd sobbed like a little girl. The invasion of privacy felt total. The idea that someone could watch him naked and vulnerable – intrude on the safe cosiness of the bathroom he'd thought he shared with his wife alone. It seemed impossible. Their cottage was not overlooked and Mrs Paddon was their only neighbour. She was a genteel woman in her eighties and was the last person in the world Jonas could ever imagine spying on him and then sneaking into the gents' at the Red Lion to scribble vicious accusations on the door.

Do your job, crybaby!

Another murder. Another note directed at him.

He hadn't heard anyone come into the bathroom since he'd entered, but then he hadn't been listening for anyone; he'd been deep in thought. Someone could have come in, written this and left. Couldn't they? He wasn't sure. He racked his brains to try to recall whether the message had been there before he entered the stall. It couldn't have been; he'd have seen it. He'd noticed it in the mirror from across the room, after all.

The door to the only other stall was closed. Jonas knelt slowly and looked under it. Empty. He pushed the door and it opened, then creaked slowly shut again. Badly hung, that was all.

Suddenly Jonas didn't want to leave the bathroom. The thought of walking back out into the bar knowing that the person who had written the message was probably there, watching him, made him shake.

The *truth* of it made him shake.

He *wasn't* doing his job.

He *was* a crybaby.

This thing with Lucy. It had taken his eye off the ball, stopped him focusing on his work at the precise moment when he needed to be 100 per cent at the top of his game.

Mark Dennis's words rang in his ears: *Lucy needs you. Now more than ever.*

Jonas wet a paper towel and rubbed the message off the door, then balled it up and flung it hard against the mirror. It hit with a satisfying splat and sprayed water across the glass in a pop-art Pow!

Other people needed him more than ever now, too.

He looked at his broken image again through the trickles of water and made up his mind.

Marvel controlled his days.

But he was still master of his own nights.

Fourteen Days

Shipcott shut down.

In the wake of two murders, the village folded in on itself with a surreal sense of disbelief.

An outsider would have noticed nothing but furtive looks; any local would have known that nothing was as it was before, and nothing was as it should be.

People went about their business. They worked, they shopped, they walked their dogs. But the Shipcott air itself had changed and all who lived there took in toxins with every breath now. Suspicion, fear and confusion started to suffuse their beings and they looked at each other with new eyes that sought clues to the killer's identity.

It was only 3.45pm but the light was already fading from the sky. The streetlamps flickered orange and warmed up slowly and, while death was still the subject on everyone's mind, life poured out of the school gates into the strange new world. Children who were used to walking home alone were surprised and embarrassed to find that nervous mothers had come to meet them with pushchairs and dogs on leads, while the narrow road outside the school was clogged with cars ready to transport children through the normally quiet lanes to other villages, rather than risk their missing the bus or walking the last few hundred yards alone in the dark. A single murder was bad enough; a second had created a sense of beyond-coincidence which justified vehicular over-protectiveness, and Pat Jones the lollipop lady bore the brunt of the fear as she tried to cope single-handedly with the sudden traffic mayhem.

Dog-walkers stopped approaching each other so readily. Women walking alone on the moor or on the playing field were nervous of men they'd known all their lives, and those men kept their distance to avoid scaring the women. Farmers who noticed walkers on footpaths kept watching until they were out of sight, and made notes of the number plates of cars parked in lay-bys. Brusque waves took the place of face-to-face conversations, and people shouted 'Hello' too loudly at each other across the street, so everyone could tell they were normal and friendly and not weird loners plotting murder.

The *Bugle* reporter came from Dulverton and attracted small knots of people nodding and looking worried on each other's doorsteps.

The Red Lion and the Blue Dolphin chip shop saw

brisk early trade, but each then closed earlier than usual for want of customers. Dedicated drinkers went home at an unaccustomed hour to discover that their children had grown up in their pub-induced absence and now insisted on watching sexually charged soaps instead of *Sesame Street*.

Steven Lamb was forbidden by his mother to go to the skate ramp after dark and was secretly relieved, and Billy Beer – who had been plagued for years by a small knot of teenagers who gathered at the bus stop outside his home every night and made Bongo bark – was so unnerved by the sudden silence that he tossed and turned all night, and woke up each morning more exhausted than he had been the night before.

*

Jonas kissed Lucy goodnight and felt like a bigamist.

She'd said she didn't mind. No, she'd been more generous than that – she'd encouraged him to go, even though she was confused about his reasoning.

'I don't think anyone was blaming you yesterday, sweetheart.'

'I could tell,' he said.

'You don't think you're being a little paranoid?'

'Why? Do you think I am?' Obviously the answer must be 'yes' or Lucy wouldn't have asked the question, but Jonas was always interested in hearing what she had to say.

'A little.' She shrugged. 'I can understand how you must feel you're somehow responsible . . . that you failed Margaret and Yvonne in some way . . . even though I don't see how. But all I saw at the pub was worried people turning to you for information.'

Jonas was silent so he didn't have to disagree with her. He didn't want to voice dissent that might turn into an argument that might lead back to the question of children. He had no stomach for it. He just hoped her contention wasn't going to turn into a suggestion that he stay at home, because his mind was made up.

Instead Lucy said, 'But I know it's not about them as much as it is about the way *you* feel about it, Jonas, and I agree that that's what's important. If going out at night makes you feel better, then you should do that.'

He didn't deserve her. He never had and he never would.

He got up and took their best knife from the block in the kitchen.

'Promise me you'll keep this with you all the time when I'm not here.'

She laughed. 'Jonas!'

'I'm serious, Lu. I have to do this, but I hate leaving you here alone—'

'Mrs Paddon's a foot away through the wall.'

'I know. And I don't want you to be nervous. But please. For *my* sake, so *I'm* not nervous.'

He held it out to her, grip-first, and after another moment's hesitation she took it.

'Promise me,' he said.

Lucy drew a Zorro-esque *Z* in the air and faked a Spanish accent. 'You have my word, *amigo*! Any mad dog will feel the edge of my blade on his balls.'

'Promise me,' he said seriously.

'I promise,' she said, and didn't smile this time because she wanted him to know she *did* take him seriously, even if she felt it was an overreaction.

Then he kissed her and left to spend the night with the village.

After he went, Lucy smiled at the knife, then took it through to the lounge with her.

She put *Scream* into the DVD player, cursing her own unsteady hands that dropped the disc twice before she managed to load it correctly; sometimes the sheer force of will it took not to be feeble was beyond her.

Ten minutes into the movie, she started to feel uneasy.

She heard a sound at the window.

She knotted her fingers into the tassels of the cushion.

She made sure the knife was close at hand.

She told herself not to be stupid.

Twenty minutes in, she realized she was missing *Desperate Housewives*.

Lucy hadn't watched it for a while but thought it would be nice to catch up, so she switched off the horror and lost herself instead in a place where bad things were made laughable by sunshine and great shoes.

*

It was only when he started to walk up one side of Barnstaple Road a little after 9pm that Jonas realized how lost he had been.

The fact that it was dark made no difference; he was back on the beat, back where he should be, and – more importantly – back where people *expected* him to be. The street was pretty empty but for a few late-night dog-walkers. He said hello to Rob Ticker and his spaniel, Jerry, and John Took – the Master of the Blacklands – thanked him for the dead pony and told him there were saboteurs in the area. They'd laid a false trail for the Tiverton hounds, which had ended up in a Tesco car park. Typical hunter, thought Jonas even as he made the right noises – two women murdered and John Took was worried about missing a fox. He asked Took whether he'd heard about Yvonne Marsh and Took said, 'Bloody awful. But that's care in the bloody community for you' – to which there was no answer except to tell Took he'd do his best to be at the next meet just in case of trouble.

Then he stopped to chat to Linda Cobb with Dixie.

'I still have your umbrella,' he told Linda.

'Drop it in when you're passing,' she said.

Jonas said he'd be back on the doorstep tomorrow and would drop it by then.

'And you're doing this *too*?' she said, waving her arm at the street.

Jonas agreed that he was, and the look she gave him made everything worthwhile – even having to leave Lucy alone. With any luck the news would be all round Shipcott tomorrow that he was making night patrols. If a killer was out there, maybe it would make him think twice.

For the same reason he dropped into the Red Lion and was greeted so warmly that yesterday's impressions did seem to be no more than paranoia. He felt foolish. Everyone in the bar now seemed to know that he had jumped into the freezing stream and tried to revive Yvonne Marsh, and clamoured to buy him a drink. When he told them he was on duty and explained about the night patrols, the atmosphere grew even warmer.

'Good thinking, Jonas,' said Mr Jacoby to general agreement, and Graham Nash brought over a coffee on the house.

The talk in the pub was all about the deaths. Murders, they called them both already, because nobody believed that Yvonne Marsh had lived all her life in Shipcott but had chosen *this* week to fall into the stream and drown. Jonas couldn't disagree, although he wouldn't speculate out loud for them. They didn't mind; having Jonas be the voice of reason would only have spoiled their theories.

'I reckon it's some nutter from Tiverton,' said old Jack Biggins of the cow-and-gate incident. His macro-xenophobia meant that everyone beyond Dulverton was a suspect.

'Could be anyone just passing through,' suggested Billy Beer, vaguely enough for the others to feel confident in disagreeing with him.

'Now if *that* were it,' said Graham Nash, 'we'd have noticed him.' Which was true, thought Jonas, because a stranger in a village this size in the middle of winter stuck out like a sore thumb.

'Maybe one of our own turned bad then,' shrugged Stuart Beard.

Beard was the kind of man whose opinion usually attracted sage nods all round, but Jonas noted that this time there were only a few careful grunts of agreement, noticeably half-hearted enough for him to look up and see that Clive Trewell – father of Skew Ronnie – was sat in the window nursing a half.

Jonas went over to him and said hello.

Ronnie Trewell had been a good kid but was growing up all wrong, and Clive Trewell was not used to speaking to Jonas Holly in anything other than an official capacity.

Clive blamed himself; he'd encouraged his son to take driving lessons, and driving lessons had been like lighting a blue touch paper for Ronnie Trewell. Some people had a calling. They were called to be missionaries in Africa; they were called to find delicate art hidden in marble blocks; they were called to open their homes to hedgehogs or stray cats. Ronnie Trewell was called to drive. Very fast. And because he couldn't afford anything faster than a thirteen-year-old Ford Fiesta with the weekly wage he earned at Mr Marsh's car-repair garage, he was called to steal those very fast cars.

Teased away from school because of his lopsided walk, caused by an uncorrected club foot, Skew Ronnie had achieved the wherewithal to steal cars, but not the guile to hide the fact. He would simply drive around in his Fiesta until he saw a car he wanted to drive. Then he would steal it, leaving his Fiesta in its place, keys in the ignition for convenience's sake. It did not take Sherlock Holmes to work out whodunit. But depending on where Ronnie Trewell had stolen the car from, it did sometimes take a little while for the police to come knocking on the door. During that time Ronnie would drive at breakneck speed across the moors, and when he wasn't actually driving the stolen car, he was modifying, tuning and customizing it in his dad's garage. Given that he didn't steal the cars to sell – and that the cars were always recovered eventually – it was this curious aspect of the crimes, coupled with his youth, which had so far kept nineteen-year-old Ronnie Trewell away from hard-core custodial sentences. Owners who had their cars returned in better condition than when they were stolen were disinclined to press charges. The owner of an old but sporty Honda CRX discovered a rusty wheel-arch had been excised, welded and expertly re-sprayed. A woman in Taunton was delighted to have her Toyota MR2 returned with a new, satisfyingly throaty exhaust fitted, and the owner of an Alfa Romeo GTV was so impressed by his reclaimed car's improved performance that he sent Ronnie a thank-you note.

Clive knew that Ronnie couldn't help himself. He had tried to teach him right from wrong but, when it came to cars, it just hadn't taken. Something in his son *needed* those cars the way other people needed braces or spectacles. Each car Ronnie stole became part of him; he put his heart, soul and all his meagre spare cash into it. And every time the police sent a tow truck to take away a stolen car, Ronnie stood in the road and cried.

PC Holly had made half a dozen visits to the Trewell home in the past two years, so Clive was prepared.

'Them other police already talked to Ronnie!' he said – and was taken aback when Jonas started to talk not about Ronnie, but about Dougie.

'Did he tell you what happened yesterday?'

Clive's heart sank. *Not Dougie too!* But then he listened in amazement as Jonas told him about the part his younger son had played in the drama down behind the playing field.

'Didn't say a word!' he said.

* * *

When he'd first stood up, Jonas had fully intended to quiz Clive Trewell about Ronnie. Where he was. Where he'd been. What he'd been doing. But when he'd got close to the man and seen the sad, wary look in his eyes as he approached, he'd lost the stomach for it.

Instead he talked up Dougie – told Clive what a good lad he had there – and then brought the surprised man a drink before saying goodnight and heading back out on patrol.

Before he did, he went into the gents' toilets.

There was no message.

The night was clear and bitter and the stars were close overhead. The street had emptied of dog-walkers and was awaiting the early exodus from the Red Lion, after which it would finally rest for the night.

Without thinking why, Jonas walked towards the Trewell home, skidding more than once on the ice that had already formed on the narrow pavement.

He had no great suspicion that Ronnie Trewell was involved in the murders. He knew he was only going to speak to him now because Ronnie was the only person in Shipcott whom anyone could logically accuse of any wrongdoing that went beyond poor parking or leaving the bins out too early. He worked for Alan Marsh, certainly, but Jonas wasn't setting much store by that. Talking to him seemed sensible – that was all. Marvel may have done it already but Marvel wasn't local, so anything anyone told him or his team was necessarily open to improvement.

Jonas turned up Heather View – a name which always made him smile because, unless you stuck your head in a cupboard, there was nowhere in Shipcott that *didn't* offer a heather view. The short, steep lane ended in a dead end of frozen mud in front of the stile beside the Trewell home, which consisted of a tiny, ugly bungalow and a vast double garage. It seemed that even the buildings of his childhood home had conspired to lure Ronnie into following his calling.

Dougie answered the door and looked concerned to see Jonas.

'All right?' he said carefully.

'All right, Dougie. Warm now?' said Jonas and the boy smiled faintly. 'Can I come in for a minute?'

'OK,' said Dougie.

The house smelled old and cold. The front room was devoid of furniture apart from an oversized green vinyl sofa and a large TV with wires pouring from the back like entrails, and connected to various speakers, games consoles, DVD players and satellite receivers strewn about the dirty carpet.

'I haven't done anything wrong,' said Ronnie instantly. He sat on the floor while a white-muzzled greyhound took up the whole length of the sofa behind his head. The dog lifted its nose and looked at Jonas with its solemn, blue-sheened eyes, then lay flat again.

'I know,' said Jonas, standing in the doorway. Dougie hovered a little nervously between the two of them, unsure of whose side he should be on.

'Then why are you here?' Ronnie put down the game control he'd been holding in his lap and turned away from Jonas to pet the dog. The vast, flat animal lifted its front leg off the sofa so Ronnie could tickle its armpit.

'She likes that,' said Jonas.

'Yeah,' said Ronnie. And then – after a long pause – 'You told me that.'

'What?'

Ronnie spoke with his back to Jonas but his voice was softened by the contact with the greyhound, which lay stiff-legged, hypnotized by pleasure.

'You told me dogs like their armpits tickled.'

'Yeah?' Jonas was puzzled. 'When?'

Ronnie shrugged one shoulder. 'Dunno. When I was a kid.'

Jonas had no recollection of it. He only vaguely recalled Ronnie Trewell as a child – marked out by his limp – hanging around on the edges of everything, never excluded but never really involved either.

He watched the teenager's callused, oil-stained fingers gently stroke the most tender skin the dog had to offer.

'How old is she?' he asked.

'Twelve,' said Dougie, relieved at this new non-confrontational turn in the conversation. 'She used to race. She had tattoos in her ears but they cut them out when they dumped her.'

Jonas saw the dog's cloudy eyes widen and its whole body stiffen as Ronnie lifted its ear to show where the delicate drape of silken flesh had been brutally sliced to prevent identification and responsibility.

'She doesn't like it when you touch it,' said Ronnie, letting the ear drop back into place. 'Even after all this time.'

'She remembers, see?' said Dougie, and he walked over, perched on the edge of the sofa and smoothed the dog's brindle flank. 'Don't you, girl?'

Jonas suddenly felt overwhelmingly sad and disconnected.

The soft thief, the unformed boy, the stale room. The old dog with its long memory of bad things.

He said something to Dougie – something about the help he'd rendered yesterday. He didn't know *what* he said or what was said in return – it was just a way to excuse himself and move from inside the house to outside, where he could breathe and be alone.

He turned left out of the front gate instead of right and walked twenty paces across the frozen mud to the stile that led to the moor. He climbed on to it and stood there, raised into the icy night sky, confused by the depth of his own feelings.

So what if the dog was old? So what if it had had its tattoos cut out? Dogs went through bad things all the time and then recovered from them and lived happy lives. Just like people did. The dog was loved and cared for *now*, so why did he feel so sad?

Because the dog remembered.

Worse than that, the dog could not forget.

Even when it had an entire green-vinyl sofa to stretch out on, and a boy stroking its armpit, the memory was right there, right *underneath*, all ready to burst through the skin, tear open old wounds and make them bleed afresh. And it wasn't just the wounds. It was the memory of the trembling, pissing terror every time a human approached and a hand reached out, in case it held not titbits but sudden sharp and selfish pain.

Jonas was dizzy with the fear of the remembering dog. He had no idea why; he just *was*.

He swayed atop the icy stile, sucked air into his lungs as if he'd just missed drowning, and squeezed his eyes shut.

He wouldn't cry. He mustn't cry. He was *not allowed* to cry.

For some reason which escaped him, that thought made his eyes burn even harder and his throat felt filled with a balloon with the effort it took to keep from tears.

It was Lucy. He knew it was all about Lucy, this new tearful streak. He tried to tell himself it was understandable – that facing the loss of someone he loved so much was sure to make him weak and vulnerable – but something in him found it merely pathetic and he hated himself because of it.

He opened his eyes and blinked at the mono-chromatic haloes around the stars above him and the streetlights below him. He made no effort to clear his vision – blurred was nice for now. Even blurred, he knew the shape of the village. He knew the light that was the pub and the light over the bus stop. A hundred feet below him he knew the yellow blob of Linda Cobb's kitchen, and the absence of light that was Margaret Priddy's home.

One light sparkled in isolation across the coombe – separate from the others. Jonas focused on it and breathed steadily. Slowly, slowly, the cobwebs faded around the single light and he saw it was a yellowish, un-curtained window across the way, only just visible above the rough silhouette of a hedge, which cut it off at the sill.

He looked down towards the village and took his bearings, then looked back up at that single pale window.

And felt his heart miss a beat.

From here.

From this place alone.

From atop the stile outside the Trewell home, Jonas Holly could see directly into his own bathroom.

Twelve Days

When it finally made up its mind, the snow came with a vengeance.

The first flakes wandered down from the black velvet sky like little stars that had lost their way, and within minutes the galaxies themselves were raining down on Exmoor. Without a breath of breeze to divert or delay them, a million billion points of fractured light poured from the heavens, to be finally reunited under the moon in a brilliant carpet of silent white.

*

Marvel woke up with a cat staring into his eyes from a distance of about three inches. He flinched and it dug its claws into his chest, keeping him just where it wanted him.

'Get off,' he suggested, but the enormously fluffy

grey ball merely blinked its orange eyes and looked contemptuous. It did withdraw its claws a little, but was certainly not going anywhere soon.

Marvel turned his head with a wince to find he was asleep on Joy Springer's hairy kitchen sofa and couldn't feel his legs. Because of the cat, he couldn't immediately see them either, which only added to the surreal feeling that his legs could be absolutely any-where. He reached down and touched his thigh. Or what he assumed was his thigh – he had no sensation in the slab his finger felt through the cloth of his suit trousers.

The light was oddly muted, as if someone had put a pale veil over the windows while he slept. It added to the air of strangeness that waking up without his legs was giving him.

It had been a late night at the mobile unit. Late and smelling of Calor gas. He'd kept his team up past their bedtimes, laying out a strategy for the two inquiries; being the swan while wanting a drink. Luckily Reynolds was on the ball. Him and his fucking little notebook, thought Marvel sourly.

Then he had come back to the farm to find that although he'd given Joy Springer money for a bottle of whiskey, she'd instead bought two bottles of Cinzano, which he hadn't even known they *made* any more.

'Get *off*!' he shouted into the cat's face and – after a rebellious beat – it rose slowly, dug in its claws in farewell, and sauntered down his body with its tail in the air, so that Marvel could see from its puckered arse exactly what it thought of him.

Marvel struggled to his elbows and looked down at his legs, which – in their paralysis – seemed to be completely separate from his hips. He actually had to lean down and pull his own feet to the floor so that he could sit up. He noticed he'd removed his shoes, even though Joy Springer's couch looked as if it had been retrieved from a tip. So did his shoes; they had been wet and dried so often in the past fortnight that the leather was going stiff. How hard could it be to buy wellington fucking boots?

He looked at his watch. Eight thirty-five am.

Bollocks.

The empty bottles on the table told their own story and as a prequel to that he had a hazy recollection of Joy Springer cackling while he told her an anecdote. He had several that he rolled out again and again and again in company – each time starting with 'Reminds me of . . .' As if he'd ever forgotten.

There was the story of Jason Harman, the Butcher of Bermondsey, who'd sliced up his wife and his mother-in-law and boiled their remains to soup on a two-ring hob; of Nance Locke, who'd murdered her three children by tying their hands and forcing their heads into a bucket of water one after the other; or of Ang Nu, who'd run as if guilty and then, when cornered, jumped from a bridge – not into the expected river, but on to the unfortunate spikes of the railings below. 'One in his arse, one in his heart and one right through the eye socket,' Marvel always finished with ghoulish glee. 'The eyeball was sat on top of the spike like a cocktail onion on a stick.'

Of course, the older Marvel got, the fewer people had ever seen a cocktail onion on a stick and the less punch the image packed. Still, he enjoyed saying it, even if the denouement was always accompanied by the guilty nudge of the untold aftermath. That Ang Nu had been beaten up twice because of his immigrant status, spoke no English, and had probably been wholly unaware that the four burly men chasing him this time were police.

That would have spoiled the story.

Which would have been a shame, because Joy Springer had seemed to enjoy that one. Old enough to remember cocktail onions, for sure. No doubt if he'd had a story about a fondue-related crime, she'd have liked that too.

Joy had a few stories of her own, Marvel remembered dimly now with a grimace. A few too many and all against the same backdrop of Springer Farm: buying the place as newlyweds, individual horses and all their little horsey quirks, the seemingly endless years of trekking and local shows and children falling off and grockles getting trampled and the stables burning down and the cottages being built in their place . . . mercifully Marvel had been able to tune much of it out entirely. Until she'd got tearful. Then he'd had to re-focus and at least *look* as if he'd been listening all along. Really, the things you had to do to get a companionable drink around here.

She'd shown him a photo of her husband. Marvel turned his head now and could still see it on the table, propped up as if it had been watching him all night. Creepy. Her husband had been called Roy. Or Ralph. Something with an R.

Debbie used to say, 'People get the face they deserve.' Another of her hippy-dippy Sting-clinging homilies that made him want to smack her with her Amazonian rainstick. Annoyingly, though, Marvel had come to the grudging conclusion that she was generally right on this one. He'd banged up enough pinch-lipped, low-browed, boss-eyed criminals in his time to become receptive to the idea. Now he thought that if Something with an R had got the face he deserved then he probably should have been banged up too.

Not according to Joy Springer, he recalled vaguely. Apparently Something with an R had been descended from angels and had returned there 'to sleep' with them once his tortured life was at an end. Marvel tried to remember what had tortured him so badly – ill health or no money or just being so bloody ugly and married to Joy Springer – but he wasn't sure she had told him. He did remember being surprised that the resilient old bird had got emotional about *anything* other than the fact that the Cinzano was finished. She didn't seem the type.

Ah well, it was all a bit of a haze now.

Marvel rubbed his eyes and face. Reynolds would muster the troops; it wouldn't be the first time. He got to his unsteady feet and saw the white outside. Snow making everything seem black and white, deep enough that he could not see the gravel of the court-yard, even through the footprints and the tyre tracks that indicated that Reynolds *had* mustered the troops, and that they had already left.

His phone rang and he found it under another cat on the corner of the table.

'I've got good news and bad news,' said Jos Reeves, and from his tone Marvel could tell that he was even happy about the bad news, which immediately got under his skin.

'Don't fuck about, Reeves.'

'All right,' said Reeves, and then proceeded to fuck about. 'The good news is there's a forensic link between the two scenes.'

Marvel stayed silent, determined not to give Reeves the satisfaction of asking about the bad news, but his heart jerked anyway, as it always did when science put the seal on a suspect.

'The *bad* news,' said Reeves, in a voice that betrayed suppressed laughter, 'is that it's one of your own men.'

*

From her bedroom window, Mrs Paddon watched Jonas clear the snow off her path. His father used to do the same thing.

Although Jonas also frequently offered to pick up bread or a newspaper for her, Mrs Paddon preferred to walk into the village, despite her eighty-nine years. She had an umbrella, after all – and a pair of stout waterproof boots.

She didn't speak to Jonas much, but she loved him dearly. Always had – from the day Cath and Des had brought him home from the hospital, all red and screwed up. Although the walls between Rose and Honeysuckle were thick and stone, she'd sometimes been able to hear him bawling, and whenever she did, she'd hold her breath until it stopped and she was sure that Cath had gone to him. Sometimes she lay awake wondering what she would do if little Jonas's crying had ever gone unchecked, and in her sillier meanderings had imagined having to rescue him and bring him back to her bed to snuggle like a little kitten.

She smiled faintly now at the memory – and at the anomalous thought of that tiny baby and the tall man below.

Every now and then Jonas would straighten up and stare across the coombe. She wondered why. Could he see something suspicious? She looked herself, but things were as they always were – the rolling moor and the other side of the village nestling at its foot, all coated in virginal white that made her eyes ache.

Terrible thing, these murders. She'd known Yvonne Marsh by sight, but Margaret Priddy and she had been friends – even though Mrs Paddon disagreed with hunting. Disagreed so strongly, in fact, that sometimes she'd pull on her waterproof boots, walk up to the common with a thermos of tea and a small wooden sign, and join the saboteurs. She'd made the sign herself: *Foxes are people too*. The young sabs with their woollen hats and their nose rings always made her welcome, and whenever Margaret rode past she'd wave hello with her sign and they'd chat for a bit. The first time it had happened, a sab had rushed over and called Margaret a 'fucking bitch' and Mrs Paddon had smacked him with her sign. Not too hard – but hard enough to make them all laugh. She hadn't driven an ambulance through the war so people could behave like *that*.

Ah yes, sabbing was a good day out.

Poor Margaret.

She had heard all the details in Mr Jacoby's shop. The pillow on the face. The body in the stream, the lack of fingerprints. Gloves, Mr Jacoby said knowingly, and she thought of the films of her youth, where the goodies wore brown-leather gloves for driving, while the baddies wore black ones for killing. Gloves made the whole thing more Hollywood. She supposed she should be frightened by two murders in a week, but couldn't find fear inside herself. She'd been in the

East End during the Blitz and had expected to die every day. Being murdered now seemed ridiculously unlikely. She felt safe in her home, and even safer because Jonas and Lucy lived next door.

She tapped on the window and waved her thanks at Jonas, then decided, despite the snow, to make the most of her clear path and go and fetch a few bits from Mr Jacoby's. Maybe pop into the Red Lion for a sherry on the way home.

'It's all go,' she told herself wryly, and went to get her brolly from the airing cupboard.

Every now and then Jonas would stop scraping at the slate and look across the tall hedge in the direction of Ronnie Trewell's house. He couldn't see it at all from the front gardens, but he still felt compelled to keep an eye on the moorland above it in case he saw anyone there. He thought again of Ronnie and Dougie with the dog. Whichever way he came at it, he couldn't see either of them writing the notes. Clive Trewell was the more obvious suspect. But Jonas had a lingering memory of Clive Trewell once picking him off the pavement after a spectacularly ill-judged wheelie had left him flat on his back outside the Red Lion, with a BMX bike on his chest.

The memory absolved Clive Trewell in Jonas's eyes.

There were a dozen homes within a hundred yards of the stile, and the moor was open to all. Anyone could have stood where he'd stood; anyone could have seen him in the bath.

Anyone.

This morning, for the first time in his life, he'd pulled the blind down while showering.

Just after Mrs Paddon waved, Lucy knocked on the front window and mimed a cup of tea at him, but he was already late, so he tapped his watch at her. She blew him a kiss instead and he grinned and blushed – too embarrassed to blow one back in front of Mrs Paddon, even though he knew that was ridiculous. But she'd known him as a child, and that made all the difference.

He turned as a car pulled up with a slushy squeak outside the front gate.

Marvel.

Jonas's heart sank. Something told him Marvel hadn't stopped by to give him a lift to Margaret Priddy's doorstep.

He glanced back at Lucy and saw her face became quizzical. She must have seen the wariness on his. Jonas didn't want Lucy seeing anything of Marvel's attitude towards him, partly for her sake, partly for his own, so he went through the old wooden gate and down the three stone steps and walked round to the driver's door. Marvel's window was open.

'What the *fuck* are you playing at, Holly?'

Jonas was confused. 'I'm sweeping my path, sir.'

'Are you being funny?'

'No, sir. I don't think so.'

'The lab called to say your hair and fibres are all over Margaret Priddy and Yvonne Marsh.'

Jonas looked blank. Why was that a shock to Marvel? He'd have been shocked if his hair and fibres *hadn't* been found on both victims.

'And the button you found in the guttering? Mass produced for the uniform trade. Probably pulled it off your own fucking trousers when you climbed up there!'

'No, sir. I—'

'Are you trying to make me look like a fucking fool?' spat Marvel.

Jonas was caught off-balance by this sudden switch. 'Excuse me, sir?'

'Those bastards in the lab are laughing at me because of *you*, you understand?'

Jonas *did* understand – that Marvel was an insecure arsehole.

So he said 'Yes, sir, I understand.' And then carefully reminded Marvel, 'But I checked that I hadn't lost a button, and I *was* at both scenes . . .' He tailed off at the immutable glare Marvel had fixed on him.

Marvel looked up – and up – at Jonas Holly. The expression on the young PC's face was utterly sincere – even hurt. Marvel pursed his lips. 'This is your last chance, Holly. Another fuck-up like this and—'

'I didn't fuck up,' Jonas said sharply, then added a considered 'sir'.

Marvel was surprised by the sudden display of backbone but it cut no ice with him. He was *so fucking angry* about the lack of progress and then that bastard Reeves giggling like a hippy down the line at him . . . Yelling at Jonas Holly was like kicking the cat: satisfying even while serving no purpose.

'Watch your fucking tone, Holly.'

Jonas knew he had to back off now or engage in open warfare with a senior officer who wielded almost complete power over him. So he swallowed some of his pride and said, 'Sorry, sir.'

Marvel grunted and put the car into gear.

'You'd better start taking your job more seriously while you still have one.'

He pulled away sharply before Jonas could answer, forcing him to step quickly out of the way.

Jonas watched the car fishtail a little in the snow. He knew it was a hollow threat, but it still made him think.

He'd have to be careful around Marvel.

*

A & D MARSH MOTOR REPAIRS read the sign on the trustingly unlocked door of the broken-down tin shack.

It was gloomy inside and Reynolds ran his hands up and down the wall inside the door until he found the light switch, then looked at his fingers covered in black smudge.

'What are we looking for, sir?'

'Evidence.'

Reynolds knew he should never have bothered asking. Marvel had no more idea what they might find than he did. Probably less. Back at the Marsh house, poor Elizabeth Rice had instructions to do the same. 'Just nose around,' Marvel had told her.

Because apparently 'nosing around' did not require a stuffy old search warrant.

Reynolds felt an ever-rising sense that they were all stagnating. They had no fingerprints and – even more curiously – no footprints. Just dirty smears and vague impressions in carpet. They were still pinning their forensic hopes on the single unidentified hair from the Margaret Priddy scene, but if that matched Peter Priddy or someone else who'd been at the scene in an official capacity then they were back to square one anyway.

When Marvel had told him about the Jonas Holly link, Reynolds had tutted in vague empathy and mentally sided with Holly.

It was just like Marvel to shit all over a guy for doing his job.

Here in the garage – for the first time since he'd come to Shipcott – Marvel felt some connection with someone local. They might be suspects, but at least it was something.

As a boy he'd wanted to be a bus driver. Not because he'd wanted to suffer the stop-and-go of

Oxford Street or get caught in a six-mile tailback on the Edgware Road. No, when the boy-Marvel imagined his life as a bus driver, he'd always seen himself bent over with his head inside the cavernous engine bay, spanner in hand. Which was probably just as likely, given London's ageing bus population, he reflected wryly whenever he thought about those times.

He felt an unaccustomed smile curl the corner of his mouth.

'Something funny, sir?' asked Reynolds.

'No,' said Marvel. A childhood ambition to be a bus driver was the last thing he was prepared to share with an over-educated prick like Reynolds.

The workshop was far neater and cleaner inside than the exterior promised. Tools were hung neatly and surfaces were reasonably tidy. The two men split automatically and walked around the premises in opposite directions.

'You think it's the same killer?' mused Reynolds.

'In a place this size?'

'Different M.O.'

'In a place this size?' repeated Marvel.

'You know Arnold Avery buried all those kids on the moors around here. Lightning *can* strike twice.'

Marvel grunted.

Reynolds ran his fingers over the sharp jaws of a bench vice and spun the lever, loving the smooth silence of its travel.

As a boy, Reynolds had wanted to be a bus driver. He had vivid recollections of cycling to school – and later university – through the centre of Bristol. Every time he was in a queue of traffic, he would stop his bicycle beside a bus, just to listen to the engine with its thudding bass covered by curiously breathy high notes. A sublime metal orchestra inside the grand theatre of what Reynolds had always considered to be the perfect method of mass transportation. Even while slaving over his criminology degree, a part of him always fantasized about giving it all up and spending the rest of his life behind the wheel, high above the traffic, sitting over the engine of a Routemaster or a Leyland National. It was a fantasy he had never divulged to anyone. No one would understand.

Marvel whistled low behind him and Reynolds turned to see him holding up what looked like a tissue box.

When Reynolds walked over, he could see that it was filled with disposable latex gloves.

Ten Days

Jonas hated the doctor.

Dr Anil Wickramsinghe was his name and Jonas had come to hold him personally responsible for Lucy's decline. Dr Wickramsinghe was middle-aged, balding and utterly inoffensive, but Jonas always felt in his guts that he was holding out on them. That, for some reason he couldn't fathom, Dr Wickramsinghe thought it would be in everyone's best interests to watch Lucy Holly in pain, fear and depression.

Like today.

Today Dr Wickramsinghe had listened to Lucy's halting description of the progress of her disease with his head cocked to one side, feigning concern. When she said she had dropped a mug of tea on Wednesday, unable to feel that she wasn't gripping it properly, he nodded and tutted. When she recounted two episodes of MS hug, which had left her writhing on the floor in agony, he nodded and made a little sound like 'mm' in the back of his throat. And when her lip trembled as she told him that her eyesight had faltered in the middle of *The Evil Dead*, he sighed as if he shared her pain.

'When?' said Jonas sharply. 'You didn't tell me that!'

Lucy bit her lip.

'Why didn't you tell me, Lu?'

'I'm sure I *did*, Jonas.'

When she used his name that way, she was lying. Not lying like criminals lie, just . . . being economical with the truth, like a politician.

'If you don't tell me these things, Lu, how can I help?'

She was too kind to say it but he knew the answer. He *couldn't* help – so what was the point?

Dr Wickramsinghe placed his palms flat on the table as if he was about to make a decision. As if he was about to get up and go to the secret safe behind the ugly sailing ships above his desk and get the *real* medicine; the *actual* pills that would put an end to Lucy's suffering. Spin the dial and Open Sesame on a cure. Every single time they were here, Jonas expected him to confess that so far they'd been giving her sugar solution and peanut M&Ms, but that now – at last – she was sick enough for them to break out the good stuff.

Instead, Dr Wickramsinghe leaned back slightly in his chair, as if distancing himself from the awkward case before him, and said, 'This is the progression we can expect, I'm afraid.'

Jonas wanted to pounce across the desk, grip him by the throat and bang his skull repeatedly against the ships until the sea ran red.

Can't you SEE? he wanted to shout. *Can't you SEE that she needs HELP?*

Lucy's warm hand on his thigh told him she knew what he was thinking, even as she agreed with Dr Wickramsinghe: 'Of course, I understand. But is there any more we can do for the symptoms?'

So like Lucy. So like her to calm *him* down, *and* to make the bastard who was killing her feel less like a shit while doing it. What can *we* do for the symptoms? As if Dr Wickramsinghe and she were both in this together. Not for the first time, Jonas imagined Lucy breaking up a fight between two five-year-olds, resolving the row, drying the tears, making them shake hands. It made him love her more than ever, even if it meant the man across the desk was getting off lightly.

'We'll try some more M&Ms,' said Dr Wickramsinghe, 'and throw in some Smarties and a big bottle of Lucozade.'

Of course, he didn't say exactly that, but Jonas thought he might as well have.

*

Jonas took it slowly on the way home. The bigger roads had been gritted but if they hadn't had the appointment he would never have ventured out in Lucy's old Beetle. It had all its weight over the back wheels, leaving the front end to wander about at will, tilting at hedges and flirting with ditches. He was so used to the Land Rover with its four-wheel drive and traction-control that the VW felt like a roller skate in the snow.

As they came down the hill into Shipcott, they could see a knot of people standing in the road roughly halfway through the village. In the brief glimpse they had before they lost sight of them again behind the hedges, Jonas thought he saw a horse, and felt unease start to pulse in his chest.

Lucy glanced at him questioningly, but he could only shrug.

They lost sight of the crowd until they rounded the curve in the road. Jonas slowed to a crawl and then parked a little haphazardly outside the shop and got out.

'What's going on?' he asked Billy Beer.

'The Marsh boy's gone mazed,' said Billy impatiently, as if it happened all the time and they were sick of it.

Jonas felt his stomach twist at the words. He hurried through the crowd and saw Danny Marsh dressed in hunting scarlet – complete with velvet hat, white britches and conker-topped boots – holding the reins of a large bay horse. It was saddled but ungroomed; there was dried mud up its legs, and its mane was a dusty tangle of dirt and twigs.

Before Jonas could speak, Danny saw him and broke into the biggest of smiles. 'Jonas! We're going hunting! You coming?' He rushed towards Jonas, making the horse throw its head up and roll its eyes. Danny jerked the reins. 'Steady up, Tigger! Stand!' Then he threw his arm around Jonas, laughing.

Jonas took in the scene. Danny and the horse, which Jonas knew wasn't his; beyond him stood Marvel and his team, including the woman – Rice, he thought her name was – who looked troubled, almost tearful. Framed in the doorway of his home stood Alan Marsh, his face blank as he watched his son disintegrate in front of him.

'What's up, Danny?' Jonas said, trying to keep his voice level.

'Going hunting,' said Danny again. 'Brilliant day for it.'

Jonas looked at the leaden sky that promised more snow.

'The hunt's not out today, mate. You've got the wrong day.'

'Aaaaah,' said Danny with a dismissive wave, 'bollocks to *that*! Who says it's got to be Thursdays? Me and Tigger are going *today*! You want to come?'

To Jonas's surprise, he saw hope shining in Danny's eyes. As if he really expected Jonas to say yes.

That's not Tigger, he wanted to say. *That's not Tigger and this isn't right.*

'That's *my* horse!' said John Took angrily from somewhere. Jonas didn't bother looking. '*And* my fucking coat!'

Why hadn't Marvel and his men just grabbed hold of Danny, thrown him down in the slushy road and bundled him back into the house? Why did *he* have to be involved? On a day like this, with Lucy sick and getting sicker? It was almost as if they'd been waiting for him.

Marvel stepped out of the crowd, looking like a man who'd seen enough and wanted to get back into the warm. The moment Danny Marsh caught sight of him, he let go of Jonas and swung the bay around in a short, clattering arc, which made Marvel – and all the crowd – recede like water to stay out of reach of its rump and heels. Danny did it again, using the horse to clear a space for himself in the middle of the road. Jonas took two nervous steps backwards. The horse snorted again and gave a confused little prance, scattering people behind it.

'STAND, Tigger!' yelled Danny and slapped the horse's muzzle, making it back rapidly into a parked car, rocking it and crumpling the door like tin foil, then skittering sideways as more of the crowd parted around it.

You've lost it, thought Jonas dully. *You've lost it in front of all these people.* Danny Marsh thought he was ten years old and they were still friends. And he was trying to drag Jonas back there with him – back to when they were kids hanging out at the farm, with their dreams and their lives intact . . .

Jonas felt anger swelling inside him like a gross burp.

He reached out and gripped Danny's bicep, pulling him close in an attempt at privacy.

'Danny,' he said tightly, 'let's go inside and talk about this.'

Danny looked at him, suddenly serious. 'You want to talk, Jonas? I'm ready. I've *always* been ready.'

Jonas dropped his arm. He had no idea what he meant, but there was a sense of threat in Danny Marsh that caught him unawares and sent a shiver down his spine. Right here in the middle of the day, in the middle of the street, surrounded by half of Shipcott and fellow officers of the law, he felt in serious danger for the first time that he could remember.

Danny Marsh opened his arms in a loud 'bring it on' gesture, flapping the reins and making the horse flinch once more, but when he spoke again it was softly – as if he and Jonas were the only ones there.

'Don't pretend you don't know what I mean, Jonas.'

Danny was crazy. They all knew that. He was stuck in some recess of his own mind. Jonas wouldn't play his game. This had to end.

'That's not Tigger,' he said brutally. 'Tigger's dead.'

'Fuck you!' cried Danny, and he let go of the horse and swung a wild fist at Jonas.

Jonas hit him so hard he felt it in his feet. Danny went down and Jonas followed him to the ground, unaware of Lucy shouting from the Beetle, unaware of the horse spinning round and bolting up the snowy road with its reins dangling – unaware of anything but the feeling of flesh and bone connecting, and hard velvet hurting his knuckles.

Until he remembered where he was and who he was and *what* he was.

Then he got up and walked away.

*

More than anyone, Lucy knew what Jonas had sacrificed for her.

He'd had his eye on Glock 17s and body armour, but her diagnosis had forced them to make other choices.

They had married in the local church with poor Margaret Priddy playing a clunking, wheezing 'All Things Bright And Beautiful' on the eccentric little organ. They had only sent invitations to *her* family and friends; he'd told her everyone in Shipcott would come anyway, whether they were invited or not. And they did – standing at the back and outside among the leaning tombstones to watch Jonas lead his bride into the sunshine.

His parents had beamed.

Desmond and Cath.

Lucy had only met them twice before the wedding and would only see them once again, before they were both killed instantly in a head-on collision on the A39 link road. The other car had rolled right over the Hollys' demure Rover, which had been so flattened that when she and Jonas were later allowed to see it in the police pound, a box of tissues in a hand-crocheted cover was still held in its place between the roof and the parcel shelf. Lucy would never forget it – or the way Jonas's hand had twitched and tightened a little around hers at the sight.

Lucy had always felt the need to protect him. It was ridiculous really. Jonas could take care of himself.

She was the one who was weak and feeble. She with her endless medications that he had to fetch and store and prepare, and administer in injected doses. She with her tears and her depressions and her dropping of crockery and her failure to cook or clean properly and her mood swings and her despair. She with her weight gain, her weight loss, the regular desertion of her libido. He would go weeks – sometimes months – without seeing her naked behind unless he was about to stick a needle in it.

Hot.

Not.

He never complained. Never got impatient. Never made her feel bad.

But today, just maybe, she'd seen the effect on Jonas for the first time.

He never talked about growing up in the village – as if he thought she already knew his business the way everyone did here in Shipcott – but she knew that he'd grown up with Danny Marsh because he'd told her after Danny's mother was killed.

'She used to make us beans and chips,' he'd said suddenly in bed that night.

She had turned to him in the darkness, even though she couldn't see his face.

'Mrs Marsh?'

'Yeah. She was my best friend's mother. When I was at school.'

'You mean Danny Marsh from the garage?'

'Yes,' he'd said.

'I never knew that. He's sweet. Why don't you hang out with him any more?'

' "Sweet"?' he'd said, and she'd heard the laugh in his voice. 'Is he sweeter than me?'

'Much,' she'd said, only too pleased to feel his mood lift, and there it was – they'd changed the subject. *He*'d changed the subject.

And today she'd watched him beat up Danny Marsh. There was no other word for it. She'd sat in the car and watched him lose control. And it made her think for the first time how much control he must have had to lose.

She wanted to hold him and tell him it was all going

to be all right. To stroke his hair like a child's. It made her think again of Jonas's face at the hospital – before he knew he was being watched. That fear. That raw, innocent fear that she'd only ever seen before on the faces of small children.

It was a face that made her wonder where that little boy inside him hid for the rest of the time.

Eight Days

'I've got a theory,' said Reynolds.

You always do, thought Marvel. Reynolds was a hotbed of theories, hypotheses and what he like to call 'proposals'.

They were sitting in the mobile unit, as close to the Calor gas as was physically possible without actually bursting into flames.

They'd had a call from the pathologist to confirm what Marvel had already surmised at the scene – that Yvonne Marsh had drowned and had almost certainly been held underwater. Marvel had imparted the news with a remarkable lack of I-told-you-so's, which had, in turn, opened the door to one of their few discussions where neither was trying to score points.

They'd been talking about the incident with Danny Marsh.

Marvel and Grey had stepped in to stop Jonas Holly,

but Jonas had stopped himself, so they had hauled Danny to his feet instead. His riding hat was askew but had still protected all the important stuff.

The horse had skidded into several parked cars on its destructive way up the road and had later been caught by someone down on the playing field.

The crowd had dispersed in almost complete silence.

Elizabeth Rice and Alan Marsh had ushered a tearful Danny inside, where the local doctor – a man who looked as if he was popping in on his way to a surfing competition – had given him a sedative.

Marvel had gone over to the Beetle and said something biting to Jonas about police brutality but hadn't really meant it. *Somebody* had needed to stop Danny Marsh and, for the first time since coming to Shipcott, he felt Jonas Holly had done the right thing, albeit a little over-enthusiastically. There might be some fallout from that, but somehow Marvel doubted it. The mood in the street had been one of relief that it was all over, rather than shock at *how*.

And now Reynolds had a theory.

'I was thinking about what you said. About the link between Margaret Priddy and Yvonne Marsh.'

'Yes?' said Marvel, mildly encouraged that this particular 'proposal' might be based on something sensible.

'There's something called the tipping point,' said Reynolds. 'You heard of it?'

Marvel hated that kind of question. If he said no, Reynolds would elucidate in minute detail; if he said yes, he'd be lying and then might not grasp what came next.

'No,' he said, in a tone that demanded that Reynolds take no more than thirty seconds to explain it to him. It was a very specific tone and Reynolds knew it well, so he did his best.

'It's something which tips the balance and creates a deviation from the normal path of events.' That wasn't wholly accurate, but it wasn't long enough to piss Marvel off.

'For instance, you know all those Japanese kids who commit suicide – a whole bunch of them, one after another, like it's catching?'

'What's your point, Reynolds?'

'The theory is that one suicide can spark others. People become aware of the suicide, and kids who wouldn't have gone that far before suddenly consider it. A few more actually do it – as if they have *permission* to kill themselves because it seems that everybody's doing it – it's no longer taboo. And before you know it, kids are topping themselves because their dog ate their homework, and you've got an epidemic on your hands. You've passed the tipping point.'

Marvel said nothing, so Reynolds knew he had his attention.

'You asked me about the link. And I was thinking of what you said about Margaret Priddy and Yvonne

Marsh both being a burden to their families. The methods are different, not consistent. Maybe the killers are different too. Maybe the killer of Yvonne Marsh felt he had *permission* because someone had already killed Margaret Priddy.'

'So you're saying Alan Marsh could have killed his wife because Peter Priddy had already killed his mother?' said Marvel.

'It's a theory,' said Reynolds a little defensively. 'You imagine taking care of someone like Yvonne Marsh for years. Stark staring mad. Wandering off. Doesn't know who the fuck you are after forty years of marriage. You imagine the strain of that. Maybe it only takes a nod and a wink in the way of permission for you to feel that it's OK to go right ahead and drown her in a stream.'

Marvel nodded. He could see the logic. 'In the way that serial killers take many years to build up to their first murder. The first one is difficult, but after that it gets easier and easier, more and more casual.'

'Same thing,' agreed Reynolds. 'Someone breaks the taboo.'

Marvel stared into the distance and nodded slowly. 'The unthinkable becomes thinkable.'

The two men sat pondering in rare harmony.

'I hope you're wrong,' said Marvel.

And, for once, Reynolds hoped he was too.

Seven Days

The ground was frozen and they couldn't have dug a hole for Yvonne Marsh even if her body had not been retained as evidence, but the funeral went ahead anyway. '*Interment to follow at a later date*' was what was written in biro under the order of service.

Jonas looked at it and was reminded of the note under his wiper, and he wished now that he'd kept it for the purposes of comparison with every bit of handwriting he came across. As the service got under way, he looked at the Reverend Chard with new eyes.

Alan Marsh sat in the front pew with his son. Danny had a black eye to go with his suit. Jonas blushed to see it.

'I should apologize,' he whispered to Lucy.

'Not today,' she whispered back. 'Today is about his mother.'

Jonas nodded but felt uncomfortable. Marvel had

hissed at him that he'd be lucky to keep his job, but all he had seen in Marvel's eyes was relief that someone had stepped up to the mark and done *something* to end the stand-off.

He looked around and caught Marvel's eye at the back of the church. No doubt he was there because of the chance that the killer might attend the funeral of his victim. Margaret Priddy had not yet had a funeral service, at the request of her family, but Alan Marsh had insisted on one.

'She's gone,' he'd told the Reverend Chard. 'She's gone and I want to say a proper goodbye.'

So here they all were.

Jonas hadn't asked Marvel if it was OK to come, and half smiled at the thought that the killer might be running up and down past Margaret Priddy's house while he was here, banging on the door and taunting the little brown dog. It was all bollocks anyway, and he no longer felt any guilt about leaving his post. The business with Danny had jolted things into new focus for him. Although he felt guilty about hitting him, at least he had taken some *action* at last. At least he had made a *decision* – even if it was probably the wrong one.

The service was sombre. They sang 'Abide With Me' and then 'All Things Bright And Beautiful', which made Lucy squeeze his hand. It brought a hard lump to his throat and he dared not look at her.

Afterwards there was tea in the church hall. Linda

Cobb and the other ladies had done it; they hadn't even consulted Alan and Danny Marsh – they'd just gone ahead and spent the money that the Reverend Chard had given them from the poor box bolted to the church door. Everyone thought it was money well spent.

Jonas and Lucy did not go to the church hall. They watched Alan Marsh support his son out of the church and then left. Jonas drove Lucy home carefully up the gritted lane, changed out of his black suit and into his uniform, then walked back down into the village to resume his doorstep vigil.

The darkening village seemed especially still. The blanket of snow and the fact that almost every adult was off eating egg sandwiches in the church hall added to Jonas's sense of isolation. Not even Linda Cobb was there to hand him his *World's Best Mum* mug.

On days such as this he felt like the last man on Earth. Sometimes he felt that way up on the moors, where it was so quiet you could hear a car coming a mile away. Last summer he'd walked up to Blacklands and sat down on the cushion of heather that covered the mound there. He could see the roofs of Shipcott in one direction, but otherwise no sign of civilization – or that civilization had even been invented.

He remembered now how the sun had warmed his eyes through his closed lids, and smiled even though he was standing in the snow on the doorstep of one murdered pensioner and had just attended the funeral of another.

If only all memories could be as sweet.

It was already dark when Jonas saw the stranger.

In summer, a stranger was a faceless part of a bigger whole, which invaded like an army, wore uniform hiking shorts and map bags, and cleared Mr Jacoby out of milk and sandwiches. But in winter, a stranger was a curious and somehow sinister thing. Why would anyone come to Shipcott in winter? Their motives *must* be suspect. If the stranger were a woman or child it was easy to imagine them to be a visiting sister or niece; if it were a man, it was tempting to imagine them to be so much more – and not all good and friendly. Prime among those winter strangers were hunt saboteurs, who came armed nowadays with everything from placards to Mace.

Jonas did not have Marvel's experience or cynicism, but even *his* suspicions were raised when the man saw him, then blatantly turned and walked hurriedly back the way he'd come.

After only a very brief inner tussle, Jonas left his post.

He followed the man at a distance of about a hundred yards, taking in all he could about his appearance. Shortish, thinnish, wearing a long green waxed jacket over dark trousers and town shoes, with a waxed Stetson which marked him out as a likely customer at

Field & Stream as he'd passed through Dulverton; locals did not wear waxed Stetsons. The wide brim shadowed his face as he passed under the orange streetlamps.

The snow showed Jonas that the man's shoes were small – probably a size seven or eight – with a distinctive herringbone tread.

The man bustled along quickly, glancing behind him once – which only made Jonas more determined to keep following him, even if he felt a bit as if he was doing this for no other reason than because he was bored and cold, and the man was a stranger in a stranger's hat.

The man walked into the alleyway beside Mr Jacoby's shop, which Jonas knew was a dead end. Jonas approached more slowly now, waiting for the man to turn around and come back out, but he didn't. After a couple of minutes, Jonas followed him into the alleyway.

He was gone.

The dark little courtyard behind the shop contained a few wheelie bins, some old beer barrels filled with soil which Mr Jacoby laughingly referred to as 'the garden', and a recycling box filled with glass bottles. The back of the courtyard was hemmed by a high fence, above which a spray of brambles formed an effective barrier. The only way out – other than through the back door into the shop – was over a four-foot-high stone wall between this property and the next.

Footprints in the snow showed that that was where the stranger had gone. Jonas's heart started to race. The man had climbed over the wall and must have gone down the matching passage that ran along the side of the neighbouring house, rather than turn around to face him. It was not the action of a casual visitor who'd taken a wrong turning.

Jonas was about to vault the wall and go after him, when he heard a car burst into life out on the road.

Shit.

He ran back down the alleyway, slipping awkwardly on the cobbles. He overshot the pavement and skidded to a halt in the middle of the white road, looking up and down the narrow street.

There was no sign of the man or the car.

Shit again.

Jonas went back to the exit of the second alleyway and followed the distinctive herringbone footprints to a new gap between the parked cars. The fresh tyre tracks were still clear and snow-free – and had a loop in them before straightening up, which showed that the car had fishtailed. A quick getaway.

Jonas felt stupid. He should have got closer and followed the man into the alleyway immediately. Instead he'd assumed he would turn around and come back out. In his head he heard his old English teacher, Mrs O'Leary: *Assume makes an ass out of u and me.*

Jonas was just not used to being that suspicious – even of strangers. The thought that he might have lost the killer because he hadn't wanted to face the social awkwardness of confronting him in Mr Jacoby's 'garden' made him squirm.

He walked briskly up to the school, then back down to Margaret Priddy's without catching a glimpse of another person, let alone the stranger. The snow kept everyone indoors. At least he'd got a look at the man: his stature, his clothing, his style of walking, with its short townie steps. Probably late thirties to early forties. He'd recognize him again. Maybe.

He considered telling Marvel, then immediately discounted the idea. On the face of it, all he'd done was desert his post on a smidgeon of a hunch and a barrowful of boredom – and he had nothing to show for it. All he'd be doing would be inviting Marvel to have another pop at him. So far the man hadn't needed any excuse; Jonas didn't feel like giving him one now.

Jonas sighed. The deaths of Margaret Priddy and Yvonne Marsh felt like his first real challenges as an officer of the law, and he was failing at every aspect of their investigation. He couldn't even tail a suspect successfully in his own village – even in the snow.

As if to mock him, the snow started again, quickly filling in the herringbone footprints.

Jonas got back to his doorstep thoroughly defeated.

As though she'd known he would fail, Linda Cobb immediately opened the door and handed him his mug.

*

Reynolds felt well disposed towards Jonas Holly for no other reason than that Marvel didn't.

He was on his way to get fish and chips at the Blue Dolphin when he saw Jonas standing on the doorstep with his hands around a mug. He pulled the car over and got out.

'Hi,' he said, sticking out his hand. Jonas took it and Reynolds could feel the residual warmth of the mug.

'You know, we haven't been properly introduced, what with all that's going on. I'm DS Reynolds.'

'Jonas Holly,' said Jonas, wondering what Reynolds wanted.

But he didn't seem to want anything very much.

'Local officers are a big help to us,' said Reynolds.

'Yeah?' said Jonas, raising a wry eyebrow.

'If you've not been given that impression then I'm sorry,' said Reynolds carefully. 'But if you have any concerns or would like to talk about any aspect of this case, please give me a call.'

He took out a card and handed it to Jonas. 'My mobile number's on there.'

Jonas looked at the card, which was too thick to be standard police issue. Reynolds must have had his own made.

'OK,' he said. 'I will. Thanks.'

Reynolds started to turn away.

'I saw a stranger,' Jonas blurted. Immediately he

realized how dumb it must sound to the ears of someone not living in a tiny village.

Either way, he described what had happened.

Reynolds listened to Jonas's story with an interested
look on his face, and made sketchy notes – 'waxed
hat', 'long coat', 'herringbone prints', 'ducked into
alleyway' – all the time feeling faintly ridiculous at the
amateur-sleuth nature of the whole thing.

'I don't know if it's relevant,' said Jonas at the end,
and Reynolds guessed that it wasn't. Hopping over a
low wall was hardly jumping the wire on a motorbike.

He thanked Jonas anyway. Let the man think he
was being taken seriously. Couldn't hurt.

Reynolds almost asked Jonas if he wanted anything
from the chip shop, but then thought that might be
taking fraternizing with the natives too far. And
there'd be the issue of whether he meant Jonas to pay
or not. It would all be a bit awkward. So he just said
goodbye and got back in his car, happy that he had
bypassed – and therefore undermined – Marvel in
even the smallest way.

*

Danny Marsh was calling his name. From somewhere.

Not grown-up Danny – boy-Danny.

Jonas hid from him. He didn't know why. He just
knew that hiding was best, here in the bales of

fragrant, itchy hay. He hid and listened to his heart between his ears. Every time it pumped, his head got hotter. His heart was pumping molten rock and he felt the pressure build and build until he thought the top of his head would blow off and the river of rock inside would shoot into the night sky like a fiery geyser. His head was burning up but his feet were freezing cold, and he looked down to see that the reason was that Danny's dead mother was draped across them, her slack grey bra pulled up to reveal her flaccid breasts pooled like pancake mix across her chest.

Jonas jolted awake with a shiver and a kick and found that Lucy was hogging the covers; his feet were exposed. He breathed heavily, his hair and neck damp with sweat.

'Jonas!' the voice hissed in his ear. He jerked his head to the side. No one was there. It was a wisp of a dream that had escaped into the real world.

The room was dark and Lucy was breathing so low that he strained to hear her at all. He glanced at the alarm clock. Just gone 3am.

Moving carefully, he rearranged the covers with his feet, and his breathing started to calm a little as his nightmare fragmented behind him.

'Jonas!'

He froze.

He took Lucy's arm from across his chest and slid out from beneath it, laying it gently on the warm sheet and covering it with the duvet.

In the flannel pyjama bottoms and T-shirt he wore to bed in the winter, Jonas crossed to the window and looked down at the front garden, glimmering pale under the stars.

Nothing.

His eye caught a movement in the lane beyond the gate.

Somebody?

Or some*thing*?

Something watching the house. Something watching *him*.

Something *underneath*.

His mind lolled between sleep and wakefulness, blurring the edges of both, as his overworked eyes sought the caller of his name.

In his gut he knew it was Danny Marsh. Come to talk in the dead of a snowy night. He felt once again the threat that had come off Danny in waves. Part of him wanted to go down there now – right now. To run out into the snow and finish what he'd started in the street. Beat him to a pulp. End it.

He must have stood half-dozing at the window a long, long time, because when he finally went back to bed and spooned up behind the wife he loved so fiercely, the first light of the late dawn was turning the world grey.

*

Jonas Holly liked to think of himself as the protector, but the killer was a protector too, in his own way.

They were trying to protect different people, that was all.

Not for the first time, he wondered whether he should speak to Jonas. Maybe a face-to-face would be useful. Let Jonas see who he was dealing with; see if they could come to some kind of agreement. He was not an unreasonable man.

Even though the killer despised Jonas for his weakness, somehow the policeman still kept getting in the way. He had been diverted twice now because of Jonas, and gave him grudging credit for that.

Still, the policeman might not be doing his job, but he couldn't keep the killer from doing *his* for ever.

He glanced at his watch and saw it was 4am. He snapped on a pair of surgical gloves and slid a souvenir letter-opener out of his pocket. By the moonlight he could see the glint of fake gold-enamel lettering on the handle: *A Gift from Weston-Super-Mare*.

He had noticed this first-floor window in the big old building. The only one that had not been replaced with plastic double glazing. He'd noticed it years ago. He'd noticed a lot of things over the years but had never really felt the need to *use* them before.

Now he felt the need.

He climbed on to the water butt and from there he swung easily on to the toughened glass roof. He braced his feet against the struts for purchase and slipped the letter-opener between the old wooden frames.

Then the killer pushed aside the catch, slid the sash up – and quietly climbed through the window into the Sunset Lodge Retirement Home.

*

Gary Liss liked the nights at Sunset Lodge. The days were all bustle but the nights made him think of old war movies where nurses moved quietly between softly coughing patients, carrying candles.

At night there were just three members of staff on duty. That was usually plenty. Mostly the residents slept through, with only occasional calls for help with the commode. They had one sleepwalker at present. Mrs Eaves had scared the shit out of him the first time he'd seen her tottering towards him in her flowing white nightie. Now he quite enjoyed the break in routine that was the silent little dance he occasionally performed with Mrs Eaves on the landing while he tried to head her off at the pass so she wouldn't dance straight down the wide stairwell with its thick, swirly carpet that hid the stains so well. Mr Cooke had invested in an infrared alarm which fired a clever red beam across Mrs Eaves's bedroom door and beeped loudly in the staffroom whenever she took to wandering through the home. When it did, one of them would bound upstairs – or squeeze into the lift in the case of Lynne Twitchett – and go and corral her back to bed.

Tonight he was on with Lynne and Jen. He liked Lynne, who was giggly and sweet, but wasn't so keen on Jen, who smelled of cigarettes and teased him about his girlfriend. *Girl*friend, she always said. How's the *girl*friend, Gary? Why don't you bring your *girl*-friend to the Christmas do? We'd all love to meet your *girl*friend.

Jen could go screw herself. He doubted anyone else ever did.

Right now she was bitching about a woman she'd seen in a pub wearing yellow stilettos. Gary thought yellow stilettos sounded hideous, but he was still on the wearer's side.

The radio was tuned quietly to Lantern – the local station – which played old chart stuff and made him drum his fingers and think of school discos.

Mrs Eaves's alarm beeped and Gary picked up his torch. Turning lights on at night could be disastrous. Residents who had only been in bed for an hour would stir like grizzlies coming out of hibernation and start to dress themselves in wobbly anticipation of another day growing older in the garden room. Torches took care of that.

There were fourteen bedrooms on the first floor and Gary knew that Violet Eaves could be in any one of them apart from her own, Gorse. All the rooms had twee names like Gorse and Heather, which were supposed to be Exmoor-centric. Whoever had chosen them had started grandly but must have quickly realized that gorse and heather were the only really recognizable flora the moors had to offer, and had been forced into crap names like Sedge and Blackthorn and – feeblest of all – Moss. Gary reckoned it was Mr Cooke's wife who'd done it. She was always putting her finger in the Sunset Lodge pie.

The old house was a maze of turns and steps and nooks and ramps. Two rooms here, three there, up two steps, round a corner to three more rooms. The beam of his little torch danced about like a firefly as he trod quietly along the corridors.

No sign of her. Gary stood still on the wide landing. He'd have to check the bedrooms; it would not be the first time Violet had tried to climb in with someone else.

'Violet!' he hissed, even though when she sleep-walked she never responded to sound. 'Pain in the arse!' he muttered, but he didn't really mean it. When she was awake, Violet was one of his favourites. Even at the age of ninety-two Violet had a sparkle. She would hold his hand and call him 'such a good-looking bay', then wink at him, because she'd been blind since she was seventy-five. It was an old joke but a good one. Then she would touch the rings that were stuck for ever on her gnarled fingers, and count off her husbands.

'Eddie – never spent a *penny* on anyone but herself.

Charlie – her was a good one, that's why her died, of course! Only the good die young. Another Eddie, same as the first – never go out with an Eddie, young man, you'll have nothing but worry and debts! And that one's Matthew. Mattie, I used to call her, and her used to call me Viola, like in the Shakespeare, see? I was seventy-two when we got married and her was seventy. My toyboy. Always save the best till last, that's what we used to say to each other. Always save the best till last.'

She'd pat his hand and look into the past, which was somewhere over his left shoulder.

Then she'd cock her head and say, 'Is that the biscuits?'

Standing here in the dark with his torch making a bright disc on the carpet, Gary smiled. Violet just looked confused if you shouted 'HELLO!' straight into her face, but she could hear a biscuit tin opening at a thousand yards.

He heard what sounded like a scrape of furniture and hissed down the corridor: 'Violet?' and set off again. He hadn't gone ten paces when he heard – from the open staffroom door below – the faint beep of Violet's alarm going off for the second time.

Miracle. She'd found her way home.

He turned back, went down two stairs and turned a corner, then up two more to Gorse.

He'd expected to find Violet standing by her bed, but she'd already got back into it.

Gary stood in the doorway. 'All right, Viola?' he said very softly. He didn't want to wake her, but if she had woken herself, he wanted her to know he was there. There was no answer. Asleep. Good.

Out of habit he flicked the torch over her sleeping form, and frowned. There was the minimal lump in the bed that was Violet's diminutive body, but he could not see her head. Like everyone in this place, Violet's hair was naturally white, but once a month the stylist came and gave all the heads a good blue rinse. He should be able to see her *head*.

Gary moved closer to the bed, angling the torch. Nothing but the white pillow.

'Violet?' he asked carefully, suppressing the silly panic that told him Violet's head had somehow fallen off.

He leaned over the old woman and almost laughed in relief. She was sleeping with her head *under* the pillow – that was all!

Gently he lifted the pillow.

Underneath it was Violet – her eyes closed, her toothless mouth puckered neatly, and a flower of blood blossoming on her forehead.

Blood.

Gary Liss stared in confusion at the blood and the pillow and the old lady. Whatever order he looked at them, they made no sense.

I have to call Paul. He'll know what to do.

That was the only thought Gary's numb brain could

come up with. Paul was the smart one. Paul would take care of this. Because *he* sure as hell couldn't work it out.

Somewhere down the long tunnel of his dulled senses, Gary Liss heard the alarm across the doorway beep one last time. He started to turn, started to open his mouth, started to think.

But before he could complete any one of those actions, everything went black.

*

There were footprints in the snow behind him leading all the way back to Sunset Lodge, but the killer knew they would not give him away.

He used the same snow to rinse his hands of blood.

The night was cloudy, without a moon, and the village slept like Bethlehem – in blissful ignorance of how it would be changed by morning.

He was about to step out of the alleyway when he caught sight of a movement at the end of the road, or, at least, under the dull orange reach of the farthest streetlamp.

Out of the blackness at the edge of the known world came a single foxhound. Its nose swept the snow ahead of it, its brown velvet ears swung as its head turned this way and that in response to the scents of the village. The hound's lean body glimmered under the light and, even from here, the killer could see the shining hide slip easily back and forth across the dog's ribs.

From the depths of a deep-sea dream, the rest of the pack came out of the darkness and into the light. Silent as wraiths, smooth as syrup, tails swaying, snouts seeking, the three dozen big hounds moved between the houses at a languid jog, as if by night the village belonged to them.

Behind the pack the huntsman took shape. Bob Coffin, with his short, bowed legs, his flat cap and his old brown Barbour, creased and crinkled. He held a whip but didn't look as if he planned to use it. He didn't have to: the hounds trotted ahead of him in perfect harmony and total silence. Even when a small dog yapped from somewhere behind them, they ignored it and moved on.

The killer stayed where he was in the shadows, hypnotized by their approach. The sight was strange, yet strangely calming. He felt himself suddenly unable to move, and disinterested in doing so, even if it meant he was seen. The hounds possessing the darkened village in the fallen snow were compelling to watch.

The first dog drew level and raised its head towards him. Their eyes met briefly, then it dropped its nose to the snow once more – as it had been trained to do on pain of death: the hound that puts its head in the air to look for the fox has no place in the hunt. The killer watched the Blacklands pack move past him in a liquid jigsaw of brown, black and white, with only the sound of eager breathing moving the air around him.

Then Bob Coffin went past him too.

The huntsman glanced briefly at the killer and touched his cap in a market-day hello, never breaking his brisk, rolling stride.

The killer watched the hounds pass under the streetlights and wink out in the darkness beyond as if they had never existed. Only a broad swathe of churned snow up the centre of the road bore testament to their reality.

The killer sighed as if he had lost something dear to him.

Then he stepped carefully into the ruined snow and walked home without leaving a trail.

Six Days

Marvel and Reynolds moved from room to room in silence.

Gorse, Hazel and Moss.

Violet Eaves, Bridget Hammond and Lionel Chard.

Each had died without waking. Their covers were untrammelled, their hands lay calmly at their sides; Bridget Hammond still held a delicately embroidered handkerchief crumpled loosely in her palm.

From cursory inspection, Marvel surmised that each had been rendered unconscious or killed outright by a single mighty blow to the head. Then the killer had made sure by smothering them with their own pillows.

Marvel thought of the killer's rough hand on the frail faces, holding it there until he was sure each was lifeless. Then moving on.

Marvel thought this, but said nothing. He did not trust himself. And he could barely hear himself think for the hoarse whispers of the dead. *Avenge me! Avenge me!*

Reynolds had his notebook out and for once Marvel was grateful. His own head was so full of the horror that he felt he'd need to empty it like a waste basket before he could actually sit down and start to make sense of the carnage.

Downstairs he could hear the sound of crying. Lynne Twitchett had been crying since they had arrived, less than ten minutes after getting the call from Jonas Holly. The other residents cried spasmodically, and when they weren't crying they were comforting others who *were*, in quavering, tremulous voices that might as well have been weeping. Rupert Cooke had arrived red-eyed just after he and Reynolds had, and had continued to burst into tears every few minutes after that. The Reverend Chard was trying to offer words of comfort, while openly weeping at the loss of his own father.

Mayhem on wheels.

It seemed the only person not actively crying was Jonas Holly, and Marvel thought that might well be because the young constable was in shock. He had been called by Lynne Twitchett, and met Marvel and Reynolds at the door. He had taken them through his preservation of the scene in a low, careful voice. He had made sure everyone stayed in their rooms as far as was possible with confused old folk, and had asked Rupert Cooke to call all his relief staff in to help organize things in case the home had to be evacuated to allow the investigation to continue.

He had ensured that there were no other casualties in the first- or second-floor bedrooms and had kept people from moving about the house unnecessarily. He had taken off his boots. 'I thought they might be able to get prints off the carpets.' He shrugged sadly.

Jonas Holly had done a good job. Dully Marvel recognized that he'd done a similarly good job in most respects at the scene of Margaret Priddy's murder, for which he'd received no credit. Ah well, life wasn't fair.

The young constable had written everything in his notebook and kept referring to it for much longer than seemed necessary – kept staring at the pages as if he'd lost his place. At one point Marvel had become impatient and nearly snatched the notebook from him, but then he'd seen the man's Adam's apple working in his throat, and he'd given him the extra time he'd apparently needed to be able to speak without his voice breaking into a million pieces.

He felt close himself. Close to tears. He had never cried on a job – never even felt his bottom lip wobble in time to the grief around him.

But this . . .

This was . . .

Just.

Tragic.

The old people, helpless in their beds, their spectacles and teeth on their nightstands.

He remembered Lionel Chard, peering at the TV.

Countdown.

Big ears.

He wanted to punch a hole in Gary Liss's face with his bare hands. The nurse had disappeared. Never come down from wreaking havoc on the first floor. It all made sense now. It always did when it was far too late. No doubt when they caught Liss he would have some ridiculous reason why he had not returned to the kitchen after going upstairs in response to an alarm. Tell them that he'd found the bodies and lost his mind, or pursued the killer across the moors at great personal risk, or checked on Violet Eaves and then remembered he'd left the gas on at home . . . Madmen were only clever in the movies; in real life they were mostly just mad – and it was usually only the inability of the sane to recognize the depth of that madness which allowed them to prosper even temporarily. Sometimes Marvel felt that being psychotic would be a great asset to a homicide detective; that possibly the Force should leave room for manoeuvre in its recruit-ment criteria.

'We should've arrested the bastard.'

'We couldn't have held him for long, sir,' Reynolds said. It wasn't his style to make Marvel feel better about things, but that was the truth.

'I don't fucking care. The sonofabitch as good as said he'd killed Margaret Priddy, and we should have taken him in right there and then and made his life hell for forty-eight hours. Maybe we wouldn't be standing here now. Maybe these three would still be alive.'

Reynolds said nothing, because he felt the same gnawing guilt that they had dismissed Gary Liss as merely a straight-talker, when now it looked as if he were more than that. A *lot* more than that.

He'd have to be a psychopath.

Yes, he would.

Marvel felt sick at the memory. They had left Gary Liss here. That meant they had left these poor people in the care of a serial killer. It was a miracle there were only three bodies, when you looked at it like that. Although he felt so far from a miracle right now that it would have taken Jesus Christ himself to come up the swirly stair carpet at Sunset Lodge and raise the victims from the dead before he'd be convinced of one.

'Should we call Gulliver, sir?' said Reynolds.

Kate Gulliver was a forensic psychologist based in Bristol and one of Marvel's least favourite people, right up there with Jos Reeves. He felt the little prick of anger at the implication that Reynolds thought he was out of his depth. Immediately after that, he realized that he *was* out of his depth – or at least wading there fast. And refusing to consult Gulliver at this point would look territorial and negligent.

'You call her.' He nodded to Reynolds. He knew Reynolds would love that – and be good at it. Kate Gulliver was his kind of person – the young, bright, First-Class-Honours kind.

He was busy enough here.

He wished he could clear the entire home properly, but transporting twenty-two elderly and frail residents was easier said than done. When he'd suggested it, Rupert Cooke – who was wearing paisley pyjamas under his mackintosh, like someone from an episode of *Poirot* – had started to list what they'd need to take with them. Medications, walking sticks, Zimmer frames, wheelchairs, warm clothing, changes of under-wear . . . When he'd got to incontinence pads, Marvel had put up a hand to stop him and had asked for them all to be moved into the garden room until the CSIs could examine the first floor and establish points of entry and exit.

He asked Rupert Cooke for the use of his office and got Reynolds to clear the desk so he had somewhere to put his elbows.

Grey said they had not yet found the murder weapon but confirmed that as soon as it was light they'd be moving outside the house to the grounds and the graveyard and starting on a grid until re-inforcements arrived. Marvel told him to take Singh to Liss's home in the meantime – just in case their man was stupid after all.

Then Dave Pollard lumbered in and said a local agency reporter had picked up the story from a loose-lipped control-room officer, and had already called him three times on her way to Shipcott. She had said some-thing about getting there 'before the circus starts'.

Which Pollard 'thought' *might* mean they were about to be besieged by the press. Marvel mentally rolled his eyes at Pollard's lack of imagination and had second thoughts about putting him in charge now that this thing looked like going national, but was too busy to start redeploying staff at this stage.

At 6am he called Elizabeth Rice to check on the Marshes. He didn't want to start going after Liss if she told him both men had sneaked out in the night and come home covered in blood. He really hoped they had; everything would be so much easier. He held while she checked that they were still in bed. She said she had last checked on them at midnight and had personally locked the front and back doors and all the downstairs windows, and had kept the keys with her at all times.

'Why, sir?' she asked.

He told her there'd been three murders at Sunset Lodge, then the doorbell rang and Marvel heard the CSIs identifying themselves at the entrance. They had a huge job ahead of them.

'Shall I come up to help, sir?' said Rice hopefully.

Marvel thought of Reynolds's tipping-point theory. If it was true then nobody was off the hook quite yet.

'No,' he told her. 'You stay there.'

Downstairs, Jonas was sitting white-faced and dark-eyed in a chair with an undrunk cup of tea on his knee.

Around him the vast black windows of the garden

room reflected the scene in all directions, making it seem that hundreds of people were standing around whispering, bending over each other; crying in relay in a cocktail party of mourning.

'You take sugar?' said Marvel.

Jonas raised his eyes slowly to Marvel's. 'What?'

'Do you take sugar?'

Jonas looked dully at his cup and shook his head. Marvel picked the sugar bowl off a nearby tea trolley, put two heaped spoonfuls into Jonas's tea and stirred it briskly, slopping it into the saucer.

'Drink up,' he said.

Jonas did, wincing at the sweetness. Marvel pulled the piano stool away from the piano and sat down facing him.

'You know Gary Liss?'

'Not well, but yeah, I know him. He lives here, so I know him.'

'Tell me about him.'

Jonas stared down at his cup for a long moment. 'I can't believe he did this.'

Marvel spread his hands and said curtly, '*You* can't believe *anyone* did it – but there are three dead people upstairs and Liss has taken off. It doesn't look good.'

'I know,' said Jonas miserably.

'He ever been in trouble?'

'Not really. Once there were some things missing. From the residents' rooms. A few bits of jewellery, that kind of thing. I came round and spoke to staff members. There was no evidence even though I suspected it might be Gary, so it was more to let them know it had been noticed than anything else. It stopped. That was all.'

'Any items recovered?' asked Reynolds.

'Not to my knowledge.'

'Could've been Liss,' said Marvel. 'Petty crime leads to bigger things.'

'But not *this*,' said Jonas. 'I don't understand what's happening here. Why this is *happening* . . .' He stopped, realizing he sounded lost and feeble, and cleared his throat.

Marvel said, 'Grey and Singh are at Liss's house but it doesn't look as if he's been back home. You know where else he might be?'

'Paul's,' said Jonas, and then sat up quickly, clattering his cup and saucer on to the trolley. 'Shit. I have to tell Paul.'

'Who's Paul?'

'His partner.'

Marvel glanced at Reynolds. 'He told us he had a girlfriend.'

'He doesn't know you.' Jonas shrugged, getting up and picking up his helmet. 'Why would he tell you?'

Marvel felt a twinge of irritation. 'Hold on. I'll send a man with you. He could be harbouring Liss.'

But Jonas was impatient. 'He lives in Withypool. I can't see how Gary would have got there by now, sir. Not in this snow, and his car's still out the back. I don't want Paul to hear it through the grapevine.' He lowered his voice. 'Mr Cooke's wife is Dr Dennis's receptionist and she's best friends with Lisa Tanner who lives next door to Paul. She'll tell him if I don't get there first.' Jonas hesitated, then remembered that he was supposed to be on doorstep duty. 'If that's all right with you, sir?'

Marvel nodded curtly. 'Come to the unit afterwards. I'll need you on other things now.'

'Yes, sir,' said Jonas. 'Will you be treating Gary as a suspect? Just want to know how to handle Paul.'

'Bloody right!' said Marvel. 'The *only* bloody suspect.'

Jonas nodded neutrally.

'Get a picture of Liss,' Marvel said as Jonas left, then added, 'preferably one where he's not wearing leather shorts.'

Reynolds and Marvel sat for a minute in the soporific heat of the garden room. God knew what it was like in the summer. Reynolds wrinkled his nose. The room was clean and tidy but it smelled of old things.

'Liss lied to us,' said Marvel.

'Only about his sexuality,' shrugged Reynolds. 'That's understandable in a small village.'

'Not in a fucking murder investigation, it's not.'

'Jonas seems to think it's beyond him,' said Reynolds cautiously.

'Bollocks to him. He's a boy scout.'

Several old ladies looked round at the language and
Marvel lowered his voice. 'You think Liss *didn't* do it?'

'No, sir,' said Reynolds – and meant it. 'I was only
keeping an open mind, that's all. As we haven't interviewed him yet.'

'Well, when we have him behind bars, I'll keep an
open mind too. Until then he's Jack the fucking
Ripper in my book.'

One of the CSIs spoke from the door: 'We've got a
trail.'

Reynolds got up, but Marvel didn't rise from the
piano stool. Instead he pursed his lips and looked
around at the remaining residents. They wept and
held each other's hands – and stared into their own
short futures with new fear.

'The old, the weak, the infirm,' he said in a low but
harsh voice that Reynolds had to lean forward to
hear . . .

'This is not a killing – it's a cull.'

*

Jonas had no fear of going to Paul Angell's alone. He
knew it wasn't Gary Liss. He couldn't have said *how*
he knew it. It was the same way he knew it wasn't
Peter Priddy, and the same way he'd known the
identity of the body in the stream; the same way he
knew that the killer of Margaret Priddy had also killed
Yvonne Marsh. He just *felt* it.

Big deal, he berated himself under his breath, as he drove carefully through the snow to Withypool. He seemed to know an awful lot about who the killer *wasn't*. But he felt no closer to understanding who the killer *was*. And although he hadn't been involved in the investigation, he also had a gut feeling that Marvel had no more insight than he did. The man had the look of someone who has just realized he has wandered off a true path and into quicksand. Something in Jonas enjoyed knowing that the abrasive Marvel was suffering.

They were all suffering.

Jonas found it hard to grasp what was happening to his village; to his friends and neighbours; to the very *life* he had always known.

He had already called Lucy from Sunset Lodge. Woken her up to ask if she had the knife with her, less than an hour since he'd taken so much care *not* to wake her as he slipped out of bed in response to the vibration of his phone. She had asked him to repeat the question, and said crossly, 'Wait a mo.' She had taken ages to groggily turn on the light and look for the knife, and, while she did, Jonas had the nutty idea that he should attach it to her with a piece of elastic the way surfers did with their boards. If an intruder broke in, she wouldn't be able to ask him to 'wait a mo' while she groped about on the bedside table for her only means of defence.

Finally she'd said, 'Yes, why?' still sounding

irritated. He didn't blame her. Even without being woken in the early hours and ordered to seek out random cutlery, Lucy's moods could be erratic nowadays. Dr Wickramsinghe told them it was 'to be expected', but Jonas never quite *did* expect it.

Briefly he'd told her what had happened, because not telling her would only have irritated her further, and she'd been shocked into silence.

'I'll be home as soon as I can,' he'd said.

'OK,' she'd answered in a voice that was not ratty or cross, only very small. 'Be careful, Jonas.'

*

'There's blood on the roof.'

Marvel followed the CSI's finger to what looked like a couple of thin smears on the glass between a small window above the garden room and the guttering over the water-butt. He wondered how they could tell from down here, or whether they'd already been on the roof.

'Might be the killer's,' said Reynolds hopefully, even though they all knew that that was a very long and desperate shot. Still.

'Looks like the point of entry and exit,' said the CSI. 'And prints going that way.'

The narrow concrete pathway around the building's perimeter was flat and a perfect surface for snow. And the flat and perfect snow held the prints like a joke trail for them to follow, starting incongruously at the water-butt.

'Can't see any patterns,' added the CSI with a petulant tone, flickering a torch over the treads. 'Maybe when it gets lighter . . .'

Marvel didn't care about the tread pattern on the killer's shoes. Only where he was going.

In the half-dark, Marvel and Reynolds followed the trail out of the Sunset Lodge grounds and on to the main street. Despite the hour, the road outside Sunset Lodge was already lined with tyre tracks from their own cars and those of the scenes-of-crime officers, but the pavements were still mostly clear and the trail of footprints was ludicrously easy to follow.

'I feel like Elmer Fudd,' said Reynolds, and when Marvel showed no recognition, added, 'Where da wabbit?'

Marvel knew what he meant but ignored him. So what if they were following a cartoon trail of foot-prints? So what if they led them straight to the killer's front door? They deserved a break in this fucking case and it wouldn't be a moment too soon.

In a small pile of snow which had been cleared from a doorstep, they saw blood.

'Maybe he's injured,' said Marvel, unable to keep an edge of hope out of his voice.

'Maybe,' said Reynolds. 'Or maybe he washed the murder weapon there. Get the blood off it.'

Marvel nodded. They stood for a moment building

the picture in their heads, then moved on briskly.

'We're heading for the Marshes' house,' Reynolds observed neutrally.

'And the bloody shop,' Marvel pointed out with an edge of annoyance as the snow started to show more prints.

They passed the Marshes' house without stopping, then crossed the road – the strangely featureless prints disappearing in the churned snow, but picking up again on the opposite pavement. They glanced at each other as the snow became dark and slushy for the ten yards either side of the door of the Spar shop. It was 7am – plenty late enough for any number of villagers to have collected their morning papers or to have topped up with breakfast milk. They lost the footprints.

'Bollocks,' said Marvel with real feeling.

'Shit,' said Reynolds.

They stood still – not wanting to risk inadvertently trampling over any print they might still pick up.

'There,' pointed Reynolds.

The killer's fragmented prints deviated into a narrow covered passageway beside the shop, where no snow had fallen. There they simply disappeared.

Both men started warily up the alleyway. It turned into a courtyard.

Nobody there.

'We fucking lost him,' said Reynolds. 'In the *snow*. How the *fuck*?'

Reynolds lifted the lid on a green wheelie bin. There was nothing inside. They looked around the edges of the courtyard carefully but there was nothing of interest. Just scraps of paper, a couple of plastic bags rustling against the wall, and broken-down cardboard boxes gone soggy in the snow.

Reynolds realized that this must be the alleyway Jonas had told him about – the one where the stranger had given him the slip. He hadn't taken Jonas seriously. He'd dismissed the report as parochial paranoia, and he had only written it down to make Jonas feel he was being listened to. For that reason, he hadn't reported it to Marvel.

Reynolds regretted that, of course. But the idea of telling Marvel about it now and being shat on from a great height was less than appealing.

They walked back to the entrance to the alleyway. People were passing regularly now, and the snow on the pavement around the shop was melting in dirty brown patches. The prints that they themselves had made were already all but obliterated. Prints made in the early hours of the morning would be gone by now for sure.

Marvel stepped into the road and stared glumly up and down as if he might still spot the killer.

'Bollocks,' he said again.

'Hold on,' said Reynolds with sudden urgency. He pointed back into the courtyard, where the Spar bags fluttered against the wall.

'Two plastic bags.'

'You found some litter,' said Marvel. 'Well done, Reynolds. Have a fucking *Blue Peter* badge.'

Reynolds ignored him. 'Two bags, two feet! He puts the bags on his feet so he doesn't leave identifiable prints. Then he comes in here and takes them off—'

'And walks back into the slush and disappears,' finished Marvel, catching up fast and hurrying over.

Reynolds snapped on gloves and picked the bags up. 'That means there could be prints *inside* the bags.'

Reynolds looked as pleased as punch, but even that couldn't stop Marvel feeling a lift in his own spirits.

They stared at the white bags with the green and red logo, and wondered whether this odd little scene would spell a change in their luck.

*

In the grey light of morning the snow on the moor looked dull and worn out, and the narrow strip of road was just a sunken impression in the bumpy landscape. All the white was disorientating and Jonas had to work hard to keep focused on the route ahead. It was as if the moor and the murders were conspiring to confuse him, using optical illusions to obfuscate the truth of the killings and the landscape alike, and to blur the two into one. A blanket of snow had descended on Shipcott, but under that coating of purity something dark and evil was going about its work, unseen and unchecked.

Jonas thought of the notes that had first alerted him to some undercurrent of discord.

He thought of that prickly feeling that he was being watched. Observed.

Judged.

He thought of staring into the small yellow square of his own bathroom while standing like a cold giant under the starlit sky; of the stiff greyhound with the cloudy eyes; and of the man in the hat and the herring-bone treads who had given him the slip.

He remembered the brittle hope in Danny Marsh's eyes as the dirty horse pranced behind him, and the irrational fear that he was personally under threat – that if the hope in Danny's eyes had shattered, the shards would pierce him too; and that he must stop Danny at all costs, even if it was with his fists.

Jonas fought sudden panic and the Land Rover slewed sideways and bumped over the invisible heather. He lifted his foot and gripped the wheel and slammed on the brakes. The car stalled and Jonas sat for a moment, high above Withypool, and listened to his own harsh breathing ruin the silence, while he slowly kept himself from falling apart.

*

After giving the plastic bags to a CSI back at Sunset Lodge, Marvel and Reynolds met Grey and Singh at Gary Liss's home – this time to break in. They had taken a battering ram with them but after they had knocked, even Marvel felt self-conscious about getting it out in the middle of a village like Shipcott and breaking down the door of a crooked little cottage with a black wrought-iron door knocker in the shape of a pixie.

'Fairy,' he grunted at Reynolds, who resolutely didn't laugh.

Instead they efficiently broke the small pane of glass in the door and Grey, who was the tallest – and had 'the arms of a rangatang' as Marvel put it – leaned awkwardly through to open the Yale.

Inside was neat and decorated with a deft touch, which made the most of the bowed walls and limited light.

'You've got to give it to these gays,' said Marvel. 'They do know how to tidy up.'

There was no sign of Liss – or that he had been here since leaving for work last night.

Marvel put latex gloves on and the others followed suit, and they started their careful search for anything that might incriminate Gary Liss.

They worked in two teams – Marvel and Singh upstairs, Reynolds and Grey downstairs.

'What are we looking for, sir?' said Singh.

'Murder weapon would be nice,' said Marvel.

They bagged up Gary Liss's shoes, then searched for an hour with decreasing levels of optimism, before

Singh found an old King Edward VII cigar box at the back of the top shelf of the wardrobe. He glanced inside and immediately alerted Marvel.

There was an assortment of jewellery: a few ladies' watches, some diamond earrings, an enamelled brooch with an ornate gold setting, five or six strings of pearls, which even Marvel's untrained eye could see were good, with clever clasps and that slight unevenness of shape and tone that marked them out as natural.

'His mother's stuff, maybe?' said Singh.

'How many watches can one woman wear?' said Marvel. He picked up the nicest of them – an art-deco face on a rose-gold bracelet – and turned it over. On the back was an inscription: *To Viola from your Best and Last.*

*

Jonas got to Withypool a little before eight, having taken twenty-five minutes to make the ten-minute journey. He dropped off the common and down the steep hill into the village, on a sweeping road of virgin snow. He hoped he'd be able to get back up it, but at least the Land Rover would give him every chance.

Like Shipcott, Withypool looked as if it had tumbled down the sides of the moor and landed haphazardly at the bottom. Houses stood where they fell – a few here, a few there, a dozen scattered along the river either side of the stone-walled humpbacked bridge that was sneakily only wide enough for one car at a time, despite the broad approaches.

Paul Angell was already in his shed. Jonas knew he would be as soon as his knock went unanswered. He went round the side of the cottage, but not before he'd cupped his hands around his eyes and peered through the downstairs windows. Paul had Venetian blinds rather than nets, so it was easy to see between the slats. Jonas had no expectation of seeing any sign of Gary Liss, but it was only sensible to be wary. He watched nothing move for five minutes before going down the narrow alleyway into the garden.

The shed was warm and smelled of gas and glue. Paul was hunched over an old school desk wearing a torch on his forehead and a magnifying visor which made the top half of his face look cartoonishly big and brainy; the bottom half was covered by an impressive salt-and-pepper beard. Jonas's eyes were drawn to a 00-gauge model of the *Flying Scotsman* that Paul held in his left hand. The desk was covered with tools, and the interior walls of the shed had been cleverly contoured and customized so that various trains ran around them in layers, each tier with a different landscape and different type of train. Jonas was no enthusiast but even he could identify the *Orient Express* on one circuit and an old Western locomotive with a cow-catcher, pulling cattle wagons and a caboose through a painted landscape of buttes and marauding Apaches. Paul Angell's shed was a 00-gauge Guggenheim for geeks.

Paul was fifty-eight – a retired lecturer in Astrophysics. Jonas had asked him about it once and then stood in a nebula of confusion as Paul had talked for fifteen minutes straight about string theory. Jonas had loved the sciences at school, but all he'd managed to cobble together from Paul's big-eyed excitement was a vague idea that all matter was made up of little vibrating hula-hoops. By the end he'd just been nodding, smiling and thinking of what he'd cook for tea. Cheese on toast, most likely.

Now Paul's magnified eyes lit up as Jonas opened the door, then changed fast when he saw his face.

'Hi, Paul. You know where Gary is?'

'Work,' said Paul. 'He doesn't get off until three. Why?'

Jonas took a breath; there was no easy way to break the news. 'There's been some trouble at the Lodge,' he said. 'Three residents are dead and Gary is missing.'

Paul said nothing. His huge eyes blinked at Jonas.

Jonas waited but still Paul did not respond, although the *Flying Scotsman* shook almost imperceptibly in his hand.

'Paul?' he enquired softly.

'Yes,' said Paul – then after another long pause, 'I don't know what to say. What can I say? I don't know. Or to think. What do you mean? What am I supposed to think?' He put the little engine down without look-ing at it and repeated, 'What am I supposed to think?'

'I don't know,' said Jonas. 'It's quite possible Gary wasn't involved, but I think we should do everything we can to find him as quickly as we can, don't you?'

'He's a suspect?' Paul was confused, with an edge of outrage. 'That's ridiculous!'

He got up suddenly and Jonas realized he had been holding a tack hammer in his other hand; Jonas took a slow step backwards.

'I thought you meant you were concerned for his safety! He wouldn't do anything to harm those people, Jonas. Never.'

'I know that, Paul.' Jonas badly wanted to glance at the tack hammer but stayed focused on the man's face. 'And I *am* concerned for his safety. Truly. That's why we need to find him.'

He thought of Marvel's offer of back-up and felt a twinge of regret that he'd been too keen to wait for it.

Paul seemed unaware that he was holding the hammer. He stood stock still for at least a minute. Jonas gave him the time. Didn't know what else he could do really.

Then Paul nodded. 'Yes. We must. He could have been kidnapped. He could be trapped somewhere, or injured.'

'He could,' agreed Jonas, and got a nasty *underneath* feeling in his belly.

*

The agency reporter arrived first and was Australian. Marvel found Australians unbearably cocky, so he told Pollard she'd have to wait until the TV news crews got there so that he could do just one press conference. The reporter – Marcie Meyrick – made such a fuss that even Pollard nearly caved in and told her everything she wanted to know right up front. Only a well-timed call from the ITN crew asking for directions kept him loyal.

By lunchtime Marvel had another six officers at his disposal: four uniforms and two DCs from Weston-super-Mare. He sent them all to assist in the search for the murder weapon.

They didn't find it.

By 4pm the BBC and ITN had joined the fuming Marcie Meyrick, and at a press conference that Rupert Cooke offered to let them hold in the garden room while the residents were at tea, Marvel told them the names, ages and sex of the victims, the fact that they had suffered blunt-force trauma, and about the 'concerning' disappearance of Gary Liss. He then distributed the good, clear photograph Jonas Holly had brought back with him from Paul Angell – Gary Liss looking like a member of a comeback boy-band in jeans and a tight T-shirt. Nothing was said about the box of jewellery. The watch had belonged to Violet Eaves, and the Reverend Chard identified a signet ring of his father's. When they found Gary Liss, it would be one of the few surprises they could spring on him.

The usual blah about what a terrible crime it was was said with far more than the usual vehemence by Marvel. Luckily for the two TV news crews, a trick of the light caught an ambiguous liquid shine in Marvel's eyes and 'A MURDER DETECTIVE WEEPS' booked the story a top berth on both the evening news bulletins.

Marvel protested too much, Reynolds was faux sympathetic and Marcie Meyrick – whose photographer had been delayed by a snow-crash on the M5 – was enraged.

*

Elizabeth Rice felt thoroughly left out.

Family liaison was a get-out clause for every senior police officer who had women to deploy, and sometimes she wished she'd never done the additional training the position required.

Marvel acting as if Alan and Danny Marsh were both still suspects was a joke; if he seriously considered them to be suspects in the latest brutal murders then he would never have left her alone with them. Marvel was an arsehole but he wasn't completely stupid – so why the hell couldn't she abandon her assignment and get where the action was? All her fancy-pants high-falutin family-liaison status afforded her was a total lack of privacy, and the honour of sharing a bathroom with two men who were too unreconstructed to bother with the niceties of flushing, let alone putting the seat down.

They barely said a word to each other, and that gave her the creeps.

Alan Marsh sat for hours staring at inanimate objects, while Danny stayed in his bedroom and read, occasionally went to the Red Lion, or wandered from lounge to kitchen and back, twitching.

'I suppose it was a release,' Alan said at least one thousand times a day, usually after a long sigh. Sometimes Danny would grunt in reply; sometimes he would snort; sometimes he would jump to his feet and say 'Bollocks!' and leave the room. He would come back ten minutes later and they would resume their positions.

Their tiny terraced house smelled of sweat, mildew and something else which she took days to identify as a bag of onions liquefying in the vegetable rack. One part of her wanted so badly to scrub the place from top to bottom that she kept opening the cupboard under the sink and staring at the bleach; another part of her rebelled at the thought that, because she was a woman, she should clean the house. She had a degree in Criminal Psychology! She'd graduated top of her class at Portishead! She was a highly trained and highly effective officer of the law!

It sucked, because she *really* wanted to clean that house.

The Marshes weren't under arrest; they were free to come and go – but they hardly did. By day Alan stared at *The Jeremy Kyle Show* and *Homes under the Hammer* as if he had common ground with unwed slags and millionaire property developers. Danny would slouch down at breakfast and attempt to make small talk over the cornflakes. Very small talk. He was no talker, Danny Marsh, but he was a surprisingly good listener. He would ask her something and then just let her keep talking while he poured milk and sprinkled sugar and crunched cereal. Now and then he would look up and make eye-contact; now and then he would grunt; now and then he would nod. It was the only encouragement she needed. Sometimes she found herself telling him things about her own life that she hadn't even told her boyfriend, Eric. *Sometimes* she told him things *about* Eric! Afterwards she was always sorry she'd been disloyal, but Danny Marsh's grunts and nods seemed to open her eyes to certain aspects of Eric's personality that she had to admit she'd never noticed before. Or if she had, they had never bothered her before. It had taken Danny Marsh and his objectivity to make her see . . .

She locked them all in every night. Back door, front door and all the downstairs windows. Alan Marsh was too out of it to notice, but Danny had watched her do it the first night and had asked, 'Are you locking some-one out, or locking us in?'

'Someone out, of course,' she'd said, but she could feel her cheeks grow warm and hoped he hadn't noticed.

Every night she kept the keys under her pillow while she slept in the tiny box room they had cleared for her. 'Cleared' was a euphemism for shoving everything that apparently wouldn't fit in the attic against the opposite wall, and Rice had to turn sideways to approach the bed at nights, down a narrow pathway of ugly green carpet.

She crab-walked down that pathway around midnight every night and woke at six. She checked on the Marshes as soon as she woke – but for the rapid application of mascara to her pale lashes, because *that* was next to waking like cleanliness is next to godliness – and she checked by pressing an ear against their bedroom doors and listening to them breathe. Alan snored; his son did not, but in the still darkness of dawn she could always hear him breathe eventually, once she focused and calmed her own breathing.

From day three onwards she had enquired of Alan and Danny whether they might like to return to work at the ramshackle little garage behind their home. She'd gathered that they kept half the cars on Exmoor running from the dingy corrugated-iron shed, and was more than prepared to jump around and stamp her feet to stay warm if only it took them all out of this stuffy little house. But no amount of encouragement would shift them into any action that was not slow or short-lived. Danny went to the pub now and then, but constantly forgot that he was supposed to have bought something for tea, and eventually Rice chose female submission over starvation and stormed down to the Spar to keep them all in the most mundane of foods – beans, toast, eggs, toast, cheese, toast and more toast. Her low-carb diet was a thing of the past and she felt the old white-bread addiction gripping her like crack, the longer her pointless occupation of the Marsh home continued.

When Marvel called about the murders at Sunset Lodge, she had wanted to rush out of the house and up the snowy road to be part of it all. Missing the buzz of the scene of a triple murder was killing her. The thought of that idiot Pollard being there when she was not was especially hard to bear.

All day she was short and gloomy and that night she sat fuming on the easy chair beside the sofa, from where Alan and Danny stared sightlessly at *Top Gear* repeats. Even *she* had seen this one and she'd only been here nine days.

Alan went to bed at 10.30pm, Danny at twelve when she did. She said goodnight with forced cheerfulness; he didn't bother to force anything apart from a mumble, and closed his bedroom door.

She did her teeth and washed her face, trying hard not to touch the toothpaste-spotted taps or even the cracked and grimy pink soap, which looked as if it might have been a pre-war fixture along with the mottled tiles.

As she opened her bedroom door, she shivered.

She sidled towards the head of her bed and shivered

again. The little room was always cold but there was a terrible draught coming from somewhere . . .

As if in answer to an unspoken question, the open curtains wafted inwards.

The window was slightly open. 'Slightly' in this winter was enough for the cold to stab its way into the room and chill it like a fridge.

A cheap office desk lamp with a flexible neck was the only makeshift light in here. Rice turned it to the window.

On the sill was a footprint showing where someone had climbed from the roof of the lean-to and into her room.

Elizabeth Rice had watched enough teen horror flicks on the sofa with Eric to know that the killer was right behind her with a steak knife.

She turned on a stifled shriek, throwing up her hands to protect her throat.

Nobody there.

She took three lurching sideways steps towards her bedroom door to alert the Marshes that there had been an intruder, and then stopped dead, even though her mind continued to click through scenarios so fast that it felt like one of those flicker-books where a thousand static images make a jerky motion picture.

The print was coming *in*.

There was no print going *out*.

If this was the killer, then the killer was still in the house.

Rice looked down at the boxes of junk and selected an ugly blue vase. She weighed it in her hand. She had always been a supporter of the British police remaining un-armed apart from specialized units. She felt that the lack of a firearm enforced the tacit notion of policing by consent, and that – democratically speaking – that was a good thing.

But right now she would give her right arm for a big gun.

Rice walked through the house – quietly, but not quietly enough to scare herself – switching on lights, checking doors and rattling windows. She stood outside the other bedroom doors and listened to the Marshes breathe.

There was no intruder.

There was no smearing of the inward-bound print. Therefore Rice felt it was fair to deduce that whoever had climbed in through this window had not climbed out through it again – and therefore they must be in the house.

Unless the person who had come *in* through the window had climbed out of it *first* before they muddied their shoes.

In which case there were only two suspects . . .

Neither Alan nor Danny Marsh had moved from the sofa today apart from brief visits to the bathroom or to the kitchen for tea.

Was it possible that between her checks last night – between midnight and 6am – one of the Marshes had crept past her bed and climbed out of her window?

Then back in?

Possible.

Improbable, of course, but Sherlock Holmes would base an entire case on improbable.

Her window was at the back of the house and there was a four-foot drop to the lean-to. With the downstairs doors and windows locked, it was the only viable route into or out of the house. It was, after all, the way the killer had entered Margaret Priddy's home.

The thought of someone in her bedroom while she slept was disturbing enough; the idea that someone might have passed through on their way to and from murdering three people at Sunset Lodge made her feel sick.

She dragged one of the boxes of junk across the room and against the bedroom door. It wouldn't stop anyone, but it would slow them down.

Then she sat on the bed cross-legged, fully clothed, with the blue vase in one hand and her phone in the other, and called DCI Marvel.

*

Jonas got home so late and so weary that when Lucy told him she'd made supper he could have kissed her feet. It was only spaghetti with tomatoes and basil but it tasted fantastic, and she'd put out a bottle of smooth red wine for him to open. She sat and watched him eat.

'You want to talk about it, sweetheart?' she said quietly.

He stared across the kitchen in silence.

'He beat them to death.'

Lucy bit her lip and her eyes filled with tears.

'Then put pillows over their faces.'

'Like with Margaret?'

Jonas shook his head but did not drop his sightless thousand-yard stare at the washing machine.

'I don't think he meant to smother them.'

'Why, then?'

'I don't know. Maybe so he couldn't see their faces.'

Lucy hated to ask, but the images in her head begged the question.

'Did they . . . was there a struggle?'

'I don't think so. They all looked quite . . . peaceful. I think he hit them while they were asleep. They died quickly. I hope they did.'

Lucy put her hand over Jonas's and looked down at the knife he'd given her, lying on the table between them. It had seemed a silly thing at first, but since his early-morning call from Sunset Lodge, she'd barely let it go.

She shuddered and her movement made Jonas blink. He focused on the washing machine and remembered it needed emptying. And there was a basket of ironing to do. Work shirts mostly, and a couple of pairs of uniform trousers. And the one or two tops that Lucy couldn't wear if they were wrinkled.

Jonas was bad at ironing and they always tried to buy wisely so he wouldn't have to do much.

Lucy stroked his hand. 'Eat, sweetheart.'

Jonas dutifully picked up his fork again.

He noticed that there was new mail propped against the fruit bowl. They'd been without mail for a few days, but now that Marvel's team and Jonas had been up and down the hill on several occasions, turning snow to slush, apparently Frank Tithecott's old red Royal Mail van was up to the challenge once more.

'Tell me about your day,' he said.

'You sure you want to hear all that boring crap?' she said in surprise.

'That's *exactly* what I want to hear,' he said with feeling.

She got it, so she told him.

Jonas felt warmed physically and spiritually as he ate and listened to his wife recounting the minutiae of her existence. Here in the kitchen, with a fire in the hearth and food in his belly, it was easy to imagine that all was well with the world.

She told him about the robin that had sat on the window sill for almost ten minutes, staring in at her as she watched giant cockroaches munch New Yorkers in *Mimic*; she described the way she'd suddenly had a manic urge to bake a cake and had collected everything on the kitchen table, which had taken her over half an hour – and then there'd been a power cut which meant she couldn't even pre-heat the oven. She'd taken another twenty minutes putting everything back much less tidily. She'd slept for an hour and been woken by Frank, who had come in and talked about Sunset Lodge. The postman knew almost everything there was to know, and Jonas and Lucy both rolled their eyes so they didn't have to say out loud: *Only in Shipcott!*

She had watched *Countdown*, where the conundrum had been 'residents' even though the same letters also spelled 'tiredness', which wasn't really fair, was it? Then she rambled on for ages about her letter from Charlie, her oldest school friend. Charlie's husband had had adult mumps, her seven-year-old son, Luca, had been diagnosed as dyslexic, while her younger, Saul, had run away from the first kitten he'd ever seen, shouting, 'Rat! Rat!'

They both laughed and Jonas stopped eating to stroke her face with the backs of his fingers.

She crumpled before his eyes, tears spilling down her cheeks so hard that they splashed on to the table as if from a faulty tap. Jonas dropped his fork and took her in his arms. There was nothing he could – or would – say that would make any of it better.

The illness, the murders, the baby-shaped hole in her life.

In the face of each of them he was overwhelmed and useless. There had been a time when he'd thought he could help, could be of some comfort; a time when he'd thought he could make a difference.

That was no longer true.

Sometimes you just had to accept what you were.

And what you were never meant to be.

He had never cried with her, but he'd never come closer than this, and they spent minutes like that, he kneeling beside her, she rigid in his arms, her hands over her face to keep her pain to herself – her refusal to let him share it properly an indication that he was to blame, in some part at the very least. He felt that burden settle like cold lead in his heart.

Slowly she quieted and disengaged herself. He gave her kitchen roll; she blew her nose.

'OK, Lu?' he asked softly.

'Frank left the gate open,' she replied without looking at him. 'It's been banging all day.'

Jonas put his boots back on and went down the dark garden path. More snow had fallen this afternoon and he needed to clear it again. He thought how frustrating it must have been for Lucy not to be able to venture the ten yards to her own front gate for fear of falling, while all the time the gate banged. The catch needed oiling really, so it would shut more easily. When he'd shut it he would get the shovel and clear the path, in case he didn't have time in the morning. Now that he was off Margaret Priddy's doorstep, he expected to be hectic instead of bored.

Oil the gate, empty the washing machine, do the ironing, clear the path, refill the bird feeders so that the robin would keep coming to keep Lucy company. He needed to remember the little things that kept their lives functioning, but he knew that by the time he went back into the house he'd have forgotten at least one of the items. He should make a list.

Home and work. Both needed constant maintenance, like an old British motorbike. Otherwise the oil squeezed through the casings and left ugly black stains on the floor of their lives.

He thought he'd keep up the night patrols. Just for an hour or so each night; give people a sense of security. A false sense, of course – events had demonstrated that only too well – but even a false sense of security was better than nothing when fear was uppermost in everybody's mind. Yes, the night patrols were good for the village.

Jonas shut the gate.

As he did, his fingers touched something papery.

By the stars he could see it was a note pinned to the outside of the gatepost.

With his second *underneath* feeling of the day coiling like slime in his stomach, Jonas reached over and tugged the paper free of the shiny gold drawing pin.

If you won't do your job, then I'll do it for you

Five Days

Elizabeth Rice watched the CSI pottering about with powder and gelatin lifts at her window, keeping up a muttered running commentary on his own methods like a fussy TV cook.

She had introduced him to the Marshes simply as 'Tim' and taken him up to her room and closed the door. She wondered whether they thought she and Tim were having sex. It couldn't be helped. When she'd called the previous night, Marvel hadn't wanted Danny and Alan alerted to the fact that they were under suspicion. He had asked her if she felt OK about remaining in the house and she'd said 'yes', because to say 'no' would have made her look weak. Actually the thought of staying there made her feel sick inside, the way she used to feel right before walking out of the wings in school plays. But being here with Tim doing his thing was fine. She hoped she would feel the same way once he left.

Tim had found a latent print going *out* of the window, underneath the visible one she'd first spotted. He had photographed the visible print with a Polaroid camera so that she could match it to the Marshes' shoes. She would have to do that in secret.

Secret stuff connected to a murder inquiry should have been exciting, but the thought of sneaking into Alan and Danny's bedrooms and going through their shoes made her feel slightly ashamed. They were bereaved; they were nice enough to her; Danny was quite fanciable in a lost-dog kind of way. She wished she didn't have to treat them as suspects while eating their cornflakes.

*

'She's great,' said Reynolds as he hung up on Kate Gulliver.

'We'll see,' grunted Marvel and flushed an old coffee filter down the Portaloo in the mobile unit.

'She says,' said Reynolds, then flicked back and forth through his notebook before finding his place. 'She says the fixation on the elderly is almost certainly a product of resentment of a parent or parents.' He looked up at Marvel, who rolled his eyes and made a little sound that said, 'Tell me something I *don't* know.'

Reynolds was undaunted. 'Gary Liss had to give up his job to nurse his father, didn't he?'

'And Peter Priddy had to give up his inheritance to

pay for his mother's care,' countered Marvel. He didn't know what it was that drove him to take issue with Reynolds even when he agreed with him. He hoped the spirit of debate was good for the investigation, but had a sneaking suspicion that it was not. He needed to try to curb that propensity for unmotivated bolshiness.

'Well yes,' said Reynolds, made generous by his fleeting contact with what he considered to be a similar intellect. 'But her hypothesis is that it might go beyond material deprivation and into the arena of physical or emotional abuse.'

The arena of physical or emotional abuse. The *arena*! Seriously, sometimes Marvel just felt like punching Reynolds and getting it over with. He wished now that he had spoken to Kate Gulliver, who was also ridiculously self-important, but at least he'd now be the one imparting information to Reynolds, instead of the other way round.

'So Liss could have been beaten by his mother and is now killing other people's mothers in revenge. In *layman*'s terms.'

'Right. Or fathers. Remember Lionel Chard.'

Marvel did. And that *did* put a new spin on things. Serial killers generally worked within certain parameters when it came to victims. Boys, or teenaged girls, or prostitutes with green eyes. The sex of the victims was often immutable.

'So if Liss is a serial killer he's changing his parameters, or had different ones all along.'

'Right.'

'Changing parameters *and* method.'

'Yeah,' said Reynolds less confidently. 'Maybe two killers? Working together? We've got the footprint at the Marsh house.'

Marvel made a face that said he wasn't in love with that theory.

'Or maybe it's not a serial killer at all. Kate says some elements feel more like the work of a spree killer due to the compact time frame and the number of—'

'She's reaching,' interrupted Marvel.

'So are we,' said Reynolds defensively.

'You'll be saying next that Liss had permission from Peter Priddy and Alan Marsh to kill!'

Reynolds looked wounded. 'I'm just trying to run through every possibility, that's all. I'm just trying to help.'

'I know,' sighed Marvel, which was as close as he'd ever come to apologizing to Reynolds for *anything* – even that time he'd run over his foot with the Ford Focus.

Encouraged, Reynolds continued to postulate. As he opened and closed his mouth like one of his precious guppies, Marvel stopped listening and started thinking.

He had felt lost on this case, but now they had a bona fide suspect. Few things pointed to a killer like fleeing the scene of a murder. It was a hard action to justify and Marvel felt relief spreading through him like liquor.

Gary Liss.

Finally!

A male nurse. Statistics showed they were not unlikely serial killers. Boredom and distaste masquerading as mercy.

Although poisoning or neglect were the usual methods employed by nurses who killed.

And Yvonne Marsh had never been in the care of Gary Liss.

Those two things bothered Marvel, he realized with a little jag of annoyance. Why couldn't he just enjoy the fact that they had identified the killer? Why did his memory have to bring up the kind of annoying details that he was more used to discounting from Reynolds?

The relief had been a con; a quick shot on a cold night, which could not keep him from frostbite – merely dull his senses while it ate his fingers and toes.

He had no time for relief.

Relief was for wimps.

He could do with a drink to focus his mind.

Marvel thought about the almost genteel murder of Margaret Priddy, compared to the efficient brutality visited on the three late residents of Sunset Lodge. The escalation was disturbing. It spoke of an increasing loss of control.

It was probably Gary Liss. He wished he could be sure. He *was* sure. The disappearance, the stolen jewellery. He was sure.

Soon they would know. Nobody was going to be

able to stay hidden for long in this weather – not without at least trying to go home – and Jonas had assured
him that Paul Angell was cooperating. Liss had no
family to run to and Angell was also insisting that Gary
Liss had no other lovers. Marvel wasn't so sure about
that but, either way, it had been thirty-six hours and
Liss was without his car – a twelve-year-old Renault
Clio which was sitting forlornly in the car park with a
foot of snow on the roof and a flapping square of police
tape around it. Marvel had moved all the new crew to
house-to-house inquiries and searching outbuildings.
It hadn't made him popular, but very little he'd ever
done had made him popular, so he wasn't boo-hooing
about *that*.

No, Liss would soon be discovered, and then they
would know the truth within seconds. A single killing
might be concealed for a short while, but five was the
work of a madman, and *this* time Marvel would be able
to sniff it on Liss like a dog trained by having a
murder-rag rubbed over its nose. He could almost
smell it now, the sour fear of a man trapped by the
enormity of his own crimes; the self-justification for
unjustifiable deeds. Marvel's jaw clenched in anger,
even before he had anyone to take it out on.

'. . . in which case the killer may not even be aware of
what he's doing. She also says some killers just stop.
They reach saturation point and don't feel the need to
kill again for years – maybe even never – depending
on . . .' Reynolds tapered off lamely under Marvel's glare.

'I stopped listening to you,' said Marvel bluntly, and Reynolds shrugged. He'd gathered that.

Marvel got up and picked up the car keys. 'This is bullshit. All these fucking theories aren't getting us any closer to finding Liss. All we know for sure is that this bastard is escalating – fast.'

Reynolds nodded. 'Knowing him is not the same as stopping him.'

'That's right,' said Marvel, yanking open the unit door and letting winter rush in, 'and we need to get our arses into gear, because something tells me that if we don't stop him, he's not finished.'

*

Lionel Chard's room had been taped off as a crime scene.

Now as he stared into it from the doorway, Marvel felt like a visitor to a stately home. Here is the bed, ladies and gentlemen, where the King took the virginity of Catherine of Aragon; and here is the Sealy Posturepedic upon which Mr Chard was beaten to death by person or persons unknown.

Through the white window he could see flakes falling from the sky.

Even the snow was against him.

The manhunt had been stalled by snow, which could now only be traversed beyond the village boundaries by 4×4s.

The footprints outside the garden room had been methodically measured and photographed, but Marvel had seen more convincing yeti prints.

And finding a murder weapon in the snow was like ... well, they might as well do it blindfolded. Grey had suggested as much after yet another Braille-like search of the graveyard, and Marvel had told him to do it again.

Marvel moved the few paces to the entrance to Gorse – Violet Eaves's room. As he did so he thought of Gary Liss doing the same thing. He waved a casual hand across the doorway and heard the faint beep from downstairs. Lynne Twitchett and Jen Hardy had heard several beeps. They couldn't agree on how many exactly. Had that stupid electronic sound been the straw that broke the camel's back for Gary Liss? Had Violet Eaves sleepwalked one too many times, in his perverse view? Had his patience finally snapped and he'd hit her and then panicked, which had led to the massacre?

'Shit,' said Marvel. It didn't fit with the careful murder of Margaret Priddy and the seemingly random choice of Yvonne Marsh.

If Gary Liss was *not* the killer, then that first beep may well have been the killer entering Violet's room, rather than the old lady leaving it. Although she *had* left her room that night, one way or another.

From *this* stately doorway Marvel could see over the graveyard next door, where the picture-perfect snow had been made hectic and muddy by the search. They were just going through the motions out there. Liss was the key. They had to find him before he struck again – as Marvel had little doubt that he would.

He heard the doorbell and a minute later Singh came to say that Paul Angell was downstairs in the garden room and wanted to talk to him.

As he walked downstairs, someone started to play the piano. Not Lynne Twitchett – someone who *could* play. Marvel knew the tune. Something by Cole Porter. 'Cheek To Cheek', he thought. It made him melancholy to hear the song of dancing and romance played in this place where such things were long gone.

The garden room was its usual melting temperature and Marvel wrinkled his nose as he entered. The place smelled faintly of rotten . . . he couldn't think of rotten *what*. No doubt Reynolds would call it *generic* rotten. He made a mental note to die before he could end up somewhere like this, smelling like that.

Paul Angell stopped playing and looked up at him, and several of the old ladies clapped and one said, 'Lovely,' and another said, 'Do you remember that one, Trinny?'

Paul got up and started to ask about Gary. Paul had been helpful to the police, but wary, and Marvel wasn't 100 per cent convinced that the man didn't know where his lover was hiding, whatever the hell Jonas Holly said. He got the impression that Paul Angell thought the police had been somehow against Liss from the outset because he was gay, instead of because he'd gone on the run after a triple murder. Idiot. Marvel had been polite to him so far, but he hoped Angell's homosexuality gave him the sensitivity to know that his well of manners was not a deep one.

Now Marvel found that, while Paul Angell asked why he hadn't been kept advised of the status of the hunt for Gary, he was suddenly transfixed by the hand of the old lady who had asked Trinny if she remembered 'Cheek To Cheek'. The hand had been clapping and Marvel had seen its palm. Just briefly. He wasn't even sure why his eye had been caught. Now he listened with half an ear and answered Angell with half a brain, while both his eyes watched the old, lined hand touch the arm of the chair, then reach for the biscuit tin, then poke at the selection with one bony finger, then lift the biscuit to the old-lady mouth—

Marvel stepped around Angell and gripped her by the wrist.

'Oh!' she said and dropped the biscuit. It fell on her chest and then to her lap. A Bourbon.

Marvel turned her palm up as though he were about to read it. There was a dirty smudge in the middle of it. Red-brown. It might have been chocolate.

'Reynolds!'

Marvel turned and looked at Angell. 'Get my sergeant for me. Now!'

He looked back at the scared-looking old woman. 'What's your name?'

'Mrs Betty Tithecott,' she answered tremulously.

'Here, leave her alone,' said Trinny next door.

Marvel ignored Trinny and softened his tone, but still held the squirming hand in his. 'I just need to have a look at your hand, all right, Betty? I'm not going to hurt you.'

She met his eyes and nodded. Her hand relaxed.

'This mark,' he said. 'What have you touched?'

'Nothing,' said Betty, her eyes watery and confused.

There was a similar, smaller stain inside her thumb.

Lynne Twitchett approached a little nervously. 'Is something wrong?'

'No,' said Marvel curtly and heard Reynolds hurrying into the room.

'What's up, sir?'

Marvel turned the hand up so Reynolds could see it, and was gratified to hear a surprised expletive. He rubbed his thumb across the smudge and a small amount of colour transferred itself. Whatever Betty had touched, she had touched it recently.

'She says she hasn't touched anything. Look around, will you?'

Reynolds did, checking the arms of the wing chair, the head-rest, the handles of a Zimmer which was on standby for take-off a few feet away.

'Can you hold your hand up for me, Betty?'

She nodded and he let go of her wrist.

Everyone in the room was watching them now. Behind him Marvel could hear a hum of low mutterings: '*What's going on?*' . . . '*What's he doing to Betty?*' . . . '*Where are the biscuits?*'

Betty shifted in her seat, careful not to move her hand much, and Marvel saw her walking stick hooked over the arm of her chair, right near the back where it would be out of the way.

He looked around for something to pick it up with and started to lift the rug off Betty's knees. Her smudged hand clapped down to her lap to keep her rug and her modesty in place, so instead he yanked his own tie off and used it carefully to pick up the stick.

'Reynolds.'

Reynolds came over and Marvel held the walking stick up to the light. It was made of stout wood, the handle of tooled brass – stained brownish-red.

And near the end was a small but unmistakable clump of white hair.

He had his murder weapon.

He had his suspect.

Marvel thought of the line from 'Amazing Grace'.

I once was lost, but now I'm found.

That was him. Lost, then found. Dark, then light. Drunk, then sober. The moment he saw those strands of white stuck to the end of the cane, Marvel knew he didn't have to drink any more. He *would*, but he didn't *have* to. Not on this case, at least.

It had been getting out of hand anyway. Last night

he and Joy had had a barney because she'd got all maudlin about Something with an R and, instead of sympathizing, he'd asked if she had any ice. She'd thrown a glass at him and he'd said something mean about Dubonnet . . .

What the hell was he doing getting into an argument with some lonely old drunk over ice and Dubonnet? He should have his head examined.

Lost and found.

As long as things progressed in that order, Marvel felt he was doing a reasonable job with his life.

All day long, while he clambered over debris and peered through shed windows on the off-chance of finding Gary Liss, Jonas worried about the notes.

The first had been oblique: *Call yourself a policeman?*

The second had been personal: *Do your job, crybaby.*

The third – in the wake of a triple murder – could no longer be seen as anything but a warning: *If you won't do your job, then I'll do it for you.*

But he *was* doing his job! This time the killer was wrong! He'd started his night patrols, and now he was properly part of the investigation by day, too. They even had a suspect lined up. How could the killer – or anyone – accuse him of no longer doing his job?

But the threatening tone of this note was unmistakable, and Jonas knew he could no longer hide behind previous ambiguity.

The time had come to speak to Marvel.

*

The killer couldn't keep hiding for ever. Things were closing in. Things were catching up with him. Memories pressed against the ceiling of his subconscious like desperate sailors in the hold of a doomed ship.

He was no longer sure he could hold it all together. Some part of him had once imagined some connection with the policeman/protector; there had been times when he had wondered if they might one day be on the same team. Work side by side.

But Jonas was still stubbornly ineffective where it really mattered.

The bodies were piling up.

The wrong people were dying and it just wasn't *fair*. It just wasn't *right*.

Something had to give.

*

Elizabeth Rice called Marvel – ostensibly to say she hadn't yet had an opportunity to compare the Polaroid of the shoe-print with all the shoes in the Marshes' house, but really to find out what was going on at Sunset Lodge.

Marvel told her not to bother. They had a suspect.

'Does that mean I can join you up there?'

'No,' said Marvel. 'Stay put for a bit. Might need

you to break the news of an arrest to the Marshes.'

'OK. Good,' said Rice, although she felt like throwing something in frustration.

Preferably at Marvel.

When Jonas arrived, the residents of Sunset Lodge had just started to make their arduous journeys from the garden room to the dining room for supper.

Although it was dark already, the room was as hot as ever, and smelled of sweet decay under hairspray and talcum powder. After the bitter outdoors it was suffocating. He wondered if they ever opened the windows so people could breathe—

The memory hit him like a ghost train . . .

He and Danny Marsh had bought maggots for fishing from Mr Jacoby's shop. In the late summer the stream behind the playing field had sticklebacks and the occasional brown trout, and there were schoolyard rumours of a pike that might – or might not – have eaten Annie Rossiter's missing cat, Wobbles. Jonas did not really buy the Wobbles theory, because why would a cat be in the stream in the first place? But he *did* fantasize about catching a pike. Or a trout.

A stickleback would do, to be honest.

So he and Danny had bought a pot of maggots. A little white polystyrene cup with a not-quite-clear plastic lid, which had to be lifted to see the fat white worms properly. Mr Jacoby took them from the fridge – from a shelf alongside the cans of Coke and

Dandelion & Burdock, which Jonas could never quite make up his mind whether he liked or not.

Jonas was stunned that he could recall such details. He even remembered now that the maggots had cost 55p and that Danny had paid because he'd owed Jonas for a comic.

They'd only had one rod between them – Jonas's little starter rod which had come in a blister-pack last Christmas, with its fixed-spool reel already loaded with line and permanently attached between the cork grips, along with two red-and-white ball floats and a bag of small, unambitious hooks.

They'd fished for one long, hot day, eating cheese-and-pickle rolls and taking turns to hold the rod for when The Big One bit.

By the time dusk fell and they went home empty-handed, they had only used maybe twenty of the hundred or so maggots, most of which had simply wriggled off the hook and made a break for it, or had been discarded for becoming waterlogged, limp and – the boys agreed – unattractive to fish.

Probably because the rod was his, when they parted ways Jonas had taken the remaining maggots home with him and put them in the fridge for the next day.

They'd never gone fishing again.

Other stuff had happened.

The little white pot had first been hidden behind the jam and then pushed to the back of the fridge by yesterday's spaghetti Bolognese.

And it was only weeks later, when his mother complained that that fridge – which was only four years old – was making a strange buzzing noise, that Jonas had remembered . . .

Through the cloudy lid of the pot, Jonas had seen that the pale maggots had been replaced by something amorphous, black and expansive, which now filled the pot so comprehensively that he could see darker patches under the plastic lid where *things* were actually pressing up against it. The whole pot vibrated in his nervous hand with a low, menacing buzz – and it was with a sick shock that Jonas realized that the small maggots had slowly turned to much bigger flies that were now squeezed together so tightly in the pot that they seemed to be one angry entity.

Angry at *him*.

He'd wanted to let them go. He was a good-hearted boy who loved animals. And flies were animals – of a sort. The thought of them inside the pot – packed so close that their wet wings could not even unfurl, while their neighbours ate them and vomited on them and ate them again – made him feel ill.

But they were angry at *him*. He could feel it in the vibrating fury running up his arm as he held the pot in his hand.

He had thrown it away without removing the lid. And until the bin men came three days later, Jonas could hear the angry thrum of the flies leading their short, trapped, nightmarish lives.

Jonas stopped thinking of it. He had to before it made him sick.

Standing at the threshold of the Sunset Lodge garden room, he wiped sweat off his face and *forced* himself to stop remembering . . .

'It smells in here,' he said from the doorway.

Marvel and Reynolds were sitting silently in the two wing chairs closest to the piano and both turned to look at him as he approached. Marvel with his sagging jowls, and Reynolds with his patchwork hair: Jonas thought they both looked quite at home.

'Yes,' said Reynolds. 'It's impending death.'

An old woman so doubled over her walking frame that she looked as if she was searching for a contact lens turned her head like a tortoise and fixed Reynolds with a withering glare.

'We're not all *deaf*, you know!'

Reynolds reddened and mumbled an apology and she continued on her way to the dining room, following the map of the carpet.

'Plonker,' Marvel told him.

'We found a weapon,' said Reynolds. Seeing Jonas's surprised look, he continued, 'Walking stick. He just took it from a bedroom, killed them all, and then put it back.'

'Bloody hell,' said Jonas. 'Prints?'

'The lab's got it now, but I doubt it. Still . . .' Reynolds shrugged. 'Any luck today?'

Marvel snorted sarcastically. 'Yes, Reynolds, he's just playing hard to get.'

'No luck finding Gary,' said Jonas. 'But there's something I need to tell you.'

There. He'd said it now and couldn't back out. He took a deep breath and told them about the notes. He was deliberately vague about the content. He told them that the first had said 'something about the police not protecting Margaret Priddy' and the second had told him 'Do your job.' He was too ashamed to tell them about the 'crybaby' accusation. He handed the final note to Reynolds inside a plastic freezer bag he'd taken from the kitchen drawer.

He'd expected Marvel to be annoyed that he'd said nothing before now. He'd expected him to tear a strip off him. What he hadn't expected was that the over-weight, over-the-hill DCI would listen all the way through with a stony face – and then come out of his wing chair like Swamp Thing and knock him backwards into the piano with a clanging post-modernist crash. One second Jonas was telling his story, the next he was half sitting on the keys as Marvel jammed fistfuls of his shirt up under his chin, trembling with rage and shouting angry things that Jonas couldn't quite comprehend. Behind Marvel, Reynolds was trying to pull his boss off, and behind *him*, Jonas was aware of a gaggle of old folk clutching each other's forearms as the three of them wrestled on and around the piano. Jonas staggered as the instrument rolled sideways under the weight of the discord. He could have shoved Marvel off him easily enough, but he was his senior officer. Plus, he understood the man's frustration, and couldn't muster the necessary affront to get really strong with him. Even as Marvel jabbed his knuckles into his throat, some part of Jonas was thinking, 'I deserve this.'

Staff rushed in, shouting and demanding a halt, but it was only when Mrs Betty Tithecott started a high, papery screaming and began pointing that they finally ended the shoving match and looked around, dishevelled and breathless.

Half wrapped in thick cloth – and stuffed between the now-displaced piano and the low wall of the garden room – was the body of Gary Liss.

*

Marvel was falling apart.

Reynolds had always known he would, but now that it was actually happening, the experience was more disconcerting than he'd expected it to be.

Even before their prime suspect had been found wrapped up like cod and chips and stuffed behind a piano, Marvel had been on a slippery slope. He'd seen Marvel's hands shaking while they examined the Sunset Lodge bodies and bedrooms. Then there'd been the crying at the press conference. Reynolds had seen the shine in his eyes, and the light had had nothing to do with it.

And losing it with Jonas Holly like something out of *The Sweeney*.

It wasn't shock and it wasn't because Marvel cared so much.

He knew Marvel was off the wagon. Even though it was a wagon he'd only ever been hitched to, never really *on*. It didn't take a genius to work it out when Marvel emerged from his cottage every morning smelling of booze and mint and covered in cat hair. Although if it *had* taken a genius, Reynolds liked to think he'd have been up to the task.

In Reynolds's opinion – which was far from humble – Marvel had made some damaging decisions in this investigation.

Prime among these was his move from the occasional pint after work to the harder liquor when he was alone. Or with Joy Springer because, in Reynolds's view, that was only being alone with somebody else in the room.

Another was his failure to use Jonas Holly.

In their business they relied on local plods like Jonas, and he and Marvel had done so in several investigations over the past year. Of course, Marvel always liked to show the locals right up front who was going to be boss. Rude, bullying, bulldozing – those were apparently Marvel's guidelines for what he sarcastically called 'First Contact', as if local beat officers were some alien race whose sole purpose was to be subdued and bent to his will.

Something must have happened *off-screen*, as they said in the movies. One day Marvel had been merely rude to Jonas, the next Jonas was standing on a doorstep like an oversized garden gnome. If Marvel had employed a ducking stool he could hardly have humiliated the man more effectively.

Reynolds felt Jonas's pain. Two cases back Marvel had been such a shit – and Reynolds had had to do so much damage control among the local constabulary – that his precious hair had fallen out in handfuls. Every night he had watched it swirling down the shower drain along with his self-esteem. He remembered vividly the rush of pure fury that had overtaken him as he watched it disappear. How he'd vowed to get revenge on Marvel, like some mythic hero in a Sergio Leone film.

Good old Sergio – he knew a dish served cold when he saw one.

And the dish Reynolds was preparing for Marvel was very cold indeed.

*

Jonas told Lucy about the notes. Now that he'd told Marvel he knew she'd hear about them sooner or later, and when she asked about the cut on his lip the moment he walked into the room, he couldn't think of anything fast enough to divert her from the truth of what had happened and why. The only thing he didn't say was that he had found the last note on their garden gate. He told her that one had also been under the wiper of the Land Rover. It was a small distinction, but Lucy was alone all day, and unwell; the last thing he needed was for her to feel even more nervous about the murders.

Everything he'd feared the notes might do to her, they did.

He saw the fear flash across her face, and then her concern was all for him, and Jonas watched miserably as the two emotions etched lines in her face that he'd never seen before. Jonas promised her he would be careful, promised not to take any risks – but those lines were there to stay.

Finally he told her that he'd informed Marvel – more to reassure her that he had police back-up than anything else.

'What did he say?' she demanded – at the same moment that Jonas realized he should have kept his mouth shut.

He was a lousy liar, so he told her the truth.

She was furious. He had to take the phone away from her to stop her calling 999.

'It was an *assault*!' she yelled.

'It was just a bit of shoving. It was a disagreement, that's all.'

Lucy shot him a fiery look that he hadn't seen for

ages. It reminded him of her soccer days, and he smiled, which only made her more furious.

'It's not *funny*, Jonas!'

'No, it's not,' he agreed hastily. 'You're right.'

She gave him a circumspect stare that meant she knew he was placating her, but then allowed herself to feel a little placated anyway; she didn't have the strength left to keep being angry.

'I'd like to kick his arse,' she told him seriously.

'Me too,' he sighed.

They were on the couch, he with his long legs stretched out and his big feet on an old tapestry footstool that showed the wear of his father before him, Lucy facing him with her back against the padded leather arm. Now she wiggled her toes under his thigh for added warmth, and he knew he was forgiven. For a minute they watched Tom Hanks having a mental breakdown on a desert island.

'This is a bit cheerful for you, isn't it, sweetheart?'

Lucy stuck out her tongue and dug her toes into him.

'What job does he mean?'

'What?'

'In the notes he keeps going on about doing your *job*. What does it mean?'

He frowned and shrugged one shoulder. 'Finding the killer, I suppose.'

Lucy nodded slowly, but Jonas could hear her brain ticking over from where he sat.

'But you're already doing that.'

'Maybe he thinks I should be doing more.'

'Maybe,' she agreed tentatively, while Tom Hanks's skin blistered off his face in the white-hot sun.

'Or maybe,' she shrugged, 'that's not the *job* he wants you to do.'

*

The day had passed in a blur for John Marvel.

Another body bag. Another crime scene. More hysterical crones. The decision to move all the residents after all, and the logistics of making that happen in a snowstorm while all roads out of the village were impassable by anything but a tractor or a four-wheel-drive.

Now – back in his little apartment with his inadequate travel kettle taking a week to boil – Marvel sat slumped and glum at the end of his bed.

So Gary Liss was a petty thief, but not a killer.

No doubt he had not been the intended target, but he'd probably been murdered for interrupting the killer – and then stuffed behind the garden-room piano like a surprise Christmas present. The thick old pile of heavy maroon curtaining had been wadded down the back of the piano for years, Rupert Cooke told them, white-faced with shock. He said it acted as a damper so the sound wasn't too loud for the residents.

In Marvel's brief experience with the residents, no sound could be loud *enough* for them.

But what it meant was that the killer had known about the curtains and therefore *must* be local. Not that that narrowed things down a lot – he imagined everyone in Shipcott had had a relative or friend at Sunset Lodge at some point in the past few years.

The killer had also dragged or carried Liss downstairs – close to the staffroom where the two women were – and had taken the time to wrap him up and hide him behind the piano. It spoke of great strength and it spoke of calmness, not panic. The killer had been interrupted, certainly – but he had also adapted to that interruption so brutally and so efficiently that Lynne Twitchett and Jen Hardy had never heard a sound from Liss.

This latest crime scene was now one that had been ravaged by heat and constant human traffic for the near forty-eight hours since the victim had died. No wonder the place had started to smell. If he hadn't spent so much time there he'd have noticed it himself. And they didn't even know yet *where* Gary Liss had been killed. Blood on the body was minimal – a single crusty smear over a depression fracture of the front of the skull, and smears on the throat where it looked as if he'd been manually strangled.

Yet another modus operandi . . .

I once was found, but now am lost.

Marvel sighed and put a tea bag into a mug, hoping

that if he took the lead, the kettle might catch up.

His phone rang; it was Jos Reeves on a scratchy line. There were no prints on the walking stick, and the blood on the roof belonged not to the killer but to Lionel Chard, so it added nothing to their well of knowledge.

Marvel was so annoyed by the crappy news that he yelled, 'I can't hear you!' and hung up on Reeves mid-sentence.

So it was back to square one. Only with more dead people.

Great.

Alan Marsh? Danny Marsh? Peter fucking Priddy? Marvel felt like having a tantrum. He'd 'liked' Peter Priddy so much; liked the hunchy feeling that he was *the one* – but now Peter Priddy felt like a best friend at school, whose name he barely remembered.

He switched off the kettle and opened a bottle of Jameson's instead. It would help him think; it always had and always would. That was what Debbie had never understood. *You're sick*, she'd told him once. *You get drunk and lie around and think about murder. It's sick!*

He'd come close to hitting her.

Marvel knocked back the first two fingers and went for a slightly larger chaser, which he sipped more slowly while watching *Newsnight* with the sound down; it was better that way.

This case was already like musical chairs, and then Jonas Holly comes out with a critical piece of evidence he'd been hoarding like a fucking *hamster* while they were all chasing their own arses.

Just the thought of it sent Marvel's blood pressure up again.

It amounted to withholding evidence in a murder investigation, and as soon as this case was over and Jonas Holly had outlived any modicum of usefulness, Marvel would file a complaint against him. Fuck the paperwork. Get the moron off the streets for good and stuck behind a desk up in Taunton, answering 999 calls for *real* cops.

Marvel had no compunction about it. Jonas had screwed up badly – and it wasn't the first time. He'd potentially contaminated the first scene by pawing the vic, and allowing others to do the same. He'd moved the second body, and although that hadn't really been his fault, Marvel was sore enough now to overlook that. The vomit had disappeared on Jonas Holly's watch and then he'd shown an unexpected lack of control when he'd laid into Danny Marsh, who'd really only needed one good smack to jolt him out of his hysteria.

And he'd kept the notes secret when they were probably the best clue they now had to the identity of the killer.

Of course, he'd also scared Marvel at Margaret Priddy's house, but he wasn't taking that into consideration.

He was pretty sure he wasn't.

Killers were a strange bunch. Some returned to the scene of the crime. Some took trophies and photos and kept detailed cuttings. Some tried to get involved with the investigation; tried to 'help' the police. Some *were* the police.

Now he had mentally laid out all Jonas Holly's transgressions in a neat chronological list, Marvel was surprised by how much involvement he seemed to have had in this case, considering he'd spent most of it on a bloody doorstep.

The more he thought about those transgressions, the less they looked like incompetence and the more they looked like a deliberate attempt to mislead.

And the more deliberate they looked, the more suspicious Marvel became, until finally – half a bottle in – DCI John Marvel started to like Jonas Holly.

But not in a good way.

Four Days

'You think we should pull Danny Marsh in?'

Reynolds broached the subject carefully because Marvel was only really receptive to his own ideas.

Marvel stared at him across the Calor gas, with eyes rimmed red from drink and lack of sleep.

Reynolds proceeded: 'We've got the gloves in the garage and we've got the footprint on the window sill. You think that's enough?'

Marvel continued to stare at him until Reynolds wondered if he'd had a stroke.

Finally Marvel stirred. 'It's not much.'

'It's more than we've got on anyone else now.'

Marvel nodded slowly. 'Let's talk to his father first.'

Reynolds nodded in relief and picked up the phone.

*

Jonas needed help.

He stood at the edge of the playing field and thought about the nature of evil.

The scenes he had witnessed at Sunset Lodge would never leave him. Margaret Priddy was sad, Yvonne Marsh was dramatic and pathetic. But the sheer cold brutality of the murders at the Lodge was something he couldn't quite get a hold of. The slaughter of the old people, defenceless in their beds, the cool killing of Gary Liss, and the bravado of the body behind the piano.

Jonas's brain skittered about the crime, peered around corners at it, ducked and dived, trying to get a better look, but ultimately was lost in the supermarket when it came to any kind of understanding of what it must take for a man to grow into a cold-blooded killer. He had spent most of a sleepless night running up and down the aisles of *why?* and it was only as he'd walked down the hill into the village that he had realized the only question he really needed to buy was *who?*

Without the killer in custody, he could theorize till the cows came home and never find the truth.

Jonas was convinced now that the killer was a local man. He had known that Margaret Priddy lay paralysed in the back bedroom of her home, he had left Yvonne Marsh in a stream that was barely visible from the road, and he had crawled through the only window at Sunset Lodge that Rupert Cooke had been too cheap to modernize, then bound Gary Liss's corpse in a vast curtain which had been there for years but which was hardly visible, stuffed behind the piano as it was. Jonas vaguely remembered having seen it before – probably because Sunset Lodge was a regular part of his beat, along with schools, pubs and village halls.

The killer must be local, which meant Jonas must know him. He knew everybody.

What would he look like?

If Jonas could stare into enough eyes for long enough, would he glimpse the killer looking back? Would his gaze burn like Holy Water on a demon? Would Jonas feel cold jelly fill his bones, and recoil in recognition of evil?

He didn't know.

How could he? He had no experience.

So he needed help.

A rhythmic sound and a pendulum blur in his vision brought him slowly back to the playing field and reminded him of why he had stopped here on his way to the mobile unit to report for whatever duty Marvel saw fit to assign him.

On the half-pipe ramp, Steven Lamb swooped through lazy arcs, turning smoothly at each lip, accompanied only by the hypnotic rumble of the skateboard's wheels. He had cleared the snow from the ramp with a rusted spade, which now stood upright in the resulting lumpy pile of white, with Steven's anorak slung over it.

Jonas walked across the crunchy snow, wondering whether he was following in the footsteps of the killer. Today was overcast and promised more snow – very different from the shiny morning that had greeted the horror of Yvonne Marsh.

He stopped six feet from the ramp and said, 'Hi.'

'Hi,' said Steven, his eyes always fixed on the next lip, the next turn, the next swoop. His face was serene with the rhythm of it all.

Jonas watched the boy swing back and forth with complete grace – the slight bend of the knees before each ascent the only visible effort in near-perpetual motion.

He wished he didn't have to do this.

'How are you?' he asked.

'Fine, thanks,' said Steven.

'Just thought I'd ask. After the other day.' He thought again of Steven sinking to the ground beside the stream, his dark eyes huge in his white face.

Steven rolled to the lip of the pipe, was suspended there for a brief moment, straight-legged, defying gravity . . . and then flicked his board round and passed Jonas going the other way. Jonas noticed that his mouth had tightened, and that the lack of eye contact now looked more like avoidance.

'I know what happened to you, Steven,' he said quietly.

Although he'd never given any indication of it, Jonas knew that four years earlier, while trying to find the body of his missing Uncle Billy, Steven Lamb had almost died at the hands of a serial killer.

The boy didn't make the turn this time. He let his board carry him backwards down the ramp and halfway up the opposite side, before slowly putting a foot down and pushing off once more.

'Can we talk about it?'

Steven said nothing, his eyes fixed on the ramp, on the lip – but a new vertical frown-line had appeared between his brows.

'I need your help.'

Steven continued to skate, but his rhythm had gone. The skateboard barely reached the lip – or overshot and made him teeter – and his arms were working now instead of hanging loosely at his sides.

'I need to know . . .' started Jonas. 'I need to know what to look for. I need to know what you see in the eyes of a killer.'

The skateboard clattered noisily and flipped over as Steven stepped off it and took a few faltering steps to stop himself falling. It slid back down the ramp towards him. He bent and picked it up angrily, and headed for his spade and anorak.

'Nothing,' he said, not looking at Jonas. He tugged the spade free of the snow, and slung it over his shoulder, yanking his anorak off the handle as he did so. Every jerky angle of his body screamed at Jonas that he wanted to be left alone.

But Jonas couldn't leave him alone. He spoke

urgently to the boy. 'I know you don't want to remember it, Steven. I *hate* to ask you, believe me. But I *have* to know. Before he kills again, I *have to know*. Please!'

Steven made to go around him, and Jonas put out a hand to halt him, but the boy stopped before he could be touched. He looked away from Jonas, his chest heaving and his cheeks high with colour.

'Nothing!' he said with low vehemence. 'You see *nothing.*'

*

Marvel and Reynolds sat side by side on a velveteen sofa so small that their thighs touched. Alan Marsh sat opposite in a matching easy chair.

Reynolds looked around the room.

The mantel held four or five sympathy cards and a couple of Christmas ones between family photos and a repeating motif of snub-nosed ceramic Dickensian boys, doing boy-stuff like whistling jauntily or selling newspapers. On the table there were more cards – opened but left in a pile. There was also an old photograph of Yvonne Marsh propped against a jumbled pile of clean laundry, like some kind of shrine to the memory of housework.

'So what was that all about the other day with Danny and Jonas Holly?' said Marvel, jerking his thumb randomly at the ugly striped wallpaper behind him.

Alan Marsh sighed and opened his hands in a 'beats me' gesture.

Elizabeth Rice had taken Danny Marsh to the pub. It wasn't difficult – she'd told them he had a little crush on her and she'd promised to buy.

Marvel said nothing further, allowing the aching silence slowly to reveal to Alan Marsh that this was not a social call.

'Well . . .' the man started haltingly, then stopped. He was in overalls even though Rice had reported that he wasn't working. Apparently the habit was just too much to break while his mind was already distracted by the murder of his wife. He was wearing slippers rather than steel toe-caps though, Reynolds noticed – as if he'd remembered halfway through dressing that his wife was dead and he wasn't going to work after all.

Reynolds sighed and wondered why Marvel was going all round the houses before asking more relevant questions about Danny. It wasn't like him.

He wished he couldn't feel Marvel's hip against his.

'Them used to be friends. When 'em were nippers. Dunno what happened there . . .'

He trailed off again.

Marvel realized he was going to have to tweeze information out of Alan Marsh like splinters. It was a job he hated. He preferred blunter tools.

'How old were they then?'

''Bout ten, I suppose.'

'Were they very close?'

'What do you mean?'

'I mean, were they best friends?'

'I don't know,' said Alan a little dismissively. 'I was working mostly. Yvonne would know that.'

Yeah, *but she's dead*, Marvel felt like pointing out, but didn't. He could be pretty sensitive when he tried.

'Would they play here much?'

Again Alan Marsh made an all-purpose gesture of 'who knows?' 'It was a long time back,' he said. 'Seemed like it. Why do you want to know, anyway?'

Marvel hadn't expected the question and was annoyed that he hadn't anticipated it. He blustered a little. 'We're always concerned when a serving officer gets into a public brawl, Mr Marsh. Aren't you?'

The man shrugged. 'Danny was mazed. *And* he took the first swing.'

That was the countryside for you, Marvel supposed. In town, Jonas Holly would already have been suspended and have a lawsuit pending. Here the victim's own *father* thought he deserved a good beating by the police.

Refreshing.

Reynolds sighed again and Marvel glared at him before turning back to Alan Marsh, who looked disinterested in life itself, let alone this particular conversation.

'Have you ever seen Officer Holly behave in that way before, Mr Marsh?'

'No, but I seen *Danny* behave like that plenty!'

'Well, he's just lost his mother in tragic circumstances.'

'Bollocks to that,' said Marsh. 'Just the way he is. Has been for years.'

Marvel was surprised and looked it, so Alan Marsh went on.

'He'd bin under the doctor sometimes. Psychiatrist. You know.'

Marvel did know. His nose for motive started to quiver.

'What's wrong with him, Mr Marsh?'

'Not much. Just a bit here and there, you know. Not *dangerous* or nothing like that. Just a bit down sometimes, that's all.'

'Depressed?'

'I suppose so. A bit down.'

'Has he ever been hospitalized for depression or something like that?'

'Oh, no,' said Alan Marsh definitely. 'He's not a *nutter*, see? Just a bit up and then a bit down.'

'Manic depressive,' suggested Reynolds, who thought he'd have to get up and leave if Alan Marsh said 'a bit down' one more time.

'If that's what you call it.'

'Always?'

'Not always,' said Alan Marsh, looking as if he was thinking about it for the first time. 'Since he were about twelve or thirteen. About then.'

'And that's about the time he and Jonas fell out?' said Marvel, back on track.

'Suppose so.'

'Can you think of any specific reason?' said Marvel, without one single ounce of hope that Alan Marsh would.

'No.'

Of course he couldn't. That would be too bloody easy.

They left.

'What's this interest in Jonas, sir?'

Marvel clamped his teeth together. Trust Reynolds to leap to the right conclusion.

He thought his left little toe was getting damp – just on the short walk to the car! He'd have to throw these shoes away. Beyond the village the snow was a Christmassy white blanket. Here it was just ridges of icy slush and running water. Wherever they went, whatever they did, they were accompanied by the gurgling of drains working overtime. At night it all froze again and made every step a hazard. Damn the doglegs that kept him from wellingtons and dry feet.

'He bothers me.'

Reynolds smiled. 'We like *him* now, do we, sir?'

Up until that very second, Marvel had only had a suspicion. A hunch. An intuitive feeling that all was not *quite right* with Jonas Holly.

But the moment Reynolds said *that* – in that

amused, condescending tone – Marvel decided that he really *did* like Holly after all. Liked him a *lot*.

And that he was *right*.

And that he would do almost *anything* to prove Reynolds wrong.

*

It was over.

Danny Marsh knew it.

He'd known it the moment he'd run across the playing fields behind his father and seen his mother lying in the frost like a downed footballer waiting for a magic sponge or a stretcher.

Danny had known it was the beginning of the end for him; that he would never make it alone.

His mother had known him. One of only two people who did.

For years she had let him know – by her look, by her touch, by the stories she pointed out casually in newspapers – that she knew, and even understood. And although they'd never discussed it properly, knowing that had helped.

Boy, 15, Admits School Arson in Exam Dodge.

Choirboy Stabbed Paedo Priest 26 Times.

Murdered Pervert Preyed on Own Children!

She would toss down the newspaper beside him on the table and mutter darkly, 'Got what *he* deserved!' or 'Poor boy. If only he'd told someone.'

Danny would say nothing. He had nothing he cared to tell. Just knowing she still loved him was enough. All through the bitter tears, the dark-tempered years and the razor-blade at the wrist, she loved him. While others started to walk away from him in the school-yard, stopped passing him the ball, whispered as he left a room . . . Through all that, Yvonne Marsh had loved him like a big anchor on a small boat in a wild sea.

And then she'd started to just . . . forget.

Forget that she loved him.

Forget that they shared a secret.

Forget even that she was his mother and he was her son.

It happened slowly and in patches, but it happened. And Danny found that *he* was supposed to be the anchor now. Dressing her, feeding her, watching her, locking her in, following her out, fetching her back . . .

A boat is not an anchor. Yvonne Marsh was deep beneath the waves with a broken rope that swayed with the tides. Sometimes he could grasp that rope and feel the old tug of her. But, mostly, once his mother's mind was lost at sea, Danny Marsh was set adrift.

Even Jonas had let go of the line that had tethered him to the rest of the world.

Now, as Danny sat in the little room where he had grown up – where the back of the door still showed a faded poster of Uma Thurman in *Pulp Fiction* – he thought about Jonas Holly.

Instead of a secret strengthening their bond, Jonas had been the first to withdraw.

No more fishing, no more crazy dares, no more galloping about the moors. Once, when Jonas had brought an injured baby rabbit to school in a shoebox, he'd looked wary and turned away so that Danny couldn't stroke it the way all the other kids had.

When Danny had finally summoned up the guts to ask him what was wrong – even though he *knew* – Jonas had bitten his lip and tried to go around him. Jonas was smaller then, younger by almost a year, and Danny had stopped him with a hand in his chest. Jonas had knocked the hand away, and before Danny realized it, they were fighting. A proper fight. Not some spat over a penalty kick or a broken Tamagotchi – a fight with bruises and blood and kicking and gouging, which went on long enough for teachers to be summoned and then to arrive. Even after Mr Yates the PE teacher had yanked them apart, they had both tried their hardest to lash out with their feet, and Jonas had pulled a handful of change from the pocket of his grey flannels and hurled it at Danny.

Nothing had ever hurt him so much. Not then, at least. Not until the day his demented mother had screamed in terror and threatened to call the police if he didn't get out of her house.

He could still feel the coin slicing his brow and the feeling of shock and the sheer *unfairness* of it all. He knew he'd done the right thing. Even if it had been in the wrong way. It wasn't his fault it had all got fucked up. Why couldn't Jonas see it like that?

Danny sighed and got up now and looked in the cracked mirror of the wardrobe. The scar was still there above his left eye.

Danny wondered if Jonas still remembered *that*, at least. He always acted like he didn't remember *anything*, but surely the scar would remind him of *that*? Remind him of being friends, and of what that really meant. It wasn't just for good times, it was for bad times too. It was about sticking together and sacrifice. It was about doing something for somebody and expecting nothing in return.

Except maybe gratitude.

Danny Marsh stared into the mirror and watched his face fight tears. Despite her inconstant love, losing his mother was like losing the last part of himself that was a blameless boy. There was nobody else in the world he could turn to now. Not even his father, who could not be expected to catch up with reality so late in life.

And Jonas Holly – who owed him *everything* – had never even thanked him.

*

Jonas gave Lucy her stuff. He'd got better at it over the years, but it was never routine to finish the washing up and then plunge needles into your wife's hip.

The little bruises never faded, just went brown and got covered up by new ones.

He looked down at her now, lying curled on her side with her bruised backside exposed, and could hardly bear her vulnerability. He wished Dr Wickramsinghe could be here, wished he could feel what *he* felt when he looked down at Lucy, wished he could feel the fear that simmered inside him that he never dared show.

She raised her head and looked round at him, a gentle smile on her lips.

'Stop looking at my bum, pervert!'

Jonas smiled. He pulled her pyjamas back up her hip, then slid on to the couch behind her, tucking his long legs against hers, tugging her tummy towards him so they were touching everywhere. She covered his hand with hers and he buried his nose in the back of her neck. She smelled like fresh laundry.

'Are you still going out?' she said softly.

Jonas froze. Why was she asking? Was she planning something? He experienced a moment of pure panic as his memory of *that day* crashed through his brain like a breaker in a rockpool. Her half-open eyes and her cold, cold hands, and the lifetime it took for the ambulance to come, while all the time he sat on the floor behind the front door and begged her not to leave him. The memory was so strong that he felt his stomach flip-flop in fear and tears burn his eyes.

He cleared his throat and made a huge effort to sound normal. 'I don't have to go.'

'I don't mind,' she said, squeezing the back of his hand.

It sounded like the truth, but who could be sure?

They lay like that for a while and he knew that they were thinking different things in different ways and that a universe separated their minds even while their bodies shared heat.

'I love you,' he whispered, so low that if his lips hadn't been against her ear she would never have heard him.

She paused almost imperceptibly, then said, 'I love you too.'

*

It had snowed and stopped again during the afternoon, leaving just a couple of inches on the ground. The moon was getting big and the fields looked ice blue under its gaze, but in the village itself the snow had been trampled to slush which had then frozen in the dropping night temperature, making for treacherous conditions.

Jonas walked carefully up the street, past the pub and the church and Mr Jacoby's shop to the school, without seeing anyone.

On the way back he stopped at the shop and looked in the window at the little cards stuck there advertising free kittens and bikes for sale. They made him think of the note that had been left under his wiper, and once again he got that unpleasant feeling of being watched. He turned but saw no one. Then, feeling slightly foolish, he backed into the alleyway beside the shop, where he could not be seen. From there he looked at the houses opposite.

Straight across the road was the Marsh home – a little two up, two down, which he knew was pale green but which looked merely grubby in the orange light of the streetlamps.

There was a light on behind the curtains in Danny's bedroom – or what used to be Danny's bedroom when they were boys; Jonas thought it probably still was. Next door to that was Angela Stirk's house, where Jonas knew Peter Priddy spent every Saturday night that her husband was away. Jonas guessed it was one of her neighbours who had split on him to Marvel, sick of the noise. On the other side of the Marshes was the home of Ted Randall, who grew giant vegetables for the county show, then the Peters' house, to which Billy Peters had never returned and where Steven Lamb lived now like a replacement . . . Jonas realized he could travel right down the street with his eyes, naming the residents of each little home, knowing their stories, keeping their secrets.

He saw Neil Randall limping his way home from the pub on the opposite pavement. He wondered what it was like to wake up in the sand and see your leg beside your head, which is what he'd heard had happened to Neil. How curious. How strange. How much easier to tie your shoelaces. Jonas smiled, and felt guilty.

He looked back up the street, but all was calm.

'*Shit!*'

The word was accompanied by a scrape and a thud, and Jonas looked across the road to see Neil on his back in the gutter between two parked cars. He hurried over.

'All right, Neil?' said Jonas, offering his hand.

Neil looked at it, then ignored it and tried to sit up by himself. Jonas withdrew his hand and let him struggle. The smell of booze came off him in waves, over an undertow of profanity.

Jonas remembered Neil Randall at school. He had been a star on the football field – quick on his feet and tough in a tackle. That was with two legs, of course.

'Fuck,' said Neil, and Jonas became aware that he was groping at his own thigh. He looked down and saw that Neil's right leg had grown about a foot longer than the left. For a second his brain couldn't adjust to the anomaly – then he realized that Neil Randall's prosthetic limb had come loose and was slowly working its way out of his trouser leg. By the orange light of the streetlamp he could see the edge of a thick sock and the start of a shiny plastic shin.

Jonas bent and started to try to push it back up, but it just bunched Neil's jeans at the empty hip.

'No'tha'way!' slurred Neil, shoving his hands off. 'Take it off.'

Feeling surreal, Jonas pulled carefully on the

slush-covered boot. The limb came so far and then stopped, the thigh caught in the narrow leg of Neil Randall's jeans.

'It's stuck,' he informed him.

'What?' said Neil aggressively, as if it was all his fault.

'It's stuck in your jeans, mate. You want me to push it back inside?'

'Get it *off*!' said Neil.

'It's *stuck*,' said Jonas, getting impatient. He was supposed to be on anti-killer patrol, not playing tug-of-war with a fake leg.

'Fuck you, get it *off*!'

Jonas stood up and yanked hard. Neil Randall bumped off the kerb and into the road on his back with the violence of the tug, but his leg stayed in his jeans.

'Watchmefuckin*head*!'

'You want me to pull it off or not?' said Jonas.

'No, leave it. Jus' fucking leave it.'

Jonas let go of the leg and it splashed down in the slush in the road. He thought immediately of Marvel dropping the leg of the dead pony.

It made him brusque enough to walk round behind Neil and grasp him under the arms.

'Leave *off*!'

Jonas ignored him and pulled him back on to the pavement and towards his house, as Neil twisted and flailed. 'Bastard! Ge'yofuckinhands*offme y'bastard!*'

Something hit Jonas hard in the side of the head, making him stagger sideways and fall to one knee, dragging Neil Randall with him. They both grunted at the fall and Jonas's helmet landed in the snow.

Groggily he put one hand down to steady himself and touched his ear with the other, as he looked up and down the street to see who had hit him.

For a second he couldn't grasp what he was seeing.

Then it all became horribly clear.

Suspended above the snow-covered, orange-flavoured street by what looked like a sheet was Danny Marsh. His kicking foot was what had caught Jonas in the ear.

Jonas got up in a dream.

A nightmare.

'Jesus!' said Neil Randall.

One second Jonas was just watching, the next he had Danny's shoes and ankles in his big hands, trying to take his weight, trying to push him upwards and against the cottage wall as he jerked, and someone was shouting, loudly and incoherently, and Jonas knew it was *him* but he had no idea what he was saying because his whole world was a jumble as he held his old friend's feet and tried to keep the pressure off his neck, tried to keep him alive, kept losing his grip . . . as Danny bobbed and writhed in the frozen air.

Jonas saw a yellow light and knew that the door had been opened.

He heard people shouting and rushing towards him.

He was dimly aware of Elizabeth Rice's shouts to get to the bedroom and pull Danny up from there, and the sound of men thudding upstairs.

But before they even made it to the window, the kicks turned to spasms and he felt the hot trickle of piss running up his sleeves – and Jonas Holly knew that Danny Marsh was dead.

They lowered him from the window on his own bed-sheet, recalling a less deadly childhood adventure, and Jonas felt his friend's body pass solidly through his arms, head lolling and knees buckling as his feet touched the pavement.

Jonas knelt beside him in the icy snow and pumped the still-warm chest, and pinched the still-warm nose, and sealed his lips to the lips of the son, just as he had to the mother. All the while Neil Randall watched wide-eyed, propped on his elbows and with one leg six feet long.

Too late. Too late. Too late. The words ticked like a clock, low and calm inside his head, and finally Jonas heard them. And from somewhere, his neglected memory salvaged the fact that the hearing is the last sense to leave the dying consciousness.

He stopped trying to bring Danny back and instead – for the second time tonight – bent so close to a warm ear that he could feel his own breath coming back at him.

'Thank you,' he said.

Then Jonas Holly got slowly to his feet and asked whether someone had called an ambulance.

They had.

He took off his jacket and laid it over Danny Marsh's face and asked people to please step back.

They did.

He watched Alan Marsh come out of his house, saw his eyes roll back and his knees buckle, just as his dead son's had done mere moments before, then Jonas heard the soft crunch as the man's head dropped almost silently into the snow.

*

There was a note.

I did it. I'm not sorry

'What do you know about this?'

Jonas stared dumbly at the note they had found in Danny's room, then slowly shook his head.

'Nothing,' he said.

It was 3am. They were in the mobile unit. The ambulance had taken Danny's body away. Jonas's sleeves were still wet up to the armpits with piss; he could feel it every time he moved and smell it every time he drew breath.

'Bollocks,' said Marvel. 'You knew it was him all along.'

'That's not true!'

It wasn't! Jonas felt panicky that Marvel could even think it! He was an officer of the law and if he was aware of wrong-doing, he would take action – whoever the hell it was doing the wrong.

Apart from Lucy.

Probably.

But that was *all*!

'I don't believe Danny killed anyone.'

'He cracked,' said Marvel. 'Under the pressure from his mother going bananas. Killed Margaret Priddy as a kind of trial run most likely, then his own mother. Then the people up at Sunset Lodge.'

'Why?' said Jonas. 'Why kill *anyone* after he'd killed his mother, if that was the problem?'

'Maybe he passed the tipping point,' said Marvel, pleased that he'd remembered without recourse to Reynolds. 'Maybe once he cracked, the floodgates just opened. We were about to pull him in. The night of the killings at Sunset Lodge, he got out of a window at his house. We've got shoe prints on the sill. Didn't know *that*, did you?'

'No,' said Jonas, and thought of the voice calling his name from the shadows beyond the garden gate that very same night, luring him out into the freezing dark . . .

Jonas!

It had sounded like Danny.

But it had been a dream. Hadn't it?

If you won't do your job . . .

He had no idea what Marvel meant.

. . . then I'll do it for you.

The mobile unit was cramped, damp and smelly. A flickering fluorescent strip made this feel like a Stasi interrogation.

'Sir, even if I believed he killed those people, which I don't, why would I cover it up?'

'You two were mates. I saw you on the playing field after we dragged his mother out of the stream. Good mates, I'd say. If *he* had something to hide, I reckon either you knew about it, or *you*'ve got something to hide too.'

'What?' demanded Jonas. 'What am I hiding?'

From the look on Reynolds's face, he'd only just beaten him to the question. Reynolds looked embarrassed even to be there.

'You tell *me*,' said Marvel, and sat back in his chair with an air of dogged certainty. 'First,' he continued when he got no response, 'first tell me why you hit Danny Marsh the other day.'

'*He* swung at *me*!'

'So arrest him. Don't beat the shit out of him!'

'I think that's a bit of an exaggeration, sir,' said Reynolds, and refused to look at Marvel so he could not be disciplined by a glare.

Jonas barely heard him. He recalled that feeling of

threat that had come off Danny. While he laughed and joked about old times, Jonas had been consumed with fear, desperate for him to back off and *stop* . . . In hindsight it seemed very minor.

'I felt threatened, sir,' he said truthfully. 'If I over-reacted, that's why.'

'Why did you fall out with him?'

Jonas was confused. 'Fall *out*?'

'When you were kids,' Marvel insisted.

'When we were *kids*?' Jonas gave a small laugh.

'Yes,' said Marvel, deadly serious. 'When you were eleven or so.'

Jonas looked blank.

'Ten or eleven. You were best mates. Then one day you weren't. What happened?'

The smell of burned things. Burned wood . . . burned hair . . . burned flesh.

Only confusing fragments.

'I don't remember, sir.'

'Bollocks. You do.'

Jonas shrugged. He didn't. He didn't want to.

He looked around. The cramped unit was dingy and dirty. He didn't think he could work in a place like this. There was a calendar on the wall that was four years out of date. Four years ago, Lu could have walked upstairs on her hands. Four years ago, Jonas was following another path to another place. Four years ago would do him nicely, thank you very much, so he let his mind linger there instead of here, where

Lucy was dying, Danny was dead, and DCI Marvel was being a prick.

'. . . to him? *Holly!*'

Jonas came back, blinking. 'What?'

'What did you say to him?'

'Say to who?'

'Whom,' said Reynolds. 'Sorry.'

They both ignored him.

'To Danny Marsh. When he was dying. Rice says you said something to him.'

'I didn't say anything.'

'Bollocks. Again.'

Marvel pushed his chair away from Jonas and went over to the fridge. He opened it and took out a can of cola. *Generic* cola.

'I think I said, "Thank you."'

'Why?'

Jonas frowned. 'I don't know.'

It was the truth. He had no idea. He'd taken his lips from Danny's mouth and slid them round to his ear without any thought of why or of what he was going to say when he got there. There was just something inside him that had to be said. *Had* to be said. And when he'd said it, it had felt *right*.

Jonas!

The voice at the gate had been Danny Marsh, he was sure.

He'd wanted to talk to him.

Had Danny left him the note?

If so, what was the *job* Danny wanted him to do?

The dead eye of the pony. The prickle of hay against his cheek. The woman's face at the dusty window . . .

Pfffftt! Marvel opened the cola and Jonas came back with a start to find him and Reynolds regarding him with interest.

'He's dead, Holly. You can't protect him. Not if you call yourself a policeman.'

Jonas couldn't breathe.

Call yourself a policeman?

How did he know? How did Marvel *know*? He'd never told him what the first note said!

Jonas sat there, staring wide-eyed at Marvel while his mind screamed at him, *Don't stare! Don't look at him! He'll know that you spotted the slip!* But he couldn't move – even his eyes.

'Get out,' Marvel said. 'I'll speak to you tomorrow.'

*

Lucy Holly was sitting halfway up the stairs when she felt death approaching.

She had known for a while that she was dying. Every new symptom was a reminder of the fact that she wasn't going to just snap out of it one day; that this thing inside her had come to stay and planned to kill her, like a psycho in the spare room. That craziness had become routine.

But she had never felt like this before.

She did not often go up and down stairs during the day. It was a chore that could take half an hour some-times. Jonas had plumbed a toilet into the little shed outside the back door of the old cottage, which she used in all but the coldest weather. But she had woken at 5am to find Jonas was not beside her. Immediately, she knew she would not get back to sleep, so she edged downstairs in the darkness to make tea and to get her book and then decided to take both back to bed with her.

On the bottom step she'd put the luggage for her journey – the cup of tea, her book, a new tube of tooth-paste, and the knife Jonas had made her promise to keep with her, even though she felt like a neurotic New Yorker every time she touched it. The thought of having to answer the door to somebody while holding it filled her with English embarrassment. But she'd promised Jonas, and mostly remembered to carry it from room to room with her, even though she thought there was more chance of falling off her crutches *on to* the knife than there was of it being of any use in repelling an invader.

She'd leaned her downstairs sticks against the ban-isters, lowered herself to the third step and started her little adventure, moving each item up a step before she levered herself on to the next tread. She got into a nice rhythm – almost laughing at how silly it was to feel that way about inching upstairs on your backside. She had good days like this, where her arms and legs felt stronger, and it always made her happy. Ever the competitor, Lucy got faster and faster, moving, hoisting, sipping tea, moving, hoisting, sipping tea . . . until suddenly she slipped, lurching sideways and banging her arm and her head painfully into the wall. She'd put the heel of her hand on *Fate Dictates*, which had skidded off the stair and now lay open and face-down in the hallway.

'*Shit!*' Lucy bit her lip while her funny bone grinningly punished her for being careless. She'd dropped the knife down a few treads too, and knocked her mug so that some tea had dotted the carpet.

Lucy had slipped before; she had fallen before; she had hurt herself worse than she was hurt now.

But *this* time . . . *This* time she understood death.

With the house wrapped in the cocoon of snow that made it quiet as a tomb, Lucy became aware that her own breathing was the only sound that demarcated her *living* from her *dying*.

She held it.

She sat halfway up the stairs and held her breath and let the silence assault her ears.

This was what it would be like.

Underneath the dirt.

Lying still and silent and helpless in a box waiting for nature to worm its way into her so that it could reclaim her for the greater good.

Lucy Holly was not stupid. She understood the cessation of consciousness that comes with death. She understood that if she were aware of anything it would be in a spiritual sense, and that her body was just meat. Meat rotting on young bones.

But this vivid preview was new. This feeling that she was lying in this house with her wedding ring on and a posy on her chest, and that death had finally arrived with the snow and was even now pressed against the windows, testing the chinks made by the mice and the sparrows, trying to slither inside to get at her while she sat halfway up the stairs without even Jonas's knife to protect herself with. This was all new.

Before – before the pills – death had been an abstract notion, a way to be relieved of the pain. The relief of pain had been the goal – and she'd barely thought about the death that would facilitate that. Now she knew she'd turned a corner. She didn't only know it was coming, she knew how it would *feel* when it did. How it would *look*. How it would *taste*.

It was overwhelming. And inconsequential.

She'd thought she would cry, but instead she got calm, calm, calm, as if someone had drugged her tea. She wished they had. She wished suddenly and fiercely that someone had drugged her tea and that she would fall asleep here on the stair that always creaked, and that they would come and kill her softly so she'd never have to bother with the rest of the stairs. They were a struggle and she was sick of them.

Her bum started to ache and she looked at her watch to see she had sat here for more than an hour.

No wonder she was so cold and desperate for the loo.

She would go outside.

Lucy left the toothpaste and the mug of cold tea on the stairs.

She picked up the knife as she slid back down past it and, when she got to the bottom, she closed *Fate Dictates* and never opened it again.

*

Jonas walked home in a daze just before 6am.

He'd felt as if he were floating ever since Danny died in his arms. Like a spacewalking astronaut whose tether has been severed, Jonas felt himself drifting slowly away from everything, and off towards nothing.

How did Marvel know?

Jonas had not been specific about the wording of the first two notes. He hadn't wanted to say the word 'crybaby', so had been fuzzy about the first note too, for the sake of appearing consistent, even if it was only consistently stupid. But Marvel's words had snapped everything back into sharp relief.

Call yourself a policeman.

Why had he said it? *How did he know?*

As sleet started to spit in Jonas's face, his mind turned slow, gravity-free circles around Marvel, looking at him from new angles and with fresh eyes.

Marvel had never liked him. He wasn't sure how,

but he'd managed to piss the man off right from the start of this investigation.

Now he began to wonder why.

Even from his doorstep viewpoint, Jonas had the feeling that Marvel had been lost on the case, that he'd employed a scattergun approach to suspects, that there was no real sense of focus in his investigation.

The way he'd over-reacted to finding Jonas on the doorstep of Margaret Priddy's told of a man who was floundering and insecure, and Jonas had thought he had smelled booze on the man's breath. Or maybe just in his sweat.

When the alleged vomit had disappeared, Marvel had told him to do his *job* – and the way he'd said it, '*crybaby*' was only a whisper away.

And now he'd repeated the first note almost word for word.

Had he seen it?

Had he *written* it?

It sounded stupid, even inside the privacy of his own head, but did Marvel have some kind of *connection* with the killer?

Jonas shuddered at the thought. He had Reynolds's card still in his breast pocket. Would Reynolds be discreet if Jonas voiced his fears to him? He doubted it. Jonas had the impression that Reynolds did not like Marvel that much, but that didn't necessarily mean he'd take sides against him.

He looked up into the sleet to see that he was almost at his gate.

He needed to speak to Lucy. Lucy's brain worked faster than his at the best of times, and right now *his* brain was stuffed so full, and was nonetheless so empty of solutions, that it was as if a super-massive black hole was expanding slowly within his head, ready to burst out and swallow up the whole world in compressed nothingness.

Lucy was on the living-room floor, weeping and gnarled up with pain and with an unopened bottle of pills beside her.

In an instant the black hole in Jonas's head shrank to a pinprick and his heart exploded into his throat with fear.

He dropped to the carpet beside her and tried to gather her into his arms, but she tucked up and resisted.

Her head was hot with tears, but the rest of her was icy from being on the floor. The fire was long burned out and had turned to white ashes. Jonas got her tartan rug and wrapped it around her, then lay down behind her and wrapped his arms around *that*. He could keep her warm, even if he couldn't keep her well.

'Did you take anything, Lu?'

'No!' she shouted. 'No, I didn't!'

He squeezed her into his chest. 'I meant for the pain.'

'If I had then it wouldn't be *hurting* so much!' she yelled at him – and started a new bout of hopeless crying.

An hour later they were in the same position but on the bed, where Lucy had allowed herself to be carried.

The silence was complete – what isolation and winter had not dampered, the snow had shushed as it fell.

Jonas had given her three painkillers and the worst of it was over.

'How do you feel?' he whispered.

'Better,' she said. Better than *what* she did not say, but Jonas understood that, and hoped she knew that he did.

Jonas stared unblinkingly at the opposite wall of what he would always think of as his parents' room.

'Tell me about your night,' she said, still with the weary trace of a sob in her voice.

She needed to forget her own. He knew that.

'I can't.'

'Why not?'

How could he tell her? He felt numb. He felt detached. He didn't know any more where lines could be drawn between past and present, good and evil, right and wrong.

'Jonas?'

Jonas felt it all starting to rise in him. Everything *underneath* was coming to the surface – however much he tried to keep it down.

Tigger for Danny, Taffy for him. The slide of polished leather against his knees and the grip-and-release wonder of a whole beast held in his little-boy hands; the bunching and bumping of muscles under his backside; watching Danny fly along beside him and hoping he looked as free as his best friend did; the eager little ears, between which he'd viewed his whole world. For a happy while.

Jonas remembered.

Although he'd spent a lifetime forgetting.

He remembered the heady smell of the coarse mix and hay; the quiet sounds of hoofs brushing straw over concrete, and the velvet breath of Taffy's muzzle touching his hair, while all the time he was held down and ordered not to cry while unspeakable things were done to him.

Unspeakable.

He shuddered against Lucy's back.

'Jonas?'

But Danny had seen. Danny had known. Maybe Danny had even had the same thing happen to *him*. He knew that must have been true, because even though they'd never spoken of it – *because it was unspeakable* – Danny had done something about it.

He'd burned the place down.

Now, here, twenty years later, Jonas's head pounded and he twitched, as he remembered like a dog.

Going down the row of smouldering stables, roofs caved in and doors thrown open for the ponies to escape. Someone had done that. Someone who loved them had thought of the ponies. But the ponies had not escaped. Terrified by the flames, the ponies had screamed and died in the fire, just as Robert Springer had. Seven sad carcasses still in their boxes. Some so charred that only their legs protruded from a pile of ash, some barely damaged, killed by smoke.

Tigger was half gone but Taffy was unmarked – collapsed against the back wall of his stable, with his legs tucked under his chest, his clever little head bowed gracefully, and his soft lips pressed against the concrete, as if he were lying in a summer meadow nibbling at daisies.

The eighth carcass had already been taken away in an ambulance with a sheet over its blackened, grinning face.

The smell of death was overwhelming.

Turning to his friend through a blur of tears to find comfort in shared misery, Jonas had instead seen pale shock – and guilt.

'Why didn't they run away, Jonas? They should have run away!'

The ponies had died because of him. Because he was too weak to stop it.

Jonas started to shake.

'Sweetheart. What's wrong?'

'Danny Marsh is dead,' he told her bluntly.

And then – finally – he started to cry.

*

'I'm glad he's gone,' said Joy Springer. 'Good riddance to bad rubbish.'

Marvel was so surprised that he sloshed Cinzano on

the kitchen table. The stuff wasn't so bad once you got a taste for it.

Joy sat on a kitchen chair, elbows on the table and her glass outstretched for a refill. The old woman's frizzy grey bun had escaped its grips and she looked like Albert Einstein on a bad-hair day.

'Why?' he said – and Marvel didn't often say that around Joy Springer. He'd soon learned in their almost nightly sessions not to use certain words. *Why* was high on the list, with its answering convolutions and explanations, although *When* was the real killer, as it allowed Joy to ramble back over what felt like the last 150 years of her life – none of it of the slightest interest to Marvel. One night she had held him hellbound, running through the names of her friends from nursery school onwards. No stories, no descriptions, no insightful recollections or pivotal moments – just a litany of meaningless names like a bore of biblical begattings.

'Nothing,' she said after a pause, and waggled her glass at him.

Marvel was instantly fascinated. All of a sudden here was something Joy Springer *didn't* want to talk about.

'You knew Danny Marsh?'

'Years back.' She shrugged. 'Something be wrong with your arm, bay?'

But Marvel withheld the bottle and took a deep breath. 'When?'

The story Joy Springer told was a good one. Everyone

has to have *one*, Marvel reasoned, even if it was bull-shit.

It was a story of flames and smoke and panic and of *murder*, which the coroner had stupidly ruled mis-adventure, after hearing of how Robert Springer was both an ardent horseman and an ardent smoker – two hobbies that Marvel gathered should be kept apart, like wives and girlfriends.

Not only was the coroner a conspiratorial fool, but Danny Marsh was the killer, according to Joy Springer. She became loud and slurred about it without ever giving Marvel any real evidence, then lost her thread a bit and went off at a paranoid tangent that included the prick of an executor, the lousy job a local builder had done on the stable conversions, and some idiot vet who said her cats needed worming.

After three more glasses of Cinzano, Joy Springer suddenly got up and wobbled across to the Welsh dresser. She opened a door on an avalanche of paper-work, old magazines, cards and photographs.

'Robert's things,' she mumbled. 'I don't like to throw them away. Memories.'

Marvel wondered again at the sheer tedium of those memories. Who the hell would want to mull over *them*?

Yet another tumbler allowed her to find what she was looking for, and she handed Marvel a photograph.

'Tha's Danny Marsh when her were a bay,' she slurred. 'Little sod would be in *jail* if your lot had done a proper job, not living here throwing it in my face!'

Although the photo was of two boys of about ten years old, Marvel recognized Danny immediately. The photo had been kept bright in the dresser, and Danny Marsh's brown hair had apparently been given the same cut its entire life – short back and sides. He didn't look like a little sod; he looked like a cheeky, happy kid, holding the reins of a shaggy red pony. The photo had been taken at a show and both boys were in white shirts and Pony Club ties. The second boy was smaller and holding a brown pony with a red rosette fluttering from its bridle.

Marvel's fingers twitched as he recognized Jonas Holly. That wide brow, dark eyes and nose that was already too straight for its age. Only the mouth here was different, and Marvel realized it was because he'd never seen Jonas smile.

He thought instantly of the dead pony on the moor. Of the way Jonas Holly had been almost pathologically unwilling to touch it – had actually refused to take a leg and help pull the carcass out of the road. And yet here he was with one arm thrown casually over the pony's neck, a hank of mane in his little hand, leaning into the animal like a friend. What did kids say nowadays? Best friend for ever. That's what the brown pony looked like it meant to Jonas.

What changed?

What changed in Jonas Holly to turn him from a boy who loved horses into a man who couldn't even bear to touch a dead one?

'Can I keep this?' he asked Joy Springer.

But he'd looked at the photo for so long that she'd fallen asleep and was snoring with her shiny-knuckled hand still around her empty glass.

From the shadows outside the kitchen window, Reynolds watched Marvel finish his drink, then 'shit' and 'fuck' his way across the icy cobbles to his room.

*

Elizabeth Rice had been too embarrassed to ask Alan Marsh whether she could go through his dead son's clothing looking for a missing button so that he could be more conclusively branded a killer. More conclusively than hanging himself and leaving a confessional note, she thought with no little irritation. But because that's what Marvel had ordered her to do by tomorrow, she was doing it now, at almost midnight, by torchlight and in secret.

While Alan Marsh was next door in a sleep induced by the local surfer-cum-doctor and his magic needle, she crept into his dead son's room and started to do her duty.

Danny Marsh had been surprisingly neat for a young man who'd never been in the army. He didn't have many clothes. Maybe a dozen shirts and T-shirts, a winter jacket, a summer jacket, three or four pairs of jeans and a cheap black suit she remembered he'd worn at his mother's funeral.

All buttons were present.

A pair of black Doc Martens with steel toecaps had matched the Polaroid of the dusty shoe-print that the CSI had taken off her window sill. Danny Marsh had passed her silently in the night. Going out and coming in. Hadn't hurt her. Hadn't even woken her.

It didn't matter now.

She found a small stash of porn under his shirts. Magazines on busty blondes and MILFs. Mild, really, by today's standards. Certainly milder than the stuff that Eric often failed to wipe clear of their computer's history.

She'd liked Danny Marsh. He was a good listener. When they'd been to the pub together that one time, he'd made her laugh. Rice sat down on the bed. It was still up against the window where Danny had pulled it so he could tie the sheet to it before jumping out.

That was where Alan Marsh found her fifteen minutes later when her loud sobs pulled him from his magic sleep.

He sat down beside her and took her hand in his and hushed her gently the way he always had Yvonne, whenever she remembered that she'd lost her mind. They sat there for a long time – the weeping police officer and the bereaved husband and father – their joined hands resting in her lap on a dog-eared copy of *Big Jugs*.

Three Days

Lucy Holly hated John Marvel, and it felt good.

She was so used to hating her hands, hating her legs, hating her memory, hating her disease, that to hate something external and tangible that might actually be able to give a shit about her hatred was invigorating in a dour, angry way.

Jonas had told her that Marvel obviously thought he had been protecting Danny Marsh in some way; that Danny was the killer, and that that made Jonas somehow complicit in the murders. And he'd told her of Marvel's repetition of the words that had been contained in the first note.

Call yourself a policeman?

That bastard.

The thought of Jonas *or* Danny being involved was laughable. Or would be if it were not potentially so serious. She thought Jonas was a little paranoid – that the idea of Marvel being involved in the crimes was also too far-fetched to be credible – but she hated Marvel anyway for taunting Jonas when he was obviously in shock, even if his words had been a lucky guess.

Danny Marsh was dead. Lucy could hardly believe it herself. Danny, who worked shifts with his dad and Ronnie Trewell at the little tin garage A & D MARSH MOTOR REPAIRS. Danny, who was so nice that she could never understand why he hadn't been snapped up by some local girl.

Jonas had not elaborated on his childhood friendship with Danny, but she thought it must have been deeper than he'd ever said, given how distraught he had been over his death.

Once he had let go and started to cry, it had been difficult for him to stop.

I'm sorry, he'd kept saying, *I'm sorry* – as if he had done something terrible, instead of finally given in to understandable grief.

Here over the remains of breakfast – eggshells and crusts – Lucy felt her eyes heat up at the memory of her big, capable husband reduced to a weeping, foetal ball in her arms.

That *bastard*!

Jonas had left already – ever the professional, even when other professionals were acting like pricks around him. He hadn't had a day off since this all started. On an uncommon whim she called him.

I love you, she wanted to say. Just for the hell of it.

But the phone just rang and rang.

Marvel would have to pass the cottage to get to the village from Springer Farm.

Before she had really thought about it, Lucy had seized her sticks, stamped her feet into her wellies and was out of the front door.

*

Jonas drove through Shipcott without stopping. He passed the mobile police unit and Danny Marsh's house without looking at either.

His head was so profoundly numb that his thoughts were only wisps and fragments, like a blizzard on his tongue. Nothing was sticking – except for the weird feeling that with the snow, the white sky and this blankness of mind, he was moving slowly through the tunnel of light that leads to death.

At the brow of the steep slope leading down into Withypool, Jonas stamped on the brakes and the Land Rover slid to a halt. He got out and locked the door.

He put one foot in front of the other, watching the snow give way under him, hearing the soft, squeaky crunch, and the sound of his own breathing as he climbed the narrow track away from the houses towards the top of Withypool Hill.

Everything disappeared in the mist behind him. The car, the knee-high blackthorn halfway up the hill, the village itself. He could not even make out the matching lump of the high common across the way, it was all so white-on-white.

At the summit, the silence was a cotton-wool-covered heartbeat. Jonas felt nothing as he listened to it fill the void.

He called Peter Priddy on a fractured line.

'Did you do it?' he asked softly.

'. . . alling?'

'Did you kill them, Pete? Just tell me, please.'

Priddy was the only one who made any real sense now – and Jonas had vouched for him; diverted Marvel *from* him. Priddy had asked him for a favour and he had granted it out of a misplaced sense of loyalty.

Call yourself a policeman?

'I understand if it was. I really do, Pete. But I have to know. Because it's my job. That's all.' Jonas was in a dream, so there was no harm asking.

'Sorr . . . c . . . hear . . . ou . . .' lied Priddy through the static.

Jonas calmly threw his phone off Withypool Hill. It spun lazily through the air like a disobedient boomerang, and landed out of sight and without a sound somewhere in the mist that was rising around him like a sea of bleach. Jonas watched the dead black heather dissolve into white in front of his eyes. No wonder he couldn't see the common.

He turned to go.

And was lost.

Just like that.

He had been here a hundred times, but he had no idea how to get back to the car. The blackthorn and the common were the only landmarks, and both were hidden by a conjurer's cloth of white damp.

He stood and watched the mist swirl around his legs. His own feet were dimmed by it. Soon it would cover him like a tide and he would be gone.

The thought was calming.

He would be gone. He wouldn't have to do his job any more – this job he was failing at so spectacularly.

Jonas closed his eyes.

Now that the adrenaline of the walk up here had worn off, he was bitterly cold. He had left his gloves in the car, along with the scratchy blanket.

No matter.

Jonas sat down.

It was cold and wet but the relief numbed him. The relief of calm acceptance.

He crossed his legs like a schoolboy and put his hands on his knees.

This was the end and it wasn't so bad.

It was the easiest thing he'd ever done.

He wondered whether he would fall over, or remain sitting for hikers to find here like an icy Buddha.

Jonas smiled.

The mist stroked his cheek like a dead lover.

His phone rang.

Somewhere in the white nothingness, it rang its

sensible old-fashioned telephone ring – like the phone they'd had when he was a child.

It rang and rang. Maybe it was Lucy. Maybe she needed him. Jonas got up to follow the sound.

He found his phone just as it stopped ringing. He picked it out of a depression in the snow, which his brain only slowly registered as his own footprint.

He followed his prints back to the car, then called Lucy, but there was no answer.

Jonas drove back towards Shipcott and the dream faded to white behind him.

As it did, he forgot all about the ice Buddha and all about Peter Priddy.

*

Marvel was late again. The cars were gone again. Déjà vu again.

He walked from Joy's kitchen across the yard to his stable. His cottage. His cottage that used to be a stable.

He took a piss and did his teeth but didn't bother changing his clothes.

They had left him the Honda this time, which was the best of the cars they'd brought with them.

Marvel was still bleary-eyed as he swung the car out of the farm driveway and on to the snowy road. Once again the slush had frozen overnight and the Honda immediately slid sideways a little. He corrected it easily and stayed in second down the hill.

Halfway down he saw someone stepping into the road ahead. Awkwardly. Someone was coming down the stone steps from the cottages into the lane. He started to brake and the car slowed gently.

He could see now that it was a woman on crutches. Not the old-fashioned under-the-armers, but those steel ones with a grip that went around the forearm. The woman was young, but her legs were crippled – he could see that much. And she didn't appear to be wearing a coat, just a thick jumper over a floral skirt. And wellington boots. Everyone had those bastards but him!

Marvel expected the woman to turn and walk down the hill, close to the hedge. He thought he'd stop and give her a lift. It was against the rules, but fuck the rules. A woman on crutches in snow. You'd have to be a freak not to stop for her.

But instead of turning, the woman hobbled slowly into the middle of the narrow lane, then turned so that she was facing him, and just stood there!

Marvel braked more firmly.

Too firmly.

Wheels locked and the Honda slid sideways. He applied opposite lock and he thought he'd caught it, then the car gripped briefly and fishtailed away from him again. It slewed once more and – all in slow motion – started to slide down the lane broadside on. Marvel turned the wheel and braked, to no avail.

He looked out of his side window at the woman standing in the road, leaning on her crutches, watching his unusual approach. Part of him was embarrassed, but an increasingly larger part of him was starting to realize that she didn't understand that he had no control of the car.

She just *stood* there! As if she was somehow expecting him to go around her!

Thirty yards from the woman, the Honda brushed the hedge and wavered, then kept on going at an only slightly different angle.

And still she stood there.

Marvel yelled, 'Out of the way!' through the closed window, then jammed the heel of his hand on to the horn.

She didn't move. The lane was narrow; the car was wide; there was no way he wasn't going to hit her unless she moved. For a surreal moment, Marvel looked into her eyes and realized how beautiful she was. And how calm.

Marvel's entire future flashed before him: the ghastly bump of the car going over the woman, the horror of the eviscerated corpse, the flashing blue lights – and the red one on the breathalyser, the humiliation of the cell in his own nick, the smug look on Reynolds's forever unpunched face, the collar of his good shirt tight around his neck as the jury foreman stood to condemn him, the slow-drip terror of a cop in prison, the halfway house, the bedsit, the menial office job he'd be lucky to get, the gel-haired teenaged boss who said things like 'Whatever' and 'Facebook' . . .

The nightmare that his life would become in a single split second.

Then the rear end hit the opposite bank, the Honda bounced off at a new angle, and – miraculously – slid past the woman in the narrowest of gaps between her and the hedge. The wing mirror actually clipped one of her sticks, and he had time to see her lurch, but not fall, as he passed her.

Another teeth-jarring bump sent the car into a shallow ditch, where it came to a halt sudden enough to throw his forehead against the steering wheel.

Marvel was dazed for a moment and stared stupidly at the unexpected close-up of the slightly retro Honda logo in the centre of the wheel. He thought of Debbie and her lava lamps and that fucking couch. Of putting his shoes on it even though it drove her nuts. Sometimes *because* it drove her nuts. What kind of prick was he?

Seriously.

What kind of prick?

He jerked in shock at a loud bang on the window beside his right ear, and squinted up at the woman he'd just narrowly avoided squashing to a pulp. He wanted to throw his arms around her and kiss her for not being dead; to cry with gratitude and become a monk and dedicate his life to others as penance for every wrong he'd ever done to anyone.

But *she* didn't look grateful. She looked so angry that he was almost afraid to roll down the window, which was plainly stupid, so he did.

'Are you Marvel?' she said grittily. And when he nodded she said, 'I want to talk to you.'

'Why are you picking on Jonas?'

What a silly thing to say to a grown-up! Marvel would have laughed, except for the fact that the woman he realized must be Jonas Holly's wife had lost none of her anger between the lane and the cosy little room where they stood now.

He had followed her in, impressed by her dexterity and strength despite the crutches. Up the three stone steps, through the wooden gate, across the uneven slate path and through the front door. She did it all with such determined energy that he dared not even offer his assistance.

She leaned her sticks against the fireplace, where a new fire was made but not lit, and lowered herself on to the couch, from where she eyed him coldly, still apparently expecting an answer.

'I'm not,' he said, trying – but failing – not to feel like a naughty schoolboy.

She said nothing, just sat there and looked up at him. Somehow the fact that she was sitting now, while he was still standing, put him at a disadvantage. His feeling of bonhomie at not having flattened her while

in the throes of a morning-after hangover had dissi-
pated surprisingly fast, and wanting to be a better
person seemed as silly now as a childhood dream to
ride dolphins for a living.

He had options now.

He could walk out. He could just turn around and
walk away. He used to walk out on Debbie all the
time. Whenever she wanted to talk or fight he would
leave the room. Sometimes she would come after him,
whining or yelling. Once she had thrown a cushion at
him. A *retro* cushion. But what could Jonas Holly's
much prettier wife do? Down him with a crutch?

But he didn't walk out. 'I'm trying to catch a killer.
That's my priority. Not keeping the locals happy.'

'I think there's a difference between keeping somebody happy and implying that they are complicit in
murder, don't you?'

So Jonas had told her everything. *Complained* to her,
more like.

Well, fuck them both.

He almost said that to her – *Fuck you both!* – then he
remembered the crutches. And the way she'd come
out into the road, no doubt to flag him down, to stop
him – if he hadn't already been on a collision course
with a hedge and a ditch and a steering wheel. Marvel
touched his forehead and felt a little bump there, but
no blood.

So he didn't want to blow her off; because of the
crutches. It wasn't politically correct. Two years back

he'd fumed silently through a compulsory course on political correctness, but something must have stuck, because instead of walking out, Marvel pointed to the easy chair that didn't match the couch.

'Can I sit down?'

She hesitated, then nodded briefly.

He sat. By the time he had completed the manoeuvre, he had decided to lay it on the line for her. If her husband had been shielding a killer she was going to find out sooner or later. Her crutches couldn't protect her from that. And maybe Jonas had told Lucy things he hadn't told *him*. If he appeared to be open with her, then maybe she'd be open back and he could glean new information to fatten up his case. God knows, it needed it.

'What's your name?' he started – then watched her struggle briefly not to tell him. He knew she thought it took away some of her strength, and she was right. That was why he'd asked.

'Lucy,' she finally said, because giving a civil answer to a civil question was in her nature.

So Marvel told Lucy all the reasons why he liked Jonas Holly. Contamination of scenes, disappearance of vomit, concealment of crucial evidence.

Lucy stared at him unforgivingly as he spoke – Marvel reckoned she probably wore the pants in the Holly household.

'You're not telling me anything I don't know,' she interrupted, although he could see by her face that

that was a lie. 'I'm hearing a lot of coincidence and circumstantial evidence and no proof at all. You don't even have proof that *Danny* was involved, let alone Jonas!'

Marvel wasn't used to anyone telling him that he was taking a flyer. When he was Senior Investigating Officer on a case he was used to people doing as he told them without questioning his choices. Reynolds tried sometimes, but Reynolds wasn't really a police-man; he had no *feel* for the job.

'Danny Marsh left a written confession,' he said. 'You don't get more *involved* than that.'

'Bullshit!' she said with spirit. 'Jonas told me what it said. *I did it. I'm not sorry?* That's not a confession to murder. He could have run over a neighbour's cat for all you know!'

Although she was giving him a hard time, Marvel couldn't help liking Lucy Holly. Her staunch defence and willingness to engage in battle appealed to him. Sitting on the couch with her eyes sparking – and with-out her crooked legs on such obvious display – Lucy Holly was quite captivating.

'Jonas says you don't even have any fingerprints!'

Marvel shrugged. 'People are wise to prints now-adays. They all wear surgical gloves. The only ones who don't are drunks and fools. We found a box of surgical gloves in the Marshes' garage.'

'And I'm sure you'd also find several boxes at Mark Dennis's surgery. And the vet's in Dulverton,' she came back at him. 'Either way, you don't have prints,' she continued briskly. 'What about the button?'

Damn. She knew about the button. The weak link in his weak chain of evidence against Jonas Holly.

'What button?' he said.

'Don't play dumb with me,' Lucy told him with a hard stare that made Marvel feel like a toddler who's just hit a playmate with a toy train.

'It's one of 500,000 produced every year.'

'For the uniform trade, Jonas said. Doesn't that mean people like security guards and bouncers might be suspects? Not people like Danny who wear overalls for a living.'

'Your husband should not be discussing the details of this case. Even with you. There are certain things which we like to hold back—'

'So only the police and the killer know about it,' Lucy finished for him impatiently. 'Everybody knows *that* from half an hour in front of the telly! But it bothers me that you don't seem to be taking the button seriously. Doesn't it bother you?'

She looked at him expectantly and again he wished he could just tell her to fuck off and walk out. Everything became easier when that was an option.

'We have no idea if the button is even connected to the murder of Mrs Priddy,' he said stiffly.

'That's not the point,' she shot back. 'The point is, why would Jonas be revealing evidence or possible evidence if he's been trying to hide the truth? Is he *finding* evidence or is he *hiding* it, Mr Marvel? You can't have it both ways. It makes no sense.'

It made no sense to Marvel either, but he'd be damned if he was going to concede that point to Lucy Holly.

'Mrs Holly—' he started officiously, but she cut him off.

'Come on, Mr Marvel. Everyone knows there's a million bits of forensic evidence that you can use to convict somebody.'

'True,' said Marvel. 'And if that vomit hadn't disappeared, we might have it.'

'Or you might have a pile of vomit without a DNA match,' countered Lucy defiantly. 'And you have no proof that Danny threw it up or Jonas cleared it away. The point is, you don't have it at all. Jonas said it was there overnight, which is pretty lax, if you ask me!'

Marvel knew it was too, of course, so he changed tack, hoping to wrong-foot Lucy.

'Did you know that twenty years ago there was a fire up at Springer Farm?'

'No.'

'Well, there was. The owner, Robert Springer, was killed.'

'So? What does this have to do with you bullying Jonas?'

He ignored her and ploughed on: 'Mr Springer's body was found in the only stable that had the door shut. The other doors had been opened –

presumably to let the horses out, although they didn't go.'

He let the fact hang there, hoping for some indication that she knew about it, or had something to hide. She just looked at him neutrally.

'The coroner ruled misadventure, but I'm not sure that's the whole story.'

Lucy waited again for him to go on. He collected his thoughts before he continued. He'd only heard of these events hours earlier, and wasn't sure how they affected his case, so he was even less sure of what – if anything – to tell Lucy Holly.

'When I told Joy Springer about Danny Marsh's death last night, she was happy.'

He could read the surprise in Lucy's eyes, along with the questions she didn't ask. He answered them anyway.

'Seems she always suspected Danny of starting the fire.'

'Why?'

'Apparently local kids would work up there in exchange for rides, but her husband was always getting at Danny for not pulling his weight, forgetting to put water in the stables, stuff like that. I don't know what; I don't know shit about horses. She says he resented it. When the fire happened, the police interviewed all the kids who rode there, but they never came up with any evidence that any of them played any part in the fire.'

'Maybe *she* did it,' interrupted Lucy. 'Aren't spouses

always the first suspects? Maybe she was pointing the finger at Danny to distract from the fact that *she* killed him.'

'I'm just telling you what she told me,' said Marvel impatiently.

'Maybe she wore surgical gloves,' Lucy murmured with a wry raise of her eyebrows.

Marvel ignored the dig. 'You know Jonas and Danny Marsh were childhood friends?'

'That doesn't mean he'd cover up for him if he knew Danny had done something wrong,' said Lucy quickly. 'Jonas would never do that.'

Marvel smiled without humour. 'You know, every wife of every criminal I've ever caught has said exactly the same thing – he'd never do that.'

'Well, it's true,' she said defiantly.

'You knew him as a boy?' he inquired sarcastically.

'I know him now,' she snapped back.

'You and your husband are well matched.'

'What does *that* mean?'

'You both think you know people. Know what they're capable of.'

'I suppose you think *you* know people.'

'Yes, I do,' said Marvel. 'And what *I* know is that people are capable of *anything*.'

Lucy looked at him with a small smile. 'I think you know the wrong kind of people, Mr Marvel.'

He shrugged and let her score that point. Proving her wrong would take time he didn't want to waste. He changed direction again. Maybe he could get something out of Lucy Holly without her even knowing it.

'Your husband tell you what happened the other night? When we hit the horse?'

'Yes.'

'He wouldn't touch it.'

'Jonas doesn't like horses.' She shrugged.

'Not *now*,' agreed Marvel.

He reached into his inside coat pocket and handed her the photo.

'What's this?' she said, but he thought he'd let her work it out for herself.

She did, but it took her a lot longer than it had taken him. He saw the exact moment she recognized her future husband – the tiny intake of breath and the way she dropped her head to get closer to the photo.

'Jonas,' she said.

'And Danny Marsh.'

She didn't say anything, her head bowed.

'Seemed to like horses plenty then, didn't he?'

Nothing.

'You know what changed?'

She shook her head, unable to tear her eyes away from the photo.

'I'm thinking it might go back to the night the stables burned down. Someone they knew died. All the horses died. Must have been traumatic for a kid.'

Lucy nodded silently.

'Maybe he even felt guilty,' he suggested carefully.

'Maybe Danny burned the stables down and Jonas knew about it.'

'Maybe,' she said, to his surprise. Seeing the photo seemed to have knocked all the spirit out of Lucy Holly, all the defence and all the defiance.

'What did he say about it?' It was worth a shot – tricking her into blurting out something by behaving as if his theory was already established fact.

'He never told me. I don't know. I never knew this.'

Her voice was dull. Dead. Marvel was a little concerned, despite himself, at the radical change in Lucy Holly. Her feisty spirit had seemed real, but he saw now that it had been a mere soap-bubble which, once popped, had disappeared so completely that he could not even see where it used to be.

He stood up, feeling oddly guilty that he had done something to her that might be irreparable.

'I've never seen a picture of him as a boy,' she said, still not looking at him.

'Why is that?' Marvel was surprised. Even in *his* fucked-up relationships he could remember the mother-bearing-photo-album routine as an early step in the courtship dance.

'I don't know. Can I keep it?'

'I'm afraid I need it.'

But she held on to it in hands that shook just a little.

Marvel stood undecided for a long moment. Lucy Holly stared at the photo in her wasted lap, as if he'd already left.

* * *

Jonas looked so happy!

That was Lucy's overwhelming first impression. She had almost not recognized him because of it. His brow, his nose, his lips – all were younger but definite versions of the Jonas she had fallen in love with. But his eyes . . . his eyes were completely different. Across the years, ten-year-old Jonas Holly grinned at her – without shyness, without caution.

Without fear.

It was all she could think of.

Nothing bad has happened to him yet.

She had never thought of Jonas as fearful until she'd seen this picture. She might have, if she'd seen others, but there were none to see that she could find. No reminders for her of how he had been as a child.

The photo was a tunnel in time. Danny was taller and bigger than the friend who would eventually tower over him and they held two proud little ponies – no doubt long dead. Lucy could see that this was a snapshot of the boys' whole lives at that moment, plucked from the past and shown to her now: they were at a summer show; they had won; they were happy. That was all that shone from their faces.

Her heart wrenched to see them, so young and so vital together, when now Danny was cold on a slab and Jonas's eyes were sunken with lack of sleep, and his body made too thin by work and fear and the burden of her; it seemed a fate too cruel to befall the two joyous children she held in her trembling hands.

'How could you do this?' she said.

'Hmm?' Marvel bent at the waist to hear her better.

'How could you do this to him?'

'I haven't done anything to him.'

'Look at him,' she said, her voice starting to strengthen once more.

Lucy turned the photo to Marvel and he looked past it to where her eyes had gone dark with anger. *Real* anger this time – not feistiness.

'I don't know what you mean,' he said.

'*Look* at him!' she said again. 'Look how happy he is! And look what you've done to him now! He's a good man trying to do his job and you're just trying to make him look bad because *you* can't catch the killer!'

Lucy got to her unsteady feet as her voice gathered pace. 'Putting him on a doorstep, humiliating him in front of the whole village, implying that he'd cover up for someone who had killed six people! It's just *sick*! *You're* sick.'

Sick.

Marvel snatched the photo from her hand, giving her a fright.

'*Fuck* you!' she hissed at him.

'Fuck *you*!' he spat back, making her flinch. 'If your husband's miserable it's *your* fault, not mine! Someone in this shit-hole village has been taking out old people like seal pups, and your yokel husband is hiding something from me. So the last thing I need is some angry cripple telling me how to do my fucking job.'

He walked out and slammed the front door behind him as hard as he could.

Lucy swayed in his wake, breathless with shock, holding the arm of the couch for support – and viewed herself in Marvel's words as if in the brightest mirror. She had seen herself reflected in Jonas's loving eyes for so long that she had forgotten what she really was.

Some angry cripple.

*

Reynolds sat in the chilly mobile unit and compared Danny Marsh's suicide note with the one Jonas Holly had found pinned to his garden gate.

There was not the slightest resemblance between the two hands. In the suicide note it was rounded and sprawling; in the other it was tight and spiky.

Reynolds was no expert, but they couldn't get the notes *to* the expert, Bob Hamilton, until the snow cleared a little. They had emailed a scan so that he could start work but he'd need the originals to make a proper comparison. In the interim, they were all having a good look – although Reynolds didn't need more than a glance to tell him that a match between the two notes was highly unlikely.

He looked up at Marvel with a shrug and a bottom lip that expressed that opinion.

'It's possible the writing in the gate note was

disguised,' said Marvel in a tone that invited no dissent. 'Hamilton may well be able to make a match.'

'He'd have to be a magician or an idiot,' dissented Reynolds.

Grey sniggered and Marvel's fist itched. Reynolds was always such a fucking clever clogs. Marvel knew the writing on the notes was never going to be a match. Hell, Stevie Wonder could see *that*. But as he saw it, it was Reynolds's job to support his decisions and to pretend to be surprised and disappointed when the expert failed to make a connection – especially in front of other people. Of course, he'd long ceased to expect such support from his DS, but *just once* would be nice.

Especially in this case.

There was still a chance, of course, that the notes written to Jonas Holly had not come from the killer – although that seemed unlikely. But if the note left on Holly's gate *was* written by the killer, and Danny Marsh *hadn't* written it, then two plus two made four and Danny Marsh could not be the killer.

And *that* made Marvel feel that he might be going quietly crazy.

By this stage in an investigation, Marvel was used to feeling as though he were in complete control. But here he was so far from control that he couldn't quite remember what control felt like.

It was the village; he was sure.

In Shipcott he felt cut off and lost. He was in this glorified horsebox, or he was staring at static in a stable. People told him everything and nothing. Everyone knew everyone else – except that nobody knew the killer. Evidence was there one day and gone the next. Suspects fell into his lap and then slipped through his fingers. Mobile connections were made and lost in the twinkling of an eye – and the cold, the rain, the snow were active and malicious participants in the slippery deception.

It was like investigating a murder in *Brigadoon*.

Every morning he got up and drove down the hill into the village and was somehow surprised to find it still there. Every day was another dose of secrecy and fuzzy disconnection, and it was only his now nightly sessions with Joy Springer that seemed to anchor him in time or space.

He snatched the two notes from Reynolds, and when Pollard held out his hand for them, he ignored him and banged them back into the battered filing cabinet euphemistically marked 'Evidence'.

*

Jonas got home and found that Lucy had changed into another person who wore Lucy's smile and Lucy's eyes like a poor facsimile of the real thing.

'What's wrong?' he asked her in bed.

'Nothing,' she said. 'I love you.'

He wanted to tell her not to change the subject, but couldn't find it in his heart – not even in that very small and stony corner where he kept all that was not kind, responsible and selfless.

'I love you too,' he agreed sadly.

*

Jonas thought he was strong, but the killer knew her was as weak as a kitten.

You can't fall apart now.

But Jonas *was* falling apart.

He left the house every morning and some nights to satisfy his own fragile ego in the name of protection – all the while leaving the most important person in the world alone and in peril. He seemed to have *no idea* about how to do his job. No *idea* who it was that he should *really* be protecting . . .

The killer got shivers at the thought.

Those shivers kept him focused – his eyes on the prize.

The killer liked Lucy Holly.

Loved her, in his own way.

But it didn't mean he wouldn't kill her given half a chance.

Two Days

As soon as Jonas left in the Land Rover the next morning, Lucy Holly got the number of the mobile unit from Taunton HQ, then called it. When a man picked up, she said she wanted to make a formal complaint about DCI Marvel.

There was a pregnant silence at the other end of the line and Lucy braced herself for a hostile request for her address so that the appropriate form could be sent. She was prepared to argue the toss; she didn't want an appropriate form; she wanted to drop Marvel in shit right up to his foul, hurtful, bastard mouth.

Instead of turning cold and official, the policeman – who identified himself as DS Reynolds – started to ask her quite pertinent questions, which allowed her to vent in the most satisfying way imaginable. She told Reynolds about Marvel nearly hitting her with the car; she told him how he had snatched the photograph of

Jonas from her; she took a deep breath and told him that Marvel had said, 'Fuck you' and called her a name.

'What name?' asked Reynolds.

'A horrible name,' said Lucy.

'I am writing these things down,' said Reynolds. 'It would be helpful if you could be specific.'

There was a pause. 'He called me an angry cripple.'

Another long silence, which the words expanded to fill.

'And *are* you disabled, Mrs Holly?' asked Reynolds gently.

'I have MS,' she told him, filling up unexpectedly. 'I use sticks to help me walk.'

'I'm very sorry to hear that, Mrs Holly,' said DS Reynolds. And Lucy was amazed to hear that he *did* sound sorry – not just as if he was giving a required response.

It allowed her to collect herself and deliver what she considered to be her pièce de résistance. She told him that throughout the encounter she could smell alcohol on Marvel's breath.

'Whiskey?' enquired DS Reynolds, as if he had some experience of Marvel in drink.

'No,' said Lucy. 'Something sweeter. But definitely alcohol.'

'And what time was this?'

'About nine. In the morning.'

DS Reynolds was quiet for a short while and Lucy

assumed he was writing. She tried to keep a lid on her optimism; she still had a suspicion that her complaint would disappear into the black hole of Masonic secrecy that she believed held sway among senior officers. But at least she'd said her piece. Even if DS Reynolds now told her that he'd be sending her a complaints form, she'd still had *that* satisfaction.

But DS Reynolds didn't say he'd send her a form. Instead he said in a serious voice, 'Mrs Holly, would you be happy to make a sworn statement about these matters?'

Lucy almost laughed with surprise.

'Happy?' she said. 'I'd be absolutely delirious.'

When Reynolds hung up on Lucy Holly he was actually shaking.

He had the contemporaneous notes in his notebook; he had his private logs, he had his own detailed reports showing that John Marvel was an unprofessional, bullying prick who shouldn't be left in charge of a chimps' tea party, let alone a murder inquiry, but until this very moment, he hadn't had the damning independent evidence that would tip the balance in a disciplinary case against the DCI.

He'd always known it would come. Always. People who behaved like Marvel were on borrowed time. For a start, he knew that Marvel had left the Met under a cloud. Quite what *kind* of cloud he'd not been able to determine, but the police grapevine had whispered of

Marvel squeezing the facts to make them fit a suspect – or squeezing that suspect to make him fit the facts. Reynolds believed it. He would have believed almost anything ill of Marvel. He hated the man's archaic approach – his reliance on 'hunches', his relaxed attitude to procedure, his personal whims and illogical vendettas; his secret drinking – none of these had any place in modern law enforcement.

Since he'd started working with Marvel, Reynolds had been shocked by his fixation on certain 'suspects'. In Weston last year, Marvel had held a nineteen-year-old homeless man for two days because he'd been near the scene of the crime and 'looked guilty'. Before that the married boyfriend of a strangled Asian teenager was terrified into a confession which took seconds to collapse once the girl's father haughtily confessed to the 'honour' killing a few days later.

Sure, Marvel did get results – even Reynolds had to admit that – and those results had kept him grudgingly secure ever since he'd left London. There was a kind of inferiority complex going on at the Avon & Somerset force which had allowed the big-city cop to bulldoze his way through conventional practice and on to cases that should have belonged to others. Even senior officers were only human, and – Reynolds knew – most just wanted things to run smoothly. Attempting to rein Marvel in and put him in his place would have taken more effort than any of the current incumbents were prepared to expend – even from behind a desk.

From his place at Marvel's side, Reynolds had been convinced that the man deserved to be kicked out. But because of Marvel's constant, dogged results, he'd always known he would also need to get good, sworn, hopefully civilian evidence of serious wrongdoing to bring the man down.

The kind of evidence that Lucy Holly had just dropped into his lap like manna from heaven. The kind of evidence that he could see the Independent Police Complaints Commission putting right at the top of the pile. The disabled wife of a serving officer alleging conduct unbecoming and being drunk on the job.

Superb.

Reynolds signed and dated his notes of the conversation and tucked them neatly into a folder with a sense of self-satisfaction. He was harassed and balding, trying to do his job *and* Marvel's, but as soon as he had a spare moment, he would go and see Lucy Holly, take her sworn statement and add it to the rest of the case he had built against his DCI in the past year.

Sergio Leone, eat your heart out.

One Day

It was gone five o'clock and Marvel was in the Red Lion nursing half a pint of piss masquerading as alcohol-free lager.

He hadn't invited anybody else along for an after-work drink. He was heartily sick of the lot of them and even more sick of being stuck here in Shipcott with what appeared to be trench foot.

Jos Reeves called to say that the prints inside the plastic bags they'd found in the courtyard were unidentifiable. Little more than muddy smears.

Marvel didn't even have the energy to be rude to him.

Someone walked through his line of vision with a lurching gait and Marvel focused. The young man had the look of someone who had put his weight and his drink on fast – florid, and with all the excess fat around his belly and his chin.

'What are *you* looking at?' said Neil Randall.

'You got a wooden leg?' said Marvel.

The young man was taken aback. He was used to people blushing and stammering when he confronted them.

'Yes,' he said.

Then he remembered his hostility and added, 'You want to make something of it?'

Marvel resisted the urge to snap back something about whittling a toy boat, and just shrugged. The young man was obviously defensive. Must be shit to lose your leg. Give up your job, maybe. Collect disability. Be a burden—

A burden. Margaret Priddy had been a burden. That was, after all, why he had 'liked' Peter Priddy so much, wasn't it? Yvonne Marsh had been a burden to her husband and son. But the three victims at Sunset Lodge . . . couldn't they also be considered burdens on their families? A financial drain, if nothing else?

Maybe the killer couldn't bring himself to kill his *own* burden and was taking it out on others?

Marvel felt his skin actually tingle. He felt so sure that he was on the right track, and his instincts rarely let him down.

Hand in hand with that came the uncomfortable feeling that this was Reynolds's territory. Reynolds and his beloved Kate Gulliver with their namby-pamby, touchy-feely bollocks about childhoods and transference and repression and guilt.

He stared unseeingly at Neil Randall's gammy leg as the man limped across the pub and propped himself up in front of the fruit machine.

And then DCI John Marvel got another, even bigger tingle as he put two and two together and made what looked very much like four to him . . .

Wasn't Lucy Holly a *burden* to her husband?

He put his so-called beer down on the table so fast that it slopped over the rim, and stood up.

He had to get back to his room. He had to be really alone so he could think about this clearly. He needed to write things down and draw little boxes and connect them with biro lines of reasoning. He needed to be *absolutely sure* before he exposed his theory to Reynolds, to give that bastard the smallest possible chance of poking holes in it.

And, more than anything, he needed a real drink to help him.

*

Jonas was pulling a ewe's head out of a tree.

He'd spent several minutes trying to get a good grip on the struggling, ice-covered sheep without luck, and made a new effort to focus before his hands got too cold to function.

The snow was falling again in a silent blizzard that threatened to obscure his view of Shipcott below. Jonas had done his best to get over to Edgcott to do his rounds but he'd had to turn back at the top of the hill when he lost the road completely. He'd spotted the sheep twenty yards away and decided to do his good deed for the day.

He spoke soothingly to the ewe but she didn't believe him for a second, and bleated in terror, while now and then raising her tail to vent hard marble-sized droppings in machine-gun bursts, as if paying out a shit jackpot.

Jonas Holly cursed under his breath but he understood the ewe's fear. He had learned to live with fear.

It didn't mean he wasn't scared.

All the time.

All the fucking time! He could hear Danny saying those words again.

Jonas felt that if he could only keep all his fear separate and compartmentalized, then he would be able to manage it, like a lion tamer performing tricks with just one lion at a time – carefully twisting his head into the sharp, fetid maw, feeling the prick of teeth on his cheek, and then herding the beast back to its cage, before bringing out the next lion, whose job was to jump through hoops.

At times, though, Jonas got the feeling that the catches on the cages were loose, that the lions were plotting behind his back – and that there was imminent danger of a great escape, during which he would be torn to pieces in his top hat and red tails.

Which was probably what this poor ewe thought was about to happen to her.

Don't be scared. I'll protect you. That's my job.

The words rushed at him from nowhere and for the first time in decades he remembered the face of the policeman who had told him that. The man had looked like a father. Not like *his* father, but like the kind of father Jonas had seen on TV – middle-aged, greying at the temples, slightly overweight. Jonas could even remember the shiny buttons on the policeman's tunic and being overwhelmed that this exciting uniform was actually in his mother's cramped little kitchen.

The policeman had asked his parents to stay in the front room. Jonas had panicked then, and imagined the policeman taking him out of the back door to prison while his parents waited trustingly in front of the TV that was showing *Grange Hill*. Or he might hurt him to find out what he wanted to know. Jonas didn't want to be hurt any more. But he also didn't want to tell. If he told on Danny about the stables, it would all come out. All the horror and the shame would come out and everybody would know about it, even his *parents*. And *nobody* must ever know that Jonas even *knew* that pathetic child – let alone used to *be* him. Even *he*, Jonas, had learned to leave that weak little boy to his fate and go somewhere else while unspeakable things were happening.

The big policeman had bent his head and asked

quiet questions about the fire. Jonas had told him the truth – that he knew nothing. But he didn't tell him the truth of what he *suspected*.

Somehow the policeman had known that he was hiding something. Like magic, he knew. *How?* He had probed and prodded and gently persuaded until finally Jonas had burst into tears.

'Are you scared, Jonas?' he'd asked with great kindness.

Jonas had nodded with his fists in his eyes. The policeman had taken one of those hot, wet fists and engulfed it in his own.

'Don't be scared,' he'd said. 'I'll protect you. That's my job.'

It was tempting. *So* tempting. To blurt it all out and be done with it and let grown-ups take charge. But Jonas never told because he knew that there was only one way now to protect himself, and that was by protecting the *other* boy – even from the nice policeman . . .

Here and now, Jonas's face was as flushed and hot as his hands were cold. He wished he could run away and never come back. He had failed the village and – now that he had cried – he had failed Lucy too. She had seen his weakness and could no longer call on him for strength.

He was falling apart on her.

The anger of that thought gave him strength and suddenly he managed to grasp the sheep's ear and a handful of dirty wet fleece in just the right place so that he could lever the animal upwards and out from where it was wedged in the V of two branches. As he did, the ewe's legs flailed wildly and caught him in the thigh. He bit his lip and grunted as he heaved it free and let it go.

After an initial panicky dash, the ewe turned and surveyed him with a supercilious yellow eye.

Jonas panted and rubbed his leg. His trousers had ripped and he could feel the cold touching his thigh. He'd have to go home and change. Again.

Even so, he wasn't angry any more; he was grateful. The kick had brought him out of it. Out of that terrifying place where memories rose like dead fish breaking the calm surface of his mind.

He was here.

He was safe.

He was Jonas Holly, the protector, once more.

'Don't be scared,' he told the sheep.

*

An abandoned Toyota had blocked the bottom of the lane to the house. Apparently the driver had been attempting to get up the hill but had slid sideways, and the car was now wedged between the spiny black winter hedges with their thick caps of soft-edged snow going grey in the fading daylight.

Jonas said, 'Shit' quietly and sat for a moment,

hating the driver, who had no doubt wandered back to the village and was probably even now having steak-and-kidney pudding in the Red Lion, while trusting that *someone* would do *something* about his misfortune while he was gone.

No local would have left his car there, Jonas reckoned. Locals knew that even in conditions like this, farmers in tractors needed to reach livestock all over the moor. Locals had more sense and more courtesy.

Fuming silently, Jonas climbed out into the snow – and was bitingly reminded that he had only just managed to get warm again after the sheep episode.

He had to slide across the boot of the car to attach the winch, getting a wet arse for his pains.

As he dropped off the other side of the boot, the Toyota's rear end broke free and the car lurched side-ways, then started to slide slowly back down the hill.

Jonas took a few faltering paces, but then stopped and could only watch as the car arced gently into his Land Rover before skating on and coming to rest against a drift at the bottom of the hill.

'Bastard,' said Jonas quietly but with feeling. He was freezing cold, it had started to snow again, and now he'd have to fill out forms explaining how the Land Rover got damaged, when all he wanted was to get home, have a steaming hot bath and share supper with Lu.

As he started down through the churned snow

where the Toyota had been, Jonas noticed what he assumed were the driver's footprints leading not down the hill to the Red Lion, but up the lane towards Rose Cottage.

He stopped and shone his torch into the prints.

The new snow was starting to soften them a little, but Jonas could still see the tread pattern.

Herringbone.

Jonas switched off the torch and ran up the hill.

The footprints led straight to his front door.

He skidded on the path despite the grit, and skidded again in the porch, sending several loud logs tumbling off the neat pile.

Shit.

Any attempt at stealth ruined, Jonas burst through the front door.

'Lucy!'

No answer.

Please be OK. Please, please, please.

He opened the door into the front room.

Lucy was on the couch under the friendly glow of the fire, her eyes closed and her head nestled on the tasselled cushion.

Jonas released a huge breath he didn't know he'd been holding. She was safe. She was fine. The driver had probably asked to use the phone, that was all—

The back door closed quietly.

Jonas's heart pumped a shot of pure ice into his system. He could even feel it in his teeth.

He grabbed the poker from beside the fire and rushed into the kitchen.

Empty.

Jonas crossed the room in three strides and yanked open the back door. By the light spilling out of the kitchen it was easy to make out the herringbone treads.

'Jonas?'

Jonas ignored Lucy and ran into the night once more. As soon as he was beyond the reach of the kitchen light, he lost the tracks, but he ran anyway, past the Beetle domed with snow, out into the road and down the hill.

In the jerking beam of the torch, he saw the indistinct shape of the man running for his life through the fast-falling snow. He was fast, but Jonas was gaining.

And then he wasn't.

He lost his footing and went down heavily, the torch flying out of his hand. He skidded again getting up and lurched sideways. It was crucial. Even as he rose, Jonas heard the car door slam. He ran blindly towards the sound as if through a snowy waterfall, but the super-reliable Japanese engine caught first time and revved furiously as the wheels spun and then caught. The lights were not switched on; Jonas never even *saw* the car go.

He stood panting at the foot of the hill. He hadn't even taken down the car's number earlier. Basic stuff. *Basic.*

He got into the Land Rover and rumbled back up the hill to home.

He came through the still-open back door.

'Jonas?' Lucy called from the other room, sounding scared.

'It's OK, Lu,' he called and locked the door behind him. Now he had stopped reacting and started thinking, the shock of disaster averted hit him like a wall, and he had to put his hand on the counter and double over to get his breath.

The killer had been here.

Right here in Rose Cottage.

While Lucy slept unaware on the couch, the killer had come into their home.

Had he seen her?

Had he already stood over his victim in life and mused on how best to make her dead?

Had he touched her hair and known that *this one* was next?

He shivered and realized he was shaking uncontrollably.

He couldn't fall apart on her now.

'Jonas?'

He couldn't tell her; it would scare the hell out of her. She must never know how badly he'd fucked up or how close she had come to being killed. He would stop going out at night. Hell, he would stop going out during the *days* if he possibly could! How could he have been so stupid? How could he have gone out to protect the village and left Lucy to protect herself? His most precious thing in the whole wide world! Was he *fucking crazy?*

Jonas suddenly thought that he *might* be crazy. Had maybe been crazy ever since he'd found Lucy behind the front door in her pink flannel pyjamas and the joke bunny slippers he'd bought her two Christmases ago. Or maybe before that – maybe when they'd sat together in that bastard doctor's office and he'd told them that Lucy Holly, his perfect wife and best friend, was going to spend the next several years dying in front of his eyes. Or was it when his parents both left him alone? One minute here, the next minute gone – their immaculate little car turned into instant scrap by a head-on collision with an idiot driver who was halfway through a text to his wife at the time: *On my wax CU soo—* They had read it out at the inquest into all three deaths.

On my wax.

If that wasn't enough to drive anyone crazy, Jonas didn't know what was.

Or maybe it was even before that. Maybe he'd always been crazy. Who the hell knew? Right now he couldn't remember the last time he'd felt completely sane.

Jonas picked up his hand to watch it shake.

Then his eyes refocused on the kitchen counter beyond it.

Between the kettle and the toaster were two mugs. Wisps of steam still rose from them and the tea bags floated just under the surface of the dark liquid like two little drowning victims.

The killer had been making tea.

One for himself and one for Lucy.

That made no sense.

No sense at all.

Why would a killer—

With a hollow jolt, Jonas realized the man he'd chased from his home could not have been the killer.

Then who the fuck *was* he?

*

Steven Lamb liked delivering newspapers. He'd had this job for almost three years now – ever since Skew Ronnie Trewell had got his driver's licence and lost interest in the *Exmoor Bugle* and the *Daily Mail* as a means to an end.

Steven liked the early mornings in the summer, and bore them in the winter. He liked the smell of the newspapers as Mr Jacoby cut the plastic tape that bound the quires, and he liked the fleeting snapshots of world news he glimpsed as he helped Mr Jacoby stuff each paper with shiny brochures advertising debt consolidation and credit cards.

Most of all he liked the £11.50 he got every week.

That was the reason he'd wanted the job in the first place, of course. What boy doesn't want to earn money and start buying? He'd had to fight for it though. Not other applicants, because Mr Jacoby had told him the job was his if he wanted it. No, Steven had had to fight his mother and grandmother to be allowed to do the job. They didn't want him getting up and walking to Mr Jacoby's shop in the dark; they didn't want him knocking on doors of a winter's evening and asking for payment; they didn't want him outside at all really – day or night.

They said it was dangerous.

Most boys his age would have scoffed and whined and dismissed them both as fussy old hens, but Steven understood that it *was* dangerous. *That* he knew as well as anyone and better than most.

He also knew in his secret heart that if he didn't *have* to go out into the world every day, he might never leave the house again; might cringe indoors and think too much about what might have been and what very nearly was.

His mum and nan had finally bowed to the sheer weight of his persistence and Steven had lain awake all night before his first day, shaking with apprehension.

He'd had therapy. He didn't know who had paid for it, but he suspected it was not his mum or his nan, because they encouraged him to go as often as possible.

But Steven Lamb still knew what fear was.

He recognized it when it whispered from the high hedges that hemmed the narrow lanes; when it made him shudder alone on the moor on a warm summer's evening; when it visited his dreams and settled over his sleep in a visceral veil. But he'd also grown adept at throwing it off, at staring it down – and at turning his back on it and daring it to do its worst. Every time he hoisted the weighty DayGlo sack over his shoulder, and every furled newspaper he pushed through springy letter boxes helped him to thumb his nose at fear.

As did the Fracture Snub skateboard he'd bought with the first £60 he'd managed to save; and the secondhand iPod shuffle he clipped to his jeans; and the first real grown-up present he'd bought his mother for her birthday – a slim gold chain with a tiny green birthstone on it.

Something in Steven understood that each of these was a trophy he awarded himself for living his life and kicking fear's ass.

And now – as the winter made day into early night – he was doing it again.

*

Jonas stared into the cooling tea for what seemed like lifetimes while his brain tried so hard to think that a headache blossomed inside it like a mushroom cloud of pain.

'Jonas?'

He looked up to see Lucy standing in the doorway between the kitchen and the living room. She was in jeans and her favourite blue sweater.

She had got dressed for the man.

She rarely got dressed for him any more unless she planned to leave the house; mostly she just wore pyjamas, her bunny slippers and a fleece.

'Who was that?' he said bluntly.

'What?'

He could see in her eyes that she knew exactly what he meant.

'Here. Just now. Who was it?'

He didn't want to hear her answer. He *had* to ask the question, but if he could have, he'd have defied the laws of physics to have missed the man so he would never have to be here now, asking again . . . 'Who *was* he, Lu?'

'Jonas—' she started and then stopped and thought hard before going on. 'It's not what you're thinking.'

'I come in the front door and a strange man runs out the back. What am I thinking?'

She was having an affair. She couldn't say it. The thought made Jonas unbearably sad. He'd have thought he would be furious, but he wasn't. He just felt like sobbing.

'Come and sit down.' She held out her hand for his but he didn't give it. Instead he tucked both hands into his armpits, as if the forearms crossed on his chest might protect his heart from the truth.

'Please, Jonas. Can we sit down?'

He recognized the tone from the few times he had been to pick Lucy up from the kindergarten before they moved. Although then she would be crouching, so she could look into the face of a tearful child.

Now he realized he was close to tears himself, and felt the image was not far removed from reality, despite the fact that she had to look up to meet his eyes. He still saw love in her face, but his heart twisted as he saw pity there too. Pity for him. Pity because she was going to hurt him.

He bit his lip and wished it were already over; that he already knew the worst and didn't have to go through the sordid shock of hearing it.

Numb with foreboding, Jonas followed her into the front room.

They sat on the sofa, but not as they always had before. This time they sat at either end, prim and upright, half turned towards each other, like insurance salesmen. The room was dark but for the silent television which tonight showed *A Nightmare on Elm Street*.

'I've been wanting to tell you . . .' she started.

He couldn't look at her. Instead he watched Freddy Krueger's arms grow impossibly long and chillingly inescapable in a silent nightmare.

'. . . I just didn't know how.'

She was stalling. It was torture. He couldn't bear it.

'What's his name?'

She looked perplexed that he'd ask.

'Brian Connor.'

'How long have you been seeing him?' Every word sounded wrong to Jonas's ears, all the emphasis, all the syntax, as if the sentence had been cobbled together by robots, syllable by syllable, from sound bites found in some alien archive. He'd had no concept that he would or *could* ever say them to his wife.

'I'm not having an affair with him, Jonas.'

Was she going to deny the fact now? Or had he just caught them before anything could happen?

She slid her eyes from his gaze, which made him suspect the latter. Jonas felt himself unwind just a little bit. It was hardly any better, but it was *something*—

'He's run from me twice, Lucy.'

'He knows who you are. He didn't want to . . . get into a conversation.'

I'll bet, he thought. Some suitably outraged, angry and cuckolded words swirled in his head for a second but never got the energy to make it out of his mouth. He just gave up on them.

'He's from Exit, Jonas.'

She glanced at him to see his response, but he looked blank. She cleared her throat and made a gesture with her hands that was half shrug, half pleading.

'They help ... I mean ... they support ... voluntary euthanasia.'

Jonas made a sound that had never come out of his mouth before. Pain and shock and fury. He stood up as if ejected and stared down at Lucy, whose face was bathed in a pale-blue TV flicker.

'NO!' he shouted. '*NO!*'

*

Lucy Holly would have been Steven Lamb's favourite customer even if her husband hadn't been tipping him £5 a month to keep watch over her.

He liked the companionship of sitting down with her in her cosy front room where the fire was almost always alight and smelled wonderfully of warmth and winter. He liked the fact that she rarely tried to make conversation. Everybody always wanted to make conversation – to ask him how he was and what he was doing and whether he was all right. Even his best friend Lewis sometimes put out feelers. But Steven always felt that they were tiptoeing around the subject that surrounded him like a moat.

He didn't like it.

He didn't like to be reminded.

So sitting in silence with Lucy Holly while fake fear played out on the TV was oddly comforting for Steven. The scenes of horror rarely affected him and when they might he closed his eyes. But the warm silence

calmed him and sometimes even made a bit of conversation pop into his *own* head. Over the years he had
shared with Mrs Holly extracts from his life, and
learned that he could be of interest to someone outside his family, for reasons other than that he was still
alive when – really – he should be dead.

Now, as he struggled up the hill in the snow towards
Rose and Honeysuckle cottages, Steven hoped Mrs
Holly was watching something good – but not so good
that he felt bad about interrupting with a titbit about
his little brother, Davey, who had just this morning
accidentally swallowed his last remaining baby tooth
and who was therefore down to the last fifty-pence
piece he was ever likely to earn from their nan for
doing absolutely nothing. As Davey had already spent
the money at least ten times over in his head, the
tragedy was compounded for him, while that only
increased the humour of it for Steven.

The snow was shin-deep in the lane and Steven
wore wellies and his black waterproof trousers and
kept his head down as he trudged uphill, staring at the
crystalline surface he was about to break with each
step, smooth and pale grey in the fast dark of winter.

He passed the telegraph pole halfway up the hill
and heard it creak under the weight of snow and ice on
the lines. Creepy.

The DayGlo sack on his shoulder held only junk
mail tonight. Frank Tithecott gave him a fiver a week
so that he didn't have to bother stuffing leaflets

through letter boxes himself, and Steven kept it for the nights when he collected the newspaper money from his customers. He liked to make Mrs Holly's his last call of the day so that he knew he could go straight home afterwards and didn't have to rush.

He finally looked up to see that he had made it to the gate of Honeysuckle Cottage. Mrs Paddon didn't get a paper delivered. He'd knocked at her door once to see if she would like to order one from him but she had waved him away as if he were a Jehovah's Witness, and told him, 'We don't want that kind of thing here.' Steven still pondered on what on earth she might have thought she heard come out of his mouth instead of 'Would you like to order the *Western Morning News*?' After all this time, he'd never been able to come up with anything that sounded even remotely unsavoury.

Steven went up the three stone steps to the second gate and fumbled in the dark for the catch. As he did he heard something coming from Rose Cottage. He held his breath so he could hear better.

There it was again. Raised voices.

Steven was surprised. He was used to hearing customers shouting at each other as he opened the letter box on their lives for a brief moment. He couldn't remember the last time he'd opened the Randalls' letter box and *not* heard Neil yelling *something* at his father.

But he'd never heard raised voices at Rose Cottage.

He stood for a moment, undecided in the cold and dark.

He liked Lucy Holly very much. He liked Mr Holly too – even though he'd splashed about in the moat of Steven's memory. Steven hadn't liked *that*, but he'd understood that it was the policeman's job to ask. Plus Mr Holly was a source of income for him.

So even though he decided to open the gate and walk the few paces to the porch of Rose Cottage, Steven had not yet made up his mind whose side he should be on when he got there.

*

Lucy's bottom lip trembled but she sat up straight and determined.

'It's my life, Jonas. It's my right.'

'No!'

This was worse than an affair. *So much* worse! If Jonas had come home to find Brian Connor buried inside his wife, if she had eloped and sent him a postcard from Hawaii, it would not have been one millionth as bad as *this*. How could she do this to him? *How?* After the pills? After the tears? After they'd worked so hard and come so far? After they'd held each other and made love and whispered *I love you* in the bed where his parents had loved each other too? After everything he'd done for her? After he'd *protected* her . . .

She still wanted to die.

He shook his head stupidly, seeing horror in his mind the way he'd never seen it in a movie.

Lucy stood up almost straight and spoke quietly.

'It's my choice.'

He hit her.

He hit her with a heavy hand on the end of a long arm that swung fast. The blow spun her round and knocked her on to her knees on the couch – her face bouncing off the wall they'd repainted together the week they moved in. Summer Dawn, the colour was called. And as Lucy curled, sobbing, Jonas noticed with detachment the smear of blood that now sullied the horizon above the back of the couch.

He leaned over her, putting one hand on the wall beside the blood, the other on the arm of the couch.

'No,' he said again.

'*Stop!*'

Jonas looked around to see Steven Lamb in the hallway.

The boy stood there tightly clutching the strap of the DayGlo sack on his shoulder with both hands, as if it was keeping him from falling from a great height. Even from across the room and in semi-darkness, Jonas could see he was shaking.

'Just *stop*!' he cried again, the words vibrating and cracked with fear.

'Steven, get out!' Lucy wept at him from between her hands.

But he didn't. He just stood there and shook, staring at Jonas.

'Leave her *alone*!'

Jonas stood up and Lucy hunched away from him.

He had to go.

Without even looking at her again, he strode across the room.

Steven Lamb backed into the hall table and knocked over the vase of drooping carnations. He watched Jonas coming with a look of resigned terror on his face, then at the last second he stepped aside as he realized he was not coming for *him*.

Jonas brushed past him without a glance, and closed the front door quietly behind him.

Steven sank slowly to the cold flagstone floor, with his back against the banister, and hugged his knees to his chest.

Lucy looked up from the couch and saw that Jonas was gone and Steven was sitting in the hallway.

She touched her mouth where warm salt leaked from her lip, and tried to stop sobbing.

She backed off the couch awkwardly and dropped to her knees and crawled across the floor, not trusting her legs to carry her across the room. She knelt beside the boy in the hallway and put her arms around him.

'It's OK,' she told them both. 'It's OK. Jonas was

just upset, sweetheart. He didn't mean it. He was just very upset and frightened.'

But Steven didn't respond to her touch or even appear to see her. His eyes were still fixed in the middle distance, a deep frown splitting his forehead. Lucy felt liquid soaking her knees. She looked down and realized it was the water from the flowers. He was sitting in it.

'Steven,' she said. 'What's wrong?'

He did not respond and Lucy started to worry seriously about something other than herself and Jonas. She shook him by the shoulders and saw him blink, so did it again and raised her voice, making it sharp – her playground-duty voice.

'Steven! Talk to me, please! What happened? What's wrong?'

Finally the boy turned his haunted eyes towards her.

His lips trembled as he whispered:

'Nothing.'

*

Reynolds laid out his case on the cheap brown bedspread.

He had almost everything he needed.

He could hardly wait until the case here was officially closed so that he could go and see the Chief Super with his damning evidence. The thought of how that interview would unfold consumed Reynolds like porn.

'*Sir, could I speak to you on a matter of some delicacy?*'

He knew there might not be an actual promotion in snitching on his boss, but he was sure there would be *some* benefits for him somewhere down the line.

He anticipated taking Lucy Holly's statement with pure pleasure. At last, hearing critical words coming out of a mouth other than his. Around colleagues he'd always been discreet, but every little eye-roll, every murmur of discontent, every sudden cessation of chatter when Marvel walked past, he'd squirrelled away like winter nuts to sustain him whenever he felt he was all alone and that nobody else noticed what was going on. Even now the Senior Investigating Officer was probably knocking it back in the musty farmhouse with Joy Springer. It made Reynolds ashamed to be a policeman.

He hoped Lucy Holly would remember lots more about her confrontation with Marvel when she made her statement. What she had told him on the phone was good enough, but he would draw more from her. Nuances, looks, implied threats. Reynolds wanted them all, like an egg collector wants to shake a rare bird through a tiny hole in a shell.

He put his notes and Lucy's statement away in their folder, then turned on *Mastermind*.

*

Steven sat at the kitchen table with his hands around the first cup of tea he had ever accepted from Lucy Holly.

He was wearing a pair of Jonas's trousers. She had told him where to find some in the bedroom cupboard. It had been strange opening the Hollys' wardrobe, but no stranger than opening their front door. He'd tried several pairs before he found some newly washed jeans which were only too big, rather than ridiculous, and rolled them up, then cinched them with his school belt.

He'd put his trousers and underwear in the laundry basket, as she'd told him to, and gone back downstairs to the sound of the kettle whistling.

Now they sat on opposite sides of the table and Steven watched Mrs Holly pretending she was OK. He knew she wasn't. He'd seen her hands shake while making tea and he'd seen her wince as she put her cup to her broken lip.

He had registered these things but had detached himself from thinking about them too hard. Instead he had become a vague little ball with a shiny shell, so that he could protect himself. He knew now that *that* was his job, and his alone.

She smiled faintly at him, so he moved his mouth in response.

'You haven't drunk your tea,' she said.

It was no longer hot, but Steven drank it anyway – for her – and saw that this gift made her smile much better.

'I want you to have this,' she said, getting up and rummaging in a cupboard. She took out a tin and removed the lid with difficulty, then handed him a thick wad of £20 notes, so he took it, even though it made his stomach roll over. It made him think of his nan sellotaping names to her nick-nacks, so they'd all know who was getting what when she died.

Then Mrs Holly said 'thank you' and 'goodbye' and hugged him so hard that it squeezed tears from his eyes, which slid down his nose and fell on to her blue sweater.

Halfway down the hill Steven stopped and took the notes out of his pocket and fanned them out. Even in the dark he could see there was about £600.

He drew his arm back and threw the notes hard into the night sky, where the biting wind whipped them away.

Then he put his head down and walked on through a blizzard of snow and money.

After Steven left, Lucy took the knife Jonas had given her, and inched slowly upstairs with it.

Steven had left the cupboard open and several pairs of Jonas's uniform trousers on the bed. Leaning her sticks against the wall, Lucy started to fold them back into the wardrobe, the familiar effort of the task making her feel warm and calm.

An errant sob emptied her of the final breath of unexpected drama.

She didn't blame him.

He had worked so hard, under such pressure, to keep her going. Nobody could have done a better job than Jonas. He was so strong, so patient.

The pills had been a bitter blow and her sense of having failed him was all-embracing. Her shame was almost unbearable. She couldn't live properly and she hadn't even been able to die properly.

And for a while she had almost believed she would never try again. Contacting Exit had only been insurance at first. So she would know better how to do it if things got unbearable. Brian Connor had talked through her options and it was a relief not to pretend that she would never consider it. But she tucked the thought away and kept going. Kept battling. Kept telling her mother she was feeling better all the time. Kept being the Lucy that everyone knew and loved.

And then Marvel had said that thing.

And she had understood how the world saw her. That at some indeterminate point she had ceased to be Lucy Holly – teacher, daughter, athlete, friend, wife, lover – and had become *that thing*. She couldn't even think the words. She was amazed she had been able to get them out to Reynolds, and thought she must have been more angry than she'd ever been in her whole life to do so.

She hoped Jonas would come home soon. He was

the only one who had never made her feel that way. She knew he'd hit her out of fear, and the pain of her split lip was nothing compared to the pain she knew he must feel at her planning to leave him alone. At the thought that she could *want* to leave him alone.

She ached with sadness and pressed a pair of his uniform trousers to her cheek, feeling her lashes brush the rough serge.

As she raised her head and lifted the trousers to put them away, Lucy noticed they were missing a button.

The Final Day

Jonas raised his face to the sky and felt the feathery snow turn slowly to needles of hot water on his skin. He opened his eyes and was surprised to find himself in the shower in the bathroom of Rose Cottage.

He shook himself. He must have drifted off and dreamed.

He noticed with surprise that he hadn't drawn the blinds on the two little windows. It had become his habit since he had stood on the stile across the valley and seen into this very room. But still, it was late; past midnight, he guessed – although he didn't know when he had last checked the time – and the bathroom was thick with steam.

He must have been standing under the shower for a good long time.

He was hungry. Starving. Even under the hiss of the water he could hear his stomach rumbling.

He turned slowly, blinking the water out of his eyes, then wiped them and looked again at the window that faced away from the moor and towards Springer Farm. Although the black pane of glass reflected only the lit bathroom, something flickered at its centre. Puzzled, Jonas looked over his shoulder to see what might give such reflection but all that was behind him was the mirrored cabinet made opaque by the steam.

Jonas stepped out of the stream of water and wiped a stripe of condensation off the little side window.

Through it he could see quite clearly that Springer Farm was on fire.

*

The missing button changed everything for Lucy.

She looked at the loose thread above the button's surviving twin, and was stunned that it could be so. That *this* – this twist of lonely black thread – was what could make her doubt the man she loved with all her heart, when the slap had failed to do so.

It made no sense. That Jonas would hand in a button from his own uniform trousers as evidence if he were trying to cover Danny's tracks. It had made no sense when she'd said that to Marvel and it made no sense now.

Unless Jonas hadn't known what he was doing.

Or what he had *done*.

Was that possible?

Lucy sat utterly still and stared at the place were the button used to be. She groped for sanity – for a finger-hold on any reality that did not sound like the plot of one of her horror movies.

The Exorcist flashed to her mind. The child trapped inside the ranting demon desperately pushing the words *Help Me* up through the tender skin of her midriff. It made her think of Jonas's face at her hospital bedside. The face of a frightened child staring into the void.

Or out of it.

Help me.

She shivered.

She had briefly covered cases of multiple person-alities in her Abnormal Psychology lectures. Patients who lived their lives as two, three – even more – dis-tinct and different people. *Alters*, they were called, she remembered now. One man had even beaten prison on a rape charge after the court accepted that he was unaware that one of his alters had committed the crime.

Was Jonas such a case? Had something terrible happened to him as a boy that had caused his person-ality to fracture into several brittle parts?

She thought of the photo of the carefree child. Something had changed Jonas; some trauma. Was it something to do with Danny Marsh? With the fire at the farm? With horses? Had Marvel actually been *right*? Lucy shuddered at the thought.

Jonas had been under pressure for years. His parents' death, her diagnosis, starting a new job all alone. And then she'd failed to kill herself, so that he'd had to come home from work every day not knowing whether he would find her alive or dead. Then Margaret Priddy had been murdered and Marvel had treated him like shit, and someone had started to leave him notes telling him to do his *job* . . .

Any one of those things could have pulled the trigger on the loaded gun of a damaged psyche.

Did Jonas clear up the vomit? Or did an *alter* do it without his knowledge?

Did an *alter* lose the button and Jonas merely find it?

She believed Jonas was telling the truth. Then again, maybe *his* truth was not *the* truth.

She still didn't fear Jonas. She trusted him with her life.

But she did fear the stranger inside him.

She stood up suddenly and nearly fell. The jelly in her legs was not all the disease. She tried *not* to be sure. In her head, in her intellect, she tried to rationalize, to hypothesize, to justify Jonas's contradictions so that she could disprove her own conclusions. But her body overrode her and made her shake with adrenaline.

Hollywood had been preparing Lucy for this for years. She had learned from the mistakes of air-headed heroines, and determined to be different. But now that the fantasy was made real, it made her feel sick, and numb with confusion.

She heard the front door open.

Jonas.

Her panic was only outweighed by her indecision. She had to hide from him! And yet that seemed ridiculous. Hide from Jonas? She would just feel like a fool.

He didn't call from the door. He *always* called from the door, to let her know it was him.

Maybe it *wasn't* him.

The thought spurred her to action.

She slid to the floor with the trousers still in her hands, and rolled under the bed.

She heard the middle stair creak and felt fear trickle down her spine. Jonas always took care to miss that tread.

Who *was* it that was coming up the stairs towards her?

Suddenly, rolling under the bed seemed the smartest thing she'd ever done, even though she felt horribly vulnerable. If he saw her, she had no defence. He would lean down and grip her ankles and drag her out like a pig in a slaughterhouse.

The man walked down the landing and into the bedroom.

Lucy held her breath.

She saw only his black trousers and boots, still with snow clinging to them. Jonas never wore his boots upstairs. Taking them off at the foot of the stairs was second nature to him.

The man crossed the room as if he owned it. There was no hesitation, no caution, no fear that he might be detected.

Lucy heard a drawer open and shut, and watched the boots leave.

After a few moments, she heard the shower go on.

She frowned.

It *must* be Jonas!

Relief made her shake.

And yet *something* stopped her from coming out from underneath the bed. It wasn't the fact that he had hit her. Somehow that seemed almost incidental now. It was something else. The missing button, the silent entrance, the boots upstairs, those things meant more to her now. Something – maybe something learned from years of horror films – made her lie there on the dusty carpet, hiding from the husband she loved until, at last, the exhaustion of fear – coupled with the familiar and homely sound of the shower – lulled her to an unlikely sleep.

*

Marvel awoke to the sound of flames.

It was not the sound of a fire in the hearth, but the crackling roar of a furnace, accompanied by what sounded like small-arms fire.

He checked his watch: 2am. He rolled out of bed and staggered straight into the wall-mounted TV, knocking himself over and almost out. His stomach protested the sudden activity and he burped the sophisticated aroma of Cinzano into his nose.

He regained his feet and yanked the curtain aside to see two or three silhouetted figures backlit by the burning farmhouse. A section of tiles exploded off the roof in a volley of shots and arced into the white-spotted snow-sky like fireworks.

He fumbled his damp shoes off the radiator, threw his coat over his vest and shorts, and ran outside – another stagger giving away just how recently he had left the house that was now an inferno.

Reynolds, Rice and Grey were throwing water at the front-door handle – apparently in an attempt to cool it down enough to open it. They were using what looked like flower pots, and scooping water from an old trough in the yard. Singh staggered about in the snow with a ladder that was too short to do anything more than be a hazard to all, while Pollard shouted, 'Mrs Springer!' repeatedly and randomly at the house between staring at the flames, mouth agape like a tourist.

What a bunch of fucking babies!

'Where is she?' yelled Marvel above the roar, but Pollard just shook his head.

'Fire brigade?' yelled Marvel again, with the obligatory mime of a phone at his ear, and Reynolds shouted, 'On their way!'

They'll never make it, thought Marvel. Not in this snow.

The snow had continued to fall and was knee deep in places. Great plumes of steam joined the smoke pumping from the roof of the house, as flakes sizzled and spat off the tiles like fat in a pan.

'Help them!' he yelled at Pollard, pointing at the others, then ran to the trough, stripping off his coat. He plunged it into the water, which was sharp with broken ice, then pulled it on once more, barely noticing the freezing cold against his bare skin. He pulled the coat up over his head, then rushed at the front door just as Singh and Grey broke it open with the ladder.

Reynolds tried to stop him, standing in his way, grabbing at his coat like a fan.

'You're drunk,' he shouted in Marvel's face, without even the nicety of a 'sir'.

Marvel elbowed him in the nose – it wasn't a punch, but it was *something* – then barged past him shouting, 'Out of the way!' and ran inside.

Inside was an oasis of calm compared to the court-yard and for a moment Marvel stopped and swayed and took it all in.

The flames were up the curtains and walls, but the flagstone floor was a daunting foe to fire. The bottles and the glasses he'd left just a few hours before were still on the table. Smoke obscured much of his view, and – not content with blinding him – now reached down Marvel's throat with long, sharp nails and started to claw at his lungs.

From outside he could hear Reynolds hoarsely shouting 'Sir!' with an irritable air – as if Marvel were a dog that wouldn't come back – and Grey yelling something about hosepipes. They sounded shockingly close for people in another universe.

He coughed and spat and shielded his face from the heat coming at him from the far end of the room as he edged closer to where he knew the sofa was.

He staggered once and caught his thigh a painful blow on the kitchen table.

Halfway there, Marvel thought maybe he shouldn't be doing this. The smoke was making it hard to breathe and steam was rising off his coat, while his exposed hands, arms and legs were uncomfortably hot.

He dithered.

He almost turned back.

But the thought of staggering back into the snow with nothing to show for his derring-do but a bit of a cough was anathema.

Buoyed by bloody-mindedness and sweet vermouth, he carried on inching his way across the room until he could make out Joy Springer lying face-down on the hairy sofa with her four cats running frantically up and down her body as though she were the last piece of flotsam in the wake of a shipwreck.

He reached out to take her arm and the big grey fluffy cat shot out a razor-sharp claw to keep him at bay.

Fuck.

Marvel dropped to his knees and huddled under his coat for a moment and he coughed until he retched – his eyes and nose and mouth streaming with fluids as his body tried to reject the killing smoke.

Down here the air was clearer, and Marvel bent and touched his head to the flagstones as if praying, so he could breathe better. When he had refreshed himself he looked up blearily and saw the writing on the wall behind the sofa.

She knew

He recognized it immediately, even though it was a foot high and on a wall. How he could ever have thought it might be a match for Danny Marsh's hand was ridiculous. He saw that, now that it was writ so large. And in what appeared to be blood.

Marvel grabbed Joy Springer's arm and yanked her unceremoniously on to the floor. Three of the cats leaped clear and disappeared; the grey one came with her – its claws firmly lodged in the wool of her old cardigan. It glared at Marvel and growled menacingly before darting away.

He rolled Joy on to her back and recoiled at the bloody sockets where her eyes had been.

He thought of Ang Nu. He thought of cocktail-onion jokes. He thought of Danny Marsh.

Danny Marsh was not the killer. The killer had been *here*.

The bastard had killed Joy Springer *right under his nose*!

Suddenly there was not enough air. He gulped for it, needing even more than usual to combat his shock, and finding so much less than he wanted that his shock became panic in a hot, blinding second.

He had to get out!

He half stood, staggered, banged his head on the table, fell to his knees, rolled, crawled, gasped at the floor, lungs bursting, head about to pop, lost his way to the door, and finally curled into a ball and retched Cinzano-flavoured bile on to his own hands.

He had to get out. He had to tell Reynolds. He had to—

Breathe. He had to *breathe* . . .

But he couldn't.

He *couldn't*—

And the door at the far end of the kitchen suddenly blew off its hinges and let in a fireball that incinerated Joy Springer and the hairy sofa as if they were one big ball of tinder, and then rolled across the room towards Marvel.

*

The Land Rover only took Jonas so far.

The blizzard was blinding and he did his best but he

needed to get there fast and he tried too hard. Halfway up the driveway to Springer Farm it came to a sudden lurching halt in a ditch that Jonas couldn't even see until after he'd climbed out and gone round to the front of the car.

He wasted no time digging it out, just headed up towards the farm on foot, just as he always had as a boy.

*

Reynolds despised Marvel. Never more than now, when the man had elbowed him aside and rushed into flames in a display of stupid bravado fuelled by liquor.

Part of him was horrified when his commanding officer disappeared through the door; the bigger part was just furious that when Marvel emerged he would be regarded as a hero instead of the selfish, stupid, alcoholic *wanker* that he undoubtedly was.

He shouted for Marvel a few times, and set his face in a worried frown. His colleagues stood, open-mouthed, exchanging looks, carrying off their worried frowns with far more skill, in his eyes, while all silently asked each other the same question: *Should we go after him?*

Grey yelled something unintelligible and ran off into the darkness.

The kitchen window blew out as if a bomb had gone off inside. Bright new flames licked out of the cavity as the fire tried its best to escape the confines of the house and reach the courtyard and the cottages beyond.

'No one go after him!' Reynolds barked. 'I don't want anyone else hurt!'

He saw their relief and was relieved in turn that no one was going to insist that they all do something heroic.

Then someone rushed past his shoulder and into the house anyway.

It was Jonas Holly.

*

Jonas had arrived just in time to hear Reynolds yell not to go after him, and knew there must be at least one person in that inferno.

He ran into the farmhouse before he'd even decided to.

The heat was like being hit in the face, and steam rose immediately from his wet clothes and hair. The smoke was debilitating. He stopped dead, then took a few blind paces – hands out in front of him in case of obstacles.

He hit the table with his thigh and at the same time stepped on something hard yet yielding. He groped at his feet and found a slippery arm. He seized it with both hands, and backed out of the door with the body bumping along behind him.

The others crowded round, helping him to drag it out of the danger zone.

It was Marvel.

Only half of one sleeve and the upper part of his coat still gave him much cover – his vest and shorts were just blackened rags. His left shin was a vivid mess of red and black, like the leading edge of a lava-flow, with the bedrock of bone showing through in places. The rest of that leg was livid and raw, with bubbles in the flesh of the thigh. His ever-damp shoes had protected his feet from the worst of it, but it was small comfort.

Singh immediately dropped to his knees to check his vitals.

'Not breathing,' he said, and started CPR.

Jonas coughed and spat before gasping, 'Is there anyone else?'

'Mrs Springer, we think,' said Rice.

Jonas turned to go back but Reynolds and Pollard barred his way.

'She can't be alive,' said Reynolds. 'Stay here.'

'She might be!' cried Jonas, bursting into a fresh bout of coughing and trying to go around them.

'Stay *here*,' said Reynolds. 'That's an order.'

Jonas looked at him in fury and Reynolds almost put up a hand in self-defence.

'It's your *job* to *protect* people!'

'Not dead people,' said Reynolds – and although it was a good answer, he took no pleasure in saying it.

'He's coming back,' said Singh with relief flooding his voice.

They all turned to look down at Marvel, who was now breathing noisily and irregularly, and jerking his arms and legs as if trying to make angels in the snow.

'Shit,' said Grey. 'You think he's got brain damage?'

'Where's the *fucking* ambulance?' cried Singh.

'Call control and tell them we need an air ambulance,' said Reynolds. 'Tell them officer down.'

Pollard opened his phone and scurried about the courtyard, seeking a signal.

Jonas started to heap snow on to Marvel's burned legs and Singh and Rice quickly did the same.

'He'll be fine,' said Reynolds with more confidence than he felt. He leaned over Marvel and said, 'Sir? John? Can you hear me, sir?'

Marvel's eyes flickered and rolled back in his head, then steadied and came to something like focus on his Task Force and Jonas Holly looking down at him.

'Murder,' he whispered hoarsely.

'What, sir?' Reynolds put his ear close to Marvel's lips.

'Murder,' he mouthed again weakly.

This time Reynolds got it.

'He said murder.'

The others looked at him, confused.

Reynolds shrugged and – with a wholly in-appropriate sense of dawning happiness – realized he was now in charge, due to the unforeseen incapacity of the Senior Investigating Officer. The fire was obviously beyond their control, even though Grey had finally arrived with a coil of heavy-duty yellow hosepipe over his shoulder. Now he needed to stop responding like a panicky man in pyjamas, and start responding like an SIO at a crime scene. He swelled visibly as he straightened up over Marvel's prone figure half buried in snow.

'Charlie, get that pipe hooked up and you and Dave do your best,' he told Grey and Pollard, then pointed at Marvel. 'Armand and Elizabeth, keep helping *him*. The whole area is a potential crime scene. Me and Jonas will take a look round, just in case.' Jonas and *I*. Jonas and *I*. Jesus Christ! One man down and his grammar was all over the fucking place.

'We're just giving up on her, are we?' said Jonas.

'Yes,' said Reynolds, thrilled by the horrible brutality of that truth. He looked Jonas square in the eye in case he was going to have trouble with him, but the young policeman just gave a tilt of his head that might have been assent, might have been a shrug. Either way, Reynolds strode away from the scene of the crime and fetched his torch and his back-up torch for Jonas, then led him across the courtyard.

They left the orange glow and the heat that was turning the snowy courtyard into a giant puddle, and moved into the darkness behind the stables. Once away from the action, it was shockingly serene. Jonas felt quite removed from the horror of it all. The farmhouse burning down sounded like a jolly bonfire; the tiles blasting off the roof like rockets and bangers. The smell of roasting meat filled the air and Jonas shivered, but got a pang of hunger that disgusted the vegetarian in him.

He felt strangely ambivalent about Joy Springer inside the burning house. He wondered if her cats had died too, and thought of the way their fur made him sneeze whenever he'd gone into the gloomy old kitchen with its towering dresser and Belfast sink.

Reynolds switched his torch on; Jonas followed suit and immediately went blind, but for the two bright shafts of speckled light which showed tunnels of falling snow. He turned it off again, without bothering to explain to Reynolds why it was easier to see without it.

They crossed the old hard standing with its ridged concrete, where the blacksmith used to shoe the ponies. Jonas could almost feel Taffy's head, heavy in his arms as he dozed, while his neat little hoofs were shaved and shaped and scorched and hammered. That strangely comforting stink of burned hair, and the yard lurcher, Nelson, darting in to snatch the biggest bits of horn, which made his breath reek and gave him the runs . . .

Reynolds said something Jonas didn't hear.

'What?' he asked.

'Could be anywhere,' said Reynolds again, shining his torch across the field behind the stables.

Jonas didn't answer. From the corner of his eye he'd seen something regular at one edge of the concrete standing. Three or four darker patches in the snow which his memory could supply no immediate explanation for.

He dropped back from Reynolds and walked over to check it out.

Footprints.

Now that he had found what he was looking for, Jonas switched his torch back on and examined the depressions in the snow.

Although the snow was filling them fast – softening them and making identification impossible – they were definitely footprints. Jonas shone his torch into them. There was no tread visible at the bottom of each twelve-inch-deep impression, just a delicate frosting of new flakes glittering in the false light.

Jonas followed them with his torch.

The prints led down the hill – straight towards Rose Cottage.

'Lucy!' he shouted into the night, as if she might hear him.

Reynolds shone his torch in Jonas's face and saw terror there.

'What?' he said.

'My house!' cried Jonas and pointed to where the bathroom light shone square and yellow two fields away. 'He's gone to my house! My wife! She's alone. I left her *alone*!'

Then he started to run, bounding through the snow in long, awkward strides.

Reynolds ran after him for a few paces, then stopped. 'Jonas! Wait!'

But Jonas ignored him.

'Fuck!' Reynolds turned and made his way back to the blackness behind the cottages. He needed re-inforcements. If the killer was indeed at Jonas Holly's house then he didn't want to be the only back-up. Once back on the flat ground, he slipped and skidded around to the courtyard once more, almost surprised that things had been going on here without him. The house was still burning, Grey was still playing with the hosepipe, and Rice and Singh were still bent over Marvel and had started CPR again. Reynolds rushed straight to them.

'How is he?'

'Dead,' said Singh between compressions.

'*Shit*,' said Reynolds. 'Shit fuck shit!'

'Yeah, I know,' said Singh. 'Should I stop?'

Reynolds thought of the months of work he'd put into the file he'd hoped would see Marvel kicked off the force in disgrace and without a pension.

Wasted.

Now Marvel had instead died trying to rescue a civilian from a burning building.

Die a hero, stay a hero.

Nothing was fair.

'Yes,' he told Singh. 'Stop.'

Rice and Singh both stopped working on Marvel, and Grey stopped his own pointless task and came over and stood beside Rice. Singh remained kneeling in the sludge that the snow had become. He took off his jacket and laid it carefully over Marvel's face. Then he noticed something sticking out of the inside pocket of Marvel's coat and carefully removed a burned and crispy photograph.

Two charred and blistered boys, damaged beyond recognition.

'Did he have children?' he asked.

'Don't think so,' said Grey.

'Right,' said Reynolds, before they could all get maudlin, 'our man might be at Holly's cottage down the hill. We all need to get there *now*!'

'How?' said Pollard, whose face was as black as a miner's. 'Even fire and ambulance can't make it.'

'Across the fields. You can see it from here. Everyone get a torch and a coat.'

They all looked at each other.

'Come *on*!' yelled Reynolds, and they all scurried into their respective cottages and out again in seconds, Singh in just a sweater.

'Get your jacket,' Reynolds told him roughly. 'You need it more than him.'

Singh tentatively lifted his jacket off the body and pulled it on.

Then Reynolds led his new team out of the courtyard, leaving DCI John Marvel to another, colder shroud, which covered him slowly from a pitch-black sky.

*

When Lucy woke there was dust on her lips and carpet-print on her cheek.

She knew the sound of an empty house and this was it.

The telephone was downstairs. She didn't know how long she had, and couldn't afford the time the return journey would take.

She remembered her first line of defence and limped to the landing and tried to move the bookcase to the top of the stairs, but with her weakened hands and wrists it was a hopeless task which she was quickly forced to abandon.

She thought of banging on the wall to alert Mrs Paddon, then decided not to. What could an eighty-nine-year-old woman possibly do to help? Lucy would only be placing her in danger. Instead she went into the back bedroom, picked up the gaff, opened the trapdoor into the attic and – after several wavering attempts – managed to hook the eye on the sliding ladder and tug it to the ground.

Then Lucy put the knife that Jonas had insisted she carry into her back pocket, picked up the camping lantern from the bedside table and put an unsteady foot on the first rung.

It took her almost fifteen minutes to climb the ladder. She slipped a dozen times – banging her elbows, grazing her fingers, once tearing a gash in her forearm – and had to take several gasping rests, clinging on to the upper rungs and kneeling on the lower ones to try to give her legs some respite. The longer she struggled and the higher she climbed, the more frantic she got to ascend into the square of darkness.

The irony did not escape her. She had tried to kill herself. Still *might*. And yet here she was, trying to hide from a killer who would do the job for her.

The instinct for self-preservation came as a shock to Lucy.

When she finally made it and hauled herself into the dry, cold space that smelled of wood and feathers and mouse droppings, Lucy could not move again for ten minutes. She retched from effort and sobbed in pain.

And then the kick in the teeth came when she found that she could not pull the ladder up behind her. She strained and wept, but her grip was limp and her arms feeble and the ladder didn't seem to be designed for such a thing anyway. There was nothing she could do about it. She tried to move a heavy wooden packing case over the entrance but it stuck on a joist and she had expended the last of her energy. She cried again with frustration. She *knew* what she should be doing! In her head she had it all worked out! The Lucy Holly that she used to be would have run, jumped, set booby traps, armed herself, been prepared. *That* Lucy Holly would have kicked zombie butt and outwitted the very devil. But that Lucy was long gone. And with the new Lucy's body the only one available to her now, it was all she could do to crawl into a corner with her unlit lantern and her knife, huddle in a musty old armchair, and wait for the killer to come home.

*

The killer did come home, although nobody would ever have guessed it.

*

Jonas was a fit man, but running through the foot-deep snow was exhausting. His lungs tore at his chest and his heart pounded his ribs like a madman in a cage. His boots and trousers were wet well past his knees and seemed to be made of something that stuck to snow and dragged at his legs every time he tried to lift them to place one foot in front of the other.

Still, he made it across the first field lit only by the stars and a slim moon, his eyes adjusting so well that he even spotted the gap in the hedge that denoted a gate, which he clambered over so fast that his legs got left behind and he dropped face-first into the snow on the other side before getting up and running again.

Despite the snow over uneven ground and the wind that drove the flakes into him, fear made him faster than he'd ever have thought possible and blurred the blizzard so that he was running through a snow globe as it was shaken up. He couldn't tell which way was up, as flakes came at him from everywhere – now in his eyes, now in his ears, now slapping the back of his head like a teacher. The only guide was that bathroom light which – mercifully – he had left on in another time and place he barely even remembered now. It disappeared and jiggled and jerked on the inconstant horizon. If it weren't for that he might have run to Withypool for all the sense of direction he had left in him.

Now and then he saw the tracks he was following, but he didn't really care about them any more. His target was that bathroom window. He didn't care where the killer was going – as long as it wasn't Rose Cottage. As long as it wasn't to Lucy.

Not Lucy! Not Lucy! Not Lucy! The words beat the rhythm of his headlong race across the snow.

He pulled his phone from his pocket and looked at the display but there was no signal. Big shock. He tossed it aside like ballast.

The prints in the snow curved slowly to the right. The gate in the second field was off somewhere to his right and opened on to the lane. He couldn't afford the detour and kept running straight down the hill. He would have to go over the hedge beside Rose Cottage. Or through it.

Either way, it wasn't stopping him.

The hedge loomed, huge and black with its happy

icing of snow. Because of his height, Jonas had done high jump at school. He wasn't much good at it but he remembered the basics. He speeded up, turned in at the last moment, and threw himself at the hedge in a not-ungraceful arc. He landed high enough to be suspended there in uncomfortable limbo. He rolled on to his stomach, reaching for anything that would give him purchase, gripping handfuls of branches and thorns, dragging himself across the five-foot expanse, which sagged and dug and snapped under him like cruel water, before dropping to the ground in a heap on the other side, right next to Lucy's Beetle. There was a crunch and he winced as he landed on his torch.

He stood, jerked forward as if to rush into the house, and then stopped and caught his breath. The killer could be there. He couldn't just rush in. He needed to *think*. He couldn't afford to screw this up. Lucy needed him. Now more than ever.

He couldn't fall apart on her now.

The front door was closed but unlocked. His fault. *His* fault. Leave it open for people so Lucy wouldn't have to keep getting up. This was the countryside; his home village. They'd felt so safe! Leaving the door unlocked had become a dangerous habit, and a bed-time oversight.

He sucked air into his burning lungs and pushed open the door.

Everything was the same.

He peered into the dark front room but the TV was

off, although the fire still burned softly behind the guard.

No light in the kitchen. He crossed quietly to it. It was empty, and the washing machine hummed.

Up the dark stairs, pausing at every other step to listen for an intruder, missing the tread halfway up that creaked so badly.

The bookcase at the top of the stairs had been moved slightly, which Jonas discovered painfully with his left shoulder. A little gasp of surprise escaped him before he could apprehend it.

No answering sound.

The light was on under the bathroom door. Jonas went in.

The air was still slightly warm and heavy with moisture from his earlier shower.

Jonas's gut lurched. There was blood on the tap.

There was blood.

On the tap.

He went closer to the basin. The smear of blood was unmistakable – as if someone had turned the tap on or off with a bloodstained hand. A little drip ran down the porcelain.

He frantically looked around with eyes attuned to this one thing, and found more. Two drops on the floor, a smear near the laundry basket, what looked like half a handprint on the outer edge of the basin – four slightly splayed strips where someone had rested their printless fingers.

Jonas turned sharply to go and caught a movement close to his head that made him flinch and put up a hand in self-defence.

He almost laughed. He'd jumped at his own fuzzy reflection in the cabinet mirror!

He stopped dead.

In the lingering condensation on the cold glass mirror was a message he had no doubt was meant for him.

She is next

'*Lucy!*' he cried in strangled horror, and ran to the bedroom, slapping on lights. She was not there. He ran into the box room. Empty. Jonas was no longer looking for, or afraid of, the killer. He only wanted to see his wife.

The back bedroom. His childhood room. She wasn't there but, behind the door, the loft ladder had been dropped from the attic.

'Lucy?' he hissed. He was wary again now. He couldn't see how Lu could have extended the ladder, let alone gone up it, without help.

Or without being forced.

Halfway up the ladder was a long smear of blood.

He bit his lip to keep himself quiet. He peered up into the black hole. There was no light in the attic; they used a camping lantern. A lantern that was no longer in its usual place on the bedside table.

Jonas gripped the ladder and slowly climbed into the dark.

*

From his secret place the killer watched with a dispassionate eye as Jonas Holly warily ascended the ladder. He knew what he would find up there, and knew that this would soon be over.

It was sad, but it was the way things had to be.

*

Reynolds and his team were lost.

They had run across the fields more slowly than Jonas because they did not have a wife in danger on the other side and because they were not as fit, as fast or as tall as him. The snow was a problem – both that which was deep underfoot and the fresh flakes that were whipped stingingly into their faces.

They followed Jonas's tracks to where they appeared to run straight into a hedge.

'Shit,' said Reynolds.

They could see the lighted window in the cottage on the other side of the hedge, but there seemed to be no way to get to it.

'There must be a gate,' Reynolds said, and so they started to look for it, splitting into two groups, each going in opposite directions down the hedge-line.

Singh tried to find a place to burrow through, but learned a quick lesson in blackthorn and sheep wire.

They reconvened at the place where Jonas's tracks were now filling with new snow, and Reynolds turned towards the lane and started a methodical circum-navigation of the field in an attempt to find a way out.

*

Lucy jumped at the rattle of the ladder. The yellow patch of light in the attic floor was darkened by a shadow and she got out of the armchair, groping for the knife.

She saw the silhouette of a man's head rise into the attic space and held the blade out towards him in hands that shook uncontrollably.

'Who's there?' she said in a tremulous voice.

'It's me!' Jonas sounded hugely relieved. 'Are you OK, Lu?'

'Don't come up here!'

His head and shoulders were already in the attic and she could see him cocking his head, trying to squint into the darkness to make her out.

'Sweetheart, what's wrong?'

He stepped up another rung so he was up to his waist in the attic.

'*Stay there!*'

Jonas stopped dead. Lucy's head spun. This was

ridiculous. This was Jonas. He had come to help her, not to harm her. But she needed some . . . explanations.

'I found the missing button!' she cried.

Of all the things he'd expected Lucy to say next, that was the stone-cold last. Jonas almost laughed. Would have, if he hadn't been able to hear the shake and the fear in Lucy's voice.

'What button?'

'The button you found on Margaret Priddy's roof. It came off your trousers.'

'No it didn't. I checked when I found it. What's this all about, Lu? How did you get up here?'

'It did, Jonas! I found a pair of your uniform trousers tonight with a button missing.'

Jonas still failed to see how that would scare his wife so badly she would hide in the attic. She'd always been so objective and sensible. He couldn't understand—

Panic suddenly made him tingle all over.

'Lu? Did you take anything? Did you take any . . . thing?'

'No! Jonas! Something's going on here, but it's with *you*, not *me*! I think . . . I think something's *not right* with you, Jonas.'

He was not convinced. The note of hysteria in her voice worried him. He started to move up as if to make the final climb into the attic, but her scream cut him short.

'*Stay there!*'

'OK. OK, Lu. I'm not moving. I'm staying right here.'

A sob of relief came from the darkness.

'Lu, do you have the lantern?'

'Yes.'

'Can you turn it on, baby? So I can see you? So we can talk?'

She hesitated, then he heard her fumble around in the darkness, sniffing back tears. He was careful not to make a move while she was distracted; she sounded brittle enough to snap at any moment.

The lantern glowed an unnatural white beside her, and made her haggard face look ghostly, while the knife in her hand glittered.

He saw the cut on her swollen lip.

'Lucy! What happened? Did you fall? There's blood in the bathroom.'

She touched her lip with one shaking finger. 'You did this, Jonas. When you hit me.'

'What?'

Lucy's voice was small and childlike. 'Earlier tonight.'

'I never hit you, Lu! I never *would*! What the hell's going on?'

'You don't remember,' she whispered.

'Lucy, please, you're scaring me. Please tell me what's happened. Why are you up here? Did he come back? Did he hurt you, Lu?'

'Who?'

'The killer! The man I chased out of the back door! Did he come back? Lucy, *tell* me!'

'You don't remember,' she said. 'You don't remember what happened. You were somebody else.'

'Lucy, I'm me. I'm just me.'

He didn't know what else to say. Lucy must have taken something. He didn't want to engage in some weird drug-induced conversation with her. He was the protector. He needed to get her to come out of the attic with him and downstairs so he could check her over and get her to vomit. Maybe he'd have to take her to hospital. The Land Rover might make it.

'Lu, I'm coming up, OK?'

'No!'

'Sweetheart, I have to, I—'

'NO! *Stay there!*'

He stopped again, still on the ladder but now more in the attic than out of it.

She tried to control the wobble in her voice. 'Jonas, you have to listen to me. Please.'

'I'm listening,' he said, although really he was wondering if he could rush her, or whether it might be dangerous with her waving that knife around in front of her.

'Jonas,' she began – then started to cry. 'Jonas, I think you lost your button the night you killed Margaret Priddy.'

'Lucy!—'

'*Listen!* You said you'd listen to me!'

'I am,' he said, and this time he really was.

'It wasn't really you, Jonas. I know you'd never, *ever* hurt anyone. I don't just believe it, I *know* it. But I think some . . . *part* of you killed Margaret and Yvonne and the others. I don't know why, but you've been under such pressure, Jonas! Your parents and the job and then me, being such a burden to you . . . And then . . . and then when I couldn't even *kill* myself . . .' Lucy trailed off, but gathered herself up again and went on. 'I know how scared you were, Jonas. I saw it on your face! You were like a frightened little boy, like a—'

'*Shut up!*'

Lucy stopped, shocked, at Jonas's words, which came out with a thick, low vehemence she'd never heard from him before.

'Jonas?' she said cautiously.

'Shut up! You'll wake him!'

Lucy swayed in disbelief. The voice was not Jonas's. It was rougher and older, and his face had changed. Lucy sought the softness in Jonas's eyes and found only black nothingness.

'Who's there?' she whispered.

'None of your business,' he snapped.

'Who will I wake up?'

'The boy. We let him sleep.'

'Who's we?'

'Me and Jonas. Although *he*'s been *no* fucking use. Won't do his job.'

Lucy caught her breath.

Do your job, crybaby.

'What's Jonas's job?'

'Protecting the boy, of course. That's always been his job. He's the protector.'

'And who are you?'

There was a long pause.

'I am the killer.'

Something in Lucy hoped she might be dreaming, but the cold and the smell of mouse droppings and the knife in her hands all felt very real to her. She made a huge effort to speak simply and gently so as not to provoke the person who was no longer her husband.

'Who is the boy?'

'The boy is us. He's who we used to be.'

'What do you need to protect him from?'

Silence.

'How can Jonas protect the boy?'

The man who wasn't Jonas shrugged, but looked sly. He knew.

'Why does the boy need protection? What happened to him?'

'Shut *up*!' The man who was not her husband put an angry foot up on to the floor of the attic. 'You'll *wake* him!'

Lucy spoke quickly and gently, trying to talk her way past the killer to reach Jonas. 'Was it something to

do with the fire, Jonas? What happened to you and
Danny up at the farm? Did somebody hurt you, sweetheart? Did somebody—'

'*Don't! Please don't!*'

Huge tears welled in Jonas's eyes and his face
instantly relaxed into something so young and vulnerable that Lucy gasped. That little boy who'd been at
her hospital bedside was suddenly standing here in her
attic as if by magic.

'Jonas?' she whispered.

The boy/man shook his head and pushed his tears
away with the heel of a rough hand. 'Please don't talk
about it. Please don't make me say.' Then he covered
his face with his hands and his young voice was
muffled. 'Where is this? I don't want to be here. Don't
make me be here.'

It broke her heart. She actually felt a pain, as if that
tender organ was being torn in two, and she put a hand
to her breast, knotting the blue sweater in her fist.

'Jonas,' she whispered, her voice hoarse with
emotion.

Jonas slowly took his hands from his face and looked
at her, and Lucy gave a huge sob of relief to see her
husband standing there once more.

'I wouldn't hurt anyone, Lu. You know that!'

It was as if the last two minutes had never
happened. No killer with his cold, dead eyes, no boy-
Jonas tortured by the memory of something so terrible
that it had split him apart. Those fragments of the

whole lived separate lives – the boy sleeping, Jonas protecting him, the killer dormant until the stress that *she* had caused threatened to reawaken the horror he'd already lived once. If something had gone wrong with that delicate balance, the only person to blame was herself. *She* had been the tipping point.

Lucy burned with shame and selfishness.

With one self-obsessed handful of pills, she had made Jonas start to fall apart.

Despite the shock of the truth, Lucy felt a sudden surge of pride in Jonas. There was one thing he had done supremely well: he had protected the boy within him like a tigress does a cub. He had become a protector both personally and professionally; his whole life – conscious and subconscious – had been devoted to keeping that small child from having to face whatever it was that had been done to him.

She realized with a sharp pang that Jonas had been more of a parent than she would ever be. He had worked so hard and done so well. The boy had grown up into a good man, had got a good job and had loved her like no other. He had suffered setbacks and sadness and nothing had broken him.

Until she had tried to kill herself.

And now she understood everything.

Tears started to blur her vision.

'I know you love me, Jonas.'

'Of course I love you!'

'But protecting me is making you hurt other people

instead, sweetheart. The notes you wrote: *Call yourself a policeman? . . . Do your job . . .* You *knew* you were hurting the wrong people . . .'

Jonas looked confused. 'What do you mean?'

Her tears were coming thick and fast now – as she knew in her heart the truth of what she was about to say.

'Jonas . . . There's somebody inside you who wants me dead.'

'*What?*'

'It's OK. I understand. You have to protect the boy. He needs you to be strong, Jonas. Now more than ever.'

'Lucy, honey, I don't know what you're talking about. Please come downstairs . . .'

He held out his hand to her – the way he had at the altar. She had given him her hand then and he had slid the ring on to her finger and vowed to love her for ever.

'You killed the wrong people, Jonas.'

She had lost it.

'I didn't kill *anyone*, Lu. I swear to you. Sweetheart, please just come downstairs with me, so we can talk properly. It's freezing up here. Please, Lu? Please?'

Lucy stared at his outstretched hand and then looked up into his eyes with an expression of such helpless agony on her face that he flinched.

'Jonas,' she choked, 'you're still wearing the gloves.'

Jonas looked down at his hand. It shone, stretched

and strange in the white light of the lantern, and he held it up so he could see it better.

He was wearing a near-translucent surgical glove.

Why?

Why?

He frowned stupidly at his own fingers, all smooth and pale and plastic. He raised his other hand and saw it was the same. He felt disorientated. Why would he be wearing these gloves? It made no sense.

'I love you with all my heart, but you can't protect me any more. It has to stop.' Lucy's voice was a dull whisper. It had lost all hope.

Jonas said nothing – still consumed by the sight of his own shining fingers.

'*This* is the job you were meant to do, Jonas,' Lucy said, and – with hands that did not shake – slid the knife into her own throat.

'NO! NO! NO!'

Jonas reached her in two seconds and caught her before she fell. The knife was lodged in her jugular, blood beat from her neck in time to her heart, while she made a very small mewling sound, like a kitten in a box.

Jonas made all the noise. He screamed her name and screamed for help and tried to stop the blood with his hands, then dragged her towards the hatch. He had to get her to hospital. He barely touched the ladder, dropping on to the landing in a heap with his wife in his arms, then down the stairs, slipping halfway, banging his head, and falling to the hallway, holding on to Lucy in a tangled mess of blood and arms and legs.

He raised his face from the cold flagstones, sat up and pulled her on to his lap, repeating her name like a talisman against bad things. If only he kept saying *Lucy* then she would not die. *Would not.*

Her copper hair was darkened by thick blood, and her face was spattered and smeared. Her eyes were still open and found his.

'*LucyLucyLucyLucy* . . .'

She looked away from him then and into a future where he could not follow.

'Don't go,' he begged her. 'Please don't go.'

But he could do nothing but hold her and watch the light in her eyes go out.

Here on the cold floor behind the front door – where Lucy Holly had already tried to end her life once – she finally succeeded.

Jonas laid her head gently on his knees and pulled the knife from her neck. Then he plunged it into his belly.

'GET OUT!' he screamed. 'GET OUT!'

Jonas repeatedly sought the killer inside him, but his job was done and he was nowhere to be found.

*

The walls were thick and stone, but Mrs Paddon was woken by Jonas's shout of 'NO! NO! NO!'

She was eighty-nine, but she had been through the war, so she got out of bed and pulled on her coat and boots.

She heard Jonas screaming 'GET OUT!' as she approached the front door, but nobody burst past her, so she went inside.

She found Lucy dead and Jonas still alive, so she fetched towels to staunch the blood.

She saw the knife lying nearby, so she didn't touch it in case it was evidence.

She called the police and the ambulance and told them two people had been attacked in their home and stabbed.

She went back to help Jonas and noticed with a puzzled frown the surgical gloves on his hands.

She had known Jonas Holly since he came home from the hospital in his proud father's arms, and she knew he was a good boy.

There could be no doubt about that.

So she pulled them off and threw them in the embers of the fire, where they stank and smoked and then melted into flames just as Reynolds and his team finally burst through the front door.

Another Day

Jonas didn't want to survive and had tried his best not to, but the doctors were skilful and the nurses relentlessly vigilant.

Reynolds insisted on driving him home. He talked all the way. About that night.

He told Jonas how fortunate he'd been that Mrs Paddon knew the basics, and that the air ambulance already on its way for Marvel had been diverted to save his life.

'You came *this* close,' Reynolds told him. 'You were unbelievably lucky.'

Lucky. Yes. Jonas nodded.

Marvel was dead. Joy Springer was dead. The farm was destroyed. The blood in Jonas's bathroom was Joy Springer's. Herringbone footprints found outside the back door had been lost in the snow beyond the shelter of the eaves. They had the knife, but no prints on it except Lucy's.

'She must have fought, Jonas,' he said, in that sick pseudo-sympathetic way that was really just prurience. 'She must have grabbed the knife at one stage. She was very brave.'

Yes, Jonas nodded. Very brave.

The snow had melted on Exmoor and the day was bright with spring.

They reached Rose Cottage and Reynolds followed Jonas in, even though he was desperate to be alone.

Mrs Paddon was just inside the door and hugged him right on the spot where Lucy had died.

'You're a bag of bones,' she said. 'There's a pie in the oven. Vegetarian.'

He nodded and thanked her and wished she hadn't bothered. Not with the pie and not with saving his life.

They both hovered but he had no more to say to them, and Mrs Paddon had the decency to leave. Reynolds kept talking mindlessly from the hallway as Jonas walked slowly upstairs, one arm protectively across his abdomen where the stitches were itchy and tender.

There was a new stair carpet.

No blood anywhere.

In the back bedroom the ladder was up and the trap-door shut. He wondered who had cleaned the house and whether they had done the attic.

This is the job you were meant to do, Jonas.

He closed his eyes and swayed.

Marvel was to receive a posthumous Queen's Commendation for bravery.

'He was drunk, of course,' added Reynolds from the hallway. 'But they're hushing that up.'

Here was the bed where he would sleep alone for ever.

Here was the bathroom, all nice and shiny.

Here was the laundry basket. Empty.

Here was the mirror.

Jonas stopped his slow inspection and stared at himself.

Lucy had said there was somebody inside him who wanted her dead.

He couldn't see it in his eyes. He turned his head towards the window, hoping to catch a glimpse of the intruder while he wasn't looking directly at himself.

Nothing.

He went downstairs.

'Thanks,' he told Reynolds.

'Will you be OK?'

Never, thought Jonas, and said that he would.

Jonas remembered how to say goodbye and held out his hand. Reynolds shook it, looking suddenly tearful. He leaned forward and pulled Jonas into a clumsy embrace, slapping his back awkwardly.

'We'll get him, Jonas,' he said vehemently. 'Don't you worry. We'll get him.'

No, thought Jonas. You won't.

Acknowledgements

Many thanks to Gill Bauer and Simon Cryer for being my first and best readers.

Also to Sarah Adams, Marysue Rucci and Stephanie Glencross for their invaluable editorial input, and my agent, Jane Gregory, for her support and boundless enthusiasm.

If you would like to know more about the strange world explored by *Darkside*, please visit my website, www.belindabauer.co.uk

Belinda Bauer grew up in England and South Africa and now lives in Wales. She worked as a journalist and a screenwriter before finally writing a book to appease her nagging mother.

With her debut, *Blacklands*, Belinda was awarded the CWA Gold Dagger for Crime Novel of the Year. She went on to win the CWA Dagger in the Library for her body of work in 2013. Her fourth novel *Rubbernecker* was voted 2014 Theakston Old Peculier Crime Novel of the Year. In 2018 her eighth novel, *Snap*, was longlisted for the Man Booker prize and won the Specsavers National Book Award for Best Crime & Thriller of the Year. Her books have been translated into twenty-one languages.

Connect with Belinda on Facebook at www.facebook.com/BelindaBauerBooks or visit her website for more information: www.belindabauer.co.uk

HAVE YOU READ THEM ALL?

BLACKLANDS

Twelve-year-old Steven Lamb writes to notorious murderer Arnold Avery, asking him to reveal where his uncle is buried. And so begins a dangerous cat-and-mouse game between a desperate child and a bored serial killer . . .

'Thought-provoking and utterly original'
Mo Hayder

DARKSIDE

Jonas Holly is working his first murder investigation, but he is taunted by anonymous letters accusing him of failing to do his job. He has no choice but to strike out alone – but who is hunting who?

'Bold, mordant, compassionate, *Darkside* confirms Bauer's reputation as a significant new talent'
Sunday Times

FINDERS KEEPERS

At the height of summer, a dark shadow falls across Exmoor. Children are being stolen – there are no explanations, no ransom demands . . . and no hope. Jonas Holly faces a precarious journey into the warped mind of the kidnapper if he is to save them – but can Jonas be trusted?

'One of the leading names in crime fiction'
Stylist

RUBBERNECKER

As a medical student with Asperger's Syndrome, Patrick's life is challenging enough – and now he's faced with solving a possible murder. With his only evidence the body on his dissecting table in his anatomy class, can he stay out of danger long enough to unravel the mystery?

'Breathtaking. I read this and wished I'd written it'
Val McDermid

THE FACTS OF LIFE AND DEATH

Ten-year-old Ruby Trick is more focused on school bullies and the threat of her parents' divorce than the murderer on the loose in her town. But helping her father catch the killer seems like the only way to keep him close – as long as the killer doesn't catch her first.

'The true heir to the great Ruth Rendell'
Mail on Sunday

THE SHUT EYE

A front door accidentally left ajar . . . and four-year-old Daniel Buck was gone. His mother will go to any lengths to find him – but how far will this desperate search push an already vulnerable woman?

'Almost indecently gripping and enjoyable'
Sophie Hannah

THE BEAUTIFUL DEAD

As a TV crime reporter, Eve Singer will go to any length to get the latest scoop. But when a twisted serial killer starts using her to gain the publicity he craves, Eve must decide how far she's willing to go – and how close she'll let him get . . .

'Will keep you up all night'
Shari Lapena

SNAP

After his mother disappears, fourteen-year-old Jack is left in charge – of his sisters, of making sure no-one knows they're alone in the house and, quite suddenly, of finding out the truth about what happened to his mother . . .

'Belinda Bauer's fiction teems with life'
Daily Telegraph

**He was only twelve, he reasoned;
he couldn't be expected to get stuff like
writing to serial killers right first time.**

'A psychological tour-de-force' *Guardian*

BLACKLANDS IS OUT NOW

READ ON FOR AN EXTRACT ...

1

Exmoor dripped with dirty bracken, rough, colourless grass, prickly gorse and last year's heather, so black it looked as if wet fire had swept across the landscape, taking the trees with it and leaving the moor cold and exposed to face the winter unprotected. Drizzle dissolved the close horizons and blurred heaven and earth into a grey cocoon around the only visible land-mark – a twelve-year-old boy in slick black waterproof trousers but no hat, alone with a spade.

It had rained for three days, but the roots of grass and heather and gorse twisting through the soil still resisted the spade's intrusion. Steven's expression did not change; he dug the blade in again, feeling a satisfying little impact all the way up to his armpits. This time he made a mark – a thin human mark in the great swathe of nature around him.

Before Steven could make the next mark, the first narrow stripe had filled with water and disappeared.

Three boys slouched through the Shipcott rain, their hands deep in their pockets, their hoodies over their faces, their shoulders hunched as if they couldn't wait to get out of the rain. But they had nowhere to hurry to, so they meandered and bumped along and laughed and swore too loudly at nothing at all, just to let the world know they were there and still had expectations.

The street was narrow and winding and, in summer, passing tourists smiled at the seaside-painted terraces with their doors opening right on to the pavement and their quaint shutters. But the rain made the yellow and pink and sky-blue houses a faded reminder of sunshine, and a refuge only for those too young, too old or too poor to leave.

Steven's nan looked out of the window with a steady gaze.

She had started life as Gloria Manners. Then she became Ron Peters's wife. After that, she was Lettie's mum, then Lettie and Billy's mum. Then for a long time she was Poor Mrs Peters. Now she was Steven's nan. But underneath she would always be Poor Mrs Peters; nothing could change that, not even her grandsons.

Above the half-nets, the front window was spotted with rain. The people over the road already had their lights on. The roofs were as different as the walls. Some still wore their old pottery tiles, rough with moss. Others, flat grey slate that reflected the watery sky. Above the roofs, the top of the moor was just visible through the mist – a gentle, rounded thing from this distance. From the warmth of a front room with central heating and the kettle starting to whistle in the kitchen, it even looked innocent.

The shortest of the boys struck the window with the flat of his palm and Steven's nan recoiled in fright.

The boys laughed and ran although no one was chasing them and they knew no one was likely to. 'Nosey old bag!' one of them shouted back, although it was hard to see which, with their hoods so low on their faces.

Lettie hurried in, breathless and alarmed. 'What was that?'

But Steven's nan was back in the window. She didn't look round at her daughter. 'Is tea ready?' she said.

Steven walked off the moor with his anorak slung over one shoulder and his T-shirt soaked and steaming with recent effort. The track carved through the heather by generations of walkers was thick with mud. He stopped – his rusty spade slung over his other shoulder like a rifle – and looked down at the village. The street lamps were already on and Steven felt like an angel or an alien, observing the darkening dwellings from on high, detached from the tiny lives being lived below. He ducked instinctively as he saw the three hoodies run down the wet road.

He hid the spade behind a rock near the slippery stile. It was rusty but, still, someone might take it, and he couldn't carry it home with him; that might lead to questions he could not – or dared not – answer.

He walked down the narrow passage beside the house. He was cooling now, and shivered as he took off his trainers to run them under the garden tap. They'd been white once, with blue flashes. His mum would go mad if she saw them like this. He rubbed them with his thumbs and squeezed the mud out of them until they were only dirty, then shook them hard. Muddy water sprayed up the side of the house, but rain washed it quickly away. His grey school socks were heavy and sodden; he peeled them off, his feet a shocking cold white.

'You're soaking.' His mother peered from the back door, her face pinched and her dark blue eyes as dull as a northern sea. Rain spattered the straw hair that was dragged back into a small, functional ponytail. She jerked her head back inside to keep it dry.

'I got caught in it.'

'Where were you?'

'With Lewis.'

This was not strictly a lie. He had been with Lewis immediately after school.

'What were you doing?'

'Nothing. Just. You know.'

From the kitchen he heard his nan say, 'He should come straight home from school!'

Steven's mother glared at his wetness. 'Those trainers were only new at Christmas.'

'Sorry, Mum.' He looked crestfallen; it often worked.

She sighed. 'Tea's ready.'

Steven ate as fast as he dared and as much as he could. Lettie stood at the sink and smoked and dropped her ash down the plughole. At the old house – before they came to live with Nan – his mum used to sit at the table with him and Davey. She used to eat. She used to talk to him. Now her mouth was always shut tight, even when it held a cigarette.

Davey sucked the ketchup off his chips then carefully pushed each one to the side of his plate.

Nan cut little pieces off her breaded fish, inspecting each with a suspicious look before eating it.

'Something wrong with it, Mum?' Lettie flicked her ash with undue vigour. Steven looked at her nervously.

'Bones.'

'It's a fillet. Says so on the box. Plaice fillet.'

'They always miss some. You can't be too careful.'

There was a long silence in which Steven listened to the sound of his own food inside his head.

'Eat your chips, Davey.'

Davey screwed up his face. 'They're all wet.'

'Should've thought of that before you sucked them, shouldn't you? Shouldn't you?'

At the repeated question, Steven stopped chewing, but Nan's fork scraped the plate.

Lettie moved swiftly to Davey's side and picked up a soggy chip. 'Eat it!'

Davey shook his head and his lower lip started to wobble.

With quiet spite, Nan murmured: 'Leaving food. Kids nowadays don't know they're born.'

Lettie bent down and slapped Davey sharply on the bare thigh below his shorts. Steven watched the white handprint on his brother's skin quickly turn red. He loved Davey, but seeing someone other than himself get into trouble always gave Steven a small thrill, and now – watching her hustling his brother out of the kitchen and up the stairs, bawling his head off – he felt as if he had somehow been accorded an honour: the honour of being spared the pent-up irritation of his mother. God knows, she'd taken her feelings for Nan out on him often enough. But this was further proof of what Steven had been hoping for some time – that Davey was finally old enough, at five, to suffer his share of the discipline pool. It wasn't a deep pool, or a dangerous one, but what the hell; his mother had a short fuse and a punishment shared was a punishment halved in Steven's eyes. Maybe even a punishment escaped altogether.

His nan had not stopped eating throughout,

although each mouthful was apparently a minefield.

Even though Davey's sobs were now muffled, Steven sought eye contact with Nan and finally she glanced at him, giving him a chance to roll his eyes, as if the burden of the naughty child was shared and the sharing made them closer.

'You're no better,' she said, and went back to her fish.

Steven reddened. He knew he was better! If only he could prove it to Nan, everything would be different – he just knew it.

Of course, it was all Billy's fault – as usual.

Steven held his breath. He could hear his mother washing up – the underwater clunking of china – and his nan drying – the higher musical scraping of plates leaving the rack. Then he slowly opened the door of Billy's room. It smelled old and sweet, like an orange left under the bed. Steven felt the door click gently behind him.

The curtains were drawn – always drawn. They matched the bedspread in pale and dark blue squares that clashed with the swirly brown carpet. A half-built Lego space station was on the floor and since Steven's last visit a small spider had spun a web on what looked like a crude docking station. Now it sat there, waiting to capture satellite flies from the outer space of the dingy bedroom.

There was a drooping scarf pinned to the wall over

the bed – sky-blue and white, Manchester City – and Steven felt the familiar pang of pity and anger at Billy: still a loser even in death.

Steven crept in here sometimes, as if Billy might reach across the years and whisper secrets and solutions into the ear of this nephew who had already lived to see one more birthday than he himself had managed.

Steven had long ago given up the hope of finding real-life clues. At first he liked to imagine that Uncle Billy might have left some evidence of a precognition of his own death. A *Famous Five* book dog-eared at a key page; the initials 'AA' scratched into the wooden top of the bedside table; Lego scattered to show the points of the compass and X marks the spot. Something which – after the event – an observant boy might discover and decipher.

But there was nothing. Just this smell of history and bitter sadness, and a school photo of a thin, fair child with pink cheeks and crooked teeth and dark blue eyes almost squeezed shut by the size of his smile. It had been a long time before Steven had realized that this photo must have been placed here later – that no boy worth his salt has a photo of himself on his bedside table unless it shows him holding a fish or a trophy.

Nineteen years ago this eleven-year-old boy – probably much like himself – had tired of his fantasy space game and gone outside to play on a warm summer evening, apparently – infuriatingly – unaware that he would never return to put his toys away or to wave his Man City scarf at the TV on a Sunday afternoon, or even to make his bed, which his mother – Steven's nan – had done much later.

Some time after 7.15pm, when Mr Jacoby from the newsagent sold him a bag of Maltesers, Uncle Billy had moved out of the realm of childhood make-believe and into the realm of living nightmare. In the 200 yards between the newsagent's and this very house – a 200 yards Steven walked every morning and every night to and from school – Uncle Billy had simply disappeared.

Steven's nan had waited until 8.30 before sending Lettie out to look for her brother, and until 9.30, when darkness was falling, to go outside herself. In the light summer evenings children played long past their winter bedtimes. But it was not until Ted Randall next door said perhaps they should call the police that Steven's nan changed for ever from Billy's Mum into Poor Mrs Peters.

Poor Mrs Peters – whose husband had been stupidly killed wobbling off his bicycle into the path of the Barnstaple bus six years before – had waited for Billy to come home.

At first she waited at the door. She stood there all day, every day for a month, barely noticing fourteen-year-old Lettie brushing past her to go to school, and returning promptly at 3.50 to save her mother worrying even more – if such a thing were possible.

When the weather broke, Poor Mrs Peters waited in the window from where she could see up and down the road. She grew the look of a dog in a thunderstorm – alert, wide-eyed and nervous. Any movement in the street made her heart leap so hard in her chest that she flinched. Then would come the slump, as Mr Jacoby or Sally Blunkett or the Tithecott twins grew so distinct that no desperate stretch of her imagination could keep them looking like a ruddy-cheeked eleven-year-old boy with a blond crew-cut, new Nike trainers and a half-eaten bag of Maltesers in his hand.

Lettie learned to cook and to clean and to stay in her room so she didn't have to watch her mother flinching at the road. She had always suspected that Billy was the favourite and now, in his absence, her mother no longer had the strength to hide this fact.

So Lettie worked on a shell of anger and rebellion to protect the soft centre of herself, which was fourteen and scared and missed her brother and her mother in equal measure, as if both had been snatched from her on that warm July evening.

How could Uncle Billy not know? Once more Steven felt that flicker of anger as he looked about the clueless, lifeless room. How could anyone not know that something like that was about to happen to them?

Desperate for more?

BLACKLANDS is out now in paperback and ebook

Snap decisions can be dangerous . . .

'Original, pacy and thoroughly entertaining'
Clare Mackintosh, bestselling author of *I Let You Go*

SNAP IS OUT NOW